Tower of Light

P.G. BADZEY

A STONE OWL PRESS BOOK

Interior Art by Matthew Bostic

Cover Art by Oladimeji

ISBN-13: 978-1-7328627-5-3

DEDICATION

To My Family, Near and Far, Immediate and Extended.
Every one of you has been part of the inspiration for the Grey Riders Series
You are immortalized in these pages.
Ad Majorem Dei Gloriam.

In memory of Joshua Page (June 16, 2003- March 7, 2022) and

Jeremy Page (October 6, 2004- March 7, 2022)

Requiescat En Pacem

Praise for the Grey Riders Series!

<u>Book 1, Whitehorse Peak</u>
"...Whitehorse Peak excels, standing out from the crowd of fantasy adventures...a riveting, emotionally powerful story line...vibrant with realistic action" – D. Donovan, *Midwest Book Review*

"...an excellent balance of worldbuilding and introduction...fully lavish and exciting, with atmospheric moments of high, epic fantasy that smack of tradition and the old favorites, but then also more modern inclusions and plenty of witty humor... Highly recommended: fantasy fiction at its best." – K.C. Finn for *Readers Favorite* (5-star review)

<u>Book 2, Eye of Truth</u>
"...a real treasure ... Think Dungeons and Dragons or Tolkien, throw in a dash of Patrick Rothfus ... recommended for any reader who enjoys high fantasy spiced with a bit of mystery" — D. Donovan, *Midwest Book Review*

"... a charming and rich tale of magic, loyalty, friendship, and secrets, ... I enjoyed the complexities of the plot and characters, and their development and alterations as secrets are uncovered...good world-building...Danger, action, threats, and camaraderie will keep the reader engaged..." – K.J. Simmill for *Readers Favorite* (5-star review)

<u>Book 3, Helm of Shadows</u>
"...wraps its cloak of fantasy around an atmosphere of mystery and intrigue... Impressively vivid..." — D. Donovan, *Midwest Book Reviews*

"...an even bigger and better addition to the Grey Riders series... Helm of Shadows is an excellent addition that once again lifts the series to new heights: a highly recommended read for fantasy fans everywhere." – K.C. Finn for *Readers Favorite* (5-star review)

<u>Book 4, Assassin Prince</u>
"P.G. Badzey has created a complex, absorbing atmosphere ...fast-paced and thoroughly engrossing... a compelling saga... satisfying action... whets the reader's appetite for more to come in later sequels." — D. Donovan, *Midwest Book Reviews*

"I am always delighted to return to the works of author P. G. Badzey and the fantastic Grey Riders series, and this new addition is no exception... As always, the worldbuilding and atmosphere are solid, and the closer we get to what is sure to be an epic conclusion, the less I want the series to end." – K.C. Finn for *Readers Favorite* (5-star review)

Book 5, The Skull Gates

"…rivals J.R.R. Tolkien's Middle Earth in cultural and genealogical complexity… will have fans clamoring for the saga's next chapter." – Kate Robinson, US Review of Books (Recommended)

"Badzey keeps this novel in perfect balance, shifting action to keep readers following the different threads of the story and giving each of the Riders time to shine with their unique skills, whilst also building to a fantastic magical conclusion. Overall, I would highly recommend The Skull Gates..." – K.C. Finn for *Readers Favorite* (5-star review)

Book 6, Gate of Stars

"…compelling… epic in scale… Readers familiar with the Forgotten Realms books will feel right at home in Badzey's fantasy environment… an entertaining adventure…" – M. Heisey, US Review of Books

"Epic fantasy surely doesn't get more epic than this… P G Badzey wastes none of the potential of this incredible setting, consistently demonstrating gorgeous prose that brings the world of Damora to life… This is a powerful and exciting adventure through a fantasy conflict like no other and is an incredible read…" – K.C. Finn for *Readers Favorite* (5-star review)

CONTENTS

ACKNOWLEDGMENTS

There are so many people to thank along this journey over (incredibly) the last ten years. The process of writing the Grey Riders saga has been an education, a marathon, and a blessing all rolled into one.

First of all, I thank my mother for instilling a respect and love of reading and literature in me from an early age, and my father for showing me that a task should receive my best effort if it's worth doing at all.

Second, I want to thank my brothers and sisters for putting up with endless, obsessive games of D&D; their playful silliness and sense of wonder has been the inspiration for much of the series. Those sessions fed my imagination. Third, I wish to thank the various writing and critique groups who have examined my work in painstaking detail through the years (OCWG, OCSFF and Realm Makers); though it was often painful, your insights have vastly improved me as a writer and helped me along my road. My journey isn't done yet, but your attentiveness, patience and friendship have provided a solid foundation upon which I hope to build in the future.

Lastly, I wish to thank my immediate family: my sons (Michael & Joshua) and my beloved wife, Siobhan. Without two young boys who eagerly awaited bedtime stories of the Grey Riders and a wife who patiently encouraged and accommodated my writing obsession, I would never have dreamed of writing the series to begin with. You have been my inspiration and the wind under my wings whenever I became discouraged or tired. To say I love you doesn't come close, but language is limited, after all. I am sure I have forgotten and neglected other important people in this acknowledgement and I apologize, but know that you have my unending gratitude and my prayers.

Pete (PG) Badzey
Huntington Beach, CA

"For the Lord your God is He that goes with you, to fight for you against your enemies, to save you."
– Deuteronomy 20:4

You are the light of the world. A city built upon a mountain cannot be hidden… In the same way, your light must shine so that it can be seen by others; this will enable them to observe your good works and give praise to your Father in heaven…
– Matthew 5: 14, 16

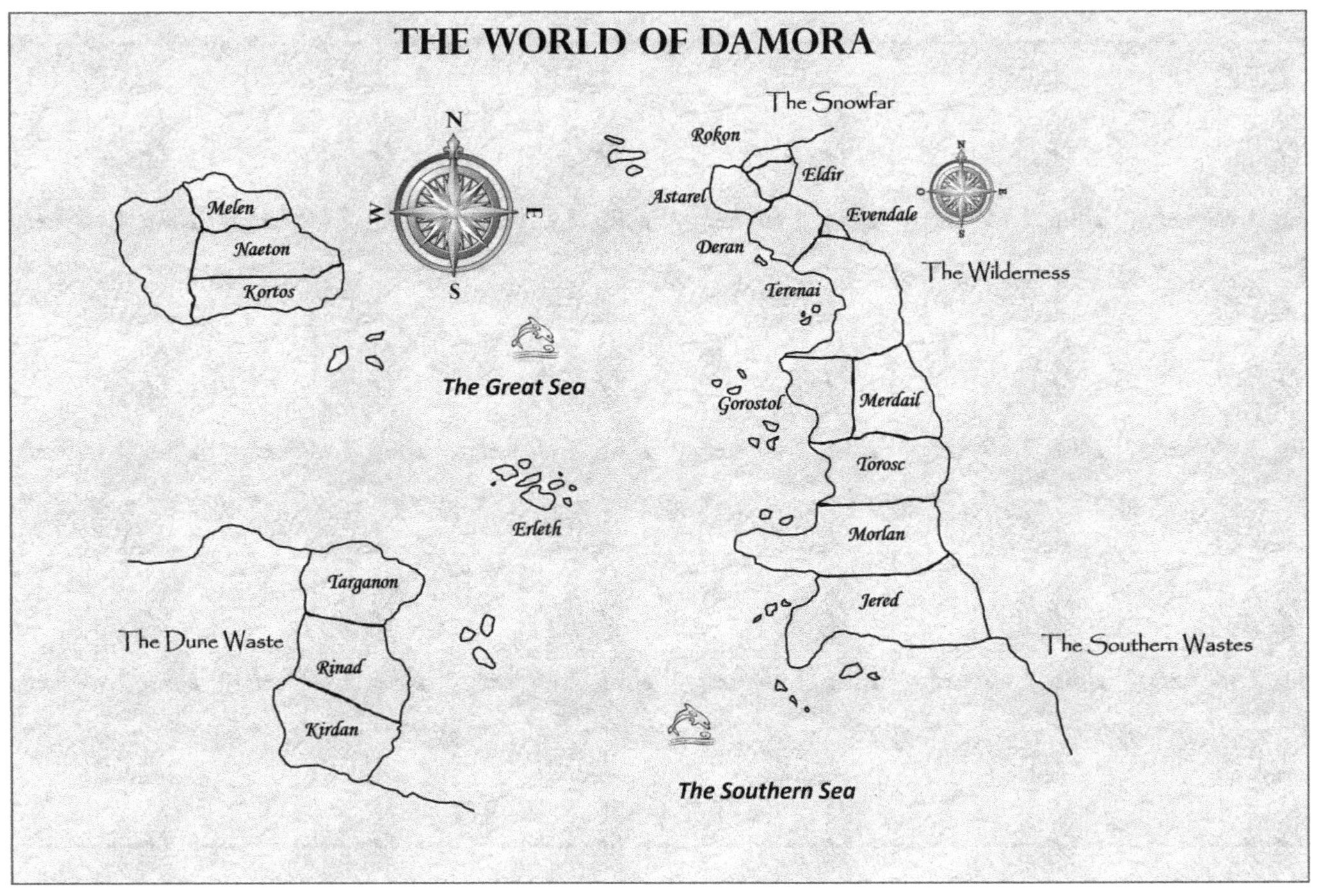

THE WORLD OF DAMORA
The Snowfar
Rokon
Eldir
Astarel
Evendale
Deran
The Wilderness
Terenai
Melen
Naeton
Kortos
N
W
E
S
The Great Sea
Gorostol
Merdail
Torosc
Morlan
Jered
The Southern Wastes
Erleth
Targanon
The Dune Waste
Rinad
Kirdan
The Southern Sea

DERAN AND EVENDALE
Eldir
Astarel
Deran
Evendale
Terenai
The Great Sea
Whitehorse Peak
The Dragonspine Range
The Crescent Range
The Greenwall
The Ridges
Silver Mountains
Twinspire
Shadow Lake
Dwarfshire
Wildford
Westfort
Lakeview
Glen
Falconshire
Darcy's Wood
Orl's Haven
Virdildris
Eldirian
Issendar
Wit's End
Forester
Athor
North Corner
Sun Lake
Sun Plains
Hillton
Deor River
Deorfast
Darlon
Tyler
Seacrest
Lonmar River
Vanguard
Oakmoor
East River
Eastridge
St Martin's
Alrihan
Old Misty River
Horizon
Fenbluff
Marolvar
N
W
E
S
KEY
Capital City
Major City
Major Town
Town
Cathedral
Hills
Mountains (Elev. >10K ft)
Mountains (Elev. <10K ft)
Plains
Fen/Marsh
River
Lake

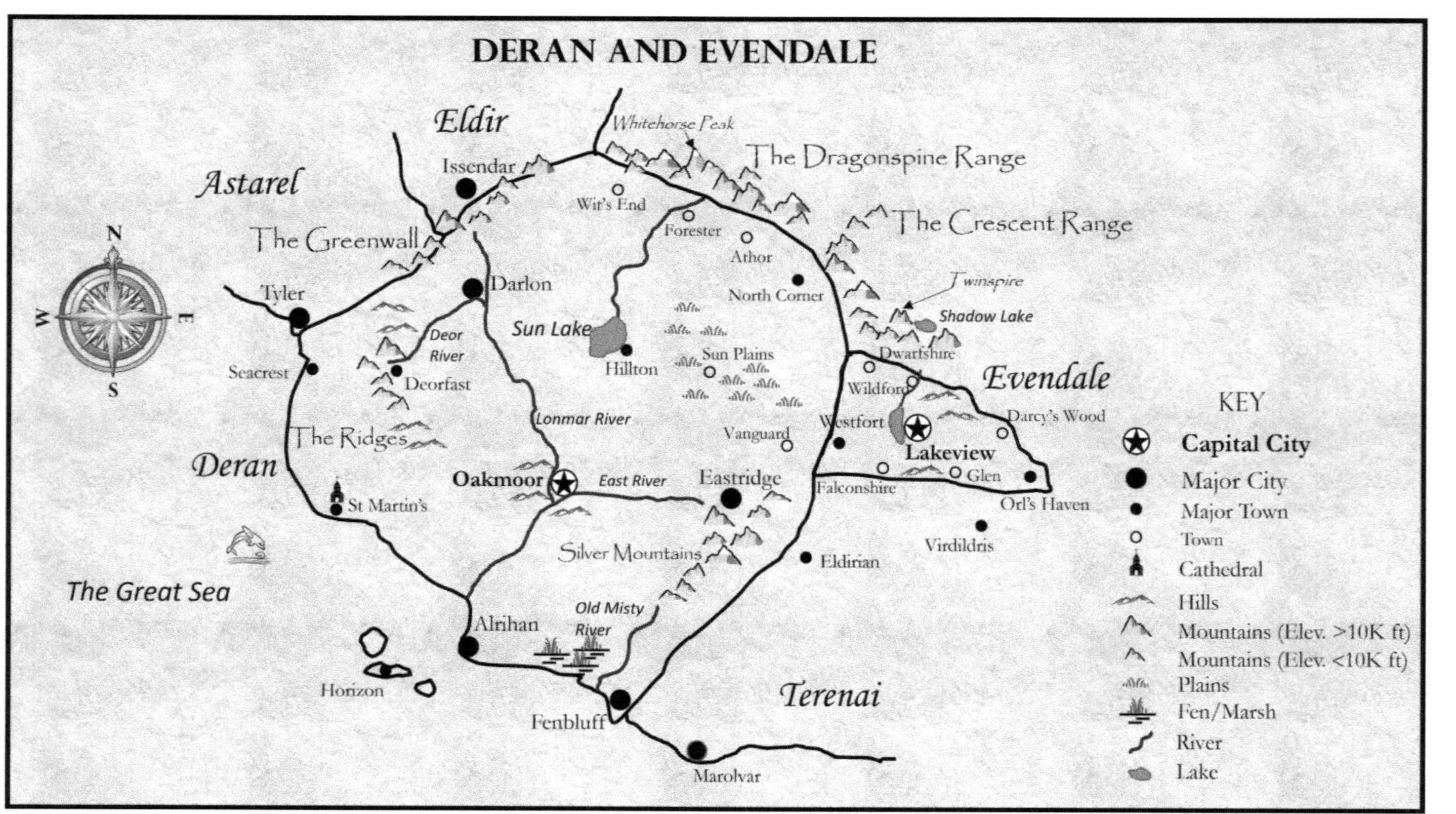

iv

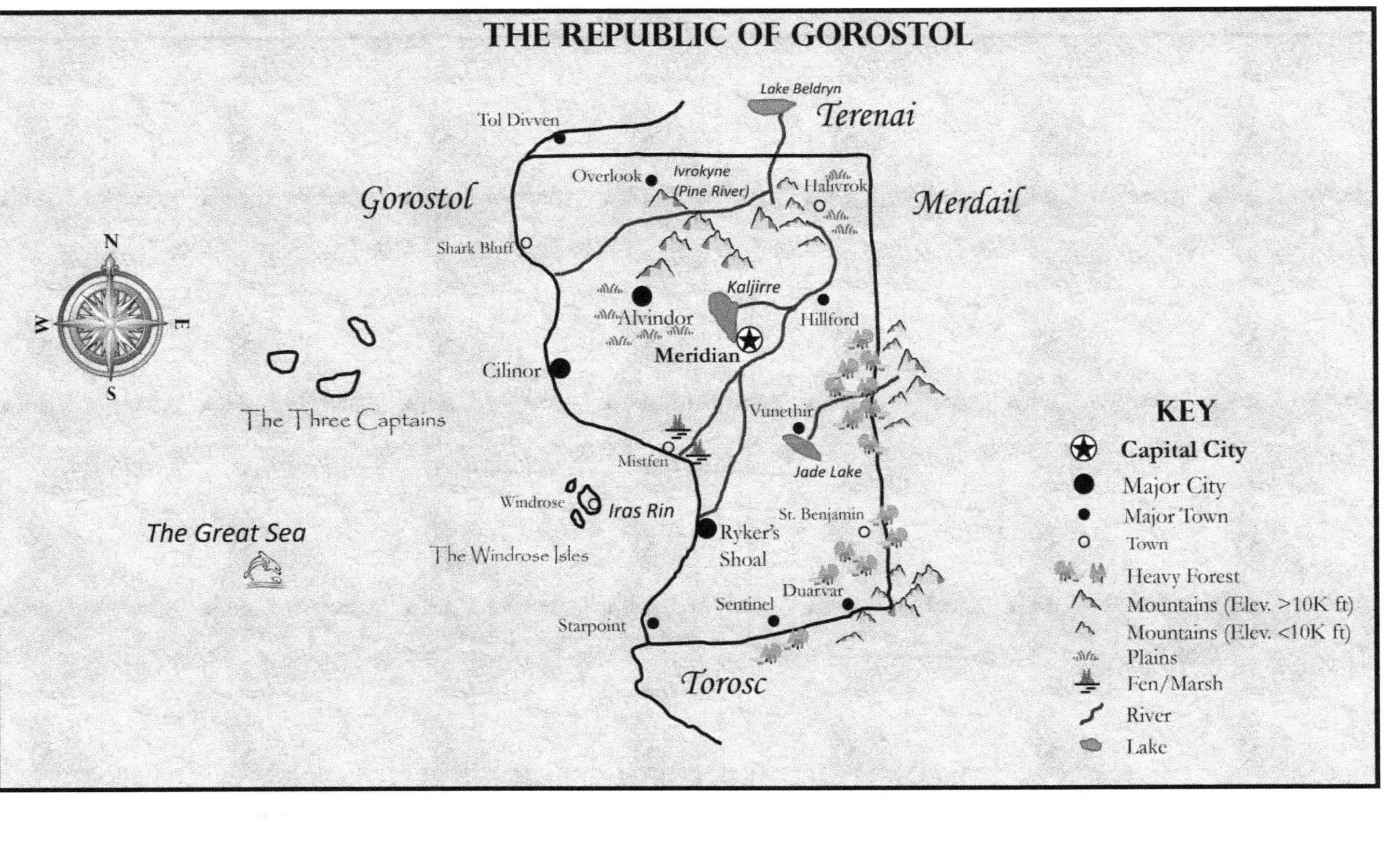

THE REPUBLIC OF GOROSTOL
Gorostol
Terenai
Merdail
Torosc
Tol Divven
Lake Beldryn
Overlook
Ivrokyne
(Pine River)
Halivrok
Shark Bluff
Alvindor
Kaljirre
Meridian
Hillford
Cilinor
Vunethir
Mistfen
Jade Lake
The Three Captains
Windrose
Iras Rin
Ryker's Shoal
Duarvar
The Windrose Isles
St. Benjamin
Sentinel
Starpoint
The Great Sea
N
E
S
W
KEY
Capital City
Major City
Major Town
Town
Heavy Forest
Mountains (Elev. >10K ft)
Mountains (Elev. <10K ft)
Plains
Fen/Marsh
River
Lake

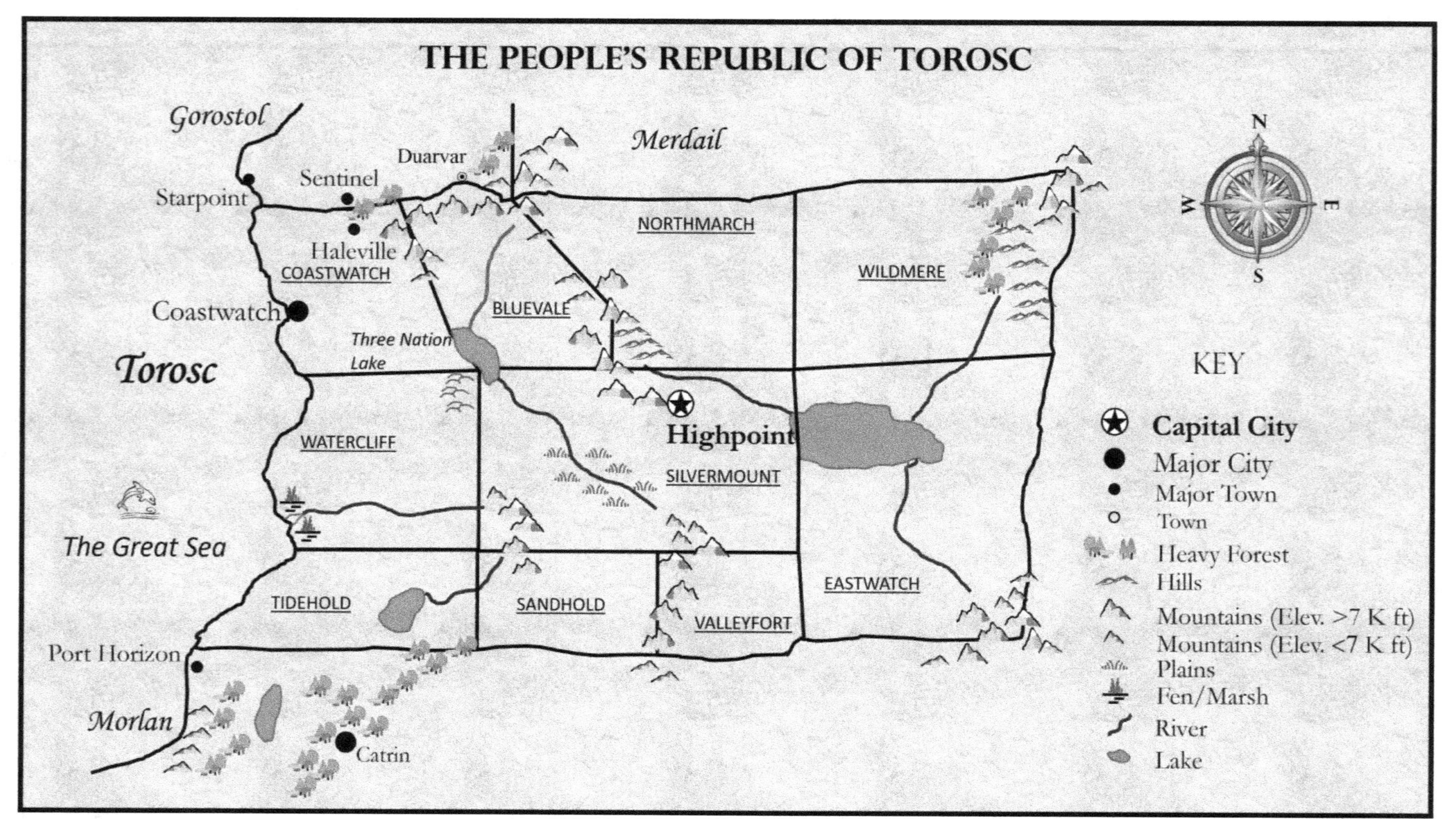

THE PEOPLE'S REPUBLIC OF TOROSC
Gorostol
Merdail
Duarvar
Starpoint
Sentinel
NORTHMARCH
Haleville
COASTWATCH
WILDMERE
Coastwatch
BLUEVALE
Three Nation Lake
Torosc
Highpoint
KEY
WATERCLIFF
SILVERMOUNT
Capital City
Major City
Major Town
Town
Heavy Forest
The Great Sea
Hills
EASTWATCH
Mountains (Elev. >7 K ft)
TIDEHOLD
SANDHOLD
Mountains (Elev. <7 K ft)
VALLEYFORT
Plains
Port Horizon
Fen/Marsh
River
Morlan
Catrin
Lake
N
E
S
W

BLUEVALE PREFECTURE, TOROSC (LOEMIN)

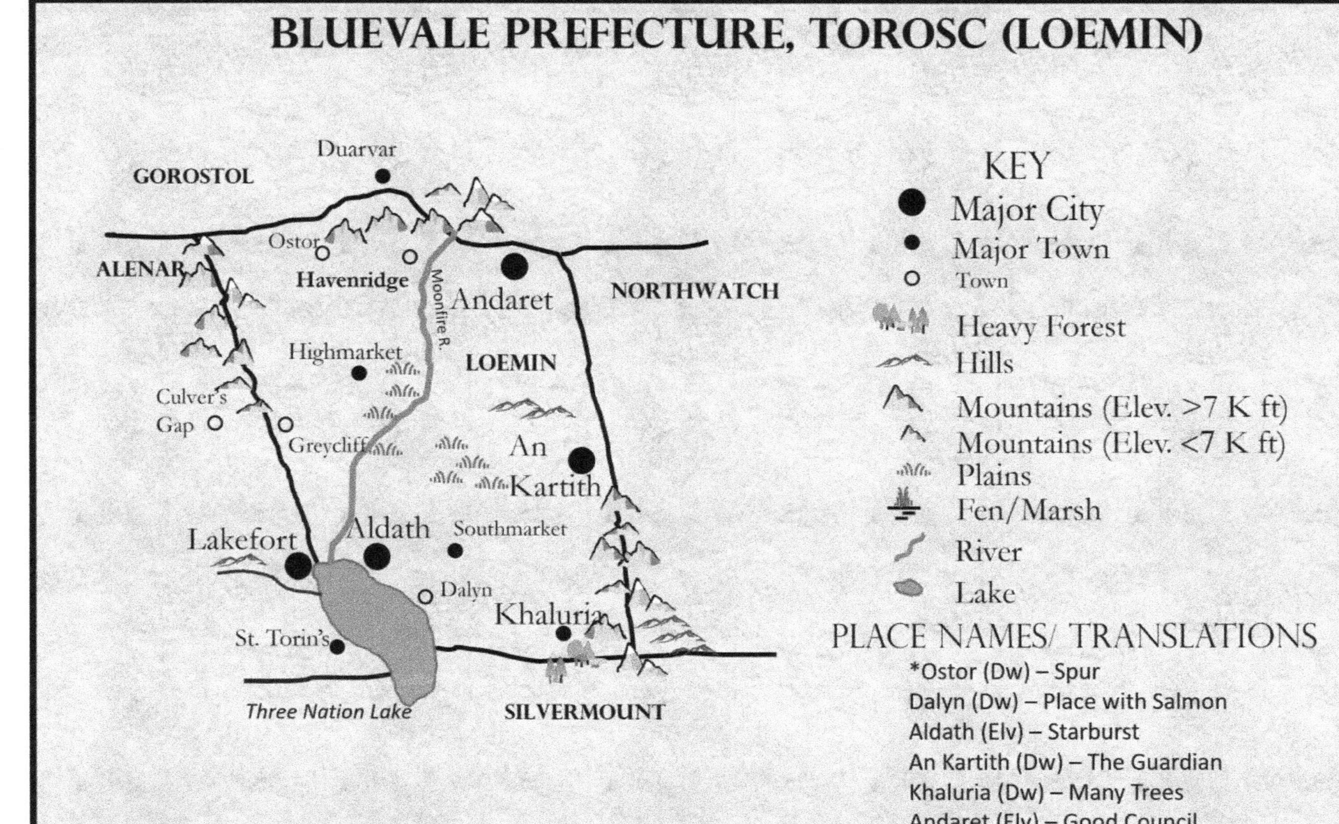

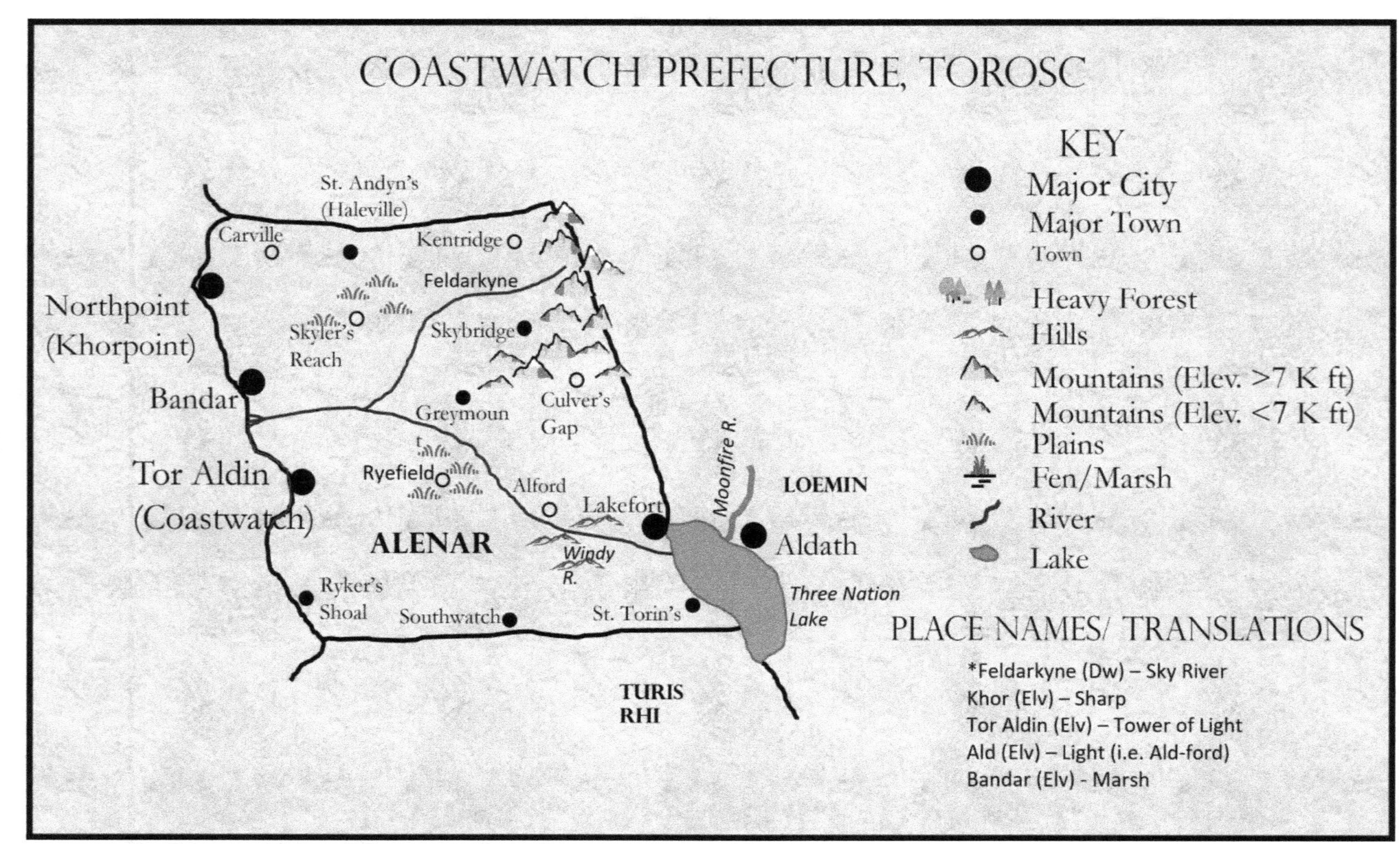

COASTWATCH PREFECTURE, TOROSC
St. Andyn's (Haleville)
Carville
Kentridge
Feldarkyne
Northpoint (Khorpoint)
Skyler's Reach
Skybridge
Bandar
Greymoun
Culver's Gap
Moonfire R.
LOEMIN
Tor Aldin (Coastwatch)
Ryefield
Alford
Lakefort
Aldath
ALENAR
Windy R.
Ryker's Shoal
Southwatch
St. Torin's
Three Nation Lake
TURIS RHI
KEY
Major City
Major Town
Town
Heavy Forest
Hills
Mountains (Elev. >7 K ft)
Mountains (Elev. <7 K ft)
Plains
Fen/Marsh
River
Lake
PLACE NAMES/ TRANSLATIONS
*Feldarkyne (Dw) – Sky River
Khor (Elv) – Sharp
Tor Aldin (Elv) – Tower of Light
Ald (Elv) – Light (i.e. Ald-ford)
Bandar (Elv) - Marsh

Chapter One – Nothing Comes Easy

Relax, Brandawyn Aldenar told herself. *Breathe. Center.*

She brushed a few snowflakes off her banded mail and stalked through the snowy woods. Mist clouded the tree trunks and curled around her boots. Despite the wintry conditions, she felt only a mild coolness on her exposed upper back. She let out a slow breath, extended her senses and put hands to her swords.

Her earring tingled and a smooth alto echoed in her head. *Ready, Your Majesty?*

As I'll ever be, Johanna, she answered mentally. *And please, no titles. You're the teacher and I'm the student. I have a lot to master.*

In her mind's eye, she imagined her mentor's wry smile. *Don't underestimate yourself. But I will defer to you and dispense with the honorifics.*

Thank you.

Now, remember what we've taught you, Johanna continued. *Patience is part of your Elohir legacy. Take time to perceive.*

I just hope you let me keep this earring after training is over, Brandi thought back. *I could really use it.*

Perhaps.

The contact faded and Brandi relaxed, slipping into a state of near-trance, reaching out with her otherworldly senses into the cold forest. For long moments, she detected nothing but the aroma of pines and spruce.

With startling suddenness, she sensed movement.

There! A woman glided on bat wings just above the treetops, a hundred yards to Brandi's right. The newcomer wore blue-black chainmail; twin scimitars hung from her hips. Wicked points of dark spines shone on vambraces and greaves. Red eyes glowed behind a chainmail veil attached to a black, spired helmet. Her dragon tail lashed the air.

A War Fiend. This will be interesting.

Brandi whispered under her breath, concentrating on her upper back and reached out to the Other Space. Slowing her breathing, she focused on an impression of light and air and flight. Energy poured into her. She opened her eyes and extended her wings. Snow-white pinions with tips of deepest black curved around her. She drew her blades.

She was about to take to the air when another creature glimmered in her enhanced sight. It lurked among the bushes, low to the ground in the mist, seventy yards away. Shapeless, it warped and shifted as it glided towards her.

Brandi paused, frowning. The amorphous creature advanced with alarming speed, resolving into a blob of dark grey fog with silvery tendrils and multiple red eyes.

Death Mist! There are two daemons!

Closing fast, the War Fiend fired two red-glowing spines from the armor plate on her forearm. Brandi leapt into the air and swerved to the left. One spine sizzled into the snowy earth, cutting a blistering furrow in the frozen ground amid a cloud of steam. The other slammed into a boulder, turning half of it into glowing molten rock.

The Death Mist hurtled up to meet her. Brandi banked away. The War Fiend pursued, unleashing an apple-sized comet of purple fire that sizzled past. The pungent odor of brimstone stung the air.

Brandi remembered more of Johanna's advice: *The Fallen Ones are aggressive and savage. Use that against them.*

Brandi dodged between trees as another of the War Fiend's fiery spines blasted a sapling in half. The Death Mist surged after her, tentacles extended. Thin lightning bolts crackled out and she spun out of the way.

The two Daemons lunged and swooped, trying to get her between them. She evaded, slashing them with her blades several times. Though she managed to keep them in line with each other, she still took a couple of hits from lightning and blade.

Cold seared her injuries, so intense that it burned. *That actually hurts… a lot. Do they have to make it so realistic?*

Brandi veered behind a copse of spruces as a glowing spine sizzled past. She stopped, hovering. The Death Mist wavered and sank towards the ground, leaking a black vapor from where she had cut it.

The War Fiend swooped around the trees. Brandi soared to meet her, slashing. They danced in mid-air, short swords and scimitars ringing like bells in the forest. The War Fiend snarled obscenities.

Out of the corner of her eye, Brandi saw the Mist rising up toward her. *Time it right…*

The War Fiend drew back. One of the spikes on its armor glowed. The Death Mist lunged towards Brandi, grey tentacles reaching. Two lightning bolts jolted one of Brandi's wings and she gritted her teeth against the pain.

The War Fiend shot the spine at her.

Brandi folded her wings and dropped straight down. The spine shot through the air where she had been and blasted through the Death Mist. Unable to even shriek, the fog-Daemon simply evaporated, its tentacles falling to hiss and dissipate in the snow. A sudden blast of sulfurous air made Brandi's eyes water.

Panting, Brandi landed near a trio of young pines, her wings tingling. She wished she could communicate with Johanna but she felt no signal from the earring.

The War Fiend stooped to follow and released her last two spikes. Brandi flinched, but the spines didn't arc towards her — they slammed into the trees.

Too late, Brandi realized her peril. One of the pines splintered and toppled over onto her. It was all she could do to protect her head. She tried to dodge, but the trunk slammed her into a drift of snow. She hit the frozen ground beneath with a jolt that rattled her teeth. Her swords flew into a nearby bush.

Her vision swam. She tried to lift herself up, but the tree trunk pinned her legs. She was glad she could still feel them.

The War Fiend alighted. "Ah, little queen. Can't fly anymore?" she said in a sultry voice, stalking forward like a panther. "That's too bad."

"I can still take you," Brandi shot back, pushing at the tree. She poured all her otherworldly strength into it. The trunk rolled aside and freed her legs. She rose, limping. Her eyes flicked to her weapons behind the War Fiend.

"I don't think so." The Daemon clucked in mock sympathy. Her scimitars made lazy circles in the air, the edges flaring crimson. "Say! I have a great idea! First, I'll cut off your ugly head, then maybe I'll take your lovely little husband next, eh? Cutting off all his parts will be entertaining."

Red tinted Brandi's vision. *No! You will NEVER have Eric!*

She extended her wings, fighting against a sudden rage burning within her. Again, she remembered Johanna's words: *Elohir nature is stronger than the Daemonic, always.*

"Nothing to say, little queen?" The Fiend sounded disappointed. "Oh well. Goodbye then. I'll give your regards to your little man-toy."

Brandi's composure broke. Wild, unbridled savagery surged into her. She shot up and backwards. The War Fiend lunged and missed.

Brandi threw out her hand, calling for one of her swords. The blade jumped to her fist and she parried.

"I'll carve out your innards, Daemon!" she screamed. She thrust out her free hand, glowing now with golden fire. A blast of light thrust the War Fiend back.

The Daemon hovered, her armor smoking. "It seems I underestimated you. But look, you're becoming one of us now! Splendid. You can join the Cause."

Out of the corner of her eye, Brandi caught a glimpse of one of her wings. The feathers darkened from white to grey. Her heart skipped a beat.

No. I can control this. She called for her other sword and let out a deep breath, willing the red haze to diminish. It started to fade.

Eyes flashed behind the Fiend's chainmail veil. "I'll have you. You and your whole family," the Daemon taunted. "Tortured, dead, chopped into morsels for hell hounds to enjoy."

The Daemon sprang forward. Brandi spun, her blazing sword lashing out. With a clanging thump, she severed one of the fiend's arms. Not even waiting for her to scream, Brandi drove the other blade into her midsection.

The Daemon fluttered to the snowy ground with her free hand pressed to the cauterized stump at her shoulder.

Brandi landed, breathing hard, battling against the remnants of Daemon rage.

The Daemon raised her good hand. "Mercy…" she managed.

Hot anger still lingered despite Brandi's attempts to control herself. *There should be no mercy for enemies,* she fumed. *I have to destroy it! It wants Eric.*

"Mercy," gasped the Daemon again. "I repent. I surrender."

Brandi fought for control, willing her fury to be still. She heard Johanna's counsel again. "*Abandonment of the virtues corrupted our people into the Fallen Ones. Do not give in to that temptation.*"

Brandi took a deep breath and let it out. *Our Father, who Art in Heaven…*

Her demon rage faded and the haze in her sight melted away. She gazed at the Daemon, who looked more pitiful than dangerous now.

"Very well," Brandi said. "Mercy is yours."

Instantly, the War Fiend winked out of existence. Brandi's injuries likewise disappeared and she sighed with relief. The ruined trees shimmered and vanished.

"That was better," announced a now-familiar male voice. Two Elohir strode out of the snowy trees towards her. Despite the cold, they wore only short robes with golden belts. Ivory wings tipped with tan curved over their shoulders. The dark-haired male clasped hands with his blonde companion.

Brandi leaned back against a tree, her hands still trembling from adrenaline. "Did you have to make it so realistic, Lord Petrus?"

"Well, you don't want to be unprepared when you meet the real thing, do you?" he replied.

"No, I don't. And I know why you're doing it, but…"

Johanna smiled, her agate eyes kind. "But it's painful. I know. Growth always is."

"I understand." Brandi straightened. She glanced up at the pair, more than a head taller than she. She opened her mouth, then closed it again.

"But?" Johanna prompted.

Brandi sheathed her swords. "I feel like I should be better at this but I'm not. The Daemon rage is very difficult to manage."

Petrus chuckled. "Brandi! You only started training after you returned from the honeymoon. That was only, what? Five months ago?"

Brandi shook her head. "Yes, but the people of the southern kingdoms — my people — suffer under the oppression of the Dark Faiths while I fumble around, trying to figure out my skills. I have to get better at this for their sake."

Johanna put a hand on her shoulder. "Leaping into danger before you're ready isn't going to help them. This takes time, especially with people of mixed blood."

Brandi bit her lip in frustration and forced herself to unclench her fists. "I can't keep training forever."

Johanna gave her shoulder a squeeze. "You're making wonderful progress. You'll be flying off with the other Grey Riders in no time."

Flying…

"Speaking of flying," Brandi said, dismissing her wings into the Other Space. "Discovering latent abilities is one thing, but I think I would have noticed something in the last thirty years that told me I had the ability to summon wings."

Petrus joined his wife at Brandi's side. "Elohir abilities have to be awakened for people with mixed heritage. It's especially difficult with you and your sister: part human, part Elven, part Elohir and part Daemon. I assure you there are very few guidelines of how to assess — much less train — people with your pedigree. Also, there is no sure formula for which abilities any given person might have, so even we didn't know until we started training you."

"I bet Megan isn't having this much trouble." Brandi tried and failed to keep the envy from her voice.

Johanna tilted her head to the side and gave her a wry look. "You would lose the bet. Ask her. Your sister has a list of complaints to rival yours. She's just more vocal about it."

Petrus' eyes flicked to something in the forest behind Brandi. "Speaking of family…Hello, Eric."

Brandi's senses tingled a split second after Petrus spoke and she spun. Her husband strode through the trees toward them, his short blond hair like burnished gold in the morning sunshine. He flipped the edge of his cloak over one shoulder and vaulted over a thick tree stump, not even breaking stride. His eyes danced when they alighted on her.

"Hello Petrus, Johanna," Eric Aldenar said.

Brandi's tension and anxiety dissipated away at the sight of him. He held out a hand. She fairly ran to meet him, drawing him close. His warm lips met hers and she lost herself in a brief and deep kiss, feeling heat and electricity surge through her all the way to her toes. She swore that the season changed to spring.

"That's a very fine hello," he said, drawing back.

She gazed into his violet eyes. The corner of her mouth curved up and she tapped his chin with her finger. "And a regular occurrence as long as you behave yourself."

"You have a deal, Your Majesty." He gave her a look that promised far more than kisses but she tore herself away and led him to Petrus and Johanna.

The Elohir stood arm in arm. "How was the meeting with King Phillip, Eric?" asked Petrus.

"He gave me his perspective on international relations. There's an entire world I didn't know about. He said Queen Ahlana wanted to meet with me but she wasn't feeling up to it."

Brandi made a face. "Morning sickness. Ugh. I am not looking forward to that."

Eric looked at her in surprise, eyebrows raised. "Something I should know?"

Longing and disappointment wrestled for dominance and disappointment won. She looked down at the snow-covered ground for a second, then back at him. "No, my love. Sorry."

Again, he gave her his knee-weakening smile. "Don't be."

Petrus and Johanna exchanged a knowing look. "Well, with that, we'll take our leave of you," Petrus said. "Keep up the good work, Brandi. You have made great progress and we are confident in your abilities."

Brandi and Eric bowed. "Thank you again," Brandi said. "I know I don't say it often enough."

Johanna laid her palm on Brandi's cheek and kissed her forehead. "Don't mention it. It is our pleasure."

The Elohir couple spread their wings and flew up through the trees into the wintry sky.

"How did it go today?" Eric asked. She felt the touch of his lips on the crown of her head.

Brandi sighed but remained quiet, memories of her rage still fresh in her mind.

"Tell me." He turned her towards a white-frosted glade. Two black, winged horses waited patiently on the far side.

Brandi strolled with him silently. Finally, she sighed and described her training session. "The worst part is that, half the time, I feel like I'm only seconds away from losing control," she finished.

"But you haven't, have you?"

She opened her mouth to answer and closed it. He had a point.

He patted her arm. "Did you talk to Saren when she was out here last week? You have something in common, after all."

"Yes, your sister has been very helpful, but information and implementation are different things. I have to get past this. Too many people are counting on me."

"Don't you think you're being a little hard on yourself? Saren has had to deal with her Daemonic side for decades and you've only been at it for five months."

"Maybe, but this is only practice. I can't afford to make mistakes in real-life situations."

They paused at the edge of the glade. The pegasi's heads came up and the mounts walked towards them, hooves crunching through the snow. Brandi refused to let go of Eric, holding him in silence.

"There's something else, Bran. I can tell."

She only nodded.

"Is it children?"

She gave him a mock scowl and pushed his shoulder. "Men are supposed to be oblivious."

He grinned. "That was an educated guess."

She waited a long moment before answering. "With the War over, I see more pregnant wives and new babies. People feel confident about starting families and I want one of our own, but how are we going to do that when my homeland is controlled by evil cults, hundreds of miles away? A campaign to reclaim a lost kingdom is no place for a child."

He hugged her. "I agree. And I want kids too, but you're right. It's not a good time."

She didn't answer, thoughts straying from children to training against mock Daemons and back again.

He kissed the top of her head. "I'm here with you all the way. Never forget that."

Brandi tried to submerge the memories of the savage Daemon rage. The intensity of it frightened her, even though she had once again conquered it, as before. *What if I lose my temper with him? What if I hurt him? God help me! What if I hurt our children?* Her stomach twisted.

Unbidden, she recalled yet another bit of Johanna's advice. *Your Elohir and Elf and human blood are far stronger than any evil.*

"I don't want to burden you or worry you," she said after a long pause. Her pegasus minced through the snow to her, nosing her shoulder bag for a treat. She smiled, stroking Amicus' nose.

"I'm here to help, sweetheart." Eric kissed Brandi's cheek. "Besides, I've seen you as a vampire. This is a lot less worrisome." He gathered the reins and swung into the saddle. "Come on. The others are waiting."

Chapter Two – Restless Lies the Crown

Connor Loemin adjusted the clasp of his cloak and pulled his gloves tighter against the cold. Despite the fire blazing in the fireplace and newly rebuilt walls, winter's chill managed to seep into their guest room.

At least they brought some furniture sized for Halflings, he thought.

"Ready?" asked Hannah Loemin, smoothing the sleeve of his velvet doublet. Her chestnut hair glowed in the reflected firelight.

"For yet another meeting? As much as I'll ever be."

She raised an eyebrow. "I know how much you dislike them and especially waiting for results," she replied. "But it will be part of the job when you eventually become king. Just remember you won't have to do it alone. I'll be there to help."

"Thank the great god Irial for that."

He ran his fingers through his hair, thinking over past council meetings. *Well, we have a backup proposal this time, just in case.*

Hannah glanced into a nearby mirror and settled the circlet on her brow. "Think of this as training. You will have to step into your father's role someday, though I pray it will not be soon."

"You and me both," he replied, taking her hand. "I'm not in a hurry to be King."

Hannah kissed his cheek. "It will come in time, love, and you'll be ready."

She accompanied him to the door of their chamber. Connor tapped on a star carved into the surface. The symbol flared white and the portal opened of its own accord. Human soldiers in blue and red hauberks of the Palace

Guards came to attention and saluted with gleaming halberds.

Connor nodded up at them and the pair proceeded along the hallway. Two guards detached from the squad and followed at a discreet distance.

"And that's another thing," he whispered to her. "I know they want to keep us safe, but having guards follow us everywhere is unnerving."

"Well, I am certainly glad they're here. So are Brandi and Megan and everyone else."

As they walked, Connor's eyes flitted to walls and ceilings under repair as well as restored areas of the Royal Palace of Deran. Though wreaths and holly no longer adorned the chambers and hallways of the palace, Connor still detected the faint aroma of pine, cinnamon and nutmeg.

Even war and devastation didn't keep the Christians from celebrating their Christmas, he mused. *Or maybe it spurred them to do so with more fervor.*

Thoughts of hearth and celebrations and home brought his thoughts to the town of Glen. He wondered how much of his family manor or his mother's temple still stood.

Knowing the Ja'al's savage and vengeful nature, he doubted much remained of either.

However, seeing life slowly return to normal calmed his mind and made it easier to forget what Oakmoor had looked like after the War. The sad part was that twenty percent of the city's population weren't alive to see it.

He continued on in silence, content to have Hannah's arm entwined in his own. At the council chambers, he squared his shoulders. "Let's pray for better results this time."

"Have faith, dearest," she replied.

They entered. A seneschal rapped his staff on the floor and announced their names.

King Phillip and seven ambassadors looked up from their seats at the horseshoe-shaped table. Connor and Hannah bowed to the King. The emissaries rose and bowed as one.

"Welcome, Your Highnesses," King Phillip said with a nod. "Please join us."

The couple climbed into high seats at the table and Connor took stock of the assembly. Emissaries sat in high-backed chairs, sifting through documents. A globe of blue crystal glittered on a pedestal at the center of the arc of the table. The area smelled of candle wax and fresh varnish.

"Well, everyone's here," Hannah whispered. "All the Northern Alliance nations as well as the realms of Gorostol and Merdail."

"Now all we need are my parents." Connor took up a sheaf of papers, scanning over the figures and paragraphs. It told him the same story as the last council: rebuilding was taking longer than anticipated and was far more expensive. Each of the represented nations struggled under the waning effects of a cold winter as well as the devastation of the War of the Dark Wave. The world needed time to heal.

Connor let his eyes drift to the ambassadors. They avoided looking at him or Hannah, concentrating on the papers in front of them. *How committed are they? Will they stand by their pledge to help us reclaim Loemin, not to mention Turis Rhi and Alenar? Will they try to back out? Or, worse yet, merely string us along with nothing but promises? We certainly don't have any resources to bear… just our names and our right to rule.*

King Phillip, of course, would support them as much as he was able. The other nations needed to be convinced, especially the ones that had taken a severe beating during the War.

A combination of impatience, frustration and lingering fears assailed him and he made an effort to control them. He knew life was difficult for everyone and that they were doing their best, but still…

"Will the Aldenar and Rhivan families be in attendance?" Hannah asked King Phillip.

"No. We had our meeting with them yesterday," the King replied.

And we've already heard about that from Brandi. Well, here it goes, then…

The seneschal's staff rapped on the floor again. "Their Majesties, King Seamus the Fourth and Queen Miriam the First of Loemin."

Connor rose as his father and mother entered, clad in the forest green and gold raiment of Loemin, coronets glittering on their heads. King Phillip and Connor's parents bowed to each other at the same time. His mother took a seat next to Connor and gave him an encouraging smile.

"Welcome, everyone." King Phillip announced. "Continuing on from yesterday's council, we are here to consider material support from the Northern Alliance to the Kingdoms-in-Exile of Alenar, Loemin and Turis-Rhi. Lady Navarre, please proceed with the summary."

A slender elven woman in a grey dress with burgundy trim bowed to King Phillip. She raised both hands overhead and then moved them down. A holographic map sparkled into being above the blue orb.

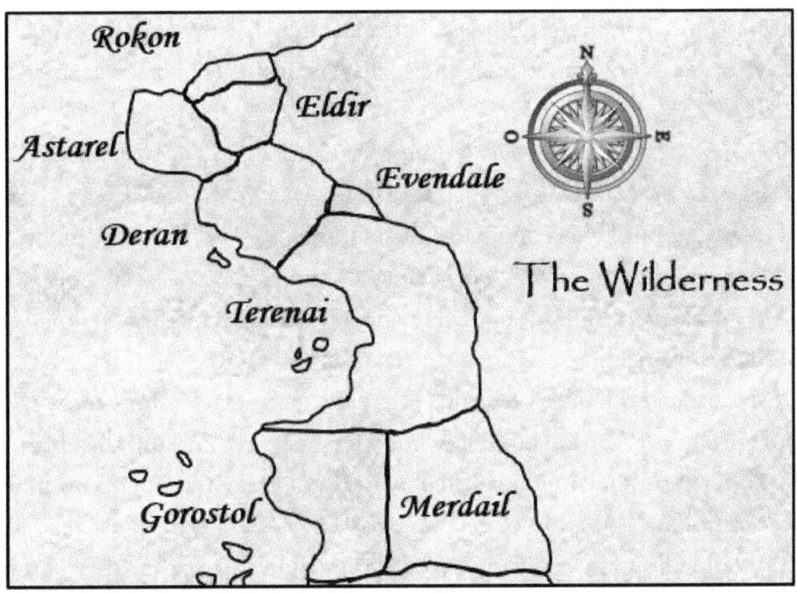

She read from a parchment. "First, we have an assessment of readiness of the Northern Alliance, Merdail and Gorostol to support the liberation of the ancient Southern Paragon Kingdoms from the rule of the People's Republic of Torosc. Turning our attention to Exhibit One, the Veriani Patriarchate of Eldir reports that their losses prevent them from contributing more than ten thousand gold northmarks and two companies of heavy infantry before Aprilis, but that they could increase this two-fold by the summer — the end of Augustus, to be exact..."

Connor's mind wandered as Lady Navarre continued reciting her notes. He knew them by heart and the conclusion worried him as much as it had a week ago. His parents and the other exiled royals could expect no significant aid before the summer's end, and probably not even by the beginning of autumn. Though the onset of winter meant less in the southern realms than it did in countries like Deran, it still presented logistical challenges, mainly in transport.

He kept quiet as the ambassadors from the other nations spoke next, outlining rebuilding projects, their misgivings about the progress of recovery efforts, and concerns about Fallen Ones potentially lurking in wild places. Connor paid less attention to their words than he did to their tone and body language. None of them addressed the Loemin family directly. Their eyes focused on anything other than the Halflings and their voices seemed a bit on edge.

They can't commit… or won't. Connor concluded. *Not unexpected, but I think it's time for the alternative.*

He waited until everyone had finished, then looked to King Phillip.

The King met his gaze. "Yes, Prince Connor?"

Here it goes, Connor thought. He surreptitiously wiped his palms on his trousers before rising.

"My lords and ladies," he said, "I feel it necessary to speak now that all the information is on the table. I acknowledge everything that has been said and I understand the situation. I feel we cannot delay the operation in order to accommodate a buildup of resources as Lady Navarre has just related. To do so would allow the authorities of Torosc time to regather their strength. If that happens, we would be set back years and miss a golden opportunity to bring freedom to the Old Realms."

"We understand your eagerness, Prince Connor," replied the ambassador from Rokon. He stroked his greying beard. "But surely you realize that the current state of affairs makes it very difficult to provide resources for major expeditions beyond our borders."

Connor's mother gave him the tiniest of smiles.

"I do indeed, Sir Alphaeus," he replied. "But I would ask all those here present: where did the Dark Wave originate? Where were the Skull Gates invented? And where did the Ja'al hide their research facilities where they figured out how to close the Celestial Gates and bar the Elohir from coming to our aid?"

No one spoke. King Phillip steepled his fingers before his face and Sir Alphaeus gazed into the distance. The Halfling representative from Evendale opened her mouth and then closed it. She shifted in her high seat, frowning.

Connor swept the council with his eyes. "Yes," he nodded. "You know it as well as I do. All of that malignancy started in the People's Republic of

Torosc, in what used to be the old Paragon Realms. If we don't excise what evil remains there, it will regenerate and hatch yet another vile plot. It may not happen in our lifetimes, but it will surely happen in our children's. We must act to retake those lands and make them safe so that our enemies cannot inflict another Dark Wave on the world."

"You leave out one important point, Highness," noted the Dwarven ambassador from Merdail. She pointed at the map and a mild shimmer outlined the section corresponding to Torosc. "The catalyst for the Dark Wave was the plan of the Ja'al, but, thanks be to Kurental, the Ja'al cult is no more. Their temples are razed to the ground, their high clergy slain, and their military units scattered. I doubt if they have even a quarter of their former strength."

Connor caught his father's eyes and bowed to the Dwarven emissary. Without another word, he settled back into his seat.

They're hedging, like before. Connor forced himself to unclench his fists. *This is the part I can't stand. Why can't they see the danger?*

Hannah rose. "What you say is true, milady," she said, gesturing to the map. "Yet you know as well as I do that nature abhors a vacuum and the Ja'al are not the only force for evil in the world. The other Dark Faiths will step in to take their place and will find ready volunteers. There are plenty of people greedy and selfish enough to join whoever promises them what they want."

"But the forces of Evil need time to coordinate," interjected the emissary from Eldir. "The region is turbulent. If they are spending half the time we are in rebuilding, it will be many months before the remnants of the People's Republic can think to mount any kind of new offensive."

Hannah sat and Queen Miriam spoke up. "True," she noted. "They face significant obstacles. But realize also that several of the Ja'al gods remain. They will not sit idly by."

"Who?" asked the ambassador from Astarel. He raised an elegant eyebrow. "Gudarta? Neralia? After the Grey Riders found the lost Gate of Stars, the forces of evil took quite a beating at the hands of the Elohir. I hardly think they'd be eager to repeat that."

"Gudarta or Neralia might not," Miriam replied. "However, do you think that other evil religions pass up the chance to absorb the remnants of the

Ja'al cult? We could potentially face new federations of evil. Do not forget that some of the evil churches stayed out of the War and are still very strong."

The Dwarven emissary waved a hand. "With all due respect, Your Majesty, that is highly unlikely. The infighting amongst the Dark Faiths is well known and one of the few things we have been able to exploit."

Again, more talk and no action… Connor just managed to keep himself from grinding his teeth in frustration. Hannah's hand covered his own and she gave him a squeeze. He let out a slow breath.

King Phillip tapped the arm of his chair. "Supposing what you say is true, Queen Miriam, it does not mean what it did previously. Even in concert with other Dark Faiths, Ja'al goddesses such as Gudarta and Neralia would have difficulty hatching another conspiracy like the Dark Wave."

"Indeed Majesty," Seamus now jumped into the fray. "However, the only factor limiting the numbers of either Elohir or Daemon agents here on our world was The Ban. When Daemons invaded at the outset of the War, that agreement between Hades and Celestia became null and void. Now there is little holding back the Fallen Ones from installing fresh forces on Damora, in wild places or even the seamy underbelly of large cities."

"But Elohir also live among us in secret," the emissary from Astarel protested. "The Daemons would be defeated before they began."

Seamus nodded. "If we or the Elohir could get at them. But Torosc is far away and still a formidable foe despite their losses. There is nothing to stop them from declaring themselves as a sanctuary state for Daemons and hosting entire platoons of Fallen Ones."

Utter silence reigned.

The ambassador from Astarel shook his head. "None of this is certain. Those are dangers that have not yet — and may never — come to fruition. Our present predicament, however, is very real: food shortages, a harsher winter than normal, illness among the population and depleted militaries. We cannot invade Northern Torosc. It is simply beyond our means."

"There does not have to be an invasion," Seamus replied.

The ambassadors exchanged glances.

"What are you suggesting, Majesty?" the Halfling emissary asked.

The King of Loemin stood. "Even during the War, we heard of disaffected elements in the People's Republic. If they can be rallied, we can turn them against their former masters. Any forces we send to the Southern Lands would not need to do all the fighting, but merely support the rebels in freeing their own lands. Then, after the people have joined with us, our allies to the North would send support — a move that would gain goodwill and enable future new alliances, I might add."

"How does Your Majesty propose to implement this plan?" asked the Eldirite ambassador, her brow furrowed.

Seamus smiled. "We can be the catalyst for the oppressed to take action. Some people in the south believe that the royal houses have been found while others do not and still others are skeptical. If we were to convince them that we are there to help them, then we can rally the countryside to our cause. I propose that Queen Miriam and I, as well as the Queen and High Princess of Alenar, travel south to lead the rebellion."

A tumult of discussion arose.

"You cannot mean that, Majesty," protested the Dwarven representative. "You cannot risk yourselves. Send emissaries instead."

Seamus held up a hand. The room quieted. "Intelligence indicates that rebel leaders will accept no one but us, personally. They have had other, false 'saviors' in their midst in the past, only to find out they were Ja'al agents sent to root out elements of discontent."

"How will you prove your identities?" challenged the emissary from Rokon.

Miriam spoke up. "The Aldenar sisters have proof positive that they are the heirs of their ancient kingdom. I can say no more without their leave."

"Are you sure that is enough?" asked the Halfling ambassador.

Seamus shrugged. "Actions speak louder than words. To prove ourselves, we will join with the rebels in their struggle. In addition, we will take with us officers from the Northern Alliance with militia experience who can serve as liaisons."

No one spoke.

"I must protest," said the Elven envoy from Terenai. "I agree with my colleague from Merdail. While the Aldenars may be able to prove their identities and you might be able to convince the leaders by word or deed, it is too risky to send all of you."

And now I play my last card...

Connor and Hannah stood, hand in hand. "You make a good point, my lady," Connor said. "How would the Council feel if the Crown Princess and I were to go in place of my Royal Father and Mother? Hannah and I are well-accustomed to the rigors and dangers of the life of a sell-sword."

The ambassadors exchanged surprised looks.

Finally, the Dwarven ambassador barked a short laugh. "Did Queen Brandawyn put you up to this? Never mind. Don't answer that. You're all Grey Riders. Of course you're working together."

A thrill of hope surged through Connor. *Now, maybe, we can end all the discussion and get on with it.*

King Seamus smiled. "Naturally. Now, I would propose that we concentrate on Loemin and Alenar first. We would use those regions as a foothold to get to Turis Rhi, farther south."

The emissary from Astarel shook his head. "It is sheer madness to thrust yourselves into the most dangerous place in the world without an army at your back."

Hannah nodded. "It is audacious, but ironically, that will be in our favor. We don't think the leaders in Torosc would suspect it. They are used to commanding from behind, not risking themselves for others."

"The Torosci intelligence service will detect you," warned the Halfling ambassador.

"They are vigilant, but if you help us, we can distract and misdirect them," replied Seamus. "All we require is supplies, intelligence, and a few well-played diversions. The Grey Riders will do the rest, but they need your help for the initial step."

"It seems you have thought all this out," the Dwarven representative said, "In my opinion, it borders on the foolhardy. However, it is your own necks that you risk so I cannot insist on you abandoning the idea."

Connor let his eyes rest on each representative. Maybe, just maybe, they would go for it. The plan required minimal investment to begin with and then a vital hammer-stroke at the right time. It needed attention to detail, great timing and commitment, but it could work.

His mind flew back to his short time in northern Torosc, when he and the Riders tried to rescue Megan. The squalor, fear and despair of the communities weighed on him. *It has to work. We have nothing else at this point. And everything we've said is true. The alternative is…*

Images of daemons rampaging through Oakmoor now came to the fore. *No. Never again.*

Seamus removed a page from his belt pouch. "This plan shows how we can accomplish our goals with minimal impact to your nations."

The Elven emissary from Terenai chuckled, shaking her head. "I do believe we've all been maneuvered into position, King Phillip. Who am I to say? Maybe this will end well for everyone. Please, Majesty, show us what you have in mind."

Chapter Three – Chess Pieces

Captain Alex Fejer gazed out the window. Troops marched in formation on the drill field below. Workers swarmed over scaffolding that embraced a tower just beyond and he readily discerned scorch marks on the walls of the citadel. He contemplated partially collapsed houses, damaged fortifications and charred neighborhoods in the vast city scape in the background.

Well, at least Oakmoor survived the War. That makes two of us.

"Were you here during the siege, Sergeant?" he asked without turning his head.

"No, sir," answered a male voice behind him. "I was up north, in Darlon."

Alex turned on his heel and clasped his hands behind his back. "Darlon…How badly was it damaged?"

The young human in a navy blue and silver surcoat averted his eyes to study the paper on the desk in front of him. "Not as bad as Oakmoor, sir, but then, the Daemon army had its eye on the capital anyway."

"So, you were a bit more fortunate."

The sergeant tapped his pen on the desktop. "Many were not, begging your pardon, sir."

"Too true," Alex murmured. A pretty face framed by golden hair flashed in his mind for a second and his heart clenched. "It is up to us to honor their memory."

Before the sergeant could answer, a tiny blue crystal on his desk flashed once.

"The Major will see you now," the sergeant said, rising to open the door to the inner office.

"Thank you."

Alex entered the office but didn't see anyone in the large chair behind the massive desk. Tall glass windows dominated the far wall. Two bookcases stood on either side of the windows, lined with neat rows of tomes and cubbyholes crammed with scrolls. He looked left and right but only saw two more empty chairs and a plain side table. The mild aroma of mint tea lingered in the air, along with a vaguely familiar musky odor.

"Captain Fejer reporting, sir," he said, coming to attention.

A dry chuckle sounded from behind the chair. "At ease, Captain," said a low, guttural voice in halting Humana. "Please take seat."

A short, wiry Goblin stepped around the chair.

Fejer's eyes widened. "Major… Gorlak?"

"Yes, I am." Sharp black eyes appraised him from a round, simian face. Three stubby horns on his forehead gleamed in the morning sunlight. He carried a long dagger in his belt. Alex's eyes flicked to the silver medallion of a pegasus resting against Major Gorlak's white and gold hauberk.

White and gold? That means he serves the Papal Nuncio. And the medallion means he's someone important to the Grey Riders. But he's a Goblin!

The Goblin vaulted into the chair, which Alex now noticed had a padded wooden platform installed on the seat. Gorlak rested his forearms on the desk and nodded at a chair opposite him.

"Oh. Sorry. Thank you, sir." Alex sat, his mind spinning.

Gorlak folded his hands and raised an eyebrow. "Something wrong?"

"I… no… beg pardon, Major. It is nothing." Memories of fighting Goblin commandos surged to the surface and Alex regained his composure with an effort.

"Nothing? Ha! I take a guess," Gorlak said, picking up a paper from the desk. "You spend much time during War of Dark Wave fighting Goblins and now you talk to me as superior officer. I am supposed to be enemy. I speak right?"

"Well, sir, I wouldn't put it quite that way."

Gorlak's amused expression didn't waver. "But I would if I am in your place. Not to worry. I understand. Much changed now."

Alex's eyes flicked to Gorlak's livery again. "Major, if you don't mind my asking, how did you come to serve the Papal Nuncio? The Church and Goblinkind haven't exactly been on friendly terms since the New Faith arrived at the time of the Skyfire."

"That is a long story," Gorlak replied. "But for now, I can tell you I changed by interaction with Grey Riders and Father Edward, previous Nuncio." His eyes grew distant and, Alex thought, a little sad.

Alex regarded Major Gorlak, trying to come to grips with this new reality. *Christianity arrived thousands of years ago and I can probably count on two hands the number of Goblins who have turned from evil and joined the Church. Now, one of them is my commander.*

Gorlak shook himself as if waking from a dream. He turned his attention to the paper in his hands. "You pronounce surname in Elven fashion?"

And he knows Elven? "Yes, sir. It's pronounced Fay-air; the 'j' is pronounced as a 'y'."

"Hmm…" Gorlak mused. "Name is very old. I think Lord Melinor tell me of a region with that name, from Paragon Era. A barony, I think, somewhere here in Deran. Hard to tell after thousands of years."

This is not your usual Goblin. "Yes, sir. My ancestors probably originated from there."

Gorlak nodded. "Name means 'those of magic' or 'the magical ones', yes?"

"Yes sir." Alex tried to square his past experience of Goblins with the calm and almost scholarly officer behind the desk. He failed.

Gorlak's eyes returned to the paper. "You served with Hannah Loemin at Siege of Meridian, in last days of War."

"Yes, sir, before her marriage. She was Hannah Lervion then."

"Yes. The wedding days were great celebrations." Gorlak smiled, showing sharp little fangs. "The Crown Princess is good officer. She not have lot of experience but that will come." His eyes flitted over the paper. "I see here you were captain in Gorostol Army, took command of militia company when commander die in battle."

"Yes, sir."

"You only four and twenty years old."

Alex took a breath before answering. "Yes, sir. I understand that I'm young for my rank but —."

Gorlak held up a hand. "I do not mean that. I mean you do good service for one so young."

"Oh. Thank you, sir."

The Goblin officer examined the paper again. "You have skill in riding flying creatures, like hippogriff and pegasus."

"Yes, sir. I was trained just as the war broke out. I did have some combat experience but then a lack of mounts put me on a list of reserves."

"Hmm…" Gorlak observed Alex for a while with piercing black eyes. "So, why do you want to go with us to Republic of Torosc and be liaison officer for Crown Princess Hannah? Torosc is dangerous place."

Alex met his gaze unflinchingly. "It is a great opportunity, sir. I have no family and I can make a name and a future for myself if I help her family reclaim their homeland."

"I see. You know you will work with the Grey Riders, yes?"

Alex nodded.

Gorlak laid down the paper carefully on the desktop. "This does not bother you?"

Alex sat up a little straighter. "Should it?" he asked.

Gorlak leaned back in his chair and interlaced his fingers, settling them on his chest. "Captain, how much you know about the Riders?"

Alex shrugged. "As much as anyone, I guess. They were free-lance sellswords who made a name for themselves in Deran. Then they found the last surviving Celestial Gate during the worst days of the War. Once they opened the Gate, they brought in an army of Elohir to defeat the Ja'al cult and their Daemonic allies. And, of course I know Princess Hannah is married to one of them, Connor Loemin."

Gorlak nodded slowly. "All true, but you should know few more things." He hopped down out of his seat and strode to a wall map. He clasped his hands behind his back. "Grey Riders have fame and title, but also many enemies."

"Not surprising, sir, considering their history."

"Indeed. They faced many evils." Gorlak pointed at various sections of the map. "They defeat lich princess, Assassins' Guild leaders, dragons, Daemon princes. You fight Daemons before, Captain?"

Alex's memory flashed back to desperate days on the walls of Meridian, fighting for his life against wave after wave of howling enemies. He forced himself to unclench his jaw.

"Yes, sir," he replied in an even voice. "Dwerrolves and Skreets made repeated assaults on our position. We repelled them but at great cost. We lost…" The faces of his friends hovered in his mind, their eyes closed in death. His voice trailed off.

Even Eleanor.

Gorlak turned to face him. "I understand sacrifice, Captain," the Goblin said in a soft voice. To his amazement, Alex saw sympathy in his eyes. "I also fight against Dark Wave, in Oakmoor."

Alex could think of nothing to say.

"I point this out because Grey Riders have equally dangerous enemies in future," Gorlak continued, raising a finger. "If you become attaché for Princess Hannah, you face same perils – become target of the enemy."

Assassins' Guild leaders, liches, dragons, Daemon lords… Alex remained silent for a while.

Gorlak studied him, black eyes impassive.

I have to throw the dice or get out of the game… Alex shook his head. "Yes, Major, but weren't all the Daemons chased back to Hades by the Elohir?"

Gorlak gave him a grim smile. "Not so. Not all Fallen Ones retreat. We just not sure where they are. Also, much of Torosc Republic government remains. They will not stand by and let Grey Riders free old kingdoms."

"I might have to end up fighting Daemons again?"

Gorlak nodded. "Perhaps, and enemies from War, and servants of Dark Powers. Not an easy assignment, this."

Captain Alex considered that. *General Watson said I could have a command in his division if I decided not to go.*

"You still volunteer?" Gorlak prodded.

Alex's thoughts drifted to the friends and comrades-in-arms he had lost — and Eleanor.

A new start.

He took a deep breath. "Major, some of my friends died in the War. If the Grey Riders succeed in what they're trying to do, we can prevent another conflict like it. Also, I grew up around orphans and I see many orphans today.

They deserve better."

Gorlak nodded slowly.

"Besides," Alex finished, "to be part of the retinue of a Crown Princess is an opportunity few people will ever get."

"Indeed." The twinkle returned to the Goblin's eyes. He selected a different parchment from the desk and handed it over. "This is list of personnel for journey. Attaché for Queen Brandawyn of Alenar is Captain Khyla Dearborn. You know her?"

"No, sir," Alex shook his head, scanning the page. He looked up at the major sharply. "We have dragons?"

"Yes. Two young dragons, grandchildren of a hero from the War. They named Tholerios and Kindriana. Not as powerful as their grandfather, but still plenty strong, I think."

Even dragons! This will be quite the mission. Alex handed the paper back. "It looks like everything is ready."

Gorlak grinned. "Almost. We needed one more liaison, and now we have you. Welcome to the Grey Riders, Captain."

Alex's smile broadened as waves of relief, excitement and trepidation competed within him. Excitement won out. "Thank you, sir! I should probably get to the quartermaster."

Gorlak chuckled and held out his hand. Alex took it, surprised at the strength of the Goblin's grip. "Good idea, Captain. We leave tomorrow morning..."

<<>>

How far the mighty Ja'al cult has fallen, Lady Arlene Culver mused. *First, they're trying to take over the whole world and now this. Maybe I should have thought twice.*

She swept into the room. Hewn stone walls festooned with Ja'al graffiti greeted her eyes. A large bed leaned against the far wall next to another wooden door. Wall sconces held guttering torches and a cold firepit occupied the center of the room. Two trunks and a table and chair were next to the bed, near a water barrel and a rickety wardrobe. She doubted the place had been dusted in a fortnight.

"This is the best they have?" she sniffed.

"Apparently," answered Arless Octavio. His red eyes swept the chamber. "From what we've seen of the rest of the complex, it's better than most." He gave her a smile, his fangs glinting.

Arlene sighed, then beckoned to a pair of Hobgoblins hauling her luggage. She waved to one side of the room and the muscular, half-simian soldiers set down her trunk, then stood at attention, hands on their scimitar hilts. One Hobgoblin's black eyes flitted to his companion and his baboon-snout twitched.

"That will be all. Return to your captains," Arlene ordered.

Both soldiers hesitated.

"Go," Arlene repeated. "We don't need to be guarded."

The Hobgoblins bowed and departed, shooting a glance at Arlene as they did so.

"Their chieftain doesn't trust us," Octavio said after they left. "Or maybe he just doesn't like humans." He grinned.

"Or vampires." Arlene replied with an arched eyebrow at him. She removed her cloak and waved a hand at the firepit. A spark leapt from her fingertips and lit the blackened wood within. A feeble flame started up and smoke rose towards a crack in the ceiling.

"See if you can get some firewood," she said. "You'd never guess there's a whole forest surrounding us. Lazy Hobgoblins."

Octavio stepped to the door, but it opened before he got there. Instead of a Hobgoblin, a golden-haired male Elf stood in the doorway. A silver medallion depicting a whip and tongs glittered against his scale mail.

The Elf bowed. "A visitor just arrived to see Your Ladyship."

Arlene sighed. "Who is it?"

"Archon Golvadu, milady."

"Really?" She exchanged a look with Octavio. "Very well. Escort him to us."

"Of course, milady." The officer departed.

Octavio looked thoughtful as the door closed behind the Elf. "Golvadu. I wonder why he's out and about — though I can guess."

"And your guess?"

Octavio smirked. "The defeat of the Ja'al Cult during the Dark Wave depleted his power base. Our esteemed Archon needs new allies."

"Agreed. The religion of the Ja'al is no more. I foresee new alliances between their remnants and the other Dark Faiths."

Octavio shrugged. "I am not so sure. Take the Church of Vardu, for example. They kept out of the War and you know they're just as likely to fight against us as they are against one of the Religions of the Light, like the Christians or Veriani. Old rivalries die hard."

If he only knew. Arlene smiled. "Do not discount greed or the lust for power, Arless. Some allies just need the right incentive."

"We will see, then."

"Indeed." Arlene folded her hands at her waist. *Golvadu. That old goat better bring something to the table besides arrogance. By the gods, he's not hiding out here if I can help it.*

As if in answer, the door opened again and the Elven officer bowed. "Second Archon Golvadu."

A Dwarven man in dark purple wizard's robes marched into the room, eyes darting around, his staff clutched in his hand.

"Your Grace." Arlene bowed and Octavio followed suit.

"Lady Arlene." Golvadu stumped to the chair by the table and settled himself in it as if it were a throne, brushing a hand over his dark beard. His face screwed up in distaste after a survey of his surroundings. Dirt stained his formerly resplendent clothes. Mud and moss crusted his boots.

She smiled. "I'm sorry we don't have the usual amenities."

His lip curled in a sneer. "Your obsequiousness does you credit."

A spark of anger brought words to her lips but her common sense bit them off. Instead, she inclined her head. "Perhaps Your Worship would like other accommodations? Maybe at another outpost? I can arrange for a travel escort."

Golvadu ground his teeth and slammed the butt of his staff into the stone floor. "Bah! You'll do no such thing."

Arlene gave him a sweet smile. "To what do we owe the honor of this visit?"

Golvadu tapped his foot vexedly, scattering bits of dried mud on the stone floor. "I am touring the provinces to see who is still loyal to the People's Republic of Torosc and who is a traitor." He fixed her with a baleful eye. "Which are you?"

Arlene maintained her calm demeanor. "To be frank, Great Archon, we serve whomever gives us greater rewards. Though I admit that accepting a vampire into the ranks is normally an impediment." She nodded at Octavio, who flashed his fangs in a broad smile.

Golvadu made a face. "Don't be daft! They will accept whomever I damn well tell them to accept."

Arlene remained silent.

With a grunt, Golvadu stared at Octavio and nodded at the table. The vampire hefted it like a child's toy and set it in front of the Archon. Golvadu waved dismissively at a chair and Arlene sat.

"Let's get to the point," Golvadu growled, pinching the bridge of his nose with two fingers. "There are still many in Torosc loyal to the Republic. I have sent liaisons to the regional governors. We have plans to raise an army to march on Gorostol within a year."

"March on Gorostol?" Arlene gasped. "That's madness!"

"It is not!" Golvadu snapped. "Our long-term plan has not changed, despite the failure of the Dark Wave. We are already starting our rebuilding efforts. The situation to the north is just as difficult for our enemies as it is for us, even more so. The regime that acts quickest will have the advantage and I mean to take it to the full."

Arlene scanned his face for any sign of irony or jesting but he looked serious. *Is he mad? The war ended not five months ago.*

She leaned back in her chair. "That will be a tall order. Some districts, like Coastwatch and Bluevale, are turbulent, particularly since word has reached them of the Houses-in-Exile to the north. The heirs to the ancient thrones of old won't wait long before trying to reclaim them."

Golvadu sneered. "As if they could just walk in here and jam crowns on their heads! We know about their plans. We have a few surprises waiting."

Arlene nodded. "I'm sure you do, but my point is that many provinces are restive and require constant monitoring and patrol. Our resources are not as plentiful as in times past."

"That may be true." Golvadu twisted his staff in his hands. "However, we can recruit from the Wild Lands. Perhaps there might be Dark Elven communities that did not join in the initial assault with whom we could negotiate."

Arlene shrugged. "I am not sure. You would have to ask one of the Dark Elves here. I imagine there might be opportunities, but it would take time to entice them into an alliance and coordinate planning."

Golvadu muttered something profane and glowered at the tabletop.

Time to play my card. Arlene leaned her forearms on the table. "With regard to alliances, at least, I think I have an opportunity. We have been approached by those who would join us in common cause."

"Who?" snapped Golvadu.

"Arless, tell the guard to go to the guest chamber and request the presence of my special visitor."

Octavio's brow furrowed. She nodded. The vampire walked to the door and spoke to a guard outside, then returned to his place at Arlene's side.

Golvadu's eyes narrowed. "What are you playing at, Lady Arlene?"

Someone rapped on the door and opened it. A burly, grey-haired human man with a neatly trimmed beard entered. He wore bone-white robes over chainmail. A medallion of pure ebony depicting a skull and crossed swords rested against his tunic, glowing with a ghostly aura.

"Greetings," he said with a bow, then swept them with cold, dark-blue eyes.

"Your Grace," Arlene announced, sweeping a hand toward the new arrival, "I would like to introduce Ilyan Kalik, emissary of the Church of Vardu. I have heard his proposal and feel it would be mutually beneficial to all concerned."

Golvadu scowled. "A proposal from Vardu? Ha! Where were you during the War? I have a hard time believing you would throw in your lot with us now."

Kalik smiled. "It is true that we kept our distance during the Dark Wave but this means we have resources you lack. My leadership believes it is time to create new alliances lest the so-called Religions of the Light gain the upper hand, as friendly realms in the Torosc region would undoubtedly enable them to do."

Golvadu didn't speak for a while, tapping his boot against the floor. Kalik returned his stare impassively.

Finally, the Dwarf grunted. "And what can you bring to the table?"

Kalik gave a slight shrug. "Five full-strength divisions of troops unmarred by the recent conflict, alliances with the Blood Star Goblin Confederacy and the Dark Elven city-state of Minrikard, plus three Troll tribes and some, shall we say, potent allies from other quarters."

Golvadu sat up. "Five divisions? You would contribute that much?"

Kalik inclined his head and Golvadu's eyes glinted.

Arlene hid a smirk. *Maybe the old goat's plan will work after all...*

The Dwarven Archon's eyes narrowed. "Your offer is very significant. What is the cost for such generosity?"

Before Kalik could answer, Arlene bowed to Golvadu. "If you will indulge us for a while, Your Grace, all this will be revealed when we go over Ambassador Kalik's proposal. I believe it has great merit. Let us discuss it, shall we?"

Chapter Four – Best Laid Plans

Dar Cabot twisted in the saddle, scanning the darkening evening skies behind him for enemies. None pursued.

The other Riders flew ahead of him through murky clouds, with Eric and Brandi leading the formation. His eyes flicked to Connor and Hannah riding above and to the right. Their pegasus labored, despite only carrying two Halflings.

A lightning bolt to the chest armor will slow you down, Dar thought grimly. *Damn it. Retreating for the fifth time in a week. We need a different plan.*

A golden-brown dragon swooped below him, turning coppery eyes in his direction. Gorlak crouched in a special saddle on the dragon's back.

Dar waved. The Goblin nodded and tapped Tholerios between the wings. The dragon swung lower, then looped around towards their back trail.

Dar cast about for Tholi's sister but saw no sign of Kindriana.

When the available light made it difficult to make out his fellows flying nearby, he tapped the pendant resting against his surcoat. His vision shifted from visible light to infrared in a heartbeat. Now he clearly saw not only the other Riders riding their pegasi, but Captains Fejer and Dearborn on their own mounts. More importantly, the dim lights of the city of Duarvar now glimmered in the distance, becoming stronger every second.

Dar glanced over his shoulder and relaxed when both young dragons came into view. This close to their base of operations, away from the dangerous borderlands, they were probably safe. He turned his face back towards the city.

The familiar, rhythmic pattern of Virasi's wingbeats followed by resting glides lulled Dar into a more relaxed state. He mulled over their last foray, twisting the reins in gloved hands.

What did we do wrong? Brandi and Megan gave us what they knew about patrols and Torosci military tactics. Lord Venris provided us with maps and scouting reports. We headed for the gap between the mountains just when the enemy riders took off after the diversion force. Yet everything went haywire anyway…

Duarvar loomed ever closer and their formation closed in on the central fortress keep. He pushed aside his musings and concentrated on landing in the barracks courtyard, a tricky proposition at best in twilight conditions. The Grey Riders swung about. Dar and Megan descended last, just after the dragons. Dar pulled in next to Megan, slowing to a stop before dismounting.

Gorlak clambered down from Tholi's saddle and immediately ran to Dar's side.

"Tholi not say anything but I know he hurts," the Goblin said with an anxious look back at the dragon. "Please go use curing magic."

Dar shot a glance at Megan. She swung down from the saddle and beckoned to Captain Fejer. "Captain, please see to the pegasi," she announced. "Prince Dar and I will help with the wounded." She took Dar's hand and they accompanied Gorlak to Tholi's side.

The dragon panted and took a deep breath as they neared. "You should see to the others, Your Highnesses," he protested. "I'll be all right."

Dar put a hand on a burn mark on his foreleg. "I'll be the judge of that," he replied. "And stop with the titles. We've been through too much together."

Megan smiled. "At least in private, Tholi."

One hand still clasping Megan's, Dar closed his eyes and slipped into a healing trance. He frowned. In addition to the lacerations, arrow wounds and burns, he detected a Daemonic poison.

"Got it?" asked Megan. He nodded.

She murmured under her breath and a wave of energy pulsed through him. He captured it, added his own healing power and then directed it into the young dragon's injuries. The wounds and venom faded. Tholi relaxed and much of his tension evaporated.

Dar opened his eyes.

Megan gave him an admiring glance. "I've spent so much time on practicing my other talents I haven't trained much in healing," she said.

"You will get there," he replied, giving her hand a squeeze.

"Thank you both," said Tholi. He laid the bottom of his jaw on top of Dar's head gently and repeated the gesture with Megan.

Dar smiled and patted him on the shoulder as Megan gave him a kiss on the nose. "You and Kindri took a lot of punishment out there," he said. "It's the least I can do when my plan goes awry."

Tholi's eyes flashed and he opened his mouth but Brandi's voice interrupted him.

"How is he?" Brandi and Eric strode to Tholi's side.

"Healed," Dar replied. "Probably exhausted, but he'll never admit it."

"I am well, Majesty – I mean, Brandawyn," Tholi interjected with an arch look at Dar. "How are Kindri and Phantom?"

Brandi smiled but her eyelids still creased with worry. "Better. Tholi, I would like you and Kindri to accompany the pegasi to their stalls to make sure everything is satisfactory. The Riders and I have things to discuss."

Again, Tholi looked like he wanted to say something but inclined his head. "As you wish. We will wait with Captains Fejer and Dearborn until you return."

Connor and Hannah joined them. Connor let out a deep breath.

"The drawing board calls us yet again," Hannah noted with a wry look up at Dar.

"With a vengeance."

The Riders trudged towards the military headquarters. Dar's mind raced as they climbed the steps and turned down a hallway towards a conference room. He formulated half a dozen altered plans and just as quickly discarded them.

There has to be another way to get into Torosc…

Once inside, Eric closed the doors behind them. "Well, again, they knew we were coming. For some reason, they're not taking the bait when the Duarvar military execute the probing attacks."

"Something we should have changed after the first two attempts," Hannah noted.

"We did," Megan added, stripping off her riding gloves and laying them on the table as she slipped into a chair. "But the enemy is obviously doing the same. This is our fifth try and we're no closer to entering Torosc than a week ago."

"We haven't tried at night," Connor said, "but something tells me that our enemies might do better in darkness."

"Their Daemon scouts certainly will," Brandi agreed. She leaned on the table, frowning. "It's almost as if they have some advance knowledge."

"With the Skreets to detect us and the attack Daemons right on their heels, I doubt if they need much," Eric said. He slapped his gauntlets into his palm. "We need a new strategy. There were just too many of them and they arrived too quickly."

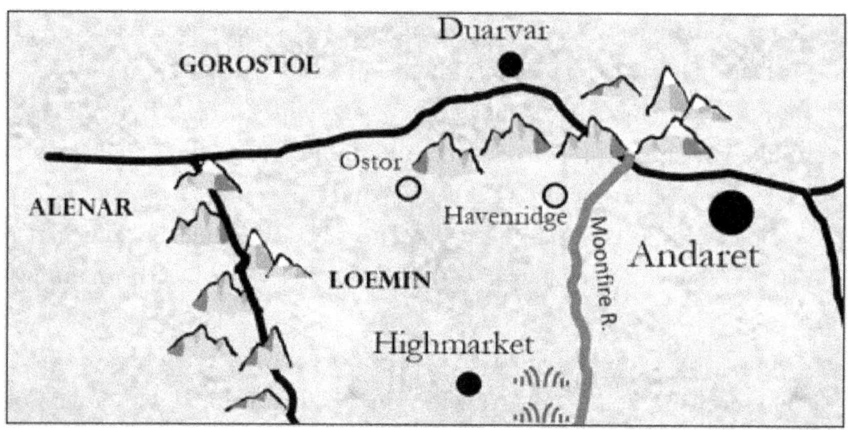

Dar's agitation returned, fueled by the added complication of a possible spy somewhere in Duarvar, reporting their every move. He took a seat next to Megan. "A dawn incursion doesn't work and neither did one at twilight. We've tried single diversions, double diversions, diversions followed by a pause, heading west and then south. They're always waiting. What other options do we have?"

The group mused in silence for a while. Dar watched all their expressions, mirrors of his own: frustrated, tired and stumped.

Boy, we're a morose group, Dar thought.

Connor caught Dar's eye. "How about in broad daylight?" he asked with an innocent expression. "We could blow trumpets and hand out cakes and ale? It might work."

That got a round of laughter.

"Sure," answered Eric with a swipe at Connor's head that he easily dodged. "You can lead the formation for that one."

The Halfling grinned back. "The cakes might not make it to Torosc." Hannah poked him in the side, smiling.

Brandi chuckled, eyes twinkling. "I believe you! Thanks, Connor, for lightening the mood."

Before anyone could answer, a knock sounded at the door.

"Enter," said Brandi.

Captain Dearborn strode in and bowed. Blonde hair peeked out from under the rim of her helmet and a bandage encircled her left forearm.

"Begging Your Majesty's pardon," she said. "The pegasi are safe in the stables and the dragons are on guard."

"Thank you, Captain Dearborn." Brandi said.

The captain fixed her with bright blue eyes. "Do we leave on the morrow, Majesty?"

"That may be a little soon, Captain," Eric replied with a grin. "But we'll see."

The captain inclined her head. "If Your Highness says so." Her eyes flashed. "But I want another crack at those Torosian brutes."

"Your enthusiasm is commendable," Brandi replied. "Please get some rest and be ready for an early departure."

"Yes Ma'am." With a quick glance at Eric, Dearborn bowed and left.

"Our young captain is certainly eager to prove herself," Connor said with a wry look at Hannah. "Reminds me of someone, not too long ago."

She made a face and bumped him with her shoulder.

"Well," Megan said with a frown, "We had best report in to the Papal Nuncio."

"Agreed." Brandi reached into her shoulder bag and set a deep green sphere on the table, about the size of a large apple. Inside, gold swirls moved in an ever-changing pattern. The globe shone with a mild amber light.

She touched the top of the orb with a finger. "Thomas Cardinal Williams, Saint Martin's Town."

A few long seconds passed. The glow of the orb intensified. A shining cloud of light hovered over it, then resolved into the image of a dark-skinned man in a white cassock with a red sash around his waist.

"Greetings Riders," the man said.

The Riders inclined their heads. "Your Eminence," Brandi replied.

The Papal Nuncio smiled. "Thank you for contacting me. The Northern Alliance Council is most anxious for a status report, as am I. Where are you now?"

"Still at our base of operations, in Duarvar, eastern Gorostol," Eric answered.

Father Thomas gave a slight frown. "Problems?"

"To put it mildly, Eminence," Eric said. "We've tried to enter Torosc five times in seven days, but so far, they have thwarted us." He quickly summarized their attempts.

The Nuncio paused for long seconds. "Well, those tactics should have borne fruit, so your suspicions of a spy in the ranks make sense."

"We were just going to brainstorm for another approach." Megan offered.

"Then I will leave you to plan. But first, there are a few things you need to know," Father Thomas said. "We have received indications that there is a high-value target in Torosc. He could be a member of the Hadean ruling class, maybe even King Selaan of Hades."

The Riders froze. Dar felt the blood drain from his face. *A Daemon god… and worse yet, the god of Treachery and Deceit.*

"Wait," Hannah protested. "I thought the Ja'al gods were killed by the Elohir Royal Family."

Father Thomas shook his head. "Just Torvu and Arachnia. No one knows what happened to Selaan."

"This doesn't change anything, does it?" Connor asked. "We still have a job to do, Selaan or no Selaan."

The silence stretched on.

"A Daemon god was not in the equation," Eric said, tapping the table absently with a finger.

Dar shook his head. "We can't let that stop us. Connor is right."

"Let's not jump to conclusions." Father Thomas said, raising a hand. "Selaan is powerful, yes, but even if he is still on our world, I don't think he would reveal himself directly."

"Why not?" Hannah asked. "He can easily overpower whatever leaders are left in Torosc and lead an army wherever he chooses."

"Not exactly," Father Thomas replied. "He is not omniscient nor can he be everywhere at once – he still has to contend with a variety of factions with their own agendas. Also, there are Elohir knights among us now. If he takes over Torosc at the head of an army, the Celestials will descend on him like hornets. He may be able to withstand seven or eight Elohir but there are many more than that on Damora. No, I think he poses more of a danger as a force multiplier. He has access to the lore of ages from Hades and can equip your enemies with powerful tools."

Dar's mind hopped from one idea to the next. "Can't the Elohir help?" he asked, trying not to show his aggravation.

"First, we are not certain it is actually Selaan," said the Nuncio. "It might not be. The Celestials also need to concentrate on finding Daemons who went into hiding at the end of the War and we suspect there are more than a few. I don't need to tell you how much havoc they can wreak. We have to keep to our mission of mopping up after the War of the Dark Wave, Selaan or no Selaan."

Dar wracked his brain, trying to remember what Petrus had told him about the Daemonic leadership of Hades. *Selaan is a shapechanger. He could be anywhere… or anyone. Even if Elohir were among us now, it would take time for them to find him.*

Urgency and apprehension warred within Dar's mind. He felt a driving need to get to the South Kingdoms and strike while the forces of evil were still reeling, but a Ja'al god somewhere on the loose made that more difficult, even if they would not fight Selaan directly.

Father Thomas raised a hand as if calming an agitated child. "It is not as dire as you might think. It might just as easily be one of Selaan's courtiers who remains on Damora — a powerful enemy, to be sure, but not as deadly as the god of Deceit."

"How will we be able to tell if this Daemonic entity is in the area?" Megan asked.

"Be aware of particularly powerful evil magic that is out of place with the surroundings. Whether it is truly Selaan or some other Daemonic leader, it will likely be a giveaway. Also, whoever it is will probably be the epicenter of any rebuilding and military maneuvering. If nothing else, you may be able to avoid confrontation by working around them."

Dar caught Megan's gaze and read the doubt, uncertainty and anxiety there.

Father Thomas smiled. As if he could detect their thoughts, he said, "I know this sounds very daunting, but take heart. Any powerful Daemon, Selaan or not, would risk much in revealing himself at this point. And you are all very capable. I know God will guide you to success. Of that I have no doubt."

Dar did have his doubts. *I've stood against Fallen Ones and liches but a Daemon king?*

"Thank you, Eminence. I hope we gave you enough information," Brandi said.

"You did. We knew from the outset that this wouldn't be easy. I think you are doing very well under the circumstances. Now, on to more practical matters. We issued you a Sending Bag. Make sure you use it to send me anything you find that you feel is significant. Brandi and Megan can show you how to use it. Try to limit usage of the Orb, but don't be shy about it either – if it is necessary, contact me."

Megan lifted the Sending Bag out of her shoulder satchel and shook it, eliciting a mild clinking sound. "We have seven tokens so that will last us for a while."

"Also," the Nuncio continued, "have you reviewed the list of code phrases I sent you?"

"Yes," Eric answered with a grin. "You didn't warn us that it was in Celestial, so Megan and Brandi had to translate."

"Good," the Nuncio replied. "When you suspect that someone might be part of the rebel community, follow the line of discussion shown in the book. If you are talking to a bona fide official of the rebel alliance, they will use one of the code phrases in replying to you. Did you burn the book after memorizing the contents?"

Lost in thought, Dar only nodded.

"I took the liberty of providing you a scroll in the Sending Bag with additional data that might help," Father Thomas added. "Brandi and Megan can use their royal signet rings to bolster their claims to their homeland, but you will likely need other resources. Since you will be heading into former Paragon realms, you should know that some of the ruling houses of that epoch hid away valuable records and magic items in safehouses. They are well-hidden but Lord Indidarc managed to find descriptions of the locations of some of them."

"How will they help?" asked Hannah.

"If you can locate one of the safehouses, you may be able to find valuable information that will prove your good intentions but useful items."

"It seems little enough to go on," replied Eric, "but we'll take any advantage we can get. Thank you, Eminence. And thank my father for providing it."

"I will." The Nuncio squared his shoulders. "I have taken enough of your time. You need to rest and replan. Remember, keep the Messenger Orb with you at all times."

He raised a hand in benediction. Dar made the Sign of the Cross as the image faded away.

"Good news with the bad," murmured Megan, laying her hand on the Orb.

Dar laid out his maps on the table. "Let's take another look at our options. Maybe there's something we missed."

The Riders pored over the parchments. Dar's eyes flitted over the lines and markings and notes, his mind busy. Nothing immediately presented itself.

"Maybe we should split up into separate teams," Connor suggested. "Team One is a decoy to attract attention while Team Two slips over the border. When the patrols go after Team Two, they land in the forest and hide. Then Team One slips in. Both teams meet up at a rally point and head to first town on our list."

Eric shook his head. "That's clever, but there's too much left to chance. The Torosci can split their force and pursue both groups, as we've seen. In addition, if something unexpected occurs and one group is diverted, we have no way to communicate. We'd have to have another Orb or at least a pair of Sending Mirrors, which we don't."

Brandi tapped on the larger map of the general region. "What if we don't try to cross here after all?" she asked. "Suppose we go to the coast and try to slip past over the ocean, then land on a beach, maybe somewhere close to where Megan was held prisoner by George Oxbridge. Then we head for one of the other objectives."

Megan disagreed. "Even if we can get past the patrols, which will be hard in summertime with clear skies, the Torosci will likely have troops on the shoreline. It won't be hard to spot pegasi."

Another knock sounded at the door. The dwarven soldier bowed and ushered in an orderly with a cart bearing tea, bread and jam.

"Thank you," Dar said, absently stirring his tea.

The dwarf waited at the door while the orderly finished up. *Is he from Duarvar?* Dar wondered. *It makes sense. The name literally means Stone Castle...*

Dar's eyes flitted to another map on the table, then back to the soldier. A sudden thought struck him and he set down his mug. "Sergeant, is Lord Vinson still available?"

"I believe so, milord."

"Please ask him to attend us."

With a bow, the soldier left.

"What's this about, Dar?" asked Megan.

"The start of an idea," he mused, half to himself. "Wait until the Baron gets here."

He felt the eyes of the other Riders on him, measuring him, but no one asked anything further. Shortly, Lord Vinson of Duarvar entered, clad in a blue tunic, breeches and soft shoes instead of his trademark plate mail and boots.

"I am sorry it took me so long, Prince Dar," Vinson said, closing the door behind him. He bowed deeply.

"Not at all, milord," Dar replied. "It was on short notice, so thank you for coming."

"How may I help?"

"What do we know about the tunnels that the Ja'al dug through the mountains to attack Duarvar during the War?"

Vinson shrugged, scratching his cheek just under the patch over his left eye. "Well, Highness, there were several of them leading from the People's Republic of Torosc all the way to the sewers and storage units under the city.

The shortest of them is perhaps two miles long and starts in a canyon on the Torosc side of the border."

Eric shot Dar a look but he held up his hand.

"How big are they?" he asked.

Vinson stroked his greying beard and hooked a thumb behind his belt. "Oh, very large. They had to fit ogres and trolls and siege equipment and carts through there, not to mention some of those pig-like daemons… what are they called? Deathhammers?"

"I see."

Vinson's good eye now swept the Riders. "You aren't thinking of going into Torosc that way, are you?"

"It might be the best option."

Lord Vinson took a deep breath. "Well, I am not well-versed in dealing with pegasi, but I can imagine they wouldn't like it very much."

"Is the area monitored?" Megan asked. "Do you patrol it?"

"Down there? Oh no. We have far too many other worries to occupy us, Highness. After the Elohir blew through here and cleared those passages, we sealed the access on our side and laid barring spells on the doors, just in case. No one has been in there for five months or more."

Dar shot a glance at his companions. They gazed back at him with expressions ranging from confusion to incredulity.

"Thank you, milord," Dar said, inclining his head. "I don't want to detain you any longer. May we confer with you in the morning?"

"Certainly, but…" the Dwarf's voice trailed off. He paused. "I would be remiss if I didn't mention that we have no idea what the Torosci have done on their side of the tunnels… or even if they're open anymore."

Dar nodded. "Again, thank you, milord. We have much to discuss, it seems."

With another deep bow, the Baron of Duarvar left.

Connor rounded on Dar. "You're not serious."

"I am."

"Dar, Lord Vinson is right," Brandi said. "Pegasi are creatures of the air, not caves."

"We've taken them into cramped places before," Dar said. "Think of our trek along the wilderness near Terenai when air patrols grounded us. We rode on them like regular horses for days. The trees were so thick in places the pegasi couldn't even see the sky."

"There's a big difference between trees overhead and tons of rock, dearest," Megan replied.

"Not if we cover their eyes and lead them through."

No one said anything for many heartbeats.

"I don't think it's a good idea," Hannah offered. "Flying horses and the underground don't seem like a winning formula. We'd have a hard time protecting them."

Dar shrugged. "Maybe if we let the dragons go first, with Connor scouting ahead…"

A slow smile crept over Eric's features. "I see. Connor and I lead the formation with the dragons, followed by the pegasi escorted by the others. We take the shortest route. If anything attacks us, they'll have to deal with Kindri and Tholi right away. If they don't intimidate attackers into retreating, they'll certainly rough them up."

The Riders exchanged looks.

"We're running out of time," Dar said. "We've tried to get into Torosc via air routes and enemy patrols are too focused for us to slip past. This is the best we have. Unless someone has a better idea?"

The silence stretched on. Connor raised an eyebrow at Brandi, who stood with hands braced against the tabletop, staring at the maps.

Finally, she nodded. "Let's do it. I have to say this is one of your more unusual schemes, Dar. I hope we don't regret it."

Chapter Five – Course Correction

Mother Mary, pray for us, thought Megan. She stared at a massive set of double doors banded with steel and inscribed with glowing silvery runes.

At her side, a Dwarven priestess bowed. "Kurental's blessing on Your Highnesses. May your mission be victorious."

"Thank you, Priestess," Megan replied.

The priestess joined a human wizard in front of the portal. The pair incanted a spell together, eyes closed and glowing hands uplifted. A squad of Gorostoli heavy infantry stood at the ready nearby, halberds gleaming in the pale light of magical spell globes.

Tholerios shifted his weight next to Megan, and she laid a hand gently on his left hind leg. Dar cast a glance at her from his post next to Tholi's forequarters and winked. She smiled back, trying to keep any nervousness from her face.

It's okay to be anxious. She counseled herself. *I haven't done this in quite a while.*

The priestess and wizard gestured in unison. A sizzling arc of light curved over the edges of the door, then down the seam in the middle. The runes faded. With a heavy grinding noise, the portal opened.

Megan kept her eye on Connor, at the head of their formation. He flipped his cloak hood over his head and beckoned them onward, then slipped off into the darkness.

Accompanied by Gorlak and the two liaison officers, the Grey Riders headed into the tall, wide tunnel. Megan took up the reins of two pegasi and led them forward. The winged horses followed her, docile, eyes covered and hooves muffled by cloth coverings.

Now, God, if You would bless us with an uneventful expedition, we would really appreciate it.

In the magical light, the rough-hewn walls of the passage looked like an otherworldly sculpture of curves, bulges and sharp angles. Megan looked up and around.

Lord Vinson was right. You could fit two carts and a pair of ballistae in here and have room left over. She eyed the ceiling about twenty-five feet overhead. *But not fly.*

Behind them, the light faded as they forged on. Then they heard the grinding of the doors again and their path plunged into blackness.

She shifted her vision to the infrared spectrum, then the ultraviolet. Now she clearly saw the shadowy outline of Connor flitting ahead of their party, bow at the ready. Soon, he passed out of her range.

Hannah walked at Megan's side, armored in banded mail, moving with only an occasional clink of armor, leading one of the pegasi. Her eyes flitted from one side to the other, then ahead.

Megan wondered at Hannah's anxiety. Hannah was no stranger to perilous situations; she had even commanded a company of infantry during the War.

"Connor will be fine, Hannah," Megan offered in a low voice. "You've seen him do this before."

Hannah's return smile looked strained. "Not really. I've never been on a special operations mission."

Megan gave her shoulder a light squeeze. "Don't worry. We've done this a lot and we're right behind him. Besides, Connor's really good at this."

"So I've heard, but it's different in practice."

"Well, to make you feel better," she murmured. "Dar and Eric are excellent scouts and Connor's favorite practical joke is to sneak up on them when they aren't looking. He gets them almost every time. Believe me, if Connor doesn't want to be detected, nothing will find him."

Hannah nodded and let out a breath, stretching her shoulders.

Ahead of them, Eric and Dar kept a measured pace next to the dragons. Tholi swept his head left and right, eyes glowing with a pale white aura. In his saddle on his back, Gorlak held a crossbow at the ready.

Megan sneaked a look behind her. Leading their own pegasi, Captains Dearborn and Fejer followed, eyes glowing mild green. Small pendants glittered against their hauberks.

Thank you, Melinor, for those medallions. I don't know how we'd get the humans through the underground without them.

The group passed through the dark expanse of the massive tunnel, the silence broken only by the occasional clink of armor, creak of leather or drip of water.

Megan's Elohir senses tingled. Without knowing why, she slipped her wizard's staff from its loop in Larinor's saddle.

Something's not right…

She shifted her vision from ultraviolet to infrared and back again but nothing out of the ordinary appeared: they continued a silent trek through a vast, empty tunnel. Now every sound seemed thunderous, even the muffled thump of pegasus hoofbeats.

She activated a spell in the wizard's staff. The wooden shaft thrummed in response and grew warmer.

Melinor also gives the best wedding presents…

Her heightened sense of smell picked up a mild sour odor with a faint trace of something metallic. "I smell something strange," she said to Kindri at her other side.

The dragon nodded. "Me too," she said. Her voice always reminded Megan of the splash of mountain streams and the hiss of the breeze through the trees. "I can't place it though."

Connor came back into view. He crouched near some dark, jagged shapes on the floor of the tunnel. The other Riders slowed.

"Someone's been here," Connor murmured.

Megan joined Brandi at his side. She recognized the jagged shapes as the massive bones of ogres and trolls. She frowned. Many of the bones lay scattered about, as if something had torn the bodies to pieces.

Brandi tapped her shoulder and pointed. Other bones looked like they had burst asunder from within, and she saw two skulls with wicked antlers on their foreheads.

"Daemons," Brandi whispered. "Curbolgs and Shock Hind from the looks of them."

"Not surprising." Dar knelt to touch one of the skulls. "The Elohir must have carved them up like a Sunday steak."

"Yes, but the bodies have been scavenged." Eric's eyes glowed mild green as he scanned the dark tunnel.

"By whom?" asked Hannah in a whisper. "Or what?"

Megan told them about the strange smell.

"Any ideas?" Connor asked Kindri.

The dragon's eyes narrowed. "No, but something's not right."

Brandi drew her swords. "I feel it too. Be on your guard."

Connor nodded and motioned them forward.

Megan's staff tingled in her grip. She heard a small sound and felt a shift in the air. Her eyes alighted on dark, oblong shapes stuck to the ceiling like barnacles.

Her Elohir senses went on full alert. "Above!" she shouted. "Light spell! Cancel your infrared!"

Her heart skipped a beat when the shapes split open. Dozens of five-legged creatures the size of large dogs descended, rappelling down via misty tendrils attached to their cocoons. They looked like a cross between a spider and a lizard with wicked claws. Each monster glared at them with five red glowing eyes.

She shifted her eyes back to the visible spectrum, casting a spell through her staff. A brilliant globe of light burst into being above them, illuminating the cavern as brightly as day.

The creatures shrieked. The pegasi whinnied, backing up and extending their wings. Megan tried to bring her staff to bear on a trio of creatures but a pegasus wing hit her shoulder and she lurched into Tholi's side. She heard the ring of steel slashing through flesh and bone. The sour metallic odor increased to overpowering intensity.

"Those are Stone Lurkers!" Captain Dearborn yelled. "Watch out for their snaring attack!"

Megan stepped back, trying to lead the pegasi out of harm's way. Kindri and Tholi snarled a challenge and opened their mouths, unleashing jets of yellow-hot flame. With echoing screams, six Lurkers vanished into clouds of glowing ash. From atop Kindri's back, Gorlak shot a Lurker through the eye with a crossbow bolt.

Hannah dashed forward, her sword out and shield up. Two Lurkers hurtled at her. The Halfling princess bashed one aside with her shield and slashed at another. Both monsters opened circular, fanged maws and spat thin, smoky tentacles at Hannah. She crouched and the strands wrapped around her shield. The Lurkers took hold of the tendrils and yanked on them, dragging her closer. Hannah lopped the tendrils off with Shriek and impaled a monster through the skull.

"Arrows on!" called Captain Fejer's voice from behind her. Two arrows whistled past Megan's head and impaled Hannah's second opponent in the chest. It flopped to the ground.

Megan backed up, trying to control the panicked pegasi. The mounts plunged from side to side, wings beating. She tried again to use her staff but every time she formulated a spell, a pegasus jostled her, breaking her focus.

They sense danger but can't see it! Damn it!

She gave up trying to cast any magic. Megan struggled with the agitated pegasi, pulling them back towards the captains. Tholi dodged to the side, clawing and biting at Lurkers hurtling at him. Megan halted and ducked, keeping a tight grip on the reins in her hand.

In the light of the globe suspended overhead, Brandi, Eric and Dar whirled in a deadly martial dance amid twenty of the snarling beasts. Eric's spear glowed with golden light. A network of ebony strands held Brandi and five of the monsters snapped at her out of the range of her flashing twin swords.

Inky tendrils wrapped around Dar's legs and torso. He tapped a hand to the throat of his chainmail armor. In the blink of an eye, he sparkled out of existence and reappeared behind the monsters. His night-black sword rose and fell, the blade glittering with stars. Lurkers dropped.

A hand touched Megan's shoulder. She paused her retreat to the back of the formation. Captain Dearborn pulled the reins from her hand. "Go, Highness," she said. "You're of better use in there."

Megan darted forward and her jaw dropped. Scores more Lurkers descended from the tunnel ceiling ahead of them. The Riders turned to meet them but the new swarm joined their fellows in a seething throng. Brandi slashed her way out of the entangling tendrils, backing towards the dragons.

Megan conjured bolts of lightning and shot fire darts at the beasts, but for every one that dropped, more came on out of the darkness.

How many are there?

Connor went down and was pulled out by Eric, who also disappeared under a dark tide of attackers. Dar slashed his way to them and touched the throat of his armor again. He reappeared next to Kindri, supporting Eric and Connor with his arms. Dar shook his head as if dizzy, his face grey.

Another twin blast of dragon fire immolated ten more Lurkers. The horde swarmed in a shadowy, roiling wave. Dar, Eric, Connor, Hannah and Brandi formed a line of blades before Megan, cutting down attackers left and right, but more came on. An occasional arrow or bolt from Gorlak or the captains whistled into the fray to strike down enemies in the back rank, but there seemed to be no end to them. Lurkers surged up the arms and legs of the dragons like misshapen cockroaches. Kindri and Tholi snapped, slashed and incinerated dozens. More came to replace them.

Megan hesitated, unsure of whether to use her Celestial powers. *What if I make a mistake? What if it doesn't work?*

Brandi stumbled and Eric pulled her up, spear darting in and out, impaling darting, snapping Lurkers. Megan caught a glimpse of Hannah's eyes: determined, fiery, but scared.

Megan's heart clenched. *It's like another Dark Wave... I have to do it now.* She closed her eyes and reached deep inside herself, into a vibrant reservoir of heavenly energy. She built it into a field of spiritual strength, then opened her eyes.

"*Irae Angelorum!*" she shouted in a voice echoing with the depths of the universe.

Intense energy burst from every part of her body, incinerating nearby Lurkers with holy light. The remaining Lurkers screamed in agony and retreated, claws before their eyes. Megan floated in a state of near euphoria, reveling in the purity of the aura.

To you, Lord, I lift up my soul...

Her focus intensified and she used the light as a shield, holding the creatures at bay.

"Now!" she commanded the Riders. "Drive them off!"

Her friends waded into the fray, dispatching Lurkers with every blow.

The monsters held up their arms, faces averted, shrieking.

Megan pointed at the Lurkers. "*Apage!*"

A wave of light shot outward, sizzling and sparking. The balance of the Lurker mob scattered. Some rappelled back up into their barnacle-like cocoons on the ceiling while others raced off into the far reaches of the tunnel with howls and a scraping of claws. The remainder, locked in combat with the Riders, soon fell and the tunnel lapsed once more into uneasy silence.

Megan's power faded and she leaned on her staff. Suddenly winded and dizzy, she reached out for Tholi and the dragon gently held her up with one massive paw.

"Highness?" he asked, voice concerned.

"I'll be… fine," she panted. Spots swam before her eyes. A familiar pair of hands caught her and lowered her to the ground before she blacked out.

Ages seemed to pass. Brandi's gentle voice murmured in prayer. A feeling like a crystalline spray of icy water hit her. Her vision cleared and she struggled to sit up, but Dar held her in his lap. Her head throbbed.

"Easy," he said. She opened her eyes and winced. The other Riders crowded around, brows furrowed.

"You gave us quite a fright," Dar scolded. "What were you thinking?" He applied a healing spell of his own and her headache receded to a dull ache.

"I was trying to help," she croaked, convinced she sounded like an asthmatic elderly woman. "There were so many of them… A minute more and they would have overrun us."

"We were holding our own," Brandi replied, helping Dar in lifting her to her feet.

Megan privately disagreed but only nodded. "How is everyone else?"

Eric smiled. "We're fine. Nothing that a lot of healing potions and spells can't fix."

"What did you do just then?" Dar asked.

"Aura of Heaven," she replied.

"Have you ever done it before?"

"In training, but never with so many targets."

"That was a bit scary." He frowned down at her. "I prefer to keep you in one piece, you know."

A spark of anger lit in her and she bit off a retort. "I'm no help if I can't use my powers, Dar. I have to learn to handle them."

He opened his mouth to say something, then closed it. "I understand," he said after a pause. "It's just… be more careful. You looked…well, like before. When you died, back in Torosc."

A sudden pang of regret twisted her heart. *Dear God! I made him relive my death all over again…*

"Dar, I'm sorry," she began, but he just nodded and gave her shoulder a squeeze. That made her feel even more miserable.

He loves me and wants to keep me safe. But "safe" really isn't an option these days.

Torn between knowing she did the right thing and empathy for his trauma, she hugged him wordlessly.

The captains led the pegasi forward. "Thanks for handling them," Dar said.

Captain Fejer waved a hand dismissively. "We were behind two dragons and the Grey Riders. All we had to do was pick off the few stragglers that got past you." Judging from the amount of Lurker ichor on his tunic, there were more than "a few stragglers."

Captain Dearborn handed Megan the reins of her mount, who now appeared much calmer. "The pegasi are just fine. No damage."

"How did you know those creatures were Lurkers?" Megan asked her.

"I've encountered them before."

"Really? Where?"

"Underground. In… other places." Dearborn smiled, turning away to go to the other mounts.

Eric watched her, brow furrowed. "Stone Lurker… that's familiar for some reason."

"Did you encounter them on a mission while I was away?" Megan asked.

"No, but the name sounds familiar. Not from anything recent. I wonder if it's something Melinor told me about a long time ago." He paused, then shrugged. "Oh well. It will come to me later, I suppose."

I wonder how Captain Dearborn <u>and</u> Melinor would both know about Stone Lurkers. Megan mused.

Dar led Megan to a large rock and remained with her as the others regrouped and checked equipment.

"How much do we know about Captain Dearborn?" Megan whispered.

Dar's eyes flicked towards the back of the formation, then back to Megan. "About the same as Fejer. Khyla Dearborn is an orphan. She joined the military in her teens, fought at the Battle of Meridian during the War, and was promoted to captain. She's been vetted, if that's what you mean. Or do you mean something else?"

"I just have an odd feeling about her."

"Celestial senses or woman's intuition?"

"That… and a dream."

He raised an eyebrow. "A dream? Like the others?"

She shifted on the rock. "Yes."

He nodded. "Jesus or Mary?"

Megan's dream replayed in her mind. "Jesus this time. He showed me an image of Captain Dearborn. She was surrounded by dark clouds but held a brightly burning candle. She turned to me and held out her hand. Tears ran down her face but she smiled. Then the dream ended."

Dar watched Khyla Dearborn as she calmed the other pegasi and led them forward. "Your dreams always mean something, even if we don't understand them at the time. Like the one about Connor and the Council, or Brandi's about coming to Duarvar instead of Sentinel."

Lord, if you want me to do something to help Khyla Dearborn, please show me, Megan thought.

Dar slapped his knee and stood up. "You and Brandi should talk. But let's get out of here first."

"Deal. Just don't get chewed up by some hellish monster."

He kissed her hand. "I'll try to remember that. You're sure you're okay?"

Megan tried not to sigh in frustration. "Yes, dear. I'm fine."

She watched him stride away to join Eric. *He hasn't worked with me as a freelance for almost two years, so he has to get used to me fending for myself,* she reminded herself. *We have a lot to work out. I have to be patient.*

Part of her didn't want to be so patient.

Megan took her place in the formation and dispelled her light globe. Instantly, the tunnel plunged into darkness and she shifted her vision back to ultraviolet.

A bit more cautiously than the first time, they continued on. The passage sloped gently downward, then leveled out. Occasionally, they halted when

Connor found other evidence of battles between the Elohir and daemons, but no other creatures assailed them.

This trek reminded her of one of her first missions with the Riders. Forced into trackless caverns by pursuing Hobgoblin warriors, they barely escaped with their lives when they stumbled upon the ruins of an ancient Dwarven community — and a path out of the underground. This situation felt similar: a quietly ominous, nerve-wracking trek into unknown territory, fraught with the possibility of sudden violence. Megan kept her senses on high alert and paid special attention to the ceiling above.

It's different now, she consoled herself. *We have a lot more help… and a map of sorts.*

The passage abruptly widened into a large chamber with a huge exit on one side and smaller tunnels along the perimeter. Ruined carts, ballistae and catapults littered the open space, along with many bones and discarded weapons.

Connor returned to the main group. "It's an assembly area. We need to scout those side passages, just in case. There are three on each side. Dar, Eric and I can check them out."

Megan watched Dar hustle off with the others, trying not to be overly concerned. "I guess the anxiety goes both ways," she whispered to herself.

Fortunately, the trio returned quickly and reported that the side passages, though smaller, held no dangers for at least a hundred feet. Just to be sure, Dar and Eric set down sentry spells in each before they departed to check the other exits. Megan's whole body relaxed when they returned with a similar assessment.

"We need a break," Brandi said. "I call a rest stop."

Eric shook his head. "The sooner we get through here, the better. We've already been ambushed once."

"Yes, but we need to be alert and ready. A short rest won't hurt."

He pressed his lips together, then nodded. "Agreed."

Everyone took seats on whatever junk was somewhat level and the dragons laid down in opposite directions, snouts pointed at the three side passages.

"Doing okay?" Megan asked her sister, handing her a packet of dried fruit and hard cheese.

Brandi nodded, taking some food. "It's tough to get back into this kind of life after so long. I don't want to step on Eric and Dar, but technically, Connor and I are in charge of this expedition."

Megan watched Dar and Eric in a discussion near a wrecked mangonel. "They had time to figure out a system of working together while we were gone. We need to trust them."

"But they need to listen to us too. We have senses that they don't."

Megan allowed a little smile and took a bite of dried apple. "Celestial or womanly intuition?"

"Yes."

The sisters ate in silence until their husbands returned. "Ready?" Dar asked.

Brandi rewrapped the packet and gave it back to Megan. "Main passage?"

Dar nodded. Without fanfare, they formed up and headed into the tunnel. After only a short while, Connor returned from scouting.

"What is it?" Megan asked.

"Well, Lord Vinson was right about one thing. No one had any idea of what the Torosci did on their end. Come and see."

They followed him, slowing to a stop when they saw what lay ahead.

"Well, that is one way to deal with it, I suppose," noted Hannah. Ahead of them, great boulders, shattered rock and splintered bracing beams blocked the way.

"I hope, Highnesses, that we're not thinking of digging past that," Kindriana said, her golden cat eyes sizing up the passage. "It would take quite a while, even with Tholi and me working together."

"No," mused Connor, "I don't think that's an option, Kindri."

No one spoke for a while.

"Well, nothing for it," Brandi said. "Back to the rest area."

Megan's mind worked overtime as they headed back.

Which way now? All the side passages are smaller, much smaller. I don't think we'd be able to have both dragons side-by-side... and the roof is lower too. All it would take would be one big magical trap to collapse it on us and it's all over.

By the time they returned to the rest area, Dar already had his map out and on a makeshift table made from the remains of a cart. He beckoned them over.

"We're going to need light," he said.

Megan obliged him with a glowing ball hovering just overhead. She leaned over the map.

"The original tunnel was going to lead out to a ravine in dense woods," Dar said, his finger tracing a path on the map. "That's northeast of here. If we want to end up in the same place, we'll have to pick one of the left-hand passages."

Brandi rested her hands on the wooden surface. "Opinions?"

Eric tapped the page. "I say we go the other way, towards the rapids."

"Is that wise?" Hannah asked. "There's likely to be traffic near the river, whereas the ravine is in a wild area."

Captain Fejer raised his hand. "Begging your pardon, milords and ladies, but the ravine doesn't allow us to fly easily. We don't know anything about the gully other than that it is heavily forested. If they have guards there, we're in trouble. The rapids are a natural impediment to patrols, so it might be the right way through."

"Good point." Megan straightened. "In an odd way, the collapsed tunnel might be forcing us into a better location."

"What? You mean the forces of evil are actually helping us out?" asked Dar. He kept a straight face but his eyes twinkled. "Saints preserve us."

Megan gave him a push in the shoulder. "Yes, for once. Don't get used to it."

"Connor?" Brandi looked at him expectantly.

The Halfling prince shrugged. "Honestly, at this point, anything that keeps us moving is preferable. Standing still seems to be inviting disaster."

"We don't need any more of that," Brandi concluded. "Very well, one of the righthand passages it is…"

Chapter Six – Odd Bedfellows

Golvadu Fellhammer let his gaze wander over the vast garden. Magical globes hovered in mid-air over the terrace of the palace, illuminating the array of dignitaries of Torosc in a kaleidoscope of finery.

They better get this over with quick. I have work to do.

He appropriated a shot of Dwarven whiskey from a nearby table and downed the vaporous liquid. "At least Ilyan Kalik had the sense to provide the good stuff," he commented drily.

"It meets with your approval, Your Grace?" asked a melodious soprano behind him.

Golvadu turned and smirked at the approach of a svelte brunette on the arm of a golden-haired human male. The couple wore matching outfits of midnight blue and red.

"Ah, the delectable Lady Adina." He inclined his head. "And Lord Berek."

"You flatter me, My Lord," Adina said, dipping into a curtsey that strategically revealed her rounded cleavage.

Berek waved a hand at the assemblage on the terrace. "I see that our newfound ally has provided gourmet drink and delicacies for all the important persons in Torosc. He is no miser, at least."

Golvadu turned from them to survey the assembly. "Important persons indeed: regional governors, Dark Elves, representatives of allied cults and churches – and a few hangers-on whom I can't really identify. I wish Kalik would get on with it, though."

Adina laughed. "What's the hurry? Enjoy the free meal and liquor, Your Grace."

Golvadu frowned. "We won't defeat the Northern Alliance with puff pastry and Halfling wines, Lady Adina." He peered at his invitation card. "And what does Kalik mean by 'special guests'?"

Adina and Berek exchanged a look and shrugged. "We will find out soon, I'm sure," she said.

A faint unease touched Golvadu's mind and the Dwarven wizard shook his head in irritation. He couldn't dispel the sense that something was not quite right — otherwise, why would Kalik be so secretive?

What is he up to?

A slave passed by, eyes averted, offering a platter of roast venison medallions on black bread with sauteed mushrooms. "What will be truly impressive is if we complete the evening without bloodshed or a magical duel," he retorted, taking an hors d'oeuvre.

Adina nodded. "Well, then, I see a fracas starting up between the Lord of Golad and High Priest Faldor from the Church of Cla'Agik. Should we intervene to break it up?"

Golvadu munched his snack and dusted off his hands. "Hardly. I never liked High Priest Faldor anyway, the arrogant little monkey. I hope the Lord Governor smacks him off the veranda."

Much to Golvadu's disappointment, Ilyan Kalik interposed himself between the arguing principals and steered the High Priest to a refreshments table. The cleric shot an imperious glare at the Governor, then focused his attention on a decanter of Elven wine. He settled his ivory-colored robes and reached for a crystal glass.

Pompous windbag, Golvadu mused.

"If Your Grace will excuse us, I see someone we need to talk to." Berek sketched a short bow, then took Adina's hand.

"By all means."

Left to himself, Golvadu let his eyes rest on each of the attendees. *Damned idiots, most of them,* he thought. *They spend more time fighting among themselves when they should be consolidating our power base now, while the Alliance is still rebuilding.*

He clasped his hands behind his back and wandered to the newly repaired balustrade. The scent of night-blooming jasmine and Vampire Roses drifted on the night breeze. Light from the twin moons washed over the city scape of Highpoint. Three of the six main gates looked almost fully repaired, and mage-fire lanterns illuminated glittering new walkways of crushed gravel in the city square. Towers and archways gleamed with fresh paint and plaster and he saw several frescoes in progress.

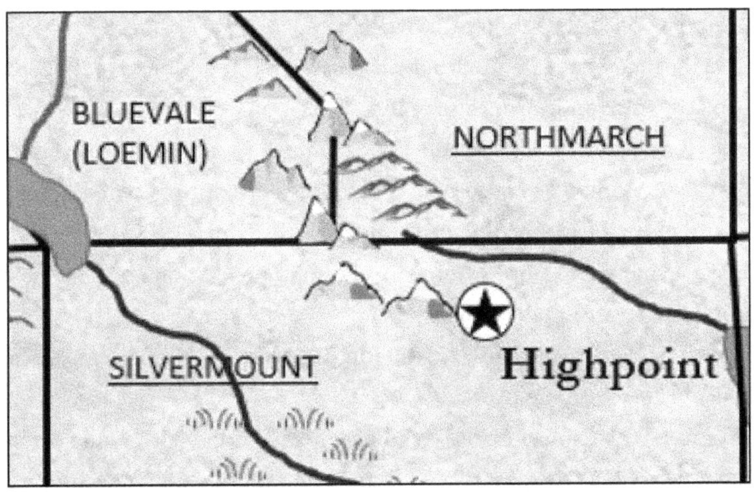

His eyes rested on the ruins of the Ja'al temple. It marred the otherwise opulent scene, looking like a black eye on the face of an alluring prostitute. *Good riddance to them, the failures. Even with Daemonic assistance they couldn't win the War.*

Turning back to the terrace, he leaned against the railing, watching the scene. Three governors huddled together near a carved stone table, involved in an animated conversation. Occasionally, someone strolled within earshot and their discussion ceased, only to pick up again when the passerby departed.

Golvadu's lip curled in a sneer. *Yes, formulate some kind of plan. Rebels conduct clandestine raids from secret outposts in your provinces and now we hear talk of the return of the ancient houses. You'll need something brilliant if you want to keep your heads.*

He observed the assembled dignitaries, noting the little cliques, furtive discussions and whispers behind hands. Most of the attendees regarded each other with thinly veiled suspicion or, at best, a guarded wariness.

He considered and discarded several ideas, then shook his head in vexation. *I've tried at least half-a-dozen times to construct coalitions, but they always fall apart. There must be some way to make them work together.*

Adina and Berek returned, carrying silver chalices.

"Kalik had better reveal his surprise soon," Adina noted, sipping from her cup, "The suspense is getting to me."

Golvadu scowled. "I care less about his grandstanding than I do about rule of the People's Republic of Torosc."

"Your Grace is not in the least bit curious?" Berek raised an eyebrow.

Golvadu snorted but didn't reply.

Ilyan Kalik detached himself from Faldor's side and headed for the carved palace doors. He clapped his hands. "My lords and ladies, Your Graces and Your Honors," he announced with a deep bow. "Thank you for coming. If I may have your attention, we may begin this conference on the future of Torosc and the southlands."

"This had better be good," Golvadu growled, accompanying Adina and Berek to a closer vantage point.

"I'm prepared to be amused," Adina murmured, a faint smile on her lips.

Kalik beamed at the assembly. "I am sure that we all have the same goal in mind, namely, to restore the power of the People's Republic. Only in that way can the nations of the northlands be justly punished for resisting our efforts to liberate them from their outmoded ways of life. Naturally, such a restoration will require powerful allies. In that vein, I would like to present our special guests for the evening." He waved a hand at the doors and they swung open. Two figures marched onto the terrace. All conversation ceased.

Golvadu felt the blood drain from his face and swore under his breath. His palms became sweaty.

The first figure stalked onto the terrace on goat's legs, towering over the tallest human in attendance by more than a foot. Black-striped purple bat wings lay against his back. A handsome face with deep red eyes surveyed the assemblage and short, twin horns like those of a gazelle jutted from his forehead. His well-muscled human torso was encased in silvery chainmail and a golden coronet encircled black hair.

"Prince Tarvener of Hades," Adina gasped.

A male Daemon with the figure of a tall Elf accompanied him, clad in bone-white banded mail. He flexed his shoulders and deep indigo batwings unfurled momentarily. Two black horns poked up from beneath honey-blond hair. Ice-blue, cat-like eyes swept the terrace.

"And Count Balris," Golvadu hissed. "Wonderful."

"Special guests indeed," Berek breathed. "How did they survive the Elohir assault?"

"No idea," murmured Golvadu, clenching his fists.

Kalik bowed to both Daemons. "We are indeed honored and pleased beyond words that His Highness and His Excellency have graced us with their presence this evening."

You mean they crawled out of their holes when they thought it safe, Golvadu thought.

Tarvener inclined his head to Kalik. "I thank you for your gracious hospitality."

The assembled crowd gaped in stunned silence.

The Daemon Prince turned his burning gaze to the assembly. "I will be brief and to the point. Your current state of disunity will doom you to defeat at the hands of the Alliance. I am as certain of this as I am that there are two moons in the sky. I, however, can lead you to victory and bring Torosc out of the ashes into a new era of power."

The attendees whispered among themselves, their faces pale or tight-lipped in anger.

Golvadu fumed but kept his features neutral. *Taking over again? This is exactly how it fell apart during the War! Damned interlopers.*

"With the Elohir on your world now in significant numbers," Tarvener continued, "I cannot declare myself openly, at least not until our victory is assured. However, Lord Balris and I have significant resources at our disposal: the arcane knowledge of countless ages from our homeworld of Hades. Magic and technology such as you have never dreamed of will be provided to you, for free, once you agree to our leadership. What say you?"

Golvadu considered this, his interest piqued. *Hmm. Hadean magic and technology, for free? The Scrolls of Kelvaros mentioned some tantalizing ideas. I wonder.*

The crowd on the veranda exchanged glances, their expressions changing from agitated to thoughtful. For all this, no one spoke.

Tarvener arched an elegant eyebrow. "Come, I sense a certain lack of faith. Let us be candid with one another. Tell me of your reservations."

"Reservations?" High Priest Faldor stalked forward, eyes narrowed. "I am more concerned about your assertion that you can bring us to victory. How do you propose to do that now, when you couldn't assure it with thousands of Fallen Ones at your back? Based on your poor performance during the War of the Dark Wave, I am not enthusiastic, to say the least."

Tarvener's left eye twitched but he smiled. "Forgive me, High Priest, but you are operating at the disadvantage of ignorance. Your Church of the Diseased One did not partake in the War, so you have no knowledge of the significant difficulties we faced. Still, for all that, I captured the Astarellian seaport of Tyler, among other cities. Which cities have you conquered?"

Faldor's eyes narrowed and the other dignitaries cleared a space around him. Golvadu prepared a potent sequence of spells, senses alert. He waited, gauging the confrontation.

"You conquered?" Faldor snapped. "Yes, and then lost again! Now our enemies celebrate and prepare to march anew. Some Dark Wave! More like a passing of dark gas, if you ask me."

"What the hell is he doing?" whispered Adina. "Those are High Daemon Lords!"

Berek nodded. "Staking his claim. Tarvener and Balris need us to succeed and Faldor knows it. He wants to take control."

"But —"

Berek lifted a finger to his lips. "He also knows that disease spells affect Daemons just like any other living being…"

Balris raised an eyebrow. "You forget that the Dark Wave left our enemies severely depleted and unable to intervene here in the southlands. That is a significant opportunity for us."

"Also," interjected Tarvener, "The Ban has now been lifted. If the Elohir can station troops on Damora, so can we, though not in the same numbers as during the War. We can craft the People's Republic and our allied nations into sanctuaries where we may summon as many forces as we like without having to worry about keeping them secret."

Faldor snorted. "Considering your incompetence, that means little. Your record is not stellar, Your Highness. I cannot and will not recommend this to the Cla'Agik High Council. As a matter of fact, my counterproposal is that we compose a War Command consisting of representatives from each of the allied faction, led by the Cla'Agik."

Ilyan Kalik shook his head, lips pressed together. "And what of our allies from Hades?"

Faldor's lip curled in a sneer. "They will be treated just like any other levied troops, to take direction from the War Command. All of them," he added with a pointed look at Tarvener and Balris.

"And if we disagree?" asked Tarvener.

"You can go back to Hades with your tails between your legs like the dogs you are!" snapped Faldor. "This is *our* world and we'll conquer it in our own way. We don't need *you* miserable failures to ruin our chances again."

Tarvener shook his head. "That is unacceptable. Either we do this our way or the hard way."

Faldor snapped off an anatomically impossible description of what Tarvener could do with his way. He waved a hand and a quintet of crackling, glowing orbs swirled around his head. A globe of sickly green fire surrounded him.

"Unfortunate," said Tarvener. He and Balris extended their hands. Blazing gouts of flame sprang forth towards Faldor, who merely sneered. His sparkling spheres flashed and the fire curved around his verdant shield of light.

The High Priest pointed one finger at each Daemon, muttering in a low voice. Shiny purple darts of crystal arced towards the pair from the whirling spheres. Both Daemons clenched their fists. A blast of blue flame erupted around their bodies and the crystal darts shattered, spraying the nearby grass with a noisome yellow liquid. The cloud dissipated. The assembled dignitaries scrambled to put distance between themselves and the belligerents.

"You really should reconsider," Balris said, stepping forward across the steaming lawn.

"I'm not afraid of you!" Faldor hissed, pointing at the Daemon Count. "You couldn't even handle Megan Alenar when you had her in your clutches!" He opened his mouth wide and a gout of pinkish-red gas burst forth, surrounding the Daemons. Two nearby slaves fell to the ground, convulsing as their skin became flushed and covered with warts. No one made a move towards them.

Balris stalked out of the cloud, his features marred by pustules and sores. "That wasn't very nice," he said, raising a fist surrounded by a corona of crackling lightning. "I sense you're not enthused by our offer."

Faldor screamed an obscenity and sawed at the air with his hands. The tiny spheres flashed again, hurling jets of sizzling, sparkling fluid at the Daemon. Balris opened his hand and a cloud of lighting surrounded him. The liquid turned to steam.

The Cla'Agik priest and the Daemon hurled bolts of fire, ice and lightning at each other.

Golvadu stalked behind a table, eyes following the battle, his hands clammy. *Faldor's stronger than I thought, but he has to deal with Tarvener even if he destroys Balris.*

Soon, Balris limped and wiped blood from his eyes, coughing as his lungs filled with fluid.

"Allow me, Count," Tarvener said, shouldering Balris aside. He slammed his fist into the ground. The earth and the nearby palace jumped and everyone lurched to keep their balance. A gaping hole opened underneath Faldor, who screamed and fell in. Tarvener snapped his fingers. The hole sealed up, trapping Faldor in the earth with only his head showing.

"Release me, you misbegotten animal!" Faldor shouted, his beady eyes wild with rage.

Tarvener strolled forward, smiling. Balris remained kneeling, panting.

Sweat broke out on Golvadu's forehead. *Faldor has skills I wasn't aware of, but it didn't matter.*

Tarvener smiled down at the imprisoned High Priest. "Are you sure you won't reconsider?"

"I am an emissary of the Most Exalted Cla'Agik, the Lord of Corruption," Faldor snapped, struggling in vain. "Release me at once or I will bring the might of my Church down on your heads!"

"Not from down there, you won't," Tarvener replied. "Well, perhaps we will just let you simmer down — after all, earth has a cooling and insulating effect."

"Let me go!" shrieked Faldor.

The Daemon Prince frowned down at him. "And you're noisy too. I'm afraid we'll have to write up an extensive report to the Cla'Agik leadership about your unseemly behavior."

Faldor responded with a stream of obscenities. Tarvener gestured with his left hand. A globe of blue light sprang up over Faldor's head. Though his mouth still moved, Golvadu only heard a tinny echo of his voice, no more than a whisper.

Tarvener regarded the imprisoned High Priest for a second, then turned to Balris, whose skin melted off one side of his face.

"Ah, that looks like it hurts. I can help you there." Tarvener placed a hand on the Count's arm and his palm flared bright red. Balris' face went pale and he gasped, falling to his knees. After a few moments, he stood shakily, his features and respiration swiftly returning to normal.

"Any other objections?" Tarvener asked.

The assembled representatives shifted nervously but no one spoke. Golvadu let out a slow breath and canceled his prepared spells.

Tarvener rubbed his hands together. "Good. Now that we have dispensed with that bit of unpleasantness, Lord Balris, I believe you have information to share with our associates."

Balris winced but nodded. "Yes, Highness. We bring news from the northern borders. We have recently learned that pegasus riders and dragons have been driven back on attempted infiltrations several times in the last week."

A murmur of conversation rippled around the terrace. "Probing for possible invasion routes," Golvadu announced. Several people nearby turned to him.

Adina shook her head. "The Alliance doesn't have the reserves to attack this soon after the War. It might be special forces operatives or reconnaissance units trying to make contact with rebels."

"Quite so, milady," Tarvener said, letting his gaze rest on Adina. "I thought of that myself."

Eyes shining, she curtseyed deeply.

"As a matter of fact," the Daemon Prince continued, putting his hands behind his back, "our spies think one special unit may be the Grey Riders."

The whispered discussions increased. Various representatives either scowled, spat or paled. Golvadu gave a slow nod.

That would explain much. We heard of the weddings and the coronations. Why wouldn't they try to see if they can get into the country?

"Even if that is true," Berek protested, "What can they hope to gain?"

"We think the Riders may be attempting to contact the aforementioned rebel elements and re-establish the old kingdoms," Tarvener answered. "The threat to the People's Republic of Torosc is obvious, as it is to our allies in Morlan and Jered and elsewhere. If the populace gets it into their heads that the royal houses have returned, they may also decide the elites are no longer fit to rule, and then…" He spread his hands in a helpless gesture.

Even Ilyan Kalik seems alarmed, Golvadu noted. *He'd better be. If the Riders raise the countryside, <u>everyone's</u> plans for domination go out the window.*

"They can't possibly succeed," objected one of the Dark Elf princes. "The Riders are few in number and our patrols are obviously effective."

Tarvener shook his head. "A group as proficient as the Riders will eventually find a weak point and exploit it. Do not underestimate them. We did so before and paid for it."

Golvadu watched the others, making note of who looked desperate and who just looked wary. The desperate he could eventually sway; the wary would take more convincing.

"What can we do?" asked one of the governors.

"We keep the population focused on preserving their own hides," Tarvener replied with a smile. "Send tax collectors to harass the rebellious provinces with additional fees and assessments, increase patrols and entice them with rewards for turning in the disloyal. Send out extra brigades of troops to each of our most unsettled regions. Use the journals guilds to spread the word that the royals-in-exile are really just elements of former oppression returned anew. In other words, make the environment so inhospitable that it will take the Riders a long time to start anything… by which time we will have deployed our Hadean resources."

"And then?" asked a high priestess of Gudarta.

"We will end them." Balris' eyes gleamed.

"With the Riders and any other infiltrators otherwise occupied," Tarvener offered, "We can consolidate our base of power here in Torosc, root out disaffected elements, and begin a program of rapid rebuilding. Torosc will become a sanctuary state for us to bring in loyal brethren from Hades. In a matter of months, we will be able to strike north into Gorostol."

"What about the Cla'Agik?" asked Berek. He flicked his eyes at Faldor, still raging inside the Globe of Silence. "They won't be pleased."

Tarvener shrugged. "For all his bluster, he was an emissary only, not their High Council. Let me handle them."

The murmur of conversation increased in volume.

"Naturally," Tarvener said over the noise, "We would not want it said that we forced any solution on this august assembly. A vote is in order, don't you think, Priest Kalik?"

Ilyan Kalik bowed low. "Yes, Highness."

Golvadu had no illusions about the outcome. Anyone even thinking of crossing Tarvener had only to look at Faldor imprisoned in the earth to see their future.

"All in favor of His Highness' plan, raise your hands," Kalik intoned.

A forest of hands — including Golvadu's — reached skyward.

"Those opposed?"

Unsurprisingly, all the hands went down. "Your Highness, Your Graces, milords and ladies," Kalik announced. "It appears the consensus is unanimous."

Tarvener beamed and inclined his head. "Then my initial assessment of the wisdom of this august assembly was accurate. We should begin preparations at once."

This isn't necessarily a bad thing, Golvadu reasoned. *If they unify under Tarvener's leadership, then they will have removed one of the worst obstacles to progress: the infighting. These idiot Daemons may have just done me an immense service.*

He envisioned a united People's Republic under Tarvener's guidance and smiled to himself. Once the Daemon Prince completed all the hard work of consolidating power, perhaps a certain group of famous adventurers might receive special, top-secret information about where to find Tarvener — from an anonymous source, of course — with the suggestion that Damora would be better off without him.

The attendees dispersed into the hallways and chambers of the palace, discussing the events of the evening in animated voices. Golvadu hadn't seen this level of energy in months.

Yes, wouldn't it be a shame if the Grey Riders and the Daemons destroyed one another? he mused. *I would have to pick up the pieces and lead everyone on my own. Perfect.*

Chapter Seven – Dark Whispers from the Past

"Well, the third time is the charm, right?" Eric Aldenar said, resting his forearm on the side of the passage. A light globe hovered overhead, casting long shadows in the mustering chamber.

Brandi leaned against him. "It had better be. We're running out of passages." He put an arm around her. Though she tried to hide it, he heard weariness and discouragement in her voice.

She has to figure this out on her own. And I have to let her. "At least we don't have to go single file in this one," he replied, peering down the tunnel. No heat signatures showed up. Unlike the previous two side tunnels, this one looked more finished, with smooth walls and level floors. He hoped it indicated a better route.

If this doesn't work, we're down to the remaining side passages... or returning to Duarvar.

The thought of retreating brought a bitter taste in his mouth. That would not be good for their collective morale. In addition, the more they fumbled around just trying to get into Torosc, the more chance they would be caught by a superior force. Their advantage lay in speed and stealth.

He forced himself to take a deep breath. *Easy. Everything is working for the good, even setbacks. God wouldn't have brought Brandi and Megan back to life just to see us fail.*

"Can you check ultraviolet?" he asked Brandi.

Her eyes glowed pale blue. "It looks clear, for what it's worth."

"Why do you say that?"

"Well, ultraviolet only go so far. If I notice something, we'll still need light to be able to see colors and details. Are your alarms undisturbed?"

"Yes. Have you decided on the marching order? Who goes first?"

Brandi didn't answer, staring down the passage. He waited, trying not to show any impatience.

"Tholi," she finally said. "He's bigger and has a hotter fire breath. Plus, he's the better swimmer if this attempt ends up in another water-filled shaft. Gorlak should go with him. Then Kindri, Connor and Dar, then Captains Dearborn and Fejer and the pegasi, then Megan and Hannah, with you and me bringing up the rear."

Brandi beckoned to Connor and explained the order of march. "What do you think?" she asked.

Connor stared down the passage, one hand toying with the hilt of his sword, his expression hidden in shadow. He shrugged. "As good as anything I can come up with. Let's just move."

Eric hid a smile. Although Connor's ability to handle delays and frustration improved daily, Eric couldn't blame him for being impatient at this point. Their list of options shrank with every passage they attempted. The first tunnel they tried had narrowed to the point that only the halflings could get through. Gorlak speculated that it had been used to bring Goblin warriors to the large assembly chamber. The second led to a huge, flooded shaft leading straight down. Megan had used an Ethereal Eye spell to scout that one, reporting that the exit was seventy feet down, still underwater.

"Okay then." Brandi said. "Let's get set."

Brandi, Eric and Connor rejoined the main group near the ruined carts in the assembly chamber.

Gorlak clambered up into Tholi's saddle and gave the passage a critical once-over. "Not much room. I wish we bring dwarf miner with us."

"So do I," Brandi sighed. "But we didn't have time to vet anyone. Best to forge on. Have everyone extinguish the lights so we don't give ourselves away."

Eric kissed her on the head and she gave him a worried smile before putting on her helmet.

All the tension is wearing us down and we need to be alert when we enter Torosc. "You're doing fine," he murmured.

"Thank you, love," she whispered.

The Riders slowly slipped down the passage, relying on their magic items and innate abilities to watch for danger. The faint scent of mold and decay from the large chamber behind them faded, replaced by a dry, dusty odor. Eric saw only an occasional glow of fungus or insects along the cold stone of walls and floor.

He kept Fidelis close, ready to transform the dagger into a spear on a moment's notice. With the roof of the passage only a yard above the dragons' heads, the Riders had few combat options other than a quick frontal assault. Only magic spells with pinpoint accuracy could be used for fear of hitting their own allies.

He adjusted the bow on his back and settled his helmet more firmly. His training mantra cycled through his head. *Focus. Breathe. Think. See everything.*

The formation in front of them slowed, then stopped altogether.

Oh Lord. Now what?

Hannah wended her way through the ranks back to them. "Another cave-in," she said, frowning. "Just like in the main passage."

Eric felt like biting one of his arrows in two. From the look on Brandi's face, so did she.

"I don't know how long ago those cave-ins occurred, but with someone spying on us in Gorostol, I can't say I'm that surprised," Brandi muttered.

"On a positive note, we found something that looked like faded carvings on the walls," Hannah said. "Megan wanted to risk some light to look them over."

"No," Brandi began, "If it's seen —"

As if in answer, a luminescent sphere sprang into being near the dragons and Eric looked down to avoid being blinded.

Brandi pressed her lips together. "We shouldn't do that. It draws attention."

Eric knew that look and took her hand. "It's probably not much of a risk now, Bran. The big chamber is a few hundred yards back."

Connor scooted between two of the pegasi and arrived at Hannah's side. "Megan thinks there's a hidden door on the left side of the tunnel, a big one, maybe big enough to let in both dragons at the same time."

"A hidden door?" Brandi asked, her eyes narrowing. Connor nodded.

Something about her expression made him take notice. "Bran?"

"Have Dar and Megan join us, please," Brandi said, leaning into the passage wall. Connor nodded and slipped away.

"What is it?" he asked.

"A dream," she whispered.

Another one? "What was it about?"

She bit her lip. "Saint Mary appeared to me. She led me by the hand to a wall that wasn't a wall. When we passed beyond, we came upon a vast space full of darkness and fangs and bones, but it couldn't touch us. I felt a stinging pain, then she smiled and the darkness vanished. She showed me a meadow with trees and the dream ended."

Eric took a deep breath. "And you think this is it?"

She turned worried violet eyes to meet his. "I don't know. Eric, I'm scared. Why is God sending me these dreams?"

He felt the weight of responsibility and uncertainty. *Why indeed? Why do I have to have a wife who gets dreams from Heaven? Well, I can guess — she's actually been there.*

He gave her a hug. "God only sends visions to those He knows can handle the outcome. Relax. Let's see what's going on first."

Connor returned with Megan and Dar.

"What do you think?" Brandi asked them.

Dar shook his head. "The map doesn't show any turnoffs from this passage and if we go left, God only knows where we'll end up. I think we should head back to the mustering chamber and pick one of the remaining ones."

"None of which lead the way we want either," Connor reminded him.

Megan put her hands on her hips. "It's the devil you know versus the devil you don't. The carvings on the wall depict skulls and flames, neither of which fill me with confidence, based on past experience. Plus, we haven't seen any decorations or symbols anywhere else, so I'm doubly suspicious."

"Connor?" Brandi asked. "Hannah?"

"Dar's idea makes sense, but there's no guarantee we'd find a way out by going back to the side passages in the main chamber," Connor replied.

Hannah nodded. "If we've been outmaneuvered, it's because the enemy is working with the same plans we have. Since they don't appear to know about this hidden door any more than we do, I say we take it."

Dar frowned. "Into an unknown area? That's not very prudent."

Connor nodded. "Maybe, but sometimes we have to take a risk. Eric?"

He watched the others carefully. They didn't look at each other and he sensed the aggravation building. *It's partly from fatigue, but they're all strong-willed people. They wouldn't be alive if they weren't.*

"Dar's suggestion is the most obvious," he replied slowly, "However, I agree that the hidden door may be the approach we need, especially if it hasn't been disturbed by the PRT."

All eyes turned to Brandi. She straightened. "I feel it incumbent to tell you I had another dream. About a hidden door."

The others stared at her. "And?" asked Hannah.

Brandi gazed down the passage. "Saint Mary showed me darkness and danger beyond it but also a safe haven."

Dar grinned. "Well, so far, these dreams are spot-on. And I can't argue with Jesus' Mother."

Connor nodded. "All right then, let's get going."

Eric took Brandi's hand and was surprised to find it trembling. "Bran?"

She let out a breath. "I'm okay. It's just a lot of responsibility, you know? This could all go terribly wrong."

He smiled. "I have faith in you and faith in the Lord. We were meant to find this new way for a reason."

She kissed his cheek and smiled. The Riders proceeded down the tunnel. Just as Megan said, Eric made out very faint outlines of skulls and flames in the light of the luminous orb hovering overhead.

Not surprising, considering that this is Torosc, he concluded.

Megan moved her hands as if pushing a door open and spoke a long, rolling word. With a deep scraping and rumbling sound, a large section of the tunnel slid to the side. She backed up and Connor took her place. He examined the walls and floor minutely, then gestured for Megan to move the light close to the ceiling.

"Looks clear," he said. "Some evidence of expended magical traps, so watch your step."

The dragons led the way. The path widened. Eric had to admit this passage was even more spacious than the one they had just left. He relaxed a little.

With more room to maneuver, they increased the pace. Eric kept his eyes on the heads of the two dragons, ready to leap into action if they adopted a defensive posture. Tholi and Kindri marched along with heads high, scanning the area with shining eyes.

The passage turned several times. Eric remembered the map, and, unless he missed his guess, they proceeded on a path around the cave-in, towards Torosc. *That's a good sign, at least.*

Captain Dearborn paused to wait for them. "Megan and Connor found alcoves, but they're empty except for a few stone or ceramic fragments," she said in a low voice, "They think this area is older than the tunnels the Ja'al made — a *lot* older."

Older? How old? What are we getting into? "What does Gorlak say?" he asked.

Captain Dearborn looked confused. "Why would he know anything?"

"He used to work for the Ja'al long ago, before his conversion. Maybe he sees something familiar."

Dearborn moved ahead and soon returned. She shook her head. "He doesn't recognize anything, but he seems really nervous."

Brandi nodded and set her jaw. "Understood. Keep moving."

The dragons halted and the column slowed.

"Open space ahead," Captain Fejer murmured to them. "Very large."

Brandi raised her hands, palms upward, and her eyes glimmered silver. A faint shimmer grew in the air, then descended on the entire party. Eric felt a light feathery sensation, as if a gauzy blanket had enveloped him. Brandi murmured soft words and the shimmering cloud repeated three more times, each with a slightly different aura. Eric felt protected, stronger, more alert, and less nervous.

"Good idea," he said.

"Helps to be prepared," she replied. "There could be anything in there."

The column started up again and they emerged into an enormous chamber. Even with his infrared vision, Eric couldn't see the ceiling or the far end. He put his hand to the nearest wall. His fingers touched inlaid patterns and he traced them, frowning.

"What is it?" breathed Brandi, her voice shot through with tension.

"The letters "T" and "M" in Elven script," he mused aloud. "And what feels like a fanged, crowned skull."

A crowned skull, T and M? No! It can't be. Could this be part of Zhinia Margoth's kingdom? Memories came back to him in a flash: war and fire and death — and a skeletal figure in rotting robes with fiery pinpoints for eyes, wielding hellish magic from a bygone age.

Darkness, evil, fangs and bones! The details of Brandi's dream stood out in sharp contrast.

"Damn it. We're in Thul Mardil," he murmured to Brandi.

"Where?"

Eric's stomach tightened and he drew Fidelis from its sheath. "You remember I told you about the Lich-princess we fought in Deran? The one who invaded with an army from the Wilderness?"

"You mean Zhinia Margoth?" Brandi whispered. "So this is the darkness and fangs and bones from my dream?"

Eric set his jaw. "It could be. Margoth's kingdom was called Thul Mardil, The Black Cage. Those carvings on the wall confirm it: this is part of her old realm."

"But I thought Andyn destroyed her!"

Eric crouched, eyes flitting from side to side. "Yes, but if this is Thul Mardil, her evil lingers."

Brandi's eyes flared golden light. "Stay alert," she said to the others in a louder whisper. "Evil, danger close."

The formation spread out, drawing weapons. The dragons crouched, tails flicking from side to side. Gorlak wound his crossbow, the bolt burning with a red flame.

"What the hell is this place?" breathed Captain Dearborn.

"The remnant of an ancient evil kingdom," Brandi said.

Dar lifted his sword and the black blade glittered with tiny stars. A sourceless, chill breeze drifted by. Now Eric smelled a subtle, sickly-sweet aroma with a hint of something vaporous, like strong whiskey. A chill raced up his spine.

"I don't see anything." Connor replied. He touched the brooch on his armor and a cloud of sparkles flowed out of it, forming into a sword hovering in mid-air. Hannah's blade, Shriek, glowed white in her fist.

"Some evil things don't have a heat signature, like undead." Megan replied. "Watch your eyes. I'm lighting up the area." After waiting a couple of heartbeats, she gestured with her staff. Three luminous spheres popped into being and drifted up in the air, casting a pale white glow over them.

No eldritch horrors assailed them from the shadows.

Eric studied the area with a wary eye. A vast chamber soared overhead to a height of over forty feet and stretched out at least a hundred to each side. Winding steps curved from level to level, four in total. Recessed doors, stone coffins, side altars, statuary of dragons and gargoyles and cold braziers lined the walls of each level. An enormous chandelier of iron and crystal, festooned with figures of nude Daemons, hung from the ceiling in the exact center of the room. The floor itself held an intricate pattern of inlaid tiles depicting skulls and flames. Unfamiliar runes curled throughout the pattern.

"It's a necropolis," Brandi breathed.

One of the fanged skulls on the floor glowed faintly and they heard the unmistakable sound of the hidden doorway far behind them grinding shut.

"Shit," muttered Connor. "This just keeps getting better and better."

Eric activated Fidelis and the dagger grew to spear-length in a heartbeat. The point flared golden light, as bright as a torch. "We need to get out of here, and fast."

"Follow me along the left-hand wall and watch those coffins and doors," Brandi said, striding to the front rank. "Keep away from the runes."

They advanced, weapons ready and eyes darting all around. The sickly-sweet odor increased in intensity as they went.

The air warped. Eric blinked, trying to refocus his eyes. He slowed his pace, uncertain of his steps in an environment that twisted under his feet. The runes on the floor glowed and undulated in a hypnotic pattern.

"What's going on?" Fejer asked through gritted teeth.

"Misdirection spell," Megan said. "Stay together." She sang a series of arcane words. A bright globe of light sprang out from her staff, shooting out to cover the entire chamber. Eric blinked and his vision returned to normal.

"Defilers," an unfamiliar woman's voice accused. The word floated out at them, echoing and ethereal, seeming to come from all directions at once.

Eric's skin crawled.

"Keep moving," said Brandi through gritted teeth.

"Intruders and defilers!" the voice repeated, more menacing this time.

A cloud of deep purple fog flowed out of an ornate coffin on the fourth level of the chamber, above the exit doors. It solidified into a form with which Eric was well-familiar: a woman with bat wings and small horns on her forehead — yet this one bore little resemblance to his adopted half-sister, Saren. The woman's eyes glowed red-orange like coals in a forge and her skin gleamed pale as death in the magical light. She wore black splint mail with white stripes and she held a flail in one hand and a dagger in the other. The medallion of a fanged, crowned skull shone against her armor.

The Riders halted.

"Who dares to enter this desecrated space?" the woman asked.

Brandi strode to the head of their formation. "Those of royal blood dare. We come to free these lands. I am Brandawyn Veronica Therese, Queen of Alenar. With me are my sister, High Princess Megan Diana Marie, and Connor Tiberius, Crown Prince of Loemin."

The Daemon smirked. "Long has it been since I have heard those lineages uttered. Still, it matters not. You have no authority or power here. This is the demesne of my mistress, Zhinia Margoth."

"No longer," Brandi declared. "Saint Alyssa defeated Margoth in ages past. She returned as a lich, but our friend Andyn Eleandir destroyed her using Saint Alyssa's Crown."

To their surprise and consternation, the Daemon threw back her head and laughed. "Do you speak truly? That wizened bitch finally met her end? Well, may the true demons of Hell enjoy grinding her foul and greedy soul for all eternity."

"Then stand aside," Connor ordered. His dancing blade drifted in front of him like a cobra ready to strike. "Flee back to Hades with your kind! The War is lost."

"War? I know of no war," the Daemon laughed. "And why would I flee to Hades? I am one of the Fallen but I am also vampire. There is no place for me on Hades."

A vampire Daemon? I thought I had heard everything, but this...

"There is no place for you here either, Fallen," Megan added, taking her place by Brandi. "Begone and let us pass."

"Nay," replied the vampire. "With Zhinia Margoth destroyed, I reign here supreme. You shall join us in perpetual vigil unto the deeps of time. So say I, Dylany, Warden of the Deathchamber."

She threw her hands to the side and her medallion flared. The earth lurched and coffins vibrated. Urns glowed red. Eric steadied himself.

Then an army of undead burst forth. Skeletons clambered out of sarcophagi, wielding hooked swords and rusted maces. Mummies lurched out of cobwebbed alcoves, red eyes glaring from behind their wrappings.

This will be a bit of a challenge, Eric thought. He prepared a series of spells.

Tomb doors swung open with a screech of rusty hinges. Blue-skinned ghouls surged forth, followed by desiccated corpses attired in scraps of chainmail, carrying battle axes and clubs. Ragged, man-like forms of darkest night floated out from the urns, their star-like eyes burning with purple flame. The gargoyle statues glowed and transformed from stony effigies into fleshy creatures of leathery skin and gleaming claws. All told, the enemy numbered over a hundred.

On second thought, we might just get our heads handed to us.

"Get ready!" Dar shouted.

A putrid stench of rot and decay rolled at the Riders with the arrival of the undead. Eric stifled a cough and his eyes watered. His hands grew sweaty on the grips of his spear.

Only Brandi stood tall, unmoving, looking every inch the ruler of an ancient house. She extended her wings and white pinions tipped with black arced over her shoulders. Eric saw no trace of fear on her lovely features. She made the Sign of the Cross and golden mist sprang up around the Riders. The undead flinched and stumbled and the vile reek abated.

"We will keep no vigil with you, Dylany of the Deathchamber," Brandi said with a beatific smile. "Let us pass or be destroyed."

God, I love you Brandi...

"So be it." Dylany's medallion flashed and her forces charged. The dragons roared a challenge and blasted flame, immolating several gargoyles and mummies. Gorlak's crossbow bolt transfixed a zombie in the eye and its head exploded in a ball of flame. Brandi held forth her crucifix and sang a single, pure note. A pale blue light burst from her hand. The undead unlucky enough to be caught in it froze, then crumbled into piles of ash.

Eric unleashed a lightning spell at a pair of leaping ghouls and burned through their skulls.

Then the wave of attackers hit.

Eric danced to the side, thrusting and jabbing, always keeping Brandi to his left and Megan behind him to his right. Zombies hacked, skeletons thrust jagged blades at him and slobbering ghouls clawed and bit. The ferocity and agility of the undead amazed him and he narrowly avoided an axe in the face.

What is happening? Eric thought, gasping. *Undead can't move this fast or strike this accurately.*

He kept his breathing regular, not extending too far from his position. Brandi's protective screens saved him more than once but soon sputtered out. Captain Fejer's well-timed stroke cut off a mummy's arm as it reached for him. Eric jammed his spear through the mummy's skull and it burst into flame, blazing like a bonfire in a cloud of black, acrid smoke.

The Daemon vampire hovered over her sarcophagus. She hurled dark fire, spears of ice and ghostly apparitions at them, but Megan stood firm at Eric's back, dispelling, deflecting and banishing everything she shot at the Riders. Perspiration streamed down her face and she gritted her teeth.

Brandi whirled through the air towards Dylany, slashing gargoyles, but every time she slew one, another took its place. Dragon fire roared. Kindriana leapt to one side of the chamber, tail lashing. She pulverized several gargoyle statues before they could animate. Delany shot her with a sizzling purple lightning bolt and she screamed, crashing on top of a trio of mummies. Tholi swooped down to her aid, ripping the undead into pieces as zombies and ghouls swarmed at them.

The two halflings stood alone against ten wraiths. Connor's dancing sword drove the attackers back time and again. One wraith lunged too close and Hannah struck, slashing through it from shoulder to hip. Her sword let out a triumphant wail and the wraith dissipated with an airy moan.

"Dar!" Eric called. "Connor and Hannah —"

"I know!" Dar whirled his sword in a deadly arc, splitting two ghouls into pieces. He touched a tiny plate at the throat of his chainmail and winked out of existence, glittering into place next to Connor. He and the halflings stood back-to-back, blades glowing in the dim light.

Eric slammed down a skeleton warrior and pulverized its skull with the butt of his spear.

"Eric!" Megan gasped. "There are too many."

"And they're too fast!"

"It's Dylany!"

As if on cue, the vampire Daemon swept her hand across the battlefield, casting a wave of greenish light. The air thickened and Eric choked. His vision grew spotty. Some of the dismembered undead knit back together and rose up, grasping weapons.

Megan desperately shouted a word and slammed the butt of her staff on the floor. A sphere of white light erupted over the Riders. Dylany's verdant fire washed over the globe, but Eric heard the scream of an injured pegasus behind him.

Brandi darted and dodged, cutting down enemies. More surged forth to replace the fallen. Dylany laughed, hitting her with a flurry of firedarts. The missiles cracked on Brandi's armor and her shields flared.

Then a small fluttering creature with bat wings darted up from the dragons, carrying a silvery, glittering dagger.

Gorlak!

"Justice comes for you," Brandi declared, her eyes changing into pools of golden light. Her weapons took on a flaming edge.

Dylany spat a profanity and lashed out. Gorlak fluttered in behind the undead Daemon and slashed her with his blade. White light flared and Dylany staggered.

With a shriek of outrage, Dylany slammed him into an alcove and whirled away from Brandi's swords. Eric raised Fidelis but Brandi charged right into his line of sight.

No! Eric sidestepped, trying to find an opening. Dylany and Brandi whacked away at each other, spinning and parrying. Gorlak struggled to his feet and hurled his dagger. Dylany dodged. Brandi danced aside to match her, giving Eric an opening.

Now! Eric threw. His glowing spear punched through Dylany's side, skewering her like a boar on a spit. With a ragged gurgle, she dropped her weapons and fluttered down to a ledge. Eric recalled his weapon and Fidelis glittered into being in his fist.

Brandi landed near the Daemon vampire. With an evil grin, Dylany clutched her medallion and healing light covered her. She thrust out a fist and a vortex of hellfire spun into being in front of her, spitting red flames in all directions. Eric twisted out of the way, but the fiery missiles tracked him unerringly. He staggered and went to one knee, his injuries burning.

"You will join Margoth in Hell!" Dylany screamed, motioning at Brandi. The vortex shot at her.

Almost faster than Eric could follow, Brandi sidestepped the whirling hellfire and lunged. Her twin swords slashed through Dylany's neck and her head fell to bounce on the stones. The Daemon's corpse exploded in a shower of flame and bone fragments. Brandi lurched backward, her shields winking out.

Below, the undead wailed in despair. They retreated to their sarcophagi and urns. Exhausted, the Riders watched them go with wary eyes.

Brandi fluttered down, thumping onto a platform and rolling over the edge. Eric jumped and caught her before she landed on a pile of mummy bits. He took her hand.

"Need to…" Brandi gasped.

"Hang on, dear," Eric said, heart in his throat. He shrugged off his backpack, drawing out his healing kit.

My God. How many times did she get hit? Eric stopped counting at twelve.

Gorlak limped off. "I get Dar to help her."

"No, you get yourself treated. I have Brandi." She lay unmoving. Submerging his growing anxiety, he methodically treated each injury with magic or medicine. He pulled out a bone fragment from her hip. It glistened with a grey slime and his heart skipped a beat.

"What the hell?"

Her hand gripped his wrist. She stared at him with eyes tinted a sickly green. "Crypt rot," she rasped.

"This wasn't in the dream, was it?" He snatched a jar of Everheal and spread it on her wounds.

"No… or maybe I would have faltered."

The magical ointment sparkled and glowed and her wounds closed. She sighed and relaxed. He felt her pulse: strong and even. *Thank you, God.*

"Hey," Connor's voice said next to him.

Eric looked up through bleary eyes. The other Riders crowded around.

"How is she?" asked Megan. She leaned on Dar for support, hobbling.

"I'll mend," Brandi whispered before anyone could answer. "How is everyone else?"

"We're fine, Majesty," said Dearborn. "Your pegasus was injured by that blast of green light from the Daemon. Dar and Megan helped her. We think she'll be okay."

"Can you stand?" Eric asked.

"To get out of this place?" Brandi rasped, taking his arm. "I'll do somersaults."

Dar chuckled and Megan laughed.

"Yes, I'd say she's going to be fine," Connor noted drily.

Eric helped Brandi up. He watched her carefully, fully aware that this was her first fight against a Daemonic entity.

"Are you sure you're okay?" he whispered.

As if she read his mind, she smiled and gave his arm a weak pat. "She didn't realize I had Fallen heritage so she couldn't tempt me. I didn't have to worry about contending with my Daemonic side. I'm fine."

Relieved but still concerned, he stayed at her side as they gathered near the double doors at the base of the necropolis.

Hannah eyed the portal. "Looks like a narrow squeeze again."

"Let's hope it's the last," said Connor.

"One second," said Megan. Though she looked worn and haggard, she raised her staff and spoke a word, then pointed with her free hand. She moved her hand from side to side and a ray of silvery light washed over the portal. Purple symbols flashed, gouts of flame and acrid smoke leapt up. Rusted metal spikes shot up from the floor and then receded. For good measure, a pool of vaporous yellow liquid seeped out onto the space before the exit. Megan gestured with her staff again. The liquid evaporated and the smoke cleared in a gust of wind.

"That's a good sign," Connor mused.

"A good sign?" Eric asked with a tired grin. "I'd like to see a bad one."

Connor smirked. "If it has that many traps, we're going somewhere the forces of evil don't want us to go." He pushed the door open. Once again, Eric found himself tramping through tunnels, glad to be free of the necropolis and praying that there would be an end to it.

After what seemed like decades, the column halted and Megan headed forward. Eric leaned on Niveral's withers, blinking against bleary vision.

Another flash of light ahead lit the passage, then the most glorious sight met his eyes: another set of double doors yawned open, letting in a stream of afternoon sunlight. Trees towered overhead, their leaves and branches waving in a brisk breeze. About two hundred feet away, a wide stream rushed over rocks and boulders, casting spray all around. The sunshine and fresh air felt like a hug and a warm bath all rolled into one.

Eric tipped his head back and reveled in it for a moment, then took Brandi's hand. "Well done, dear," he said, giving it a squeeze.

Her answering smile shone brighter than the sun.

Chapter Eight – First Steps

"Come along." Khyla Dearborn led two pegasi back from the stream. She paused, watching Eric.

He stood next to the campsite and clasped a brooch on his tunic. A glittering stream of light flowed from the brooch and materialized into a brown-tailed hawk sitting on his forearm. He swept a hand skyward and the bird soared up into the air.

Khyla watched him. A curious ache crept into her heart and she twisted the reins in her hand. *Everything fits. He looks like father and his magical skills could be from his mother… or is it just a coincidence?*

Eric stood still, eyes distant and glittering with a faint silver light.

Well, standing here won't help anything. She tramped back to the camp, tied the reins to a nearby tree, then removed two saddlebags and joined the others. Alex and Dar wrestled a fallen log into place for seating, then headed off for another. Megan put the last few pieces of wood onto a pile at the center of the camp. Gorlak perched on a branch high in a tree, peering into the woods to the west. Near the massive doors that led to the underground, the dragons lay coiled like cobras. They stared at the portal, tails flicking occasionally. Connor and Hannah took seats on a stump, leaning into each other. Hannah tried to stifle a yawn and failed.

Khyla let out a deep breath and some of her residual tension left her. *We're well-guarded, at least.* She headed over to Megan.

"Do you need anything, Highness?"

"Not really." Megan sat on the log and brushed a stray lock of red-gold hair off her forehead. "We've spell-warded the doors so we'll have an alarm if anything tries to sneak up on us, plus the dragons are a wonderful deterrent. If you want to help, you can arrange the bedrolls."

Khyla laid out the bedrolls in a ring around the pile of firewood, separated by enough distance to keep away from stray embers.

She straightened to find Megan smiling at her. "Lots of practice at setting up camp?" Megan asked.

"Yes, ma'am."

Dar crouched down by the firewood. He removed a striker from his belt pouch and arranged a pile of kindling. Soon, he had a fire started.

He then removed food packets and a flatiron griddle from a saddlebag. "Dear, we need to shield the fire. I'd like to get started."

Megan nodded tiredly and gestured with her hand, fingers waving like tall grass blown by the wind. A shimmering wall of air grew above and around the fire. Its light dimmed significantly, though Khyla still felt the heat. What little smoke issued from the flames vanished before even reaching the treetops.

Khyla shook her head. *I've heard many stories of their skills — and gear — and they were all true.*

"Have you never seen a Screen of Air before?" Megan asked.

"No, ma'am. I know there are many magic spells, but that's a new one for me."

"I understand. Don't be shy about asking questions, especially about magic you don't recognize."

She seems to have so much power. But why didn't she use her most potent magic in the necropolis? I thought we were going to die for sure. Khyla opened her mouth to say something, then closed it.

"Yes, Captain?" Despite her obvious fatigue, Megan's steady gaze didn't waver.

"It's nothing important, ma'am. You need your rest."

"Actually, talking will keep me awake long enough to get something to eat and then collapse, so ask away." She indicated the log and Khyla sat next to her.

"Well, we were in deep trouble in the necropolis but you didn't use the magic that you used against the Stone Lurkers. Surely it would have been effective."

"Ah. That. Well, my mentors cautioned me against using Aura of Heaven more than once a day. As you're probably aware, it is very draining. At sunrise, I will be rested enough."

Visions of Stone Lurkers from another time and place played out in Khyla's mind but she cut off that line of thinking. Instead, she mulled over another question, based on rumors she had heard prior to their departure from Gorostol.

Surely those can't be true…

Megan tilted her head to the side. Khyla got the distinct impression that she could sense the unspoken question. Then Megan smiled. "I can tell there's something else."

"I don't think I should ask," Khyla replied.

"Nonsense, Captain. You are part of the team."

Khyla waited in silence for the span of several heartbeats as the evening deepened. "Well, then, the rumor is that you and the Queen were raised from the dead. Is there any truth to that?"

"Yes."

Khyla stared. "I… really?"

"Really and truly." Megan leaned back on the log, hands braced behind her, her eyes focused on something far away. "Brandi and I were both killed, but the other Riders preserved us within milliseconds of our passing by using Preservation Nets, so our bodies were suspended in time. Weeks, even months later, it was as if we had just died."

"What did you see?"

Megan smile became peaceful, beatific. "We saw God. He told us it was not our time and that He had important work for us to complete yet."

Khyla's jaw dropped. "You saw a god? What did he look like?"

"It wasn't so much anything visual as it was a Presence: a warm, caring, compassionate, merciful Presence Who loved me no matter what I had ever done wrong."

Khyla stared into space, trying to come to grips with what she had just heard. "Then what happened?" she asked finally.

"Then I heard Saint Mary. She kissed us and told us to get up."

"Who is that?"

"The mother of Jesus."

"Who?"

Megan smiled. "That's a much longer conversation. Just suffice it to say that God sent His most powerful saint to help us."

"So this Mary person just said 'get up, Megan'?"

"Basically. I opened my eyes and Brandi was there and the Papal Nuncio and Sister Karen Mercato. It was a bit confusing at first, but…" She sighed. "Dar showed up a little while later and nothing really mattered after that."

She saw a god — and he sent her back from the dead! Stunned, Khyla looked up into the darkening sky. "And you still remember it?"

"Not as well as I'd like." Megan frowned. "As time goes on, I find myself recalling less and less. It's maddening really. When I really get frustrated and anxious, once I calm myself down — or Dar calms me down — I remember the love and happiness and peace. Then things don't seem so bad."

"Is it the same for Brandi… I mean, Her Majesty, too?"

"Yes, it is." Megan paused for a long while, her expression still distant. "I dream of God sometimes, and Mary." She looked at Khyla sidelong. "Would it alarm you if I told you that you were in one of the dreams?"

Khyla stared at her. "I… I was?"

Megan nodded. "Not to fear. It wasn't anything bad. Just that you needed help."

Khyla's mouth went dry. "A god sent you a dream of me?"

"Is that so incredible? God loves all his children, and you're one of them. Everyone is."

Khyla fell silent, those last words echoing in her ears. *My mother derided those ideals and father laughed at them. Yet Megan is here, alive, and they're not.*

She remembered her mother's contemptuous glance and her father's indifference — dark punishments, dark deeds and an even darker home. The bitterness of her childhood surged, threatening to dispel the wonder of Megan's tale.

Megan turned to face her. "I think the dream was meant to encourage, not warn of danger. Be at peace."

Khyla clenched her fists. *Peace? When will I truly have peace? She has a family and saints and gods and I have…* Her eyes flitted to Eric, gazing into the distance after his hawk golem. "I can only wish for something like that."

To Khyla's amazement, Megan actually took her hand. The traumatic memories fled. "Peace comes when we unite ourselves to God's will and let Him handle what we cannot."

The High Princess took my hand! As if I were a friend — I, who come from — Khyla swallowed with difficulty.

"No matter what has happened in our lives," Megan continued. "God can repair it. Don't be afraid. You have friends."

"Are part-Elohir mind readers too?" Khyla murmured.

Megan chuckled. "I wish! It would make my marriage easier. Men can be so unfathomable sometimes." She patted Khyla's hand and released it.

"Yes… um…" Unsure of what else to say, Khyla stood. "Dinner will be soon, Highness. I should go wash up."

Megan closed her eyes and nodded. "In case I'm asleep when you get back, wake me. Dar is cooking and I don't want to miss that."

Khyla bowed and left for the nearby river. Her mind went over her conversation with Megan again. *She seemed so calm. Is that a blessing from her god? Does she fear death at all?* A thousand questions raced through her mind.

She knelt at the water's edge and laved her hands, face and arms.

A twig snapped behind her. She whirled, hand flashing to her sword, then relaxed.

Alex grinned, raising both hands. "Steady on, Captain."

"Sorry. It's been a long day."

"No argument there."

He knelt next to her and washed. "It's a good thing we have dragons with us, isn't it?"

"That's a serious understatement," she replied, drying her hands in her cloak.

"Ever seen dragons before?" he asked, rising as well.

"Not up close," she said, glad for other conversation to distract her from wildly careening thoughts about gods and resurrections. "There were a few lesser dragons helping out at Meridian during the War — and good thing too. I think they were Sarkany."

"I'm just glad Tholi and Kindri forage their own meals," he said. "It's hard enough to feed ourselves." He turned towards the camp and she joined him.

"Forage?"

He pointed towards a clump of hartberry bushes. "They're nice enough to conceal the carcasses, but they caught a couple of wild deer when we started setting up camp."

The appetizing aroma of roasting meat, vegetables and spices wafting from the cookfire as they approached. Khlya's stomach rumbled. "From the smell of what's cooking, it seems they decided to share."

"We're all one team, after all."

The pair walked in silence for a while.

"I saw you talking to Princess Megan," Alex said in a casual tone as they neared the camp. "I can guess the subject."

She gave him a sidelong glance. "And what was that?"

"About being raised from the dead. It wasn't part of our briefing but the rumors have been running rampant for months. I asked the Queen before we left Deran."

"Oh." She slowed her pace.

He slowed too. "I wondered why it took you so long to ask."

She felt his eyes on her and shrugged. "Didn't think it was my place. I'm not that important."

"No, Captain. You're very important. You wouldn't be here otherwise."

Thinking of Megan's tale, she shook her head. "That's what scares me. If the Christian god sent them back, and now I'm working for them…"

"That's frightening?"

She shuddered. "The very idea of a god watching me like that…"

"Why?"

She remembered flickering braziers, dark tunnels, darker chambers and deeds darker still, then echoing screams and the stench of blood. She shuddered. "My experience of gods and religion is not very positive."

He halted and she stopped with him. He fixed her with warm brown eyes. "We will have to widen the breadth of your experience. The God I follow is very, very positive."

Something in his expression riveted her: a combination of empathy and compassion. "Captain, I wouldn't even know how to start," she stammered.

He smiled. "Stick around the Grey Riders long enough and you will."

She nodded wordlessly.

His eyes twinkled. "And please, we've been working together for weeks. No need to be formal all the time. My name is Alex."

Despite the scraps of dismal childhood memories still in her head, she felt herself smiling back. "I'm Khyla."

"Let's get a move on, then, Khyla. You've seen Dar and Connor eat, so we'd better be quick."

Stifling a laugh, she accompanied him. As they approached, the hawk golem soared down and landed on Eric's forearm. At his word, it transformed into a coppery stream of light that streamed back into the brooch on his tunic. "Not to put a damper on our rest period," he said, face grim. "But there are two columns of troops moving to the west, about a thousand strong. I saw banners for both Gudarta and Vardu."

Gudarta... At the mention of the goddess of torture and suffering, Khyla's hands clenched again and she forced herself to take a deep breath.

"Gudarta *and* Vardu?" Brandi asked. Eric nodded and she frowned. "They were at odds before the war. Now they're allies?"

"How far away?" asked Dar.

"About five miles and heading west, away from us. Still, if they're present in those numbers, we'd better be careful."

"More importantly," Megan added, "Why are they on the move? Maneuvers? Or something more sinister?"

"I wonder if our previous attempts are the cause," Connor mused. "Maybe they think we're scouting for raids?"

Megan pushed herself up from her seat. "We'll have to make sure we watch the western approaches as well as the doors."

Brandi nodded. "Good idea. Gorlak and I can take over for Tholi and Kindri while they eat and then the dragons can have first watch — one on the doors and one closer to the stream."

Connor flicked a glance at his wife. "Guardian Rod?"

Hannah dipped a hand into her backpack. "Guardian Rod." She withdrew a short cylindrical bar about the thickness of her thumb and as long as her forearm. Bluish metal made up half its length, with the other half a clear crystal. She gave the area a once-over, then planted the metal end into the earth near the fire.

Hannah murmured a phrase and the crystal flashed, then a low hum reverberated in the clearing. A swarm of tiny red lights skittered over the ground in a vast circle, passing by the Grey Riders, the tree in which Gorlak perched, and the dragons. Once the crimson dots reached a distance of about seventy feet from the rod, they disappeared into the grass and earth.

Khyla gaped. "What was that?"

"A monitoring device," Hannah said, closing her backpack. "If anyone or anything who isn't us tries to get past those little dots of light, we'll hear an alarm — and a bright flash will blind the intruders for good measure."

"Is there no end to their toys?" Khyla whispered to Alex.

Alex grinned. "As long as they work in our favor, I'm just glad to watch the show."

Connor plopped back down on the log, looking satisfied. "All right, Dar. Time to deliver. Let's try these grilled venison sandwiches you were talking about..."

Chapter Nine – A Homecoming of Sorts

So, this is Havenridge, thought Hannah. *It doesn't look any different from the last two towns… unless it's more bleak.* She leaned against the doorpost of the general store, eyes scanning the darkening, damp streets.

Halflings, humans and Dwarves slouched through the thoroughfares past weather-beaten shops and rickety wooden stalls. No one spoke to each other. Oil lanterns glowed from black iron lampposts. Most people kept their gaze on their path or the objects in front of them. Bolder ones sized up Hannah with narrowed eyes.

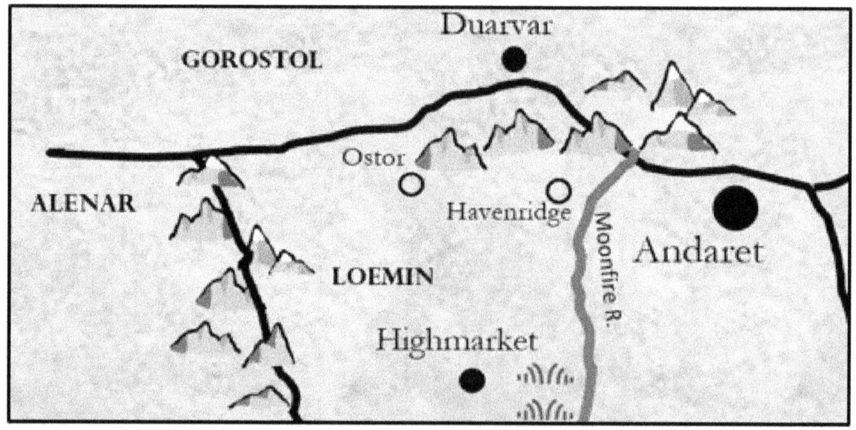

Soldiers in black and red livery patrolled in groups of two or three, spears and halberds at the ready. Their scale armor, though serviceable, looked worn.

Her practiced eye assessed them. *Their discipline is pretty good, they're reasonably attentive and their equipment is better than average.*

Then she saw a red-eyed hound trotting at the side of one particular group. Its barbed tail lashed the air as it loped along, steam issuing from a fanged mouth. Hannah suppressed a shudder and dropped her gaze, turning away.

Damned Fell-Hound! That's all we need. Don't react.

"You there!"

Only her military discipline prevented her from flinching at the harsh tone. She turned.

Just act tired and beaten-down. She kept her eyes on the muddy boots of the three troopers in front of her. "Yes?" she said in as meek a voice as she could muster.

"Look at me when I'm talking to you, woman!"

She raised her chin. A Halfling with the three spears insignia of a sergeant glared at her, fists on his hips. One of his hands held the leash of the Fell Hound.

"What's your name?"

"Erica Highwater."

The sergeant spoke over his shoulder to two troopers behind him. "Either of you know that name?"

A Dwarf with a scarred face and a Halfling with a scruffy mustache shook their heads.

"Not from around here," the Halfling said.

"What are you doing here, girlie?" the sergeant demanded.

Girlie? Hannah felt her anger rising and forced herself to remain passive. "Waiting for my husband."

The patrol leader leered at her. "Husband? Well, maybe we can keep you company while you wait."

Her mind flicked to Shriek, strapped to her back under her cloak and jacket. She slid her hands behind her. "No thank you. He should be done in the store momentarily."

"Oooh, Sarge, she used a big word," the Halfling guffawed. "Maybe she's more my speed. What do you say, Erica? Maybe we take a little trip down by the mill pond, eh?"

Hannah's anger turned to fury. One hand inched closer to Shriek.

"Ah, Sergeant, so glad to see you!" Connor announced, closing the door of the shop behind him.

The guard blinked. "Er, what?"

Connor smiled. "The shopkeeper mentioned that the local garrison might have need of some work on locks and mechanisms. My wife and I are locksmiths, recently arrived from Chilverton, Northwatch. Would you know how I can get in touch with the quartermaster?"

The sergeant shot a glance at his soldiers and rubbed his jaw. "Well, maybe I would and maybe I wouldn't."

Connor stepped closer. "Perhaps this will jog your memory in the future." He pressed some coins into the sergeant's free hand. "I'm sure we can help each other."

The sergeant's eyes narrowed. "Is this a bribe?"

"Oh no! Wouldn't think of it. It's an investment. If you would like me to invest further, let us get settled at the Black Falcon and we'll come and see you at the fort in the morning. Who should I ask for?"

The sergeant hesitated. "Sergeant Minter."

"Until tomorrow, then, Sergeant." Connor took Hannah's elbow and hefted his pack. She lifted hers to her shoulder. Without another word, they strode away.

Hannah seethed, acutely aware of the guards' eyes on her body as they walked away.

"Stay calm, dearest," Connor whispered.

"Trying. Let's just get to the Inn before anything else happens."

"Else?"

"You didn't see that Halfling in the store undressing me with his eyes? That's why I went outside."

"Which one was he? There were a few unsavory types in there."

"The one with the pale hair and light eyes. He was in the back near the herbs and medicinals."

Connor nodded. "Yes. Him. Well, he could be a spy or he might just be curious about new people in town." He gave her a sidelong look, eyes twinkling. "Especially if one of them is drop-dead gorgeous."

"Connor…"

He bumped her with his shoulder. "Can't help it if you're beautiful."

"Just stop." Hannah's cheeks grew warm and she shook her head. "Let's get to this Black Falcon, please. I hope there are no vermin."

"Good point. I think I saw a Fell Rat in the alley behind the store."

Fell Rats _and_ *Fell Hounds? Irial preserve us!* "Wonderful."

She accompanied him down the muddy street towards a two-story building. A pale grey sign decorated with a black raptor swung in the mild breeze. The couple dodged a bleary-eyed human slouching by the entrance. A pair of Halfling women near the corner sized them up and whispered to each other.

The odor of stale beer and pipe smoke assaulted them the instant they entered the foyer. A Dwarven woman stared down at them from the higher level of a two-tiered desk. She moved to the lower tier. "Rooms are four silver plus an extra silver in room tax," she announced without preamble. "Taproom is open until midnight. No funny business or we call the guard, period."

Connor nodded, producing fifteen silver coins. "Three nights."

"Write your names in the ledger. Room 2H."

Connor and Hannah signed, using their aliases. The woman gave them two small brass keys and turned away without a second glance.

Hannah surreptitiously surveyed the inside of the inn. The door to the tavern hung open and she saw the flickering lights of oil lamps and candles. Hushed conversation reached her ears.

She followed Connor up the stairs to a landing. One sign reading "Elves & Humans" pointed to the right down one corridor while a second with the words "All Others" pointed to the left. Connor led them to a door that could have easily accommodated a dwarf or shorter. Once inside, he dropped the backpack on a nearby chest and sat on the bed with a sigh.

Hannah locked the door and set her bag down. She eyed the bed suspiciously. "We should check for vermin. The very idea of a Fell Rat nearby makes my skin crawl."

He grinned. "Agreed. But don't forget we have Handor's trusty anti-vermin remedy, just in case."

A sudden wave of melancholy came over her at the mention of her brother's name and his face hovered in her memory. Hannah eased herself onto the bed.

His last thought was for me to get to safety. She stared at her hands in her lap. *Even though he knew enemies surrounded us. And I failed him.*

A pair of gentle hands covered hers.

"Hey."

She raised misty vision to meet her husband's eyes and gave a tremulous smile. "I'm okay."

"I'm sorry. I shouldn't be so casual about mentioning him like that."

She sighed, wiping her eyes. "Why should you walk on eggshells where his memory is concerned? He was your companion and a Grey Rider long before you met me."

Connor scooted next to her and put his arm around her. "That doesn't make your grief any less."

"It was over a year ago, sweetheart." She nestled into his embrace. "I need to move on."

"Moving on doesn't mean forgetting. It means making them proud of the way we carry on without them. And I'm sure your brother is proud of you."

She smiled, imagining Handor at peace at last. *Yes, he might just be proud of me after all.* Her melancholy faded.

She kissed Connor on the mouth. "Such a philosopher-king you will make! You've been hanging around your mother too much lately, or Brandi."

He kissed her back. "I have to grow up sometime."

"You've grown up quite well, thank you."

Their kisses deepened and she pulled him tighter into her arms, her heart rate accelerating. Her hands explored him, loosening belts and ties. His did the same, awakening her in a warm and familiar fashion.

Abruptly, the suspicious looks of the townsfolk, the leering guards, and the red eyes of the Fell Hound intruded on her romantic ardor. *By Irial! What are we doing? We can't be thinking of this in enemy territory!*

"Connor, wait," she whispered as his lips ran down her neck. "This…this isn't a safe place."

He pulled back and opened his mouth to say something, then closed it.

"There could be spies anywhere," she whispered, pulling her blouse back over her shoulders. "You saw those people in the town, and the guard. If they have Fell Hounds, there's a wizard nearby. For all we know, they have magical scrying devices in the room just to watch us." She stifled a shudder at the thought.

"You have a point," he replied slowly. "Let's give the room a once-over."

Fortunately, the room didn't hold much. She watched, bemused, as he inspected the furniture, walls, door and windows with an expert eye.

"You're sure good at that. Though I'm not sure what you expect to find in a chamber pot."

"I'm just thorough. Your brother's influence, in part." He moved aside the curtain and peeked out the window. "Hmm…what do you know?"

"What is it?"

He nodded. "Is that your admirer from the shop?"

A blond Halfling man strode down the street beneath their window, his black cloak billowing behind him. Hannah set her jaw and her eyes narrowed. "Yes, that's him."

"Well, he's heading away from the inn."

Hannah frowned. "I don't know. If he's a spy and suspects some-thing…"

"What's to suspect? Most of the inhabitants of this town are Halflings and we've seen a lot of through-traffic as well. We're just tradespeople."

"I don't know, Connor." She sighed, unconvinced. "I sure hope we find a rebel agent in this place who recognizes the keywords. I'm beginning to wonder if they're only rumors."

"In a place like the PRT, I'd be suspicious if we had an easy time finding them."

Hannah couldn't put the light-eyed Halfling's stare out of her mind and she shook her head.

When she didn't answer, Connor patted her hand. "We're on the second floor and the wall is sheer down to the street so he'd have to be able to fly in order to get up here. Don't forget that the other Riders are keeping an eye on us."

He's right. Dar is posing as a traveler in the other inn and Eric said he'd have Stealth on overwatch patrol too. She let out a breath and relaxed.

"You're right, dear. Go ahead and set the alarms."

He set a flat, glittering yellow jewel at the windowsill and another next to the doorjamb. Something nagged at her and she removed Shriek from her pack, laying it under her pillow.

"You're really spooked, aren't you?" Connor put his arms around her from behind.

She shivered, partly from his lips on her neck and partly from the environment. "This town is creepy."

He sighed. "Yes, it is."

"Sweetheart, I know you want to make love and I really, really want to but —"

"No, you're right. It isn't safe. Let's get some rest. We have a lot of scouting to do tomorrow."

Turning around, she gave him a tight hug. "But we better make sure there are no vermin first. I'm not enthused about getting some disease."

He kissed the top of her head. "Well, then, it's time for some anti-vermin concoction, isn't it?"

<<>>

Hannah's eyes popped open. She lay still and quiet, her right hand and her head resting on Connor's chest. Her leg lay across his hips and his arm curved around her shoulders and back. He felt as he always did: strong, warm, and safe.

Everything as it should be, yet…

Her senses sharpened and she became aware of every little sound and smell and sight. Light from the street lamps outside the inn leaked in around the shutters of their window. The wind hissed and she heard the faint scrabble of an animal in the street below.

She shifted to the infrared spectrum. Nothing moved. Without knowing why, she pulled her brother's sword out from under her pillow and laid it alongside her hip and leg.

Connor slept beneath her. She considered waking him up but paused.

What if it's nothing?

Her eyes flicked to the chair next to his side of the bed. *His tunic is there with his magic brooch, within easy reach.*

Then a mild, spicy but heady aroma reached her, different from Connor's familiar scent.

Shriek vibrated. The air chilled as if she had entered an icehouse.

Her eyes darted all around the room, seeking an enemy, but she saw nothing. Then Megan's words echoed in her head. *Some evil things don't have a heat signature, like undead.*

Oh, damn it! She was about to draw Shriek when a soft voice spoke from the corner of the room.

"Ah! Love! It's a wonderful thing, is it not?"

Her skin crawled and she dearly wished she hadn't left her shield with the other Riders.

She swallowed and replied in as calm a voice as she could. "Yes, it is a beautiful thing to be loved."

A candle flared to life in one corner of the room. A golden-haired, pale-skinned Halfling man robed in black sat in a chair next to the table. He fixed her with light grey eyes now glowing red and leered, showing fangs. "Yes, the pair of you are quite fetching."

How in blazes did he get past Connor's wards?

Hannah forced herself to remain calm. "What the hell are you doing in our room?" she asked.

The man examined his fingernails minutely. "Serving the People's Republic of Torosc, of course. I have to admit it was a little difficult. The warding gem by the window was a chore and that… substance is very irritating to bats. I had to transform rather quickly."

Oh Great Creator! A vampire! Why doesn't Connor wake up? He can hear us. She nudged her husband and he stirred.

"Oh, don't worry about him. He'll sleep for a bit," the man said, touching a hollow bone tube on the table next to a metal plate with a dark powder. He frowned. "You, however, seem to be oddly resistant."

She remained silent and drew Shriek under the covers. The sword hummed in her fist.

The Halfling stood, his eyes narrowing. "What's this? A weapon of power? Well, we can't have any of that, my dear."

His eyes transfixed her. A curious lethargy settled on her and Hannah gritted her teeth.

"Why don't you just leave that aside and come to me?" he purred. "I can offer you far more than that feeble man in the bed."

Shriek hummed in her grip like a captured, angry wasp and the lethargy faded. "I think not," she growled back. "You had best leave if you know what's good for you."

"I do know what's good for me," he sneered. "And it's you. I need another pretty little thrall to help me with my duties."

He strode forward, his robe swirling around him. She rolled over Connor and slipped off the bed, throwing the covers at the vampire.

"Connor!" She hissed. "Wake up!"

Shriek flared bright white. The vampire snarled and jumped over the bed. She dodged and slashed but he shot past.

He took a backhanded swipe at her and she ducked into a roll, heading for the opposite side of the room. She barely regained her feet when he swooped at her, reaching with clawed hands. She thrust and cut and he sprang back.

The brooch!

Hannah vaulted over the bed and snatched up Connor's tunic, pressing the brooch into his hand.

Connor's eyes popped open. He stared at her for a split second, then rolled into a crouch on the floor a moment before the vampire's clawed hands ripped apart the bed linens.

Hannah lunged, stabbing the vampire in the shoulder and leg. He swore and recoiled.

Connor spoke a word and his guardian sword glittered into being in front of him and Hannah. The vampire dodged left and right but the sword matched him.

"Who's your friend?" Connor asked, drawing his other blade. The edge rippled with orange fire.

"Never said his name. And he's not the room service."

The vampire stepped back, then hurtled into the air and flew at them. Connor's guardian sword stabbed and missed. The vampire twisted in midair. Hannah cut shimmering gashes in his undead flesh.

"You'll pay for that, you bitch!" the vampire raged, lashing out. Hannah dodged and he smashed a nearby chair into fragments.

The dancing sword darted at him again and he slapped it into a corner. It stuck into the wall and vibrated with captive energy, straining to pull itself out. Connor recalled it to him and it once again floated in midair.

The vampire waved his hands and a night-black cloud of fog burst from his palms. Hannah raised Shriek and the blade's light formed a glowing ball of luminance in the murk.

"Back-to-back," Connor murmured. She nodded, pressing her shoulders and hips into his as they turned a slow circle. From deep in the inn, they heard raised voices.

"Give it up," hissed the vampire from within the cloud. "Become my thralls and taste immortality."

"We can't fight what we can't see," Hannah said to Connor, trying to keep moving and her eyes alert. The black cloud stung her vision.

"No," Connor said grimly. "But this can."

He touched the brooch and whispered a word. The hovering sword transformed into a stream of light and flowed into the brooch.

"Got you!" chortled the vampire, leaping forward out of the mist. Half-blinded, Hannah and Connor slashed and thrust and their assailant dashed back into the cloud. Hannah's shoulders and chest stung and her nightshirt clung to her in rags. She put a hand to her arm. It came away bloody.

The vampire darted out again. Connor tossed the brooch behind the undead, then spoke the recall word. The sword glittered into being and impaled the vampire in the lower back. He let out a hissing screech, lurching to the side.

Wow! Never seen Connor do that before!

Connor ducked a swipe from a clawed hand and cut the vampire's thigh. The undead staggered, giving Hannah what she was looking for.

Her blade whistled through the air and beheaded the vampire like a sickle cutting a marsh reed. Shriek sang its wail of triumph and the corpse toppled over. Connor pounced on a piece of the shattered chair and drove it into the vampire's chest for good measure.

The voices from the lower floor raised in volume as Hannah stood over the corpse of her opponent, trembling.

Connor recalled his ghost blade and it flowed back into the brooch. He took her face in his hands. "Sweetheart? You still with me?"

She nodded, dazed, heart still racing, staring into his eyes. Blood trickled down her breasts and hips and what was left of her nightshirt stuck to her legs and arms.

"Here." Connor fished a vial of clear liquid from his backpack and pressed it into her hand, taking another for himself. She numbly popped the stopper and drank it down, grimacing from the taste of walnuts, hot pepper and licorice.

With a cool flow of energy, the burn of her wounds faded. Exhaustion and shock set in and she fought to keep her hands from shaking.

A vampire. I just slew a vampire! I thought the necropolis was bad, but this —

She heard the pounding of feet below and on the stairs. Connor snatched up a tunic and tossed one to her. "He ripped our nightshirts to ribbons," he said, "let's at least get presentable." Wordlessly, she stripped off the bloodied remnants of her shirt and slipped the clothing over her head.

A fist pounded on the door. "Hey you in there! What's all the racket?"

"Nothing to worry about," Connor called out. "My wife had a terrible nightmare."

"Open up or I call the guard!" That was the Dwarven clerk.

Connor opened the door and the Loemins stood blinking in the light of multiple lanterns. The clerk stood in the doorway, wielding a spiked mace. A couple of human men armed with swords towered behind her.

The clerk's eyes shot to the headless corpse on the floor. "What in the Nine Hells —?"

"A vampire attacked us in the night," Connor said calmly, sheathing his sword. "He tried to enthrall my wife."

More people gathered in the hall, craning their necks to see, most of them horrified. However, an older Halfling man with a scar along one side of his face watched with intense blue eyes. His appraising gaze flitted to the Loemins.

The Dwarven clerk's eyes grew wide. "You… you slew a vampire?"

Hannah nodded.

"How? You said you were locksmiths. How do locksmiths defeat one of the undead?"

Connor said, "I am the locksmith. My wife is a retired mercenary warrior and has a weapon that is deadly to them."

The clerk took a deep breath and her eyes narrowed. "Well, that may be so, but I think you have a few things to explain to the guard."

No! Any attention from the authorities could ruin everything. Hannah clenched her fist. Her eyes alighted on the vampire's head, rolled into a corner.

"Maybe so," she replied, sheathing her sword. "Perhaps you can explain how vampires manage to sneak into your guest rooms. I'm sure visitors will flock to Havenridge when they learn they can become undead thralls just by spending the night. That will do wonders for the tax receipts."

The clerk's mouth opened and closed. She looked up at the two humans, who shrugged.

Connor nodded, reaching for his trousers. "Actually, my wife is right. By all means, summon the guard. Please call in the town council while you're at it. I'm sure they'll be keenly interested."

The Dwarven clerk blanched. "No! No, there's no need for that." She waved at the two humans behind her. "You two, clear this mess out of here."

She bowed Connor and Hannah. "Please accept our sincerest apologies for the disturbance. We will refund your fees."

Hannah smiled. "No need. Just make sure no one else disturbs us from now on."

"Of course. We will move you to the Lord's Suite, number 2A, and will have a guard at the foyer. No extra charge."

"You are too kind."

The humans hauled the remains of the vampire out.

"I would burn that tonight if I were you," advised Connor. "Best to not take chances."

The clerk bowed again and retreated. The crowd at the door dispersed but the blue-eyed Halfling nodded to them before leaving.

Hannah let out an explosive breath as Connor shut the door again. "That was close."

He smiled and sat next to her, taking her hand. "You are one smooth talker under pressure! All those years working for your family business came in handy, didn't it? I'm proud of you."

"Then why do I feel like I'm going to have a heart attack?" She closed her eyes, trying to calm herself. His arms encircled her and she relaxed.

"Come on," he said after a while. "Let's pack up and go to the Lords' Suite. Sounds like we'll be in the lap of luxury for the rest of our stay."

She took a good look at the ripped bedsheets. "I won't sleep a wink," she said.

<<>>

As Hannah suspected, the blue-eyed Halfling paid them a visit in the common room at breakfast, though the other guests gave them a wide berth with awestruck expressions and much whispering behind their hands.

"Gregory Shamlin," the man said with a short bow. "May I join you?"

Hannah exchanged a look with Connor. "Please do," Connor said. "I'm Devyn Highwater and this is my wife, Erica."

Shamlin slipped into a seat in their booth opposite them. A serving girl brought them a tray with brown bread, butter, honey, crisp bacon, cheese and three mugs of spiced wine. When Connor held out five silver coins, the girl shook her head.

"Compliments of the manager, sir."

Connor pressed the money into her hand. "Then this is a gratuity."

Her eyes shone in gratitude and she bobbed her head, then fled.

"Quite the to-do last night," said Shamlin, taking some bread and cheese.

"Indeed," Connor replied. "Common occurrence?"

"Sometimes. It might explain a couple of recent disappearances. The people of Havenridge owe you a debt."

Hannah shrugged. "Just saving our skins. I was lucky to awaken when I did."

"Thinking of settling down here?" Shamlin asked, eyes measuring them.

Connor smiled. "If that's your only vampire, we might. Wouldn't want that to be a regular event, if you catch my meaning."

The trio ate in silence for a while. Hannah went over the keyphrases in her mind, debating whether to try them out or not. *Could he be a rebel? Or a spy of the government?*

She tapped Connor's thigh under the table and he tapped back.

"How is life here in Havenridge?" she asked.

"Tolerable, most times. Weather behaves most days, though we do get some frightful *rainstorms* from time to time."

Hannah's heartbeat skipped. *There's a keyword.*

Connor sipped his wine. "Is there another locksmith in town?"

Shamlin shook his head. "There was, but he moved on when the *rains* started, last spring."

There's another keyword. "So, it looks like we may have plenty of work then," Hannah said.

"Oh, aye. Business was good for the old locksmith. He had customers all over town and in the countryside roundabout — and they'll be yours too. But mind when the *rainstorms* hit. Sometimes the main street floods. And always carry an *umbrella* in the month of Aprilis. That's the wettest." Shamlin took a long drink from his mug.

More keywords! Hannah felt a thrill of excitement. *He's with the rebellion!*

Connor broke a piece of bacon into sections and laid them over his buttered bread. "I think we can handle that. There's weather all over, when you think of it. A little *rain* never hurt anyone."

Good. Acknowledge the keyword back to him.

Shamlin nodded. "That's good news. You'll be staying then?"

Now it's time for our own keyword. "I think so. Havenridge looks like a good place for a *new home*," Hannah replied.

Shamlin slid out of the booth. "If you'd like to see what the area offers, I have a small farm outside of town to the west, off the main road. Look for a sign with three yellow clovers. When you get there, turn off the road and follow the path for about a mile."

"We'll be there this afternoon," Connor promised.

Shamlin tugged his forelock and nodded, then headed for the exit.

Thank you, Irial! Hannah exulted. It was all she could do to restrain herself from rushing out of the inn to tell the other Riders the good news.

Connor's eyes met hers and he winked. "Let's make sure we're ready for our first job then."

Chapter Ten – Deeds, Not Words

"Nice place," said Connor. He put his hands on his hips, surveying the large fields and sturdy home atop a nearby hill. Workers moved among the greenery in teams of two or three, some tending goats or small cattle hitched to plows.

Gregory Shamlin gave him a genial smile. "It's not the biggest in the county, but I like it well enough."

I'd like to see the biggest, then, thought Connor.

"What do you grow?" Hannah asked.

"Oh, a little of everything: wheat, barley, feed corn, peppers, tomatoes, squash, onions, some herbs, a few peach and apricot trees…" Shamlin pointed across his widest field, where a stream led to a lower, more marshy area. "I even have rice down by the little wetlands."

Not bad at all, though Connor. *Either he's paying someone off or the local officials just don't want to disturb a productive farm.*

"Well, come along," Shamlin said, beckoning them to the farmhouse. "You can meet the family – those of them who are at the house at any rate."

He stomped the mud off his boots at the front porch and took a stiff brush to the sides and bottom. He grinned back at them, as he did so. "Marilla keeps a tidy house." He nodded to another brush by a rocking chair. "If you don't mind?"

"Oh, certainly." Connor brushed the worst of the dirt off his own foot-gear while Hannah did the same.

A mild tingle raced over Connor's body and he started, staring down at a fading luminance on the floor. He looked up.

That was a magical scan!

Another tingle hit him and he saw a flash of light from the lintel of the front door. His eyes rested on the carving of a crouching panther that had two tiger-eye gemstones.

Hannah's hand touched his and he met her gaze. *She felt it too.*

Careful not to show any further reaction, his mind raced. *It makes sense, if they're really rebels. Of course, the government probably uses magical detectors at their clandestine outposts too.*

The front door swung open and a sturdy Halfling matron with reddish brown hair cocked her head to the side, fixing Gregory with a pair of bright green eyes. "Who have you brought home this time, Gregory Shamlin?"

"Visitors, Marilla, visitors! Devyn and Erica Highwater from Northwatch. And they have quite the tale."

Marilla gave a curt nod to Connor and Hannah. "I am eager to hear it."

Gregory joined her at the door and gave her a peck on the cheek. "Is Timothy about? I think I'll need him to ready the wagon as we'll be heading to the south fields."

"South fields?" Marilla's expression changed ever so slightly. Connor had the unnerving impression that she could see right through them.

"Yes, my dove. A bit of, er, company business."

Her eyes narrowed. "Tim!" She called over her shoulder.

"Yes, Mam?" responded a voice from the depths of the house.

"Go prepare the wagon for a trip to south fields."

She eyed the Loemins and nodded towards the house. "Well, what are you waiting for? Tea's set in the kitchen."

Connor and Hannah followed the Shamlin couple into a tidy home with clean wooden floors, colorful rugs, white-painted walls and a multitude of passages and rooms. They passed through a large door leading into a kitchen where gleaming copper and steel pots and pans hung above a massive wood-burning stove. A set of steps led down to another door.

A young Halfling man looked up from wrapping roasted meat in white paper. Like his mother, he had chestnut hair and green eyes. "I'll just take this down to the cold room, Mam, and then I'll get everything set."

Marilla acknowledged this with a humph and moved to a steaming pot.

"Settle round the table there and Tim will have everything right in a bit."

Tim disappeared out a back door as Connor and Hannah joined Gregory at the table. Without another word, Marilla poured tea for them and brought a plate of small buns studded with nuts and dried fruit.

Connor surveyed the contents of the kitchen as he sipped his tea. *Rich farm, neat home, excellent equipment… very different from the town.*

A sudden doubt gnawed at him. He wondered if their exchange of passwords had been a fluke, or worse. What if the Republic had somehow gotten a hold of the passwords and the Shamlins were their agents?

He considered all the facts. Shamlin had plenty of opportunity to betray them and yet had made no move to do so. The Torosci weren't infallible or omniscient and the Riders' information came from very reliable sources. *Fortunately, Eric is keeping an eye on us with Stealth. At the first sign of trouble, the others will fly in from the woods south of here. No, we should play the cards we're dealt.*

Marilla raised an eyebrow at Gregory. "Well then?"

Gregory set down his teacup. "Ah, yes. Devyn and Erica are newly arrived in Havenridge to take up for the old locksmith. I'm afraid their first night in town was not the best. One of the undead came for them. A nightwalker agent of the PRT."

Marilla rested her forearms on the table and fixed the Loemins with a piercing gaze. "Well, now, I apologize for such a rude welcome, but the Intelligence Service uses some of the more powerful undead to keep the people in line. Once in a while they go a bit rogue and decide they need a, um, special companion or two. I see it ended well for you."

"Not so much for the vampire," Connor said with a smile.

Marilla leaned back in her chair. "So, you can handle yourselves against powerful enemies. You're not an average locksmith."

Before Connor could reply, Hannah jumped in. "I am a retired freelance warrior. My brother bequeathed me a magic sword with special power against the unliving."

"Handy." Marilla sipped her tea. "What did the constables think of that?"

Gregory shrugged. "I doubt if they heard of it at all."

Tim poked his head in. "Ready."

Connor and Hannah followed Gregory outside to a plain but serviceable cart drawn by two ponies. They climbed in the back as Tim and Greg took their seats in the front.

"We won't be long," Gregory said.

Marilla shielded her eyes against the afternoon sunshine. "See that you're not. Supper is at sundown."

The cart set off, heading down a path through the fields towards the forest looming in the distance. Not inclined to talk, Connor held Hannah's hand and watched the countryside. His assessment of the Shamlin holdings increased.

Impressive acreage…

The air hung humid though not hot, a sign of late winter in the southlands. Soon, they traveled into the shadows of the woods. Leafy boughs closed in above them. Here, in the southern climes, Connor saw more lichens and vines growing on trunk and branch. *More jungle than woods… very different from Evendale or Deran.*

The wagon rattled and bumped over the rough ground.

"I'm sure we were scanned," Hannah said in a low voice. "The gemstones in the panther carving?"

"Most likely." Connor leaned back on his hands. "Well, I can't say I'm surprised. These people are cagey, but I don't blame them, based on what we've seen so far."

"Do you think they're spies for the People's Republic of Torosc instead of rebels?"

And wait all this time to apprehend us? Connor shook his head. "No. If they were PRT agents, they would have tried to take us out as soon as possible, not give us a wagon ride to some other location. I think they're legitimate, but suspicious. Give them some time. We knew it would take effort to gain their trust."

They rumbled through the forest along a dirt path that wound and curved until the sky disappeared behind verdant boughs overhead. Shafts of sunlight shot through the green, creating a pattern of light and dark among the bushes, vines and shrubs along the road. The greenery turned more and more jungle-like the further they went.

"It's pretty," Hannah said, taking his hand and squeezing it. "I'm going to like living here."

He relaxed a bit. "You're very optimistic."

She rested her head on his shoulder. "I have reason to be. Your father will be a good king and so will you. And Irial's blessing is upon us. He does not forsake his faithful ones."

God, how did I ever deserve her?

The wagon halted and swayed as Greg and Tim hopped down. Connor and Hannah also clambered out.

"Now, I apologize for this," Greg said, with an abashed look on his face. He held two strips of dark cloth in his hands. "This is a necessary precaution dictated by both recent circumstance and policy. I hope you will understand."

Connor's stomach tightened at the idea of not being able to see, but he nodded. "It is a prudent thing to do, since you know very little about us."

The scenery vanished behind the blindfold. Greg pressed a rope into Connor's hand. "Hold to this until I give it three sharp tugs. It will keep you from stumbling as we go."

"Blindfolds?" whispered Hannah behind him.

Connor kept a firm grip on the rope in his hands as their escorts led them further into the woods. "Do you blame them?" he whispered back. "They are rebels in an oppressive regime, after all."

"I thought all the magical scanning would have convinced them we're not spies."

"They're just being cautious. I would be too."

"No talking, if you please," said Greg's genial voice ahead of them.

Connor fell silent and he continued feeling his way along the path. The scent of willows, whitestar vines, kalaca flowers and rich earth surrounded him. He felt the warmth of sunlight, then coolness of shade in alternating, random patterns. The ground rose beneath their feet and they climbed steadily for a couple of minutes.

"All right, stop here."

Connor halted. Someone tugged thrice on the rope and he released it. The blindfold dropped from his eyes and he blinked in the patchwork of sunlight and shade.

"There now," Gregory Shamlin said, "that wasn't so bad, was it? I'll let the others know you're here." He beckoned to his son and whispered to him. With a glance at Connor and Hannah, Tim Shamlin nodded and trotted off.

Connor's eyes followed the lad and he gave an involuntary start. "Well, that's a sight," he murmured.

The ruins of a temple loomed up out of the jungle ahead of them. Connor's eyes roamed over the rents in the walls, the missing roofs and piles of rubble. Judging by the trees, vines and bushes growing in profusion among the stonework, whatever brought about the destruction had happened long ago.

"Pick a block of stone or a log and make yourselves comfortable," Gregory offered. "There's plenty enough of them."

Connor joined Hannah on a tree stump.

"How do I look?" she asked.

He hid a smile at the wild tousle of her hair. "Fine."

She rummaged in her shoulder bag. He tapped her hand. "You don't need to look in the mirror. We're not entertaining ambassadors or royalty."

She gave a sniff, running a comb through her hair. "I'll not bring shame on us by looking like a ragamuffin, thank you very much."

Motion from the ruins caught his eye and he stood. "That will have to do for now, dearest."

A group of Halflings marched through the bracken towards them, clad in camouflage tunics over the dull gleam of chainmail. They carried spears, crossbows and swords and their eyes showed no emotion. Tim Shamlin strode at the side of a bearded Halfling with an eye patch.

"Colonel Whitson," Greg Shamlin announced as they approached. "I would like to introduce Devin and Erica Highwater. I believe they are interested in helping us."

The Colonel's lip curled in a half-smile. "If that indeed are their real names."

Connor took a deep breath. "For obvious reasons, we need to conceal our identities until we are sure of who we are dealing with."

Whitson nodded. "That is wise." He sat on a stone block and his troops arrayed around him, some of them watching the woods and others keeping their eyes locked on Connor and Hannah.

"You have to understand why we are cautious," Whitson continued. "A while ago, PRT intelligence agents arrived, claiming to be representatives of the Northern Alliance. We didn't quite buy it and it was a good thing. They led us into what they thought was a trap, but that came to a crashing halt."

Hannah raised an eyebrow. "You were ready for them, I take it?"

Whitson smiled back, his eye cold. "Let's just say I was the last thing they saw before they took the trip to meet whatever devils they serve. I hope, for your sakes, that you're not more of the same."

Connor shook his head. "I can assure you, Colonel, we are not in the slightest way connected with the PRT. In fact, we are here to help you rid yourselves of their tyranny."

Whitson shrugged. "What proof have you? Words are cheap."

"Of course. If I may?" Connor gestured to Hannah's shoulder bag.

"Certainly. Just no sudden moves. My troops are a little on edge after the incident with the PRT agents."

Hannah withdrew a small velvet bag and handed it to Connor. He removed a small piece of paper and a round platinum token from his belt purse and dropped them into the bag. Energy surged in the glade and for a split second, the universe seemed to warp. The bag pulsed and tingled in Connor's hands.

Whitson and his soldiers gave a start but Connor raised a hand. "It's all right, I assure you."

He smiled and slowly withdrew a scroll from the sack. "Here. A letter of introduction from the leaders of the Northern Alliance nations and all the major religions."

"Lieutenant Ashford?" Whitson nodded to a female trooper.

She lifted a hand over the scroll and murmured a few words. Her palm flashed amber light. "No traps or beguiling spells, sir," she said.

Whitson unrolled the parchment and stared at it, then at Connor and Hannah. He measured them for several long heartbeats, tapping the scroll in his hands.

"Documents are easy to forge," he replied, standing. "This says that you are two of the Grey Riders. Prove it."

"Allow me," Hannah said. She removed a gold coin and a small slingshot from her purse. She aimed up into a huge gap in the canopy overhead and loosed. The coin shot up, spinning and winking high over the treetops. It fell and Hannah deftly snatched it out of the air.

Silence reigned.

Whitson glared at them. "And what is that supposed to do?"

Connor smiled. "Wait for it."

The rush of wind sounded in the distance. Kindri and Tholi shot past overhead. The colonel and his soldiers scrambled for cover. The Riders followed on their pegasi.

Lieutenant Ashford raised a fist glowing with mage-fire.

"It's okay," Hannah said, raising both hands. "They're with us."

Whitson and his troops remained on alert but didn't attack.

The dragons swooped down through the trees and landed behind Connor and Hannah.

"Hi Kindri. Hi Tholi," Hannah said with a wink.

Tholi winked back. "Hello, Your Highness."

Connor swept a hand at the winged horses and riders as they, too, landed in the glade behind him. "Our dragon friends are Kindriana and Tholerios. I would also like to introduce our companions, the Grey Riders. Perhaps we can begin discussions?"

Colonel Whitson chuckled, waving a hand to his soldiers. They emerged from cover. "This certainly changes things," he said, a wry look on his face. "Kindly follow us into the ruins, Highnesses. We have a more suitable place for discussion."

The Riders dismounted and joined Connor and Hannah.

"Any problems?" asked Brandi, handing the reins of Connor's pegasus to him.

"Not really. They're a bit wary from a recent infiltration attempt but otherwise, they seem legitimate. Dar told you about our little adventure with the vampire?"

She nodded. "He did. Stay sharp. If Selaan really is still on our world, his ability to deceive knows no bounds and these people could still be an elaborate ruse."

The Riders followed Whitson and the rebels deeper into the remnants of the temple. They arrived at what looked like it had been the inner sanctum, with a crushed altar at the far end and broken statuary scattered about.

Connor remembered his mother's temple back home and wondered if it looked similar. *Evil seeks to destroy all semblance of light and good*, he mused. *But it will always fail in the end.*

Whitson took a seat on a fallen block. "Please, make yourselves comfortable." He watched them with his good eye as they did so. Connor remained quiet, waiting for Brandi or Whitson to make the first move.

Finally, the colonel nodded to Brandawyn. "Your bona fides are certainly impressive. I am willing to concede that your identities are as you claim. However, deeds, not words, are what make the difference in Torosc these days, Majesty. You and your companions must prove yourselves."

Brandi smiled and inclined her head, not to Whitson, but to Connor. "Agreed, but I believe you are addressing your request to the wrong person."

Whitson raised an eyebrow.

"You should be speaking to Prince Connor," she continued. "He represents his father, King Seamus, and it is patently clear that we are within the borders of the former Paragon Kingdom of Loemin. The Crown Prince and Princess hold authority. I am merely a guest."

A mixture of gratitude and affection surged through Connor. He gave her a warm smile.

Whitson inclined his head. "Well said, Majesty."

He addressed his attention to Connor. "Your Highness, although I believe in who you are, the general populace will be split between skeptics and fanatics. If the revolt is to succeed in freeing Loemin, we need a way to convince the vast majority of our people."

Connor frowned. "How do you propose we do that? I only have one copy of the letter of introduction. If we need to make more…"

Whitson waved a hand. "That would not be the way. No, I have something more particular in mind."

Something in Whitson's expression piqued both Connor's interest and his suspicions. "And that is?"

The colonel stood and began pacing. "The last King of Loemin was Liam II, a man of great personal courage and wisdom. He was also a pragmatist. Near the end of his reign, he realized that Loemin would be swallowed up by nearby kingdoms that had already come under the sway of the Archons. He and his wife, Queen Siany, vanished. With them they took two symbols of rulership: a sword named Glittershard, and Steelwing, the Queen's magic cloak. If you can find them, the people will acclaim you as the rightful rulers and flock to your banner."

"And these two items will convince the people to join us?" Hannah looked skeptical.

Whitson stopped pacing and set a boot on a nearby rock. "The appearance and properties of both the sword and the cloak are well-known and stories about them have been passed down through generations. In addition, legend has it that Queen Siany enchanted both to respond only to people of their family. If you were to take the field wielding those two, there would be no doubt that you are the true rulers of Loemin."

"How are we supposed to find them?" Connor asked. "We haven't been in Loemin very long."

"According to legend, they are both held in a location called the Vault of Safety, which was mentioned in a letter to their son, Prince Carl. If you can find this Vault, I am confident you will also find Glittershard and Steelwing."

"You'll need to provide the location of the Vault then," Dar noted, leaning back on his hands.

"Unfortunately," Whitson replied, "we can't. Legends are all we have. When Loemin fell, the Archons confiscated all records of the Paragon Kingdoms and moved them to a fortress in Hellsfont, which is a city in the far, southeastern province of Eastwatch — or Golad, as it was known in the days of the Paragons. You would have to somehow travel there, infiltrate the fortress and find the vaults and retrieve the records."

Go farther into hostile lands? We're in territory with some friendly elements and even here it's not safe! How much worse would it be in Golad? Connor's heart sank. *We can't find a lost hideaway without any clues. There must be another way.*

No one spoke. Insects buzzed in the silence and the scent of exotic plants wafted on the breeze.

"That hardly seems like something we can accomplish," Hannah protested. "To be perfectly frank, any place named Hellsfont seems like a tall hill to climb even if we had allies there, which I presume we don't. Besides, we don't have the resources to begin the search."

Whitson stopped pacing and smiled. "But you do. The letter you provided shows me that you have powerful friends in the world's mightiest alliance. Surely, with their resources, they will have something to go on."

"I don't know," Eric said, sitting on a nearby tree stump. "They rely a lot on research in libraries or from documents brought to them by freelance sellswords. If these records are all in Hellsfont, I doubt that even Melinor

Indidarc would have anything on them."

That's just great. Connor fought against a feeling of despair and aggravation. The jungle seemed to close in on him. He forced himself to take a breath. *How do you find a legendary location without any records to go on? We might as well be searching for one of the ancient safehouses — wait a second. Vault of Safety — safe house!*

He sat bolt upright. The others stared at him. "Colonel," he said, "the King and Queen spirited the relics away to the Vault of Safety. Might that mean that they took them to a safehouse?"

Whitson gave him a blank look matched by the confusion on the faces of his officers. "I don't know what that means."

Brandi slapped her knee. "Connor! That's brilliant! The Vault of Safety is one of the Paragon safehouses!"

The other Riders grinned and Hannah squeezed Connor's hand. Whitson and his troops still looked mystified.

"Highness, I must admit I am completely lost."

Quickly, Connor related the information about Paragon Era safehouses they had received from the Papal Nuncio. Megan laid down the list on a nearby stone block and everyone crowded around.

"Do any of these locations mean anything to you?" Connor asked, heartbeat accelerating with anticipation.

The rebel Halflings shook their heads. Suddenly, Whitson snapped his fingers. "Oldfather Malcolm!"

"Who's that?" asked Eric.

"He's a sage, a librarian from Aldath, the capital," Whitson said. "He's very knowledgeable. He might know something."

"Aldath?" Hannah asked. "That's far from here, and I doubt if we can just waltz into the capital and start asking around."

"Ah, but you won't have to." Whitson smiled. "His granddaughter, Fiona, owns a house close by, in the town of Greenvale. He visits her often and just so happens to be there right now."

"Then it looks like we will have to meet this Fiona," said Hannah.

Whitson's smile broadened. "You already have." He gestured to Lieutenant Ashford, who grinned and stood.

"May I present Lieutenant Fiona Ashford?"

Chapter Eleven – True Sight

It's quiet, thought Alex Fejer, crouching by the base of the tree. *Too quiet for my taste.*

"Anything, Captain?" Hannah asked.

He shook his head, eyes locked on the cottage near the stream. "The house is easily monitored from the road, but the People's Republic Army could have a platoon in those bushes and trees on the other side and we wouldn't know it."

Hannah slipped up next to him. "Well, Eric used Stealth and didn't see any traffic on the road to Greenvale. We'll have to wait until Fiona and her grandfather come to us. That's the plan."

Alex remained silent. *If Oldfather Malcolm is as much of an expert as they say, how is it that he has this much freedom of movement? It doesn't sound like the People's Republic of Torosc we all know and hate.*

"What is it?" Hannah prodded.

"I can't believe they'd just let him wander around the countryside, grand-daughter or no granddaughter."

He heard the smile in Hannah's voice. "I don't believe they do. That's why Fiona's going to bring him to us instead of all of us traipsing off to his cottage. Any spies watching the cottage are used to seeing her take him on walks in the forest to pick flowers."

"All this makes me wonder if there are other magical automatons like the one Prince Eric uses, except spying on us for the PRT."

"Yes, the enemy could have something like Stealth," she replied. "That's why Kindri's on patrol."

He was about to answer when the back door of the cottage opened and Fiona Ashford stepped out, leading the hunched figure of an elderly Halfling man using a cane.

Hannah clapped Alex on the shoulder. "Time to get back."

Alex slipped through the underbrush after Hannah. Her camouflage cloak and small size made it hard to follow, but he managed keep her in sight until they arrived in a little clearing under the shade of towering willow trees. There, the other Riders waited, except for the dragons and Gorlak. Khyla finished hitching the last of the pegasi to a nearby tree and gave Alex a nod.

"Fiona and her grandfather are on their way," Hannah said.

The Riders arranged themselves on nearby rocks and logs. Soon, Fiona and her grandfather emerged from the underbrush with only a whisper of sound.

"Here we are, grandfather," Fiona said.

"Ah, excellent," said Malcolm, raising a round, wrinkled face to them. He smiled.

Alex's jaw dropped at the sight of Malcolm's milky-white eyes. "He's blind?" he blurted before he could stop himself. Khyla gave him an annoyed look.

Malcolm's head pivoted to Alex's location. "You are indeed observant, young Human. But there are many ways to see, as I am sure you will acknowledge."

"Greetings, Oldfather," Connor began. "I am —"

"Forgive me, Highness," Malcolm interrupted, settling himself on a nearby log that he somehow found unerringly. "The pleasantries will have to be curtailed, I'm afraid. My minders will note my absence and begin to search if I am not back soon. Besides, Fiona gave me the rudiments of the situation already."

He set his cane against the log and swept them with his gaze as if he could physically see them. Alex felt a mild tingle touch his mind, almost as if a feather brushed his consciousness. Malcolm nodded. "You wish to find the Vault of Safety."

"Yes," Hannah answered.

"Very well," Malcolm replied. "There are several possibilities from what I remember of ancient records. Hopefully you can help narrow them down."

"I thought all the records were removed to Hellsfont," Connor noted.

Malcolm smiled. "And who says that I didn't review those records in younger days, Highness? Come, tell me what you know."

Dar opened a parchment and rattled off a set of coordinates.

This is madness. A blind librarian? And Dar is just reading to him?

Malcolm pursed his lip. "I can tell you that the last one is not valid. The Red Veils have a fortress in that location, likely with facilities underground. I doubt if the Vault is there."

Alex suppressed a shudder. *Red Veils? I sure hope we don't run into any of those murderous bitches.*

"And the others?" prodded Brandi.

Malcolm frowned. "I would need something more to go on. Do you have any details about any of those locations?"

"There was nothing other than the coordinates," Dar said.

Silence reigned for a few minutes, broken only the buzz of an occasional insect or a chirping bird.

"Maybe Melinor can help," Megan said. "In his notes to us, he mentioned that the Northern Alliance has ongoing expeditions to recover treasures and knowledge looted by the Dark Wave. That's the way they found the coordinates, so maybe they've found something else since then."

Malcolm cocked his head to the side. "You know Melinor Indidarc?"

"Er, yes," Eric said with a glance at Brandi. "Do you?"

"From long ago. He has probably forgotten about me."

Brandi beckoned to Alex. "Captain Fejer, the Messenger Orb please."

"Of course, Majesty." Alex drew out the Messenger Orb from his pack and handed it over. He watched with interest as she set the Orb down on a tiny hillock of soft earth. He felt a pang of longing, knowing that he had little, if any, magical talent himself.

But I'll never get tired of watching this.

"Melinor Indidarc," Brandi intoned, touching the orb with her forefinger.

A misty cloud formed above the sphere and resolved into the figure of an old man with a short-cropped white beard, sitting in a chair behind a table.

Sunlight streamed in through a nearby window. His lined face creased in a smile.

"Brandawyn!" he said. "And Eric! And the Riders...good to see you again."

Alex strained to hear Melinor's voice. It seemed reedy and wispy. *I wonder if it's the effect of the Orb.*

Then he saw the stricken expressions on the faces of the Riders. He shot a glance at Khyla, who looked confused.

Something is wrong.

"How are you, Father?" Eric asked in a gentle voice full of concern.

"Oh, I'm fine, just fine. More importantly, how are you?"

"We are well and are making great progress," Eric continued. "I'm sorry to cut it short this time, but we need to ask you about the coordinates that Father Thomas sent us."

"Ah. What do you need to know?"

"A scholar named Malcolm might be able to help us if we can get some more details." Fiona ushered her grandfather into Melinor's field of view.

Melinor peered at them and his expression brightened. "Malcolm Ashford? Is that you?"

Malcolm nodded, smiling back. "Seems that time eventually catches up with us, eh, Doctor Indidarc?"

Melinor chuckled and paused to cough. "It does indeed. How can I help you?"

"I have several coordinates from the Riders," Malcolm said, "but there is nothing indicate any one of them is better than the other and they are separated by no small distance. If you have anything that might connect one of them to the Vault of Safety, it would help."

"Ah! Well, you are in luck." Melinor pulled himself out of his seat and shuffled out of view. He returned and eased himself back into the chair, gently laying a tattered parchment on the table.

He placed a pair of spectacles on his nose. "A friend of the Riders, Andyn Eleandir Demaris, sent this to me a couple of weeks ago and I just got around to examining it. One of their mercenary teams took it off a band of Red Veil assassins who were running a clandestine operation in Andyn's county. This does say something about a vault."

He peered at the parchment. "Here it is. There's a reference to a 'Vault of the High Ones' — definitely a candidate for a safe house. There's a symbol of a crescent moon surrounded by a circle of flames. Hmm. And some faded text about something called 'Silver Doom'. That sounds ominous."

Malcolm sat up straighter. "A moon surrounded by flames? That could be the Moonfire River. The second set of coordinates on the list are near that river. It is only about fifty miles from here."

"Well, that is good news then." Melinor put down the spectacles and pinched the bridge of his nose. To Alex, he seemed to grow a bit paler.

Is Melinor sick? Alex shot a look at the other Riders. They looked grim and a bit distressed.

"Are you sure you're all right, Father?" Brandawyn asked.

Melinor gave her a luminous, gentle smile that removed years from his countenance. "I'm fine, dearest girl. These spectacles just give me a headache if I read for too long."

"Grandfather?" Fiona asked. "Do we need anything more?"

Malcolm stroked his chin. "No, I think we have enough. Thank you, Lord Melinor. Once this is all over, maybe we can have a leisurely discussion about formulae for invisibility potions. If you recall, our last debate on the subject was interrupted."

Melinor sat back in his chair and let his hands fall in his lap. "I would like that, Professor Ashford. Until then."

"Until then."

"We'll let you go for now Father," Eric said. "You need your rest."

Melinor took on a faraway look. "I suppose I do. Contact me when you can, son."

"I will."

Brandawyn reached out and touched the Orb with her forefinger. She flicked a tear from one of her eyes.

"What's wrong with Lord Melinor?" Alex asked.

Brandawyn replaced the Orb in her pack, then looped her arm around Eric's waist. "He is very sick," she said in a tight voice.

"It was all the stress of the War of the Dark Wave," Eric said. "He was everywhere, trying to thwart the Ja'al's plans, fighting at the siege of Oakmoor, taking on Daemon royalty… it's taken its toll. Soon after Brandi and I returned from our honeymoon, we noticed he started to go downhill… the doctors don't think he has much longer."

Dar gave a quick, sad smile. "I keep forgetting how old he really is."

"Indeed," added Malcolm. "He was in his sixties when I met him, and that was over twenty-five years ago, unless I miss my guess. Gentlemen in their eighties or nineties should be taking their ease, not fighting evil cults and Daemons." Malcolm gave a slight frown and turned towards Eric. "By the by, you both called him 'Father'."

"He and his late wife, Ann, adopted me when I was a teen," Eric replied. "When Brandi and I married, she became his daughter-in-law."

"I see."

He must have been like a father to all of the Riders, Alex realized, looking at all their expressions. *I wonder how my own father would look, if he had lived.*

Birds chirped in the peacefulness of the wood. Connor gave Eric and Brandi a sympathetic look, then addressed Malcolm. "Do you think we have enough to go on?"

Malcolm clapped his hands on his knees and stood. "It will have to do. While the coordinates aren't precise, they give you a much smaller area in which to search."

Malcolm said it's within fifty miles, Alex thought, relieved. *With pegasi, that won't take more than a day. Minimal exposure to potential patrols.*

"Let's get you home, Grandfather," Fiona said, taking his arm.

The Riders gathered around to thank him when a whoosh of air overhead interrupted them.

Alex reached for his bow, then stopped when he realized it was Kindri. The young dragon hovered over their refuge for a few moments while everyone cleared a space.

"My apologies, Lords and Ladies," she said, landing on the soft earth of the clearing. "I think you have been noticed."

"What makes you say that?" asked Hannah.

Kindri dropped a dark, metallic object on the grass. To Alex, it looked like a mangled black fox. Upon closer examination, he saw seams, tiny rivets and eyes made of garnet.

"An automaton," Khyla breathed.

Dar knelt and examined the object. "It's just like Stealth. Someone nearby has a Companion Pin. Where did you find it?"

"About a hundred yards away, near the cottage. It didn't behave like a normal fox and it glowed brightly when I used a magic detection spell." Kindri said.

Connor scooped the remains of the fox golem into a sack and put it in his backpack. "We have to get you out of here, Oldfather."

To Alex's surprise, the old Halfling chuckled. "Certainly not."

"Why not?" Hannah demanded.

"Do you think this is the only time that the PRT has put me under surveillance, Highness? I can tell you for a fact it is not. This is just their latest attempt to watch me secretly. I must act as if I don't realize a thing."

Fiona bit her lip. "What if they take you in for questioning? Someone will realize that something destroyed the automaton."

"And what of it? I certainly didn't do it. I'm very valuable to them and they know I'm old. They don't dare torture me for fear of killing me before they can extract anything useful. Besides, all they know is that I went into the woods with you to collect wildflowers." Malcolm grinned and took hold of a clump of flowers next to his tree stump and gently pulled them up.

How did he know they were there? He can't see. Alex had an uneasy feeling that Malcolm had an arcane means to detect things around him. Based on Fiona's magical skill, he readily believed it.

"Come," Malcolm said, handing the flowers to Fiona. "I believe there are more flowers on the way back to the cottage. Pick them and we will have enough for your grandmother's ceramic vase by the front door."

He bowed low. "Farewell, Grey Riders. Until we meet again."

With a nervous smile, Fiona led him away.

"How can he be a blind librarian?" asked Khyla as they departed.

"I asked Fiona," Hannah said. "He has three assistants who read to him. Apparently, he can tell the time period of a manuscript just from a few paragraphs and has a phenomenal memory. She said he could find anything in the Archives just by feeling his way through the stacks... that is, if they'd let him wander around freely."

No one said anything.

"I should send up Stealth," Eric said.

"No, Highness, let me go back," Kindri protested. "I can watch for pursuit."

Brandi shook her head. "Too risky. You may have given away too much if the owner of the Dark Fox automaton caught a glimpse of you. Find Tholi and Gorlak and scout our path to the south as far as the nearest hill. Wait for us there."

Kindri looked as if she had bitten a rotten log, but she dipped her head in acquiescence and flew into the air.

Eric sent up his hawk golem. "Stay sharp," he said to the Riders.

Alex set an arrow to his bow and Khyla followed suit. He nodded, trying to project an outward calm, but inside, his stomach knotted, remembering the Battle of Meridian. *Dear God, please no Red Veils. I know the Grey Riders are with us, but we may never see the Veils before they're on top of us. And they run in packs.*

"Let's get moving south, then," Connor said. "Ground travel only. We don't want to draw attention."

They mounted their pegasi and rode away. Eric's eyes focused on something far away. "Oldfather Malcolm better be right about the location of the Vault," he announced after a little while. "Fiona just left and I see three Skullhead soldiers riding on the road, heading to the cottage."

Skullheads? Damn it. Those bastards will roast him alive just for fun. Alex felt a momentary panic for the old man. "We should go back."

Megan shook her head. "No. I am also concerned for him, but as far as the Torosci know, they just have a missing spy automaton, nothing more. Our advantage — and his protection — lies in maintaining an environment of normalcy."

"Agreed," Brandi said. "Oldfather Malcolm lives here and he hasn't survived this long by being foolish. We have to trust him."

Eric recalled Stealth and the automaton flowed back into the brooch on his tunic.

They left and Alex rode in silence, eyes flicking to the mossy trees and crowding undergrowth.

If there are Skullheads nearby, no one is safe.

Chapter Twelve – The More Things Change…

Alex Fejer reined in his pegasus and patted her on the neck. "See anything, Onyx?"

The flying horse shook her head. Alex grinned. "Sometimes, I think you're human, girl."

He spurred her into a trot and they moved through the waving marsh reeds at the shore of the Moonfire River. To the north, trees crowded up to the water's edge. Here, a wide expanse of reeds by the river led to a grassy sward that stretched to meet a looming cliff of grey rock. He slipped his bow from its case and nocked an arrow, alert for any sign of ambush.

Only birdsong broke the silence. He reached the edge of the meadow near the cliffs and paused, scanning the heights for anything that might indicate something made by hands instead of nature. Cold stone greeted his eyes.

I hope Dar, Eric and Khyla are having better luck than I am.

Turning his mount, he tracked southwards along the cliff face. He was about to turn back to the mustering point when he saw deep shadows behind some trees.

"What do you think, girl?" he asked Onyx. The pegasus bobbed her head.

He slowed her to a walk and approached to within about a hundred feet, then halted.

That's quite a cave, he mused. *As big as a barn, at least.* Unsure of whether to investigate further, he hesitated. If a trap of some kind guarded the Vault — as he suspected it might — the last thing he needed was to be incapacitated before he could bring back word.

"All right, Onyx, let's head back. We may have found something."

Urging her to a canter, he took off and flew some five miles to the east, keeping low above the trees. There, a glade shone in the sunshine on a hilltop, ringed by trees, its verdant surface broken only by the occasional troll-sized boulder. He trotted to a stop near the edge. He nearly rode Onyx over the top of Kindri, who lay hidden under some massive bushes near their camp.

"Damn it. Sorry Kindri."

She gave him a toothy dragon-grin. "I would have gotten out of the way. Besides, Onyx knows I'm here, don't you?"

The pegasus tossed her head in response.

Alex patted Onyx on the neck. "Anybody back yet?" he asked.

"Captain Dearborn just rode in," Kindri replied.

"Where's your brother?"

"Out with Gorlak watching our back trail." Kindri settled back down under the bushes. "I have to admit I'm getting a little bored. I need some action."

"Careful what you wish for," Alex said with a wink.

He trotted Onyx into the camp. Brandi, Megan, Connor and Hannah sat on logs or rocks at the edge of the woods, well-camouflaged in mottled green-and-brown cloaks and tunics over their armor. The pegasi placidly waited nearby. Brandi and Megan looked up from a map. "You're the second one back, Captain." Brandi said.

"So I heard." Alex nodded to Khyla and dismounted. "What did you find?"

"There's a ruined tower in a marshy area about six miles to the east," she answered. "I rode Nightflame around for a while but it looked completely deserted."

"What about you, Captain?" Brandi asked.

"A possibility. There's a really big cave to the south."

"Anyone nearby?" asked Megan.

"I didn't see any. And Onyx would have reacted if anyone were there."

Brandi rolled up the map and put it into a bone tube. "Hold off on the details until Eric and Dar get back. I don't want you to have to repeat your-self."

Alex reached into his saddlebag and Khyla approached.

"What do you think?" she asked. "Is this a wild hootling chase?"

He chuckled. "Good choice of metaphor. I don't know that anyone has actually found a hootling. Ever."

This got him a little smile. "But it keeps children busy looking for them," she admitted. Khyla patted Onyx on the neck, eyes distant.

"Is everything okay?" he asked.

Khyla made as if to say something, then clamped her mouth shut.

When she didn't respond, he faced her. "Khyla?"

Her cheeks flushed a little. "Oh, all right. I was just wondering… how much does anyone know about Prince Eric. I mean, really know."

"I'm sure the Queen knows quite a bit," he said with a wink. "In many ways."

The flush in her face intensified. "That's not what I meant. Where does he come from? Where did he grow up?"

Alex shrugged. "He's the adopted son of Melinor Indidarc, a famous wizard lord and King's Counselor from Deran. He came from difficult circumstances, made his name as a free-lance sell-sword. He helped fight off an invasion from the wilderness by a rogue lich about a year ago. And you know all about the Gate of Stars and the Dark Wave. That's about all anyone knows about his past for sure, aside from the occasional wild rumors about pirates or escaping from slavers."

Khyla bit her lip.

Alex regarded her intently for a while. *Why such interest? It's almost as if she's fishing for information. Is she a spy?* For a moment he considered the possibility. He had heard of ways to magically mask a spy or traitor.

Well, she's had ample opportunity to betray us so far, if she really is working for the enemy. If she's a spy, she either has very specific instructions or she's not a very good one.

Her face and posture gave him a different impression; namely, that she was afraid of something.

No, if she were a spy, Megan or Brandi would have at least sensed something by now. They are part Celestial, after all.

"Is there anything you want to talk about?" he asked.

Khyla shook her head, eyes still distant. He watched her for a few heartbeats, but she didn't move.

"Hey," he said gently.

She turned, eyes widening at his tone.

"You're one of us." He moved closer to her. "If something is bothering you, you know you can trust the Riders."

She looks scared. "And you can trust me," he added.

She stared at him for a long time and he held still. "Can I really?" she asked, eyes suddenly soft and warm. "It's been a long time since I could really trust anyone."

He smiled. "We're shield-mates, Khyla. We've been through a lot in a short time, wouldn't you say? That has to count for something."

The corner of her lip curled upward but it had the effect of making her look sad and forlorn. To his surprise, she took his hand and squeezed it. "Yes, it does."

"Then tell me."

Pain flashed in her eyes and she gave her head a little shake. "I… can't. Not now. Maybe later."

What's wrong with her? He wanted to insist that she tell him, but past experience — particularly with Eleanor — taught him the value of discretion and tact.

"Well, I'll accept your answer for now," he said, gathering Onyx's reins, "Just know I'm always here to listen."

She smiled and nodded, then turned away.

He watched her go. Her golden hair reflected the sunlight and she moved with athletic grace. Keenly aware of his growing attraction to her, he turned away and led Onyx to the other pegasi.

I wonder if Eleanor would have liked her. He pondered that idea. *Yes. She would have. Khyla is brave and kind and smart. They would have been friends.*

"Riders coming," announced Hannah. "Looks like Eric and Dar."

Soon, two pegasi swooped down into the camp. Dar and Eric dismounted and embraced their wives.

Remembering similar embraces with Eleanor, Alex looked away, swallowing with difficulty. *Eleanor is at peace now. God embraces her.*

"Anything?" asked Connor, breaking Alex's train of thought.

"Not much," Eric reported. "I saw what looks like an empty training camp."

Dar waved a hand. "I saw what could have been the outlines of a set of buildings but they were really overgrown. Not very promising."

"I think Captain Fejer has something more interesting," Brandi offered.

Alex described the cave to them.

"Hmm," Hannah said. "Sounds like a bandit hideaway or a place to protect livestock in case of bad weather."

"Except there are no farms or ranchland for miles," Dar said, patting the neck of his pegasus. "And most bandit groups would have attacked you for sure, since you're only one scout."

Connor shot him a look. "Are you thinking what I'm thinking?"

Dar nodded. "It sure sounds familiar."

"What do you mean?" asked Megan.

Dar sat next to her. "When we were on a quest for the Eye of Truth, we were forced down in bad weather and took shelter in a similar cave. Dark Elves swarmed out from a secret door in the back of the cave and captured us in the middle of the night. It turned out the cave was an entrance to one of their cities."

Dark Elves? Alex's eyebrows went up. "How on earth did you get away?"

Connor smiled, patting Hannah's hand. "Hannah's brother, Handor, escaped and followed them in, using an invisibility spell to scout the complex. He freed us from their torture chamber and we fought our way through the Underdark."

Alex gaped at them. Connor described the entire incident as if they had gone shopping at the market. "I'm sorry, Highness," he managed. "But you fought your way out of a Dark Elven city _and_ the Underdark?"

Dar snapped a twig in two. "One of the worst times of our lives, honestly. I wondered how we made it, but now I see God's hand in it. It wasn't a Halfling tea party, I can assure you — no offense to Connor or Hannah."

Hannah smirked. "You haven't been to enough Halfling tea parties."

Alex grinned despite the serious subject.

"Tea parties aside," Connor said, "we have to pick an option."

"The tower?" asked Khyla. "Or maybe the ruined buildings?"

Megan shook her head. "Too unprotected or exposed to too much groundwater. I think Captain Fejer's is the most promising. It's in a hidden area and, if the vault is there, it's in solid rock."

"All right," said Connor, rising. "When Gorlak and Tholi return, let's try it. At least there won't be Dark Elves. I hope."

Alex took the time to get a snack and check his gear while they waited. He didn't have long. Tholi soared in at treetop level, looped around and landed near a giant boulder.

Megan explained the situation to Gorlak. "We think Captain Fejer's find is our best bet," she concluded.

"Sorry to head out just after you got back," Connor apologized, "but we should take a look while we have a chance. Night will fall in a few hours."

Gorlak shrugged. "Not problem. Best to get moving."

They mounted up and soared up in the sky, heading south with Alex leading. He landed at the edge of the river and the other Riders followed suit.

Gorlak pointed at the cliff. "That good place for Goblin tunnels, so maybe Vault here," he said. "Ground too soft and wet in other places."

With the dragons watching their backs, the Riders cautiously approached the opening, weapons at the ready, with Connor and Dar leading the way.

Nothing assailed them. Only a very large cave greeted their eyes, the roof towering fifteen feet above the floor. They spread out, searching. Alex cast about, looking for signs of habitation. From the shape of the walls — very rough with many indentations and protrusions — it looked as natural as could be. He began to doubt his initial optimism.

"Old campfire," Eric said, rising from a spot near one side of the entrance. "A few months at the least."

"I sure wish we had the Eye of Truth," Dar muttered.

"You mentioned it before, Highness," Khyla said. "What is it?"

"Magical gemstone," Connor answered. "An heirloom from ancient times. With it, someone can see the true nature of whatever they view. It reveals good and evil, truth and lies, illusion and reality. It made looking for secrets a whole lot easier."

What? That's incredible! Stunned by the sheer power of such an item, Alex gaped at them for the second time that day. "Wow. Where is it?"

Eric gave a half-smile. "In Astarel near the Deran border, in the keeping of its hereditary owner, Buck Bydecy, a Grey Rider. A bit far to go if we want to borrow it."

"We'll have to do this the old-fashioned way," Dar said, eyes roaming the cave. "We'll search for it. The back wall looks like our best bet.

Remember, be careful. We have had bad experiences with places like these."

After a fruitless hour of searching, Alex put his hands on his hips, leaning backward to stretch, staring at the rough walls in distaste. "Maybe this isn't the right place after all," he said.

Dar flung down a piece of burned wood. "We'll find it. I know it. We just have to be patient."

Alex frowned and twisted his hips to loosen them. A pale yellow light glinted near the top of the wall and he paused.

Wait a second…

"Do you see something up there, Highness?" Alex asked. Dar followed his eyes and froze. He peered for several heartbeats.

Khyla came to Alex's side, gazing up. "Did you find something?"

"I don't know."

"Gorlak?" Dar called over his shoulder, moving to the base of the wall. "Can you fly up there, please?"

The Goblin tapped the brooch of his cloak and bat wings spread around him. He fluttered upward as the other Riders crowded around.

"What is it?" Connor asked.

"Remember a certain tunnel near Forester?" Dar mused, "In an old mine, where we almost got trapped? Remember how we got out?"

"No," Brandi retorted. "That would be too much of a coincidence."

"What are they talking about?" Khyla whispered to Alex.

"No idea." Alex watched as Gorlak hovered near the ceiling close to where he saw the glint.

Gorlak fluttered down and landed near them. "I see three yellow gems set in the wall and a grey metal plate with outline of a hand on it. Wall is very rough and could be climbed by someone who knows how." His eyes flitted to Connor.

"How big is the hand outline?" Megan asked, eyes narrowing.

Gorlak pointed at Connor and Hannah.

Brandi and Connor exchanged a look. "That certainly makes sense, if it's a vault for keeping heirlooms related to a Halfling Kingdom."

Connor nodded, reaching into his backpack for a set of climbing gloves and boot spikes. "Be careful," Hannah said.

He kissed her. "Always."

Connor clambered up the wall, reaching the spot in seconds.

Damn. He's fast. Alex shook his head.

Connor clung to the top of the wall like an oversized spider.

"Remember what happened last time," Megan called. "This one looks like a much farther fall."

"I'm not worried," Connor replied with a grin in his voice. "Gorlak will catch me." He pressed his hand to the wall.

At first, nothing happened. Then a distinct rumble echoed in the cave and Alex heard the sound of metal on metal. Connor clambered back down as the wall slid aside, revealing a yawning opening as wide as the entrance to the necropolis.

The Riders regarded it, unmoving, as Connor alighted and removed his climbing gear.

"The usual?" Megan asked him. He nodded.

She murmured quietly, holding her staff out horizontally. Two symbols flared on the floor just inside the opening and the yellow gemstones near the hand-plate flashed twice.

Connor stepped to the doorway, eyes flitting around. He peered at the edges and ran his hands gently over the door jamb. When he came within a foot of the entrance, a globe of light popped into existence just inside. Connor retreated.

What the hell was that? Alex drew his sword and raised his shield. Next to him, Khyla did the same. The Riders stepped back, weapons out and alert for danger. The dragons crouched, jaws open.

Nothing attacked them. Finally, Dar straightened and sheathed his sword. "This is just like Moridan's Tower. Remember, Connor?" he asked. "The same thing happened with Buck. Magical lights showed up wherever he went."

"What does that mean?" Alex asked, eyeing the light warily.

Eric relaxed. "It means that this location is attuned to Connor, much like Buck Bydecy found in the ancient tower of his ancestor. We've seen this before. But stay sharp. It's been many years since this place was last used. Anything could have happened."

Unconvinced, Alex exchanged a nervous glance with Khyla and she gave his shoulder a squeeze.

"We follow their lead, right?" she asked.

He nodded. *We don't have another choice.*

Connor regarded the brightly-lit tunnel for a few heartbeats, then stepped just inside the doorway. Another light burst to life near the ceiling about a dozen feet away. "It looks clear. Eric, you'll probably need to send the pegasi away."

Eric led the flying horses outside the cavern. He made a circular motion with his arm and pointed at the sky. With a few whinnies of protest, the pegasi trotted out into the afternoon sunlight and flew off.

As during their underground trek near Duarvar, they arrayed with the dragons at the front. Gorlak mounted his special saddle on Tholi's back.

Hannah joined Connor, who activated his brooch. The dancing sword swirled up before him. Dar and Megan talked quietly as they waited for Eric to return.

"I wonder what other surprises are in store," Khyla murmured, her eyes narrowed.

"Me too," said Alex.

He felt an odd sense of foreboding, as if something lethal waited just inside the vault, hidden, unseen.

Megan addressed them all as they readied to enter. "Remember, Melinor mentioned something about a 'Silver Doom'. If this really is the Vault of Safety, it's from the Paragon Age. We could encounter something the world hasn't seen in over two thousand years. Stay on your guard. We're no use to the people of Loemin if we're dead."

Khyla flicked a nervous look at Alex and set her jaw. "Let's do this."

Alex took a deep breath and followed the others inside. *Okay God. A few extra guardian angels, if You Please.*

Chapter Thirteen – Silver Doom

Khyla peered down the corridor, hefting her round shield on her arm. Luminous globes hovered in mid-air just under the ceiling, bathing the area in a pale white glow. Elegant carvings of Halfling farmers, warriors and mages decorated smooth stone walls. Filigreed scrollwork meandered along baseboards and crown molding carved from marble edged the ceiling. Each floor stone held the engraved image of a badger. She saw little dust.

Despite the grandeur and artistry, her hands felt clammy.

Those lights just pop into existence wherever Prince Connor goes. That's unnerving.

She nodded at the orbs of light. "Don't those things bother you?" she whispered to Alex.

"Well, yes," he responded. "But good news for us. We don't have to use our infra-red visual gear. Let's be thankful the tunnels are wide enough for the dragons."

She frowned. "Yes, but why? What would they bring into here that would be that large?"

He shrugged. "I have no idea. To answer that, we'd need to know what they did here thousands of years ago."

She didn't answer, but the unique architecture and the autonomous lights still bothered her. "This place is bothers me."

"Me too." He gave a companionable smile. "But the Riders have a lot of experience in this kind of environment. I believe in them." He clasped her shoulder and marched down the passage.

She followed. *He has a point. I have to trust in the Riders. They are in their element, so to speak.* She cast a glance towards the entrance yards behind them. *At least Connor closed the door so we don't have to worry about anything sneaking up on us.*

Alex's confidence helped her relax and she found her unease diminishing. His friendliness and cheerful demeanor calmed her.

Why am I so drawn to him? Part of her wanted to push him away, but another, more basic emotional part yearned for a connection. She felt a distinct attraction growing and sensed that he felt the same. *He's not hard on the eyes and he seems like a good person. But how much can I trust him?*

Her ruminations about trust led her to think of Eric and she gritted her teeth. *Why am I worried about a relationship with Alex? I have a bigger problem: how to talk to Eric alone somehow, to find out if he really is who I think he is. Suppose he is? How will he react, or Brandi or Alex? Will they cast me out? Oh gods, I'm a mess.*

Lost in thought, she almost tripped over Kindri's tail as the passage took a turn.

Damn it, woman! She settled her sword at her hip. *Soldier up already. Enough with the wool-gathering.*

With renewed determination, she continued on. Connor and Hannah led the way, accompanied by Gorlak riding in his special saddle atop Tholi. Khyla craned her neck to see them around Kindri, just in front of her, accompanied by Brandi and Eric. Only the sound of boots and an occasional scrape of dragon claws broke the silence. Khyla kept her hand on her sword despite the quiet surroundings.

The lighting sequence repeated as they continued down the corridor. Their path curved to the right but the passage remained dark despite Connor's presence. They stopped.

Khyla's eyes narrowed. *Why no lights this time?*

Brandi gestured and a luminous sphere hovered just ahead of them, below the ceiling.

"Hmm… well, that's different all right," Connor said, pointing. Khyla's eyes followed his finger. Ugly cracks marred the elegant walls. One particularly thick fissure traced across the hallway from the left wall to the ceiling, then to the right wall. There, the crack split and one branch led to a dark rectangle where a hand-plate should have been. Next to the dark rectangle, a massive doorway gaped open.

What the hell?

Connor knelt, then held up a bent hand-plate. "Okay, now it's even more disturbing. This looks like the one that guarded the entrance to the complex. I'll bet it came off when the hallway got cracked."

"What this mean?" asked Gorlak from his perch atop Tholi.

Megan's brow furrowed. "The room beyond the doorway is unprotected. However, I'm more worried about why the walls are ruptured."

"Well," offered Eric. "There are occasional earthquakes in this part of the world. It could have just occurred naturally."

"Maybe," Hannah's eyes roamed around the area. "But if that's so, don't you think the builders of the Vault would have designed safeguards to deal with that possibility? Like a redundant hand-plate? Reinforced tunnels?"

Great. Does this mean there's a creature strong enough to crack stone on the loose? Khyla's jaw tightened. "You mean something else could have caused it?"

"Maybe." Brandi said. "No matter what happened, the way is open, but we're not sure what lies beyond. Stay alert."

Connor minutely inspected the doorway, running gloved hands gently over the frame and tapping in places. He nodded to them and stepped inside.

Megan waved her staff and three more lights popped into view just under the ceiling, illuminating everything. Khyla followed the others into a large chamber with a vaulted ceiling, about fifty feet across. Oblong, rocky shapes attached to the ceiling immediately drew her eyes and she reached for her sword.

"Stone Lurkers again?" she asked.

Eric nodded. "But the cocoons are open, see there? And look. Lurker bones on the floor. I don't think there are any left alive."

A few yards away, a marble desk sat near the right wall and a massive, dry fountain in the shape of a hippogriff loomed to their left. Five large covered stone jars decorated with enameled golden badgers stood near the desk. Three large stone tables butted up against the left wall and fragments of wooden furniture littered the floor near the right wall.

"What is this place?" Gorlak asked.

Connor shrugged. "Looks like a delivery room or an inspection area… maybe even could have been a guard room."

"Lurkers broke in here somehow," Dar said behind him. "Probably after the crack disabled the hand plate at the entrance."

"Yes," said Gorlak, holding his crossbow at the ready. "But what kill Lurkers?"

As they crept into the area, Khyla noticed that alternating patterns of black and silver ceramic squares, each about two feet across, covered the walls. They seemed very much at odds with the exquisite carvings decorating the corridors.

Something is different. Her senses on high alert, Khyla drew her sword and raised her shield, sensing Alex do the same next to her.

Several of the silver squares slid aside. Pale lights glowed in the space behind the doors, then slim metallic forms slithered out.

Her heart leaped in her throat. "Look out!" she shouted.

They looked just like very large cobras made of metal. Each measured at least six feet long. Fiery orange eyes locked on the Riders. One of the serpents pivoted its head around to glare at her. It opened its mouth and she saw a glowing amber light in its throat, encased in a tiny wire cage. More of the doors slid open.

And here's where we meet the Silver Doom. Wonderful.

Without a signal, the snakes shot forward. A crowd of more than a dozen swarmed Kindri and Tholi, trying to sink their fangs into their hide. The dragons backed up, lashing out. Two metal serpents slammed into the walls, writhing like earthworms. Gorlak activated his cloak and fluttered over the melee, firing glittering red bolts from his crossbow.

One serpent struck at Khyla, but she met it with a stout blow from her shield. The snake lunged back at her immediately. She swung. Her sword stroke pinged off its metal skin, leaving only a small dent.

Well, that did next to nothing. How the hell do I fight one of these things?

The snake darted at her. She dodged and stepped on its tail, then tried to sever its head. She might as well have tried to behead an anvil. The serpent snapped at her and caught its fangs on the edge of her shield, trying to rip it off her arm.

Not today! Fury built within her and she slammed the thing against the wall, pinning it. The serpent opened its mouth wide and again she saw the amber light within.

Instinctively, Khyla stabbed inside the thing's gullet, aiming for the wire cage. Her sword point ripped through. An electric charge jolted her arm and she gasped, nearly dropping her sword. The light in the snake's eyes faded and it slid to the floor with a metallic clatter.

"Their mouths!" She yelled, shaking her arm to try to get some feeling back into it. "Stab them in the mouth! Beware the electric shock!"

Four serpents attacked Eric. He impaled one with his spear and it veritably exploded in a cloud of sparks. He backpedaled, slashing a second one in half but the other two fastened onto his shoulder and throat. With a cry of pain, he went down, one hand gripping a serpent's throat.

Khyla froze. A memory sprang up. In her mind's eye, she gazed up through teary eyes as a kindly, half-elven lad smiled and reached out a hand to her.

"No!" Khyla charged, slamming the serpents off Eric. They sprang at her. She blocked one but the other bit into her left side. An icy pain ripped into her and she stumbled. Her shield arm went numb and her leg buckled.

A fanged mouth reached for her neck. Despite the pain, she jammed her blade into the serpent's maw and it collapsed. She lost her grip on her sword as her other arm went lifeless.

She fell back, her helmet ringing as her head hit the floor. She saw stars and the sounds of battle faded into a jumble of disjointed clangor and voices. Her eyelids fluttered closed.

She struggled to regain consciousness. Faint voices reached her. She tried to say something, to find out if Eric was alright, but she couldn't make a sound. She screamed for him to come back, but only managed a faint whisper.

Seemingly ages later, a single voice cut through the fog. She strained to hear it.

"Khyla," Brandi said, her voice gentle. "Come back to us. All is well."

She opened her eyes and blinked several times to clear them.

First, she saw Queen Brandi, smiling at her, laying a hand to her forehead. Then, Alex's face came into view, brow furrowed and a worried expression in his eyes.

"Better?" Brandi asked.

To her surprise, Khyla felt no pain. She nodded and tried to sit up. "Yes, Majesty, I —" The world spun and she put a hand to her head.

Alex curved his arm around her upper back and shoulder. "Easy, Khyla."

She tried to ignore how comforting it felt to be held by him and failed miserably. "Thank you, Captain," she said in a much weaker voice than she intended. She stared at the room. The unmoving, battered forms of metal serpents lay scattered all around.

Wait! She thought in a panic. *Where's Eric?*

As if in answer, his face appeared over her. "You gave us a bit of a scare, Captain," Eric said. He had a bandage around one shoulder and looked a bit pale, but as cheerful as ever.

"I'm sorry, Highness." She made as if to stand and Alex helped her up, his strong arms holding her, his eyes warm with concern. Her eyes stung and she bit the inside of her cheek.

Her internal battle over her feelings for him started up again. *Please, Alex, don't be kind to me. I can't handle it right now.*

"I'm fine," she continued. "How is everyone else?"

The other Riders crowded around. "Thanks to you, doing very well," said Eric. He kicked aside a metal cobra. "Your discovery worked wonders, though those little shocks were as much fun as a Goblin wedding. No offense, Gorlak."

Gorlak chuckled. "None taken, Prince Eric."

Brandi peered into Khyla's eyes. She stared back, unable to break the connection. A warm, tingling sensation floated through her head, comforting, calming, yet probing. As suddenly as it started, it faded.

Without turning her head, Brandi said, "Why don't the rest of you search the area while I tend to Captain Dearborn?"

"Already done, dear," Eric responded. "Captain Fejer and I inspected those stone jars. They have some kind of white powder in them, a mineral, I'm guessing. I have a sample in an empty potion vial for us to look at later."

"Good," she replied. "Connor, would you mind arranging a watch on the area?"

"Sure." Connor headed off with Gorlak and Hannah.

"Come with me, Captain," Brandi said, beckoning to Khyla. "It's alright, Captain Fejer. She'll be fine."

Butterflies flipped around in Khyla's stomach as she followed Brandi to the dry fountain. The queen sat on the rim and patted it.

Khyla joined her, eyes focused on her hands. "I'm sorry I gave everyone a scare, Majesty."

"That's quite all right. I carry Everheal with me at all times and my Elohir skills allow me to augment medications. I analyzed the automatons' venom prior to healing you. The poison has the effect of paralysis and eventual death if untreated, but it is not immediately deadly."

"Is that what those were? Automatons?"

"Yes, just like Prince Eric's Stealth, but more advanced. These probably had an instruction set that told them to protect the chamber from unauthorized individuals — in other words, anyone who entered without using the hand-plate."

Khyla let her eyes roam around the room. More than forty of the metal snakes lay in pieces or as heaps of melted slag. *No more Silver Doom, I suppose...*

"Why didn't the dragons just burn them all to begin with?"

"The serpents were among us too quickly. Kindri and Tholi were afraid of hitting us with their fire breath. They had to fight them in close quarters and settled for slamming them aside or biting them in half."

Brandi fell silent and Khyla tried not to fidget.

"Captain," Brandi began, then paused. "May I call you Khyla?"

For the second time in the last few weeks, Khyla's eyes widened at the concept of a royal addressing her by her first name. "Of course, Majesty."

"Good. Khyla, when I was treating you, you drifted into a kind of delirium. You said some things that were a bit, well, unusual to say the least."

Khyla broke out in a cold sweat. "M-Majesty," she stammered, "If I gave offense —"

Brandi put her hand over Khyla's, just as Megan had done. "You offended no one. Only Captain Fejer and I heard you. While you were hovering in that state, you said Eric's name several times, then something like 'don't leave me' or 'take me with you'. What did you mean? Did you know Eric previously?"

Gripped by sudden panic, Khyla clutched her sword handle with a white-knuckled hand. *Oh no! And Alex heard it too? What will he think?*

"Khyla? What is it? I acknowledge that Eric had a life before I met him. Plus, I was out of action for a while during the War. Whatever the explanation, I promise you I won't get angry."

The thought of revealing everything at that moment made Khyla's stomach churn. *I have to be strong.* "Majesty, I promise that there is no threat to Prince Eric or to you. I have no designs on him. I think I did know him before, but I am not sure, nor am I sure that he remembers me. When we get to safer surroundings, I promise to tell you everything. Please believe me."

She wrung her sword handle. *I can't believe I said that. I wanted to talk to him first, in order to make sure. I'm messing up everything!*

Brandi measured her with her eyes and Khyla felt a faint shadow of the warm probing sensation from before. "Hmm. Well, Khyla, I believe you and I trust you. I will defer to your judgement, but I need you to explain everything to me when we get a chance to rest."

A wave of relief washed over Khyla and she stood. "Yes, Majesty. I will."

"Good. And Khyla?"

"Yes, Majesty?"

Brandi's expression showed only compassion and gentleness. "Difficult burdens only get more difficult the longer you bear them alone. And you are not alone."

Can I do this? Now? What will they say when I tell them? Fear of the unknown warred with hope in Khyla's heart. She saw Brandi's smile and hope won.

She smiled back. "Thank you, Majesty."

Chapter Fourteen – Trial of Kingship

Hannah marched at her husband's side next to the dragons. She cast a glance back at the open doorway to the room with the metal snakes and shuddered. The level of magical sophistication in the Vault of Safety intimidated her and she felt completely out of her element.

Give me a battalion to command or a cavalry charge any day to this creeping around underground. That's Connor's area of expertise, not mine.

Kindri and Tholi halted, eyes flaring. Everyone slowed and stopped.

"What is it?" asked Gorlak.

"A strange metal is somewhere nearby," Tholi said. His head swung left and right, eyes scanning the hallway.

Wait. What does that mean? Hannah wondered. She eyed the corridor. Here, as in the metal snake room, large cracks and fissures tracked across stone and marble.

"What kind of strange metal?" asked Brandi.

Tholi just shook his head.

Brandi turned to Alex. "That's not encouraging, especially in a place like this."

She waved to the other Riders. Soon, they clustered near Kindri. Gorlak and Tholi stood guard: the Goblin aiming his crossbow down the passage from his perch and Tholi eyeing the corridor ahead.

"What do you think, Kindri?" Hannah asked.

The dragon frowned. "I've never encountered this one before."

"Dragons can detect metals?" Hannah shot a questioning look at Kindri.

"Yes." Kindri nodded. "Female dragons are particularly good at it. Most common materials, even alloys, are familiar to me, and even some uncommon ones, like Starsilver and Starsteel, but this one…" Her voice trailed off and her frown deepened.

Hannah's brow furrowed. *If they don't know what it is, what else is there down here that we won't know about?*

"Tholi didn't recognize it either," Connor offered. He stared down the corridor. The furthest circle of light only let them see about thirty feet ahead. Beyond lay only blackness.

Eric focused his gaze down the corridor and raised a hand. His eyes glowed amber and he dropped his arm to his side. "I have nothing," Eric said. "What do you think the metal could be, Megan?"

She shook her head. "I have no idea. We have precious little information from the Paragon Age as it is; it could be some kind of special material lost in the mists of time."

"Well, we won't find out standing here," said Dar, his tone confident and relaxed. "This place is part of your legacy, Connor. We'll follow your lead."

Connor remained lost in thought. Finally, he nodded. "Let's keep going, but Kindri, if you or Tholi detect something else that might be dangerous, call a halt."

Kindri nodded and the Riders re-formed their marching order again, wary but unruffled. After about forty more feet of travel, Kindri halted. Connor held up a fist and the Riders slowed and stopped.

"That metal is closer. It is different now, biting, sharp. Like…" Kindri murmured.

"Like what?"

"Like poison." Her tail flicked in agitation.

Hannah frowned, unsure of what to make of it. She dearly wished she'd paid more attention when her brother had tried to tell her about traps and mechanisms. "Maybe there's a metal trap with some kind of poison gas or something."

"Good point." Connor considered this. "If it's poison gas, we'd need to know what kind so Brandi can counteract it. I should probably go take a look."

A nameless anxiety seized Hannah. She grasped his arm. "Kindri's worried, and that makes me nervous. We have magical means to scout, don't we? Let's see what the others think."

He hesitated, then beckoned to the Riders and they gathered around. Connor explained their concerns.

Megan tapped her chin. "I could use an Ethereal Eye spell, but it has a limited range and I have to remain still for it to work. If the source of the gas is beyond, say, forty to fifty feet, I won't be able to see it."

"How about Stealth?" Brandi suggested.

Eric shook his head. "No good. I'd have to send him ahead into areas without lights. Even though I can see in the dark fairly well, Stealth doesn't have that ability and I'm using his visual sensors."

They remained lost in thought. Hannah shot a glance at Connor. She knew him well enough to realize he chafed at the delay, but he remained calm. She gave his hand a squeeze. *Very good, dear. There is a time to think and not act — a lesson that has cost me in the past.*

"Any ideas?" Connor asked.

"Can you put a light spell on Stealth?"

They all turned to look at Khyla. She smiled shyly. "Sorry. I'm probably not qualified to speak about magic, but I saw Her Majesty conjure a light earlier. Can you put it on Stealth so Prince Eric can see when he uses it?"

A slow smile spread across Connor's features and the Riders exchanged pleased looks.

Now why didn't I think of that?

Megan patted Khyla on the shoulder. "That's brilliant. You go right on making suggestions."

Khyla lowered her gaze. Alex elbowed her, grinning, and she blushed.

"Light spell it is," Eric said. He tapped his brooch and soon his hawk golem sat on his forearm. Brandi used her spell and a ball of light sprang into being on the automaton's chest.

"Now, let's see what's out there." Eric's eyes took on a faraway look and the hawk flapped away, its light shining down on the passage. The corridor took a turn and it soon disappeared from view.

Hannah took several breaths to calm herself.

"More passageway," Eric murmured. "An open doorway with more cracks in the wall next to it. The hand plate is twisted and warped. Now, a large, open room with, let's see, there are Lurker bones near the entrance. The floor is square tiles with a reflective sort of liquid in the seams. It looks like molten silver or something. No, it's shinier. There are multiple cracks on the wall and ceiling. On the other side of the room is a door with an intact plate and a body slouched against the wall. It's small, like a Halfling and looks like it has, wait, four arms? That doesn't make sense."

Hannah's frown returned. "Four arms? Only trolls have multiple arms." *What the hell is going on?* She shot a glance at Connor, hoping that he might have experienced something in his many previous missions.

He caught her eyes and shrugged, shaking his head.

"Bring him back, Eric," said Megan, an odd tone in her voice.

"What is it, dear?" Dar asked.

"I know what's going on," Megan replied, leaning against Tholi's flank absently. "And it's not good."

The automaton soon returned. Eric spoke the keyword and it flowed back into his brooch in shimmering sparkles.

Megan took a deep breath. "I know what that silvery substance is. It's mercury."

Something in her tone made Hannah's stomach clench. "I'm guessing that's the poison."

"Exactly. It's a deadly liquid metal. The fumes alone can kill you in the quantities that Eric is describing. That's probably what happened to the Lurkers. We can't go anywhere near that place. We have to find another way around."

Connor put his hand to the wall and closed his eyes. Hannah felt a mild tingle in the air.

He opened his eyes and shook his head. "There is no other way around."

"Maybe there's a secret passage somewhere," Eric said.

Again, Connor shook his head. "I would have felt it. I'm sure of it." He drummed his fingers on the elegantly carved wall.

This can't be the end. We must be close. Hannah wracked her brain, trying to come up with some kind of alternative. "If it's that deadly, the makers of this Vault would have kept something around to neutralize it," she reasoned. "It doesn't make sense otherwise. What can neutralize liquid mercury?"

Connor took her hand and gave it a squeeze. "Good thinking, dear."

Megan tapped her chin. "I can think of several things, but I don't see any of them around. For instance, if we could make a paste of sulfur mixed with lime and water, that would work, but I didn't see those substances here. There's also powdered zinc."

Alex and Eric exchanged a sheepish grin. Eric handed her a vial of white powder. "Like this?"

Megan seized it. Her eyes glowed yellow for a second and she closed them, entering a trancelike state.

After a few heartbeats, she opened her eyes. "Yes! This is powdered zinc. Where did you get it?"

Alex jerked a thumb back the way they had come. "Those jars back in the serpent room are filled with it."

Connor looked very pleased. "Just as Hannah thought. This is how the makers of the Vault could keep themselves safe in case of a malfunction of some kind. Captain Dearborn, please go back with Captain Fejer and bring back two large sacks of the zinc powder."

He is acting more and more like a prince every day. Hannah put an arm around him and leaned her head against his. "You're showing patience and fortitude, even though I know you really want to get going."

"Does it show that much?"

"Probably not to the others, but to me. And I'm proud of you."

"Thank you, dearest."

The captains soon returned with the bags of powder.

Tholi extended a claw. "Let us do it, Majesty."

Hannah held up a hand. "Hold on. If that substance is poisonous —"

"We can hold our breath for some time, enough time for us to neutralize the mercury near the entrance," Kindri interrupted. "Then we can step back, take a few breaths and neutralize the next section. Little by little, we'll clear the room."

Eric hefted the two bags for the space of a couple of heartbeats. "As much as I don't want to admit it, this is the best option. Stealth isn't equipped to manipulate a bag while flying."

Each dragon took a sack. "Just make sure you're careful." Dar cautioned with a sardonic smile. "I wouldn't want to deal with your grandfather's ghost lecturing me if any harm came to you."

Kindri winked. "If so, tell Grandfather it was our idea."

The dragons disappeared into the darkness ahead. Hannah tried not to fidget, but the longer they were gone, the more her nervousness increased.

Easy. It's just like waiting for the start of a battle. Focus. They'll be fine.

After what seemed like a decade, Kindri returned. "We used up almost all the powder but every seam with the mercury has been covered. We can go in. Tholi is guarding the chamber."

The Riders heaved a collective sigh of relief and followed Kindri into the room. Here, the walls held faded frescoes depicting industrious halfling cities and prosperous farmland. One scene showed a king and queen carrying a sword and cloak towards a castle. On the opposite side of the room, Hannah glimpsed a closed door with an intact hand-plate. A layer of white powder coated the seams of the floor stones.

Hannah gaped at the beauty of the artwork. *Is that what Loemin used to be like?*

Gorlak pointed at the many-armed figure from his perch atop Tholi. "Another automaton," he announced as they approached.

The contraption resembled a metal Halfling man with four arms. Loops and compartments on the chest and waist of the automaton held an assortment of tools.

Connor knelt next to it. "What's this used for?" He ran his fingers over one of the tools. "I wish Handor was here. He'd figure this out in no time."

She knelt next to Connor. "He's watching over us," she whispered.

"What do you think?" Dar asked Connor.

Before he could answer, Tholi flicked his tail at a wall. "The metal flowed out from there."

Hannah shot a glance in that direction. The wall had a small hole down near floor level with some sort of blocky structure around the hole. The crack near the entrance wandered across the roof and met the block squarely.

"Any guesses?" asked Eric.

Megan waved a hand at the automaton. "I bet this is a maintenance device, probably meant to keep the Vault in working order. When it broke down, it was unavailable to repair things like the mercury leak after the crack in the stone appeared."

"Why did it break down?" Alex asked. "Someone tampered with it?"

Megan shook her head, rising. "I don't think so. We've only seen Lurker skeletons and they aren't that smart. This vault has been here for thousands of years. Eventually, the devices would stop working without someone to tend them regularly, no matter how well the Paragons built them."

Connor approached the closed door.

"Does the hand plate work?" Eric asked.

"One way to find out." Connor placed his palm on it. The door slid open and light flared in a passage beyond.

"Kindri and Tholi, if you please?" he said.

The dragons snaked through the doorway. Hannah followed at Connor's side. Once again, the corridor lit up with the pale glow of ethereal lights.

I sure hope this is the end of it, Hannah thought.

Their path led to an arched opening. As they neared, Hannah observed bas-reliefs carved into the arch. They looked like an alternating series of Halfling figures and open hands. Her brow furrowed.

Now what does that mean?

"Careful now," Connor hissed over his shoulder. "This is the only entrance without a door or a hand plate."

Hannah took a deep breath and followed the dragons inside. Bright light washed over the interior of a massive, domed room. Her jaw dropped.

A ten-foot-tall metal statue of a Halfling man in armor loomed in the exact center of the circular chamber, motionless. Behind it, a dark wooden chest banded with silver stood against the wall next to a glass display case. A crystal chandelier in the shape of four eagles hovered in midair just below the ceiling. The eyes of the birds glowed, shining down on them.

Her eyes wandered to the walls. Bright mosaics depicted country scenes, cityscapes and mountains. Gazing at the artwork, Hannah thought she would hear birdsong and lowing cattle, the calls of artisans and street vendors, the clank of plate mail and clop of centaur hooves. She expected to smell wheat and grass, the aromas of roasted meats, and the scent of flowers.

Her mind grappled with the level of beauty and craftsmanship. *How long did it take them to fashion all that? And who made this?*

Hannah's eyes flicked to one mosaic of a king and queen holding court in a manor, their hands raised in benediction. She caught herself holding her breath, as if awaiting the pronouncement of the royal couple.

"Is that one of the Loemin kings?" Alex asked, pointing at the statue.

Connor stepped inside, eyes darting all around. "No idea. Keep your eyes open, everyone. There may be more safeguards."

The Riders entered, spreading out and giving the statue a wide berth.

"Maybe you should try something, Connor," Megan suggested as the Riders filed around the perimeter.

As if in answer, the statue's eyes snapped open, revealing small orange fireballs. It raised an arm and held its palm toward them.

"Halt!" A deep voice echoed in the chamber. "By what authority enterest thou here?"

Everyone froze. "Is that coming from the statue?" Khyla whispered.

Connor took one step forward. "By the authority of the Kings of Loemin!"

The automaton's head swiveled around to regard him. Its eyes flashed and a red light passed over Connor's body. The statue paused as if thinking. "Thou hast the lineage in thy blood. Therefore, if thou art rightwise an heir of the Kings of Loemin, come forth and provide proof positive. Speak ye the command word."

Command word? No one said anything about a command word! Hannah gripped the handle of Shriek and sized up the automaton. It looked like it weighed several tons.

Connor shook his head. "Many ages have passed since the creation of this Vault and I do not know the command word. Is there no other way to prove my lineage?

The statue paused again, as if considering. "By trial of kingship. Knowest thou the proof of control?"

Honestly? How many safeguards did they place on this Vault?

"I do not," Connor replied.

This is not good.

"Then thou must prove thy worth against me." The statue raised a fist and opened it. A curtain of stone flowed down over the entrance archway. A surge of gale-force wind blasted out at the Riders, slamming them against the walls of the chamber, even the dragons. Mosaic tiles fell like rain from the impact. Only Connor remained unscathed.

No! Hannah grimaced, pushing against the force pinning her. She managed to keep her hand on Shriek.

"What are you doing?" Connor demanded in a commanding voice. "Release the others at once!"

"Nay. Until thy lineage is verified, they remain. Come thou forth!"

Connor drew his sword and tapped the brooch at his shoulder. His guardian blade materialized in midair. The statue thudded towards him, massive and implacable.

Lord Irial, help me! Panic arose in Hannah's chest at the sight of the behemoth bearing down on her beloved. With a shriek of rage, she forced her hand to draw her blade. Every muscle screamed with the effort and she panted, her vision growing spotty.

The statue halted its advance and fireball eyes focused on her. "Who is this one with such strength? Wherefore does she strive so mightily to join us here?"

Connor stalked to the side and his ghostly blade matched his movements. "You look upon my lady wife, the Crown Princess Hannah. She is also of the House of Loemin. You must let her pass."

The automaton's eyes flared and a red light washed over Hannah. The construct returned its gaze to Connor. "Nay, for she is not of the blood of Loemin, though she may produce worthy heirs. Now, prove thyself."

The statue swung its fist overhead. Connor dodged. The attack hit the tiled floor instead, cracking the marble. Connor's guardian blade slashed at the statue but only managed a few scratches on the metal surface.

Hannah struggled, but her arm flopped down by her side though she still held Shriek.

"Steady on, Connor!" Brandi shouted. "We can't join you but we can still help!" She began a prayer. Megan, Dar, Alex and Eric joined in.

The air lightened. Though Hannah remained pinned to the wall, her pains melted away. Connor's form glowed faintly with a silver aura.

The automaton pursued Connor around the chamber, swinging at him. Connor dodged and rolled with an agility she had never seen before, striking at knee and ankle joints with his secondary blade. His phantom sword also slashed at the automaton but it seemed to have little effect. The statue barely slowed.

The statue machine swung a barrel-sized fist at Connor's legs and he jumped over it. Landing, he stumbled and tripped. Another fist whooshed through the air inches above his head. He spun and dodged but a backhand caught him in the side and he flew across the room, hitting the floor and sliding into the wall. Hannah's heart flew to her throat.

"Connor!" she screamed, fighting against her invisible bonds.

Connor shook his head as the metal behemoth thudded towards him. He flicked his hand and his phantom sword darted at the automaton's fireball eyes. The statue threw up both hands to ward off the animated blade, giving Connor enough time to get to his feet and lurch out of the way.

"Kindri! Tholi!" Hannah shouted in desperation. "Can you breathe fire at it?"

"Sorry… Highness," Tholi panted. "The statue is too far away!"

Lord Irial, how do I help him?

The chanted prayer from Brandi and the others intensified. A blue glow flashed on Connor's leg and side. His limp disappeared. The automaton swatted the guardian sword into the wall and swiveled around at him.

Connor ran towards the chest and display case, summoning his guardian sword to his side again. The statue crunched off to intercept, blocking his way. As it turned its back, Hannah saw a hand-shaped depression in the statue's back.

Her mind flashed to the carvings on the archway. "It's back! Connor! There's a hand plate on its back!"

He nodded and backpedaled. His opponent followed. Connor flicked his hand at the statue's head again. As before, two metal arms came up to deflect the guardian sword. Connor raced at the statue and slid under it, between its legs. It swiveled its head around. Connor leapt up, planting one foot on the thing's metal hip and reaching high. His hand slapped the imprint on the statue's back.

A mild ringing tone echoed in the chamber. The automaton knelt down before Connor, presenting a hand to him. Connor labored for breath but staggered forward and placed his hand on statue's palm.

"Release them," he panted.

The wind switched off like a snuffed candle and the stone curtain over the exit melted away. The iron bands holding Hannah dissipated and she raced to Connor's side. She wrapped her arms around him. "Sweetheart? Are you alright?"

"I'm fine." He smiled and returned her embrace. She gave a sigh of relief. *Thank the Worldmaker!*

Connor addressed the automaton as the other Riders gathered around. "How are you called?"

"Sentinel Five."

"Open the chest and the display case, Sentinel Five, then stand down. Your vigil is ended."

The automaton straightened and walked to the mosaic of a castle just behind the chest and case. It placed a finger on the figure of the king. The lid of the chest and the door of the case opened without a sound.

Finally. Hannah felt another wave of relief.

"Hmm… now let's see if this is what we came for." Connor peered into the chest. He lifted out a short sword in an ornate scabbard of silver and sapphires decorated with motifs of snowflakes.

Hannah's heart skipped a beat at its beauty. "Is that…?"

Connor grinned, reaching in and pulling out a case stuffed with scrolls. "I think so. Megan and Brandi, I will need your help to decipher all this."

Chapter Fifteen – Lost and Found

Khyla tossed a stick into the fire and shot a look at Megan and Brandi, deep in quiet discussion over a handful of scroll cases as Dar and Eric looked on. Brandi passed a hand over the bone tubes and both sisters closed their eyes. A misty light shone briefly. Megan nodded and Brandi added the cases to an assortment of items from the Vault of Safety lying on cloaks nearby.

The Guardian Rod was planted in the ground next to the campfire, gleaming. Khyla's gaze wandered to the cave entrance. Kindri and Tholi lay at the extreme edges of the yawning opening, their snouts pointed at the night sky beyond.

What am I worried about? The Rod will warn us, and besides, we have two really good sentries watching the glade. Khyla stretched and stifled a yawn.

"Tired?" asked Alex. He plopped down on the log next to her.

She gave him a wan smile. "Isn't everyone?"

"I know what you mean." He offered her his waterskin and she took a drink.

His nearness simultaneously comforted her and made her nervous. *How can I feel both at the same time? Could I be falling for him?*

Brandi's voice echoed in the cave. "That was the last of it. Everyone gather around so we can tell you what we found out."

Khyla gave Alex what she hoped was a warm smile and handed back his waterskin. They walked over to join the other Riders.

Brandi gestured at the items on the cloaks. "Many of these won't mean a lot to us at the moment," she said. "There are several books, scrolls and

Heritage Stones, as well as the coronation regalia of Loemin. We even found summaries of the laws of Loemin and surrounding kingdoms, like Alenar."

Connor knelt and reverently brushed his fingers on a set of Halfling-sized crowns and coronets, shining with gold and emeralds. Hannah smiled, her hand on his shoulder.

"Oh, and you can have Glittershard back." Megan's eyes twinkled and she handed the ornate short sword to Connor. "We're done analyzing it and now know what it can do. It's your father's by right, but I don't think he'll mind if you borrow it."

Connor rose and took the weapon. He turned it over in his hands, peering at the designs as if trying to memorize them.

"By all the saints, Connor!" Dar said. "Stop staring at it. Draw the blasted thing." Megan elbowed him, eliciting a grunt.

Khyla hid a smile.

Connor raised an eyebrow at Dar, then slowly drew the sword from the sheath.

An ice-blue metal blade hummed with energy and lit up the area with a pale azure light. Wispy trails of vapor floated up from the sword's edge. A sapphire in the pommel flashed once, then settled down to a wintry glow.

The Riders gasped.

"Finally. An heirloom of my house and my father's house," Connor murmured. "A blade of legend."

Hannah looped her arm around his waist, smiling gently.

"It was fashioned in the middle Paragon Age with Celestial assistance," Brandi added. "It can conjure a wall of ice on command, freeze opponents, and is especially deadly to creatures that use fire. You just have to remember that the command words are in Dwarven."

Khyla shook her head. "It's gorgeous," she murmured.

Eric handed a hooded, silvery-grey cloak to Hannah. Designs like feathers decorated the hem and the hood gave the distinct impression of an owl's head. "This is Steelwing, meant for Loemin's queen. But, again, I don't think your mother-in-law will mind."

"How do I use it?" Hannah asked, swirling the cloak around her shoulders and fastening the clasp. She lifted the hood over her head.

"Touch the clasp and say 'Steelwing, protect me'. You'll see."

Hannah did so. The cloak snapped into the form of a stiff metal bell that curved from her neck to her shins. The hood shimmered and formed into a visored helmet very much like an owl's head, with a tiger-eye gem above the nose.

Wow! Khyla blinked, unable to believe her eyes. *All this from the Loemin family of old.*

"It forms this armor and helmet when you need extra protection," Brandi said. "It doesn't allow you to attack, but it is strong enough to deflect a ballista bolt or a light catapult round, even a magically augmented one. It resists fire, cold, electricity, acid and poison. If you say 'Enemies desist', the gemstone flashes with intense light, blinding enemies in your line of sight temporarily. If you want it to return to cloak form, say 'Done, Steelwing' and it will change back into a cloak."

Hannah spoke the command word. Steelwing returned to a silvery fabric and the hood resumed its normal shape.

Gorlak shook his head, eyes round. "I hear of Paragons from Papal Nuncio and Melinor, but never think to see anything from that time."

Alex nodded at the books, scrolls and other items on the cloaks. "Was there anything of tactical or military value besides Steelwing and Glittershard?"

"There was an interesting book of spells, including an intriguing one called 'Lay of the Land'," Megan answered. "It can cast a convincing illusion over a large area to make it appear like rolling hills and forest. It's enough to hide the Grand Market in Oakmoor, if you had a mind to do it."

Dar grinned. "Of course, no one would believe the Market disappeared and hills and forest took its place, but you get the idea."

Khyla shook her head. She saw the Grand Market in her mind's eye, at least a hundred yards across. "Tavern tales and legends are coming to life, right here," she whispered, "and I'm a first-hand witness."

Alex bumped her with his shoulder and smiled down at her. A warm feeling spread in her chest and she smiled back before she could stop herself.

"We also found some items that we still use today, like Heritage Stones," Megan continued, "The ones in the Vault are linked to the royal and noble houses from the Paragon Era for several different regions. Along with the other scrolls and books, they are extremely valuable. We'll send them to Lord

Melinor tonight in the Messenger Bag."

Brandi put her hands on Connor and Hannah's shoulders. "Congratulations on finding heirlooms of your House. May God guide you in using them."

Connor and Hannah nodded. Connor sheathed the sword and Hannah gently folded the cloak.

Eric clapped his hands together. "Let's get some rest. We'd better assign a watch rotation to help out Tholi and Kindri. Captain Dearborn, please take the first."

Khyla nodded and headed to the entrance of the cave, setting herself up next to a flat table-shaped boulder.

Magic from an ancient time! Who would have thought I would ever see something like that? Maybe we really can pull this off — a few of us against an entire empire! Khyla leaned against the wall at the cave mouth, gazing at the peaceful night sky. Diamond stars spangled the velvet beyond. Insects chirped and night creatures rustled the reeds and bushes near the glade.

She activated her infra-red vision amulet. Only the familiar heat signatures of small animals and bugs glowed in her sight. The smell of grasses and lake water drifted to her. Woodsmoke mingled with the aroma of marsh reeds and trees. She listened to the others talking around the campfire, discussing their recent ordeals and the amazing heirlooms.

The heirlooms of an ancient house, she thought. *Connor and Hannah have found something special from their family heritage.*

The sound of hooves made her turn and she smiled. Her pegasus approached and nosed at her side. "I'm okay, Nightflame," she said, stroking the flame-shaped white marking on her mount's head.

Family heritage. The words stayed with her and she grew simultaneously agitated and morose.

Her eyes flitted to Eric and Brandi, smiling and talking as they removed their outer armor and laid it next to their bedroll. Brandi laughed at something he said and swatted at him playfully with a hairbrush. Connor and Hannah prepared a pot of tea over the fire, not speaking but clearly comfortable with silence.

Family is something I don't have. Will I ever?

The yearning for belonging grew stronger. Yes, the Riders accepted her as one of their number, but watching the Aldenar couples and the Loemins, Khyla wanted something more. *Do I dare take the chance? No matter what, I have to square things with Brandi. I owe it to her. I can't leave matters as they are.*

As if sensing her eyes on them, Brandi met Khyla's gaze and gave her a beatific smile.

All at once, a realization hit Khyla. *That could be my sister-in-law.*

Brandi said something to Eric, patted his knee, and strode towards Khyla. "Does your pegasus join you on watch?" she asked as she drew near.

"Not all the time." Khyla patted her mount's neck, trying to calm a sudden bout of nerves. "Though she has a mind of her own. She was my first training mount, so when I was chosen to come with you, they let me have my pick of the herd."

The pair stood silently. Butterflies fluttered in Khyla's stomach and she struggled for something to say, suddenly awkward. "What was that chant that you and the others used in the chamber with the metal statue?" she asked.

"The chant? That was a prayer, actually, called the Our Father. I combined it with a bolstering spell called Providence to help Connor."

"I felt something."

"You were supposed to. It's meant to aid the righteous." Brandi combed her fingers through Nightflame's mane. The pegasus bumped her head against Brandi's shoulder.

Righteous? Me? After everything in my life?

Brandi said nothing further, looking out at the night sky.

My sister-in-law? Khyla finally spoke. "Highness, I would like to continue our previous conversation."

Brandi's eyes never left the peaceful scene outside the cave. "I'm glad."

Khyla laid her hand on Nightflame's shoulder. For several heartbeats, she struggled against uncertainty, doubt and fear. The pegasus nosed Khyla in the side as if prodding her to speak.

"I appreciate your courage in talking," Brandi finally said, turning her eyes towards Khyla. "I can sense your struggle." Once again, Khyla felt that gentle probing and with it, a wave of empathy and concern. "Just know that no one will condemn you, no matter what it is."

Memories surged. Khyla's vision grew misty. "I…my…" Khyla's mouth went dry. "You aren't going to like me very much. You might even cast me out."

Brandi's mouth curved up in a tiny smile. "After what you've done for us? Fought bravely at our side? Used your wits to solve the problem of the silver cobras? Hardly."

Khyla swallowed with difficulty and looked at Brandi for a long time. She closed her eyes and tears rolled down her cheeks. *Do I dare?*

Brandi took Khyla's hand and drew her down to sit on the boulder. "Tell me everything."

Suddenly, Khyla felt an overwhelming urge to be done with it, to let everything be known, to stop holding it in. She clenched her fists and took a deep breath. *All right then. I'm done hiding.*

Her heart pounding, she nodded. "Very well, Majesty. It has to do with the Crossed Swords Assassin's Guild. The Guildmaster, Harkin Hylar, was my father. I believe Eric is my half-brother."

<<>>

Alex watched Khyla Dearborn talking to Brandawyn by the cave entrance, then averted his eyes. The memory of Khyla lying helpless on the floor in the serpent chamber brought back the pain of past losses.

As much as he tried to deny it, he felt his intense attachment to her and her growing trust in him. *Lord, I can't go through that again. Why am I destined to care for women who are always in mortal danger?*

Alex lifted his eyes beyond the cave entrance to the glittering stars. Eleanor's voice echoed in his mind. *"I don't want you to deprive others of your good heart because of me. I couldn't bear it."*

He let out a slow breath. *Eleanor died. But Khyla is alive. She's fine.* Her whispered words haunted him. *What did she mean? Does she know Eric from somewhere? Where was he supposed to take her, and why?*

Alex's eyes flicked to the two women by the entrance. He tossed another branch on the fire. Khyla's hand went to her mouth and it took a moment for Alex to realize she was sobbing.

"God, what is going on?" he murmured.

"Steady Captain," said Eric softly. "Brandi has skills that are beyond me. Captain Dearborn is in good hands."

"Yes, Highness." Alex took a breath to steady himself.

Brandi laid a comforting hand on Khyla's shoulder. Khyla shook her head, covering her eyes.

Alex blinked rapidly. Torn between sympathy for Khyla and the pain of his own memories, he wavered between going to her and staying put.

"Trust me." Eric said with a tiny smile. "Khyla will be all right."

<<>>

"Do you really think so?" Khyla asked, a flicker of hope coming to life in her chest. She wiped her eyes.

Brandi smiled. "I know Eric very well, Khyla. I suggest you speak to him privately first, then tell everyone else. Don't be afraid. You're one of us and nothing can take that away."

Khyla swallowed past a lump in her throat, desperately trying to hold herself together. *A place to belong, with people who care.*

Brandi held out her hand. "Come."

Khyla stood and walked with Brandi to where Eric and Alex waited. Her heart skipped a beat at the expression on Alex's face: empathy, pain and real concern.

"Eric, Captain Dearborn has something to tell you."

Eric gave Khyla a reassuring smile. "Very well."

"Alone," added Brandi with a raised eyebrow at Alex.

Eric paused, then nodded. "Of course."

Brandi and Alex retreated, but not before Alex gave Khyla a gentle pat on the shoulder that threatened to start the tears again.

Eric sat on a boulder. "Now, Captain, what was it you had to tell me?"

Khyla summoned her courage. She inhaled and exhaled slowly. *I am not a little girl or a swooning debutante. I am a soldier. My fear is just like any other enemy. Face it down and it will yield.* "Highness, I understand that you were adopted."

"Yes. By Melinor and Anne Indidarc, God rest her soul."

"I also understand your biological father was not a good person."

Eric's expression turned somber and a little bitter. "That's one way of putting it."

"Please, I need to know his name. I think I may have known you from before."

Eric's eyebrows went up and he watched her for long seconds. Finally, he said, "Harkin Hylar. He was the leader of an assassin's guild, the Crossed Swords."

"Did you have any brothers and sisters?"

Eric's laugh took on a tinge of bitterness to match his expression. "Well, yes. My father had several legitimate children, including me, by his legal marriage to my mother, and illegitimate ones by other women. But they all died during the War of the Dark Wave, fighting for the forces of evil, or, in the case of the more innocent of them, killed outright to prevent capture. Many of their bodies were recovered from the siege of Oakmoor."

Khyla hesitated and fear of rejection gripped her. She clasped her hands together to keep them from shaking. *I have to do this or I'll never be able to live with myself.*

The words came out of her almost before she realized she said them. "Not all of them died, Highness. I still live."

Eric stared at her.

Afraid that she might falter if she stopped, she poured out the words in a rush. "Your father was my father too. I am the child of Harkin Hylar and Liselle Leforge, a priestess of Gudarta who served the Crossed Swords Assassins Guild."

He stood and his jaw dropped. She continued. "I know you don't recognize me, but I lived in the complex in Harlinsville. You were the only one who ever showed me any kindness. Everyone else either looked down on me or feared me or tried to get something from me. My mother..."

Her voice trailed off and the memories came back: beatings, harsh training, taunts, verbal abuse, even worse...

His expression softened and he nodded slowly.

Tell him everything. "I was used as a spy when I was small," she whispered. Her head drooped as the weight of her memories pulled her down. She stared at the cave floor. "As I got older, I was used as a lookout or a thief. Sometimes, they forced me to poison people whom I enticed into my bed. Mother used me as a, well, a gift to important guests when they came to visit."

The silence dragged on. Her heart thudded in her chest. *He's not saying anything. Why? What if he rejects me?*

A pair of strong and gentle hands lifted up her tear-streaked face. Eric gazed at her with a combination of pity and empathy and, to her surprise, joy. "You're my half-sister?"

She nodded.

"What was your name back then?"

"Varani."

Slowly, recognition dawned in his features. "Varani! Yes! Now I see it! I thought you had died like all the others! But your hair was brown, or black or — God, I don't even remember."

She blinked and more tears ran down her face. "But I remember you! You held me as I cried in the darkness in the cell under the stairs when I was only six and Mother punished me for getting a poison mixture wrong. And another time you sneaked me food when they locked me in the dungeons for refusing to kill a teenaged boy. You were the only one who cared."

His eyes lit up. "That's how you knew about the Stone Lurkers! Father used them to guard the magical storerooms in Harlinsville!"

She nodded.

"Why didn't I recognize you?" he murmured, his hands cupping her face.

She gave him a tremulous smile. "The hair color might be part of it: I'm a natural blonde. Mother kept changing my hair so I would fit into whatever role I was to play. And I was a slender little thirteen-year-old then."

He chuckled and his eyes glistened. "Well, you've certainly grown up!"

She laughed through her tears and wiped her eyes. "I hope so."

"I thought Father told everyone I had died."

She scowled at the memory. "He did, but I didn't believe him! If you were merely dead, he wouldn't have moved everyone out of that hideout to the newer place in the north end of the city. No, he was afraid you would tell the authorities and they would raid the complex. That's how I knew it was a lie."

A sharp wave of anger hit her and she spoke before she could stop herself. "Why didn't you take me too? And the others?"

His face showed such a bleak despair and regret that she felt her stomach clench. "God! I wanted to!" he muttered with a shocking intensity, a stricken look on his face. "How I wanted to take all of the younger ones! But I had no idea how to get all of us out of there without being discovered. On my own, I could hide well enough and misdirect them, but to try to hide four or five of you? We would have been caught for sure! I knew what they would do to you, to all of us, when they caught us again."

Struck by his anguish and remorse, she imagined what it must have been like to leave the others behind. Knowing Harkin and Taramis Hylar, not to mention Liselle, Khyla shuddered at the thought of the punishments they could have inflicted on her and the others. *He did it to protect us.*

Eric's eyes shimmered with unshed tears, his expression full of apology and inner torment. "I'm so sorry, Varani! I really wanted to. And I didn't tell Melinor for months. He said there was little I could have done."

Her anger evaporated. "It's okay," she soothed, touching his cheek. "I don't blame you. I understand." *Now I'm comforting him?*

He took a deep breath and wiped his eyes. "Why didn't you say something earlier?"

"I wasn't sure. I kept trying to figure out whether you were really my half-brother or just someone who looked like him. You've changed too, you know. I knew that if I were at least part-way certain, I would mention our father and you would remember. And I was afraid."

He took her hands. "Of what?"

"Rejection. Because…" her voice broke. "Because of who I was and what I did. I should go to prison for all my crimes. If you're the High Prince of Alenar, how could you accept me?"

He stood and embraced her tightly. She froze and her heart soared.

"It was not your fault," he whispered. The last vestiges of fear in her soul vanished with a weak sigh. An inner light swept away the dark memories and she felt light as a feather.

"You were just a child," he continued, "I know what they did to you, to all of us. They forced the unwilling to do evil. No one blames you."

She wrapped her arms around him and buried her face in his chest, not trusting herself to speak.

"Oh Varani," he managed. "This is a gift from God! I don't know how you survived, but to find you alive after all this is a miracle."

She tried to say something, anything, and failed. Wildly joyous thoughts echoed over and over again in her head. *He loves me. He loves me! I have a family!*

"Don't worry about anything," he continued in a tight voice. "You're my family. I'll never let you go. Never."

The floodgates burst. Her body shook with sobs.

"It's okay, Varani. You're safe now."

Footsteps nearby made her look up. Brandi smiled radiantly, with the other Riders at her side. Alex and Gorlak and the dragons stood behind them, looking worried.

Khyla tried in vain to clean up her face. "M-Majesty —" She began, then broke it off when Brandi also enveloped her in a hug.

"Welcome, sister. Welcome home."

How many tears do I have in me? Khyla wondered as drops rolled down her cheeks again and she drew in a shuddering breath.

"What does this mean, Eric?" Dar asked. Megan took Khyla's hand.

Eric put one arm around her and the other around Brandi. He smiled down at Khyla. "I'll leave it up to you."

Khyla gazed at their concerned faces and knew what she had to do. *I'm not afraid any more.*

"My real name is Varani Hylar. I'm Eric's half-sister."

Chapter Sixteen – A House Built on Sand

Adina Tenspire reined in her horse at the top of the rise, glowering at the ravaged village on the plains below. Acrid smoke billowed up from burning buildings, obscuring the afternoon sun. Bodies lay strewn in the streets. Her troops methodically removed their own dead and piled the corpses of the villagers in the town square. A platoon of Halfling soldiers in red and black livery rounded up survivors: a motley, weeping clutch of old people, women and children. Corporals sorted the civilians and chained them, then loaded them on wagons. A squad of Goblin warriors on Fell Wolves stood guard nearby.

That's what they deserve for helping the rebellion.

An errant breeze brushed the smoke in her direction and she absently waved a hand in front of her face, wrinkling her nose at the odor of burning wood and charred flesh. A Halfling Skullhead Legionnaire in scale mail waited at her side on an armored war pony. She shot a glance at him.

"Sergeant," she said, "Bring Lady Arlene to me."

"Yes, milady." The soldier trotted his mount down the hill, heading for a squad looting a shop. Adina watched as the trooper spoke to Arlene. With a gesture to Arless Octavio, Arlene mounted a warhorse and the pair rode towards Adina's vantage point.

She's Golvadu's favorite for now. Gathering support for him in the northern provinces helped her cause, particularly now that we have an alliance with the Vardish and Cla'Agik, but what's her real game? Maybe she needs to be put in an uncomfortable situation to show her mettle, or lack thereof.

Adina's eyes roamed over the destruction as she mulled over the situation.

"Idiot peasants," she muttered. *This is going to cause me a lot of headaches, not to mention paperwork. Well, at least taxes are collected, this particular town is no longer a safe haven and we have all the property as booty. The troops will be happy.*

A two-headed Cerberus hound loped upslope to her, its yellow eyes bright and muzzles red with blood. She smirked. Her pet feasted well today.

It stopped at her side. "Enjoy your treats?" she asked. One of the heads whined at her.

Arlene and Octavio reined in and bowed in their saddles.

"Well?" Adina asked.

"The village is pacified," Arlene reported. "We should have everything onto wagons in less than an hour. We've managed to salvage something out of this for Lord Golvadu."

Adina measured Arlene with her eyes. No matter how many times she dealt with her, she felt the other woman always held a trump card in her sleeve – or a stiletto dagger.

Well, she did manage to spy for the Ja'al and assassinate her husband without King Phillip's Intelligence Service suspecting anything. She bears watching, that's for certain.

"Indeed." Adina gestured for Arlene to ride at her left. "How did the battle go?"

"We killed about seventy, some of whom were undoubtedly rebels and others who simply got in the way." Arlene wheeled her horse around. She waved a hand at the wagons with their Halfling cargo. "The balance of the village occupants are ready to be sent to the slave markets."

Adina sniffed. "Not a very enticing assortment."

"They will bring some coin. And your message has been sent, loud and clear: supporting the rebellion leads to ruin."

Adina cast a sidelong look at Arlene, noting the way her hands gripped her reins. "What did it cost us?"

Arlene hesitated just a second before answering. "Twenty dead and thirty-one wounded, including eight Fell Wolves and two ogres killed."

Adina's face heated and she gritted her teeth. "Simple villagers did all that? Explain yourself."

Arlene shifted in her saddle. "Many of the towns and villages sympathetic to the rebellion have been spying on the roads, looking for our troops. This particular place was prepared — and they had help. A significant number of the enemy were former militia. They had traps and ambushes laid out long before we arrived."

"And we blundered right into it!" Adina gritted her teeth. "This was supposed to be a simple mission to clamp down on restive communities and collect taxes, not a pitched battle. Which of our fool company commanders led the attack? I want his head on a plate."

"That will be easy enough," Octavio offered. "He was beheaded during the initial action."

"Small favors," Adina huffed. She glared at the scene before her. *Golvadu will want an explanation.* "The incompetence of our company officers aside, it doesn't explain the level of resistance. I want answers."

Arlene inclined her head. "From what we've been able to glean from the survivors, I can say that the people are more motivated. Connor of Loemin has a substantial number of militia on his side now. News of his latest victories have spread and the common folk are inspired to resist."

"There is also the sighting of the Loemin royal heirlooms on the battlefield," Octavio added.

That shouldn't matter. We should be able to rampage through a community of farmers like a hot knife through cheese, Adina fumed, but she kept her expression neutral.

"My lady!" her sergeant called, pointing to the eastern sky. "They come."

Adina's spirits rose, watching the forms of three dragons soaring towards them. "Excellent. Now, maybe, some news of the 5th Division."

"Hmm. Is something wrong?" Arlene asked in a mild tone, studiously keeping her eyes on the dragons. "Do we need reinforcements?"

Adina ignored the undercurrent of insubordination in her remark. "No, just awaiting a report from General Blake, near Highmarket."

They waited as the dragons approached and landed. The largest one, a deep purple and grey striped Drake, stalked forward while two red and black Sarkany remained behind.

A Dark Elf officer in the saddle atop the Drake bowed. "Lady Adina. I bring word from General Rocco."

Adina nodded, then did a double take. "General Rocco? He's 11th Division. You mean General Blake of the 5th."

The officer straightened, his red-tinted eyes wary. "General Blake is no longer in service to the People's Republic of Torosc. He and his division have joined the rebel ranks."

Adina blinked and her heart skipped a beat. "What?"

The Drake licked his lips with a forked tongue. "General Rocco's scouts saw them heading off to link up with the 1st Division," he rumbled, "which, as you know, has already turned traitor. They observed a meeting between their respective officers near Highmarket. They also saw a group of pegasus-riders and two young True Dragons."

Adina's mind raced. *This is a disaster! Now we have not one, but two divisions in rebellion? With those stupid Halfling heirlooms, Connor and Hannah Loemin are a lightning rod for defections. Golvadu will blow his pancreas out of his ass. And the Daemons!*

She had a sudden vision of Lord Balris showing up on her figurative doorstep and her mouth went dry.

"Hmm." Arlene rested her hands on her saddle horn. "It appears that the influence of the Sword of Blue Ice and the Steel Cloak reaches far indeed."

Adina almost snapped off an angry retort but thought better of it after a glance at the Dark Elf. It wouldn't do to have underlings see conflict among their superiors.

"Take your dragons and riders to the rear of the formation," she ordered the Elven messenger. "We will be done here soon. I want you flying top cover as we return to base."

The courier bowed in the saddle and the Drake inclined his head. The pair left.

Just wonderful, Adina seethed. *In the last week, eight supply caravans have been hijacked, the contents of the local army treasury in Greycliff mysteriously disappeared, and the rebels defeated two battalions at Havenridge and Ostor. Now the 5th Loemin has turned traitor. And pegasus-riders can only mean one thing: the Grey Riders.*

"Do you have any final orders for me before I depart to Hellsfont, Lady Adina?" asked Arlene. "His Grace is expecting me."

And I'm sure you'll take every advantage of that. Adina managed to keep from gritting her teeth. *Damned trollop. I need to keep her away from him until I can rectify the situation here.*

"Perhaps." Adina took a slow breath and settled back into her saddle.

The defections didn't look good, but even Golvadu would have to admit that Adina couldn't prevent them from twenty miles away, even if she had command authority in the area.

She drummed her fingers on the saddle pommel. "Lady Arlene, you will write a report to the First Archon. Make sure you present it to me for approval. He will want an accounting for our recent challenges. I hope your report will offer him some successes."

"Yes," Arlene offered. "Our victory here sends a message to anyone contemplating supporting the rebels — and that doesn't count all the booty and overdue taxes we've collected from the other towns. You will recall that rebel raids on storehouses near Southmarket were thwarted, and fifteen enemy collaborators were executed yesterday. I will detail all this in my report and explain it to Lord Golvadu in person."

Adina shook her head. "No, I need you here. These latest defections require our immediate attention."

Arlene stiffened in the saddle. "Milady, I am expected in Hellsfont within a week."

"Are you contradicting me?" Adina asked in a mild tone of voice. She prepared a set of attack spells in her mind.

Arlene bowed in the saddle. "No, milady. It's just that my standing order is to provide Lord Golvadu with regular updates in person."

"I will explain your tardiness to His Grace in an addendum to the report," Adina replied, twisting her reins in her hands. "We need to deal with this now, and I need as many officers loyal to the People's Republic as I can get. He will understand once we get everything under control and suppress the rebellion."

Arlene fell silent. Adina waited, gauging her, trying to determine any sign of resistance, but neither she nor Octavio said anything further.

"Well, we now know what we're up against," Adina continued. "Furthermore, we know the general location of the turncoats. That should help us in counteracting them."

There must be a way to trap Connor and Hannah Loemin. Adina sifted through various scenarios, trying to come up with a way to earn a quick victory and gain influence with Golvadu and the Council. Her eyes wandered to the looted supplies from the town being loaded onto wagons. A sudden inspiration struck her. *Supplies. The rebels need a steady supply line.*

Highmarket! That's the key. "I know how to destroy the rebel army," Adina stated, sitting up straighter in the saddle. "Highmarket."

Arlene and Octavio exchanged a glance.

"You think Highmarket is an opportunity?" asked Octavio.

Adina nodded. "The rebels now have at least ten thousand troops plus mounts and draft animals to supply. Highmarket has warehouses stuffed with everything an army could need. If we move on the city, the rebels have to respond. We have three divisions within two days march of the city, plus support from the Vardish and Cla'Agik churches. We can trap and overwhelm them."

Arlene shifted in the saddle. "Yes, milady, but I feel it important to remind you that the Grey Riders can upset the balance easily. We will need our own specialists to counteract them."

"Of course," Adina smiled. "Like you."

Arlene started. "Me?"

You stepped right into it. Now you have to stay here instead of whispering lies to the First Archon. "Of course," Adina replied. "You have field command experience and I understand you are an accomplished assassin in your own right. Plus, you can Shadow Jump. Isn't that how you managed to escape Deran after killing off your husband?"

Arlene stared straight ahead and Adina smirked. *Didn't know I knew about that, did you?* "You will command the 8th Division and Lord Berek will direct the 9th Division. I will be in charge of the operation, as well as commanding the 3rd Division."

Octavio frowned at Arlene and she shook her head. "Are you certain this is what you want?" he said. "Surely the current commanders are more than capable."

"In massed warfare, yes. In dealing with high-ranking specialists like the Riders, no. Any one of them can easily turn the tide of battle with their skills and their effect on morale."

Arlene fidgeted in her saddle. "At last count, there were six of them. We are only three."

She has a point. The image of Balris and Tarvener came into Adina's head and she realized how to counteract the Riders and curry favor with the

Daemons. "I think we can prevail upon our allies from Hades to assist us. They did, after all, offer us much in the way of ancient magic and military support, didn't they?"

Arlene's expression turned from doubt to wariness. "They did. However, while a Daemon can fly to Highmarket, I cannot."

Adina smirked. "I have a solution." She pointed at the rear of her formation. The Drake and two Sarkany preened themselves while the courier spoke with a Halfling officer near the slave wagons. The Drake caught her eye and inclined his head with a toothy smile.

Adina smiled. "I hope you're not afraid of heights, Lady Arlene."

<<>>

Thomas Cardinal Williams, Papal Nuncio to Damora, dreamed.

He walked along a bluff by an unfamiliar coastline. Dark clouds covered much of the land and yet he made out the form of a mighty port city and harbor through the murk.

He tried to walk faster, but as often happens in dreams, he made little progress. Then the sun rose in the east and he saw bright points of light advancing on the shadowed land. With supernatural vision, he peered at the lights, finally distinguishing forms. To his amazement, he recognized Connor and Hannah Loemin, accompanied by the Alenar sisters and their husbands.

A warm, friendly voice spoke. "Go forth. Preach the Gospel." A shining golden crown hovered over the city. A gleaming tower reflected the light.

Then eight flags advanced from the north and wherever they moved, the shadow faded.

Father Tom's eyes fluttered open and he blinked, disoriented. Slowly he recognized the details of his bedchamber. Early morning light peeked in through the curtains.

Another dream. Much like the others.

He sat up. In spite of the images still in his head and his state of bemusement, he felt energized and eager to discuss his latest visions.

But with whom? Sister Karen is still in Alrihan.

Father Thomas swung his legs out of bed and dressed quickly, splashing water on his face. He ran a razor over his cheeks and chin, racking his brain for someone else in Saint Martin's Town who might understand.

Melinor. He snapped his fingers and snatched up his skullcap, settling it on his curly black hair.

Without another thought, he set off into the pathways of the Chancery, heading for the guest wing on the other side of the gardens. Birds sang overhead to herald the arrival of spring and a gentle wind brushed the greenery in the garden. A particularly plump male pigeon cooed at him from a tree branch as he passed and he couldn't help smiling.

"Good morning, Puup. I trust everything is well?"

As if it could understand, the pigeon bobbed his head and cooed again.

"Keep up the good work," Father Tom said. He moved quickly to Melinor's door and rapped on it with his knuckles.

"Enter."

Melinor leaned on the frame of a tall window, awash in morning sunshine. His white robes and mantle made him seem almost angelic.

Melinor turned to face him and the Papal Nuncio quickly schooled his features to neutrality. *He looks older every week.*

"Is this a good time?" he asked.

The wizard smiled. "Of course, Your Eminence. I'm usually up at this time anyway. Good of you to come and see me. Is this a social call or something requiring more focus?"

Despite Melinor's cheerful words, Father Tom saw weariness in his eyes. "A little of both," he responded. "How are you feeling?"

"Much the same. But that's not important. I can see from the look on your face that something is amiss. Tell me. Break the monotony of people inquiring into my health and recommending I rest. I need something more stimulating." His eyes twinkled.

Father Tom chuckled. "Still the same Melinor. All right then. How are you at dream interpretation?"

Melinor gestured at a padded chair and took a seat opposite it. "Middling. Are you sure you don't want to ask another cleric? Sister Karen or Sister Carla perhaps?"

"I thought of that," said the Nuncio, easing himself into the seat. "They're both on assignment in Alrihan and Deorfast, respectively, and won't be back for a week at least."

"Well, let me have it," Melinor replied, laying his hands in his lap, eyes twinkling anew. "And don't spare the juicy details."

Father Thomas described the dream in full. "It's similar to others I've had lately," he finished.

"Hmm. You're sure you saw the Riders?"

"Very sure. Though they were small figures, my vision in the dream was ridiculously sharp."

Melinor took a deep breath. "Well, I can readily assume that the darkness is the oppressive People's Republic and that the Riders symbolize a bright new future. How was this dream different than the others?"

Father Tom chewed his lip. "There was no crown in the other dreams. Plus, I saw all of the Riders this time, not just one or two."

Melinor sat in silence for a while. "What do we know of conditions in Torosc now?"

"My spies report that Loemin — or Bluevale as the Torosci call it — is in great turmoil. Rumors abound of the finding of ancient heirlooms of the royal house and of a rebel army growing by leaps and bounds. They tell of skirmishes and pitched battles near small villages. It appears that Connor and Hannah are meeting with success."

"But…?"

Father Tom frowned, unable to shake a sense of urgency. "The Riders are up against steep odds. The last surviving Archon, Golvadu, will not sit by and let the Loemins retake their kingdom, let alone the Aldenar sisters."

Melinor tapped his fingers on the arm of his chair. His gaze wandered to the window and Father Tom followed his eyes. The flags of Deran and the Church fluttered from guard towers atop the walls.

"Flags." Melinor murmured. He turned sharp eyes to Father Tom. "How many did you see in your dream?"

"Eight."

Melinor gave a little smile. "Ah. Now I see."

"See what?"

Melinor stood. "The Northern Alliance is composed of Deran, Astarel, Eldir, Rokon and Evendale."

"Yes, but that's only five."

Melinor hobbled to his desk and picked up his staff. "The other three are Terenai, Merdail and Gorostol."

Tom stood, his mind sifting through this latest information. "So the flags represent allies coming to help the Riders?"

Melinor nodded. "Just as King Seamus requested before the Riders were sent on their mission." He waved towards the door. "I believe we need to pay the Alliance Council a visit in Oakmoor."

"Oakmoor is several days ride," Father Tom reminded him, following him out into the garden pathways.

Melinor smirked, removing a ring of blue metal from his belt purse. "I have ways. Just be glad you haven't had breakfast yet."

"Your Eminence!" A young priest in a black cassock jogged towards them, a bone tube in his hands. "A message for you by Telepost! It's marked Urgent."

"Thank you, Father Steven," Father Tom answered, taking the scrollcase. He tapped the seal on one end with his signet ring. A mild orange light flashed for a split second.

He withdrew the scroll and read it. As he did so, his heartbeat quickened. *Yes! Thank you, Jesus!* He handed the scroll to Melinor.

"Father Steven," the Nuncio said, "please bring my pectoral cross and mantle from my room. Be quick."

The priest hurried away.

Melinor looked up from the scroll. "This is the last piece of information we needed. The dream itself may not be enough, but this," he handed the paper back, "will certainly convince the Council. Connor and Hannah are winning."

"So quickly though!" Father Thomas mused, eyes roaming the text once again. "They have conquered Ostor and Havenridge in a matter of a few days. The entire northern pass to Gorostol is open. We could have a support force in Loemin within a few weeks."

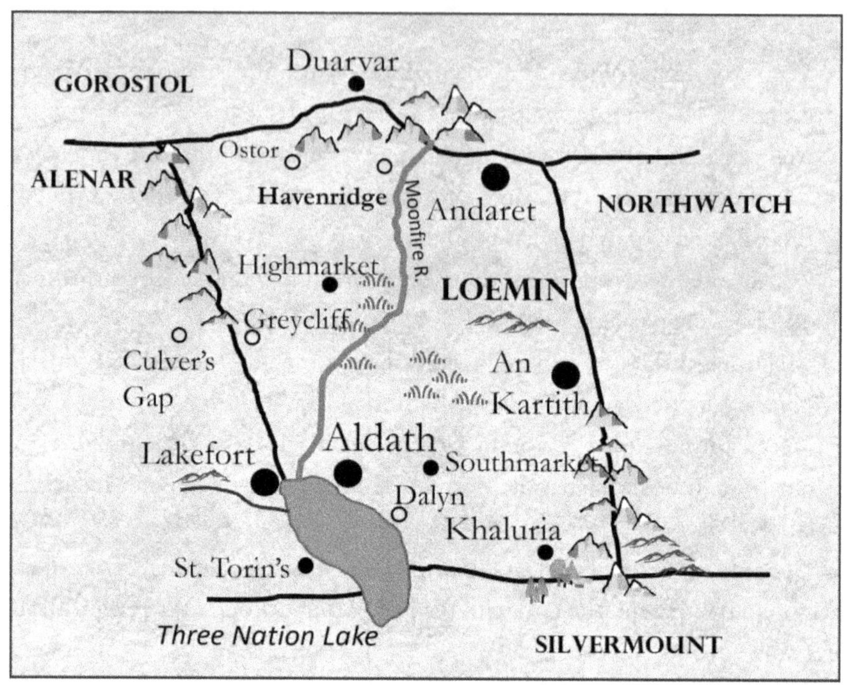

Melinor squared his shoulders as Father Steven hustled back with the Nuncio's mantle and cross. "The time has come to act."

"Can we get help to them in time?" Father Thomas asked, fitting on his white mantle and settling the cross on his chest.

"We will have to." Melinor slipped the blue ring onto his index finger and took Father Thomas' hand. "Hold on."

"Wait, what are you —"

The universe flexed and warped. The gardens melded into a riot of color, then resolved into the palace courtyard in Oakmoor, Deran. Father Thomas fought nausea and disorientation, staring uncomprehending around him. Guards came to attention and an orderly gaped, then took off sprinting.

Melinor smiled. "That should get their attention."

Chapter Seventeen – Lift High the Banners

Connor ran a hand over his new black leather brigandine, fingers pausing on the etched symbol of a golden badger. Magic tingled under his touch. Phantom pawed the ground and tossed her head. An honor guard of seven armored centaurs waited silently nearby. "What a difference five weeks makes," he mused.

"It certainly does," replied Hannah from her seat behind him. "And the people of Ostor and Havenridge are better off for it, don't you think?"

A vast array of troops spread before him on the hills. Orderly blocks of infantry, archers and cavalry waited quietly in the late winter sunshine. He lost count of the many pennons and flags.

"You have two whole divisions of regulars, eight regiments of militia, two companies of engineers, and two centaur tribal bands," Hannah noted.

He shook his head in admiration. "I'm glad I have you around. I have no idea how you keep all the military units straight."

He heard the smile in her voice. "Go easy on yourself. It's a lot to re-member."

"*You* don't seem to have any trouble."

"I have my training and Alex Fejer to help me. He's worth his weight in gold ingots, I tell you. Speaking of remembering, don't forget that some Sun-coast Clan dragons arrive today."

"Thank Irial!" Connor scanned the nearby units, his eyes alighting on the familiar figure of Alex Fejer. The captain gestured to a Halfling militia colo-nel, pointing out something near their artillery formations.

Alex and Varani have worked so hard to coordinate between the various military units. I don't know where we'd be without them. I'll make sure everyone knows it, too.

Connor's eyes drifted to the city of Highmarket spread out before them on the plains. Flags depicting a gold badger on a green field fluttered above the stone walls, signifying the city's new allegiance to the House of Loemin.

"That's a wonderful sight, isn't it?" Hannah said, pointing at the flag. "I must have seen that in more than a dozen towns and villages in the last month, but it never gets old."

"Now it's up to us to make sure it stays our city, no matter what the PRT brings against us," Connor replied. *And they'll bring plenty.*

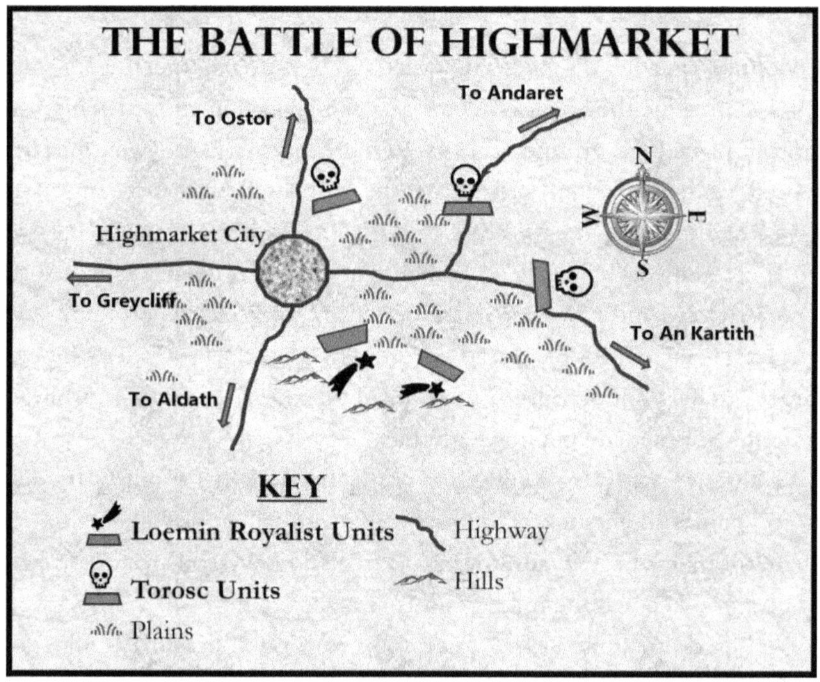

Connor scanned beyond the city. Three highways curved in across the plains from the north, northeast and southeast. Along each, a glittery snake of enemy soldiery advanced, accompanied by their own artillery and, worst of all, by several dragons circling lazily in the air.

They sure moved fast when they figured out Highmarket had joined the rebellion.

He lapsed into silence, his stomach in knots, watching the enemy approaching. He knew the battle plan well: attack the nearest formation at first opportunity to prevent it from linking up with the other two, then drive them towards the city to get the advantage of fixed artillery there.

And what happens if the plan doesn't work? He tried to relax, breathing evenly. *We have fallback plans, but what of the people in Highmarket? The PRT has shown its wrath against people who support us.*

Brandi drifted down out of the sky near them on her pegasus. Connor's centaur bodyguard drew back to let her land.

She cantered Amicus up to Connor's side and halted, her mount's chain-mail barding jingling. "Well, we're as ready as we'll ever be. The generals have the battle plan set. And Gorlak's eager to spring his little surprise."

Connor took a glance at a copse of trees near the southern road by a small pond. "We're going to need it." He twisted the reins in his hands.

Come on. You've been in battles before.

"What did Eric see with Stealth?" Hannah asked behind him.

Brandi squinted into the sun. "We're up against three full-strength Republic divisions that include Red Veils, Skullheads and Vardish Death Army. He also saw Cla'Agik priests and sorcerers, ogres and Goblins. Our instincts were right. The forces of evil have formed a new alliance."

"A very big one," Connor muttered. Hannah gave him a pinch in the side.

"Yes, but we have the advantage in terrain, the approaches are trapped — though I'm sure they've also realized that — and we have a few surprises in store," said Hannah.

She looked up at Brandi. "Anyone special in their command structure?"

"Well, one you already know: Lady Arlene Culver, the Deranese Ja'al agent who assassinated Lord Dunston Culver before fleeing to join the enemy for the War. Eric also recognized Adina Tenspire."

"Who?" Hannah asked.

Brandi's eyes flashed but her voice remained even. "A Ja'al sorcerer who captured Megan and me before the War. Her troops killed my aunt and uncle."

"I'm so sorry," Hannah said.

Brandi looked down and gave her a sad smile. "Thanks. I know Aunt Daphne and Uncle Stephen are looking down on us right now and praying for our success."

Connor frowned. "Adina seldom goes anywhere without her lover, Berek Lordwain, another Ja'al wizard. He's out there somewhere."

Brandi nodded. "We need to take care of both of them, honestly."

Connor gave her a look. "Settling a score? She's the one who turned you into a vampire."

Brandi shook her head. "I'm more interested in preventing her from harming the people of Loemin. She's the one who's been burning villages."

Connor bit his lip. *What if we forgot something? And, more importantly, where are the Suncoast dragons?*

Brandi seemed to read his mind. "Don't worry, Connor. It will all work out. You just lead by example."

"Is that my job?" he said, distracted. "Can I still abdicate?"

Hannah poked him in the side and he smirked. "Scratch that. I have a job as a figurehead."

That earned him another poke. "You're here to inspire them and take out targets of opportunity," Hannah said. "Be glad the generals don't expect you to command large units in massed warfare."

She's right. Part of leadership is delegation. I have to have confidence in the divisional commanders and their subordinates, or I'm lost anyway.

A dark blue mage flare rose up out of the plains from the tall grass.

"That's the signal. The enemy have reached a trip point," Brandi said, pointing. A trio of scouts wearing Connor's livery pelted on horseback towards them.

Brandi raised her hands over them and murmured soft words. A filmy net of blue light settled on Connor and Hannah. "That should give you a little added protection."

She smiled at Connor and raised a hand in benediction over him and Hannah. A sparkling cloud sifted out from her palm and came to rest on them. "Speak to your people, Connor. Tell them how you feel and why you're here. They will follow you anywhere."

She turned her mount. "Take heart. I see our dragon friends approaching from the west." She lifted off and soared towards the right flank.

Connor glanced westward. Four large dragon forms winged in their direction and his spirits lifted. Their tan-gold hide, striped with blue, glimmered as they banked around towards the rebel army. "Just in the nick of time."

Hannah gave Connor a hug. "Go inspire them," she whispered.

Connor fitted his helmet on his head. "Let's do this." He tapped his heels into Phantom's side and the pegasus bore them aloft to hover over the army. His heart hammered in his chest.

He gazed down at the myriad of faces looking up at him. *My people, willing to give their all for me.* His nerves calmed. *Can I become their prince in reality as well as in name?*

"People of Loemin!" he announced. His magically augmented voice boomed over the field, carrying even to the city of Highmarket. "I come to you from a faraway land and claim to be your Prince, acting on behalf of my father. For that is who I am. But do not believe my words alone. Believe my deeds! See Glittershard, Sword of Kings! See Steelwing, Cloak of Queens! Ostor and Havenridge and Pentak and other communities are free for the first time in hundreds of years! My Princess and I are here with you, fighting alongside you, risking everything. For you, my people, we will lay down our lives. Fight alongside us! Fight for our future! For Loemin!"

For a couple of terrifying heartbeats, he wasn't sure he had inspired anyone. Then the army broke out in cheers and chants of "Loemin! Loemin!" Infantry banged their spears and swords on their shields and bannermen waved their pennons in the wind.

Will it be enough to carry them through the battle? Connor wondered, watching the enemy advance.

"I'm proud of you, love," Hannah said, kissing the back of his neck armor.

Drums rolled, pipes skirled and officers bawled orders. In large, orderly blocks, Connor's army moved out.

Hannah's arm tightened around his waist. "We'll be fine, dear. Trust to Irial the Benevolent and to our commanders."

Connor swooped back towards his royal guard contingent.

"Captain Brightgrove," Hannah announced to the lead centaur, her amplified voice carrying over the sound of drums and trumpets, "we leave you for the time being. Make sure you pick out a safe landing spot in case we need to return quickly. If you see an advantage to joining in the fray or danger to us, attack at your best discretion."

The centaur saluted and motioned to her command. They cantered off to a cleared grassy space below.

Connor turned his attention to the battlefield. The commander of the nearest Torosci division apparently decided to force the issue. Howling Goblins led a charge, mounted on Fell Wolves. Ogres in brigandine thundered after them, chanting in low, harsh tones and wielding massive axes and clubs. Skullhead cavalry rode at their flanks, nightmarish helmets gleaming in the sunlight. Enemy wizards chanted and some of Connor's carefully-laid traps flashed and faded out.

They won't get all of them, Connor thought grimly. As if in answer, other rebel traps went off, flashing in bright explosions of fire, electricity or ice, carving holes in the charging enemy force. Just as quickly, enemy spellcasters cast waves of sparkling purple light over the grassy plains and the remaining traps dissipated.

Phase one.

Arrows and glittering artillery rounds arced from both sides. Magical shields flared, explosions bloomed and figures dropped. Lightning sizzled and firedarts riddled the ranks of soldiery. Then the two forces collided with an impact Connor heard from five hundred feet above.

His heart ached for the troops he knew would die. *They will fight for me, for our Kingdom, and gladly. I have to be worthy of them.*

As if reading his mind, Hannah squeezed him. "We will win. We will make sure their sacrifices are not in vain," she said over the wind.

Near one of Connor's generals, wizards thrust forth their hands in unison and a large fog bank billowed from the ground on the right flank of the enemy army. Centaurs bearing Halfling warriors raced out. They wheeled about into the fogbank. Though enemy sorcerers unleashed wind to blow away the thick mist, the cavalry erupted out the other side, crunching into the Torosci lines, throwing them into confusion.

Hannah pointed. The other enemy divisions hustled towards the battle.

It won't be long before this gets really ugly.

"Aim for a ballista team," Hannah called. "Taking out their artillery will give us an advantage."

Connor veered Phantom around. Clasping his legs around his mount, he drew an arrow to his bow. The enemy soldiers scrambled to ratchet their weapon to bear on them but Phantom's rate of turn made it impossible. A sizzling yellow ballista bolt shot past, missing by forty feet. Hannah and Connor loosed, dropping the team sergeant. Connor swung around again and repeated the maneuver, felling another soldier. The rest of the ballista team scattered. Enemy archers raced to help and returned fire. Phantom easily avoided the shafts, pulling upward.

Out of the corner of his eye, Connor saw a flash of dark green and red and snatched the reins with his free hand, banking left. A jet of steaming green acid shot past, followed by a twenty-five-foot long Sarkany with red glowing eyes.

Well, now they play some of their high value cards. Connor spurred Phantom in pursuit. The enemy dragon wove left and right. Connor stayed on its tail. Hannah loosed twice but missed.

Connor saw a flash of black pegasus wings out of the corner of his eye. Dar swooped in, hitting the dragon in the side with two arrows and zipping past. The dragon flipped on its back, gliding. It gestured with one claw. A storm of fire darts snapped out at them. Four exploded on Connor's magic shields and Dar swung around in a loop.

Connor and Hannah loosed glittering arrows as one. They thumped into the dragon's belly, bursting with networks of tiny lightning bolts. The dragon roared in pain and swung around towards them, breathing another stream of acid. Connor dove and the jet sizzled past.

"It's on our tail!" Hannah screamed into his ear.

Connor banked left and right, then climbed. More acid lanced at them and this time droplets burned his wrist and neck. *That was a little close.*

He shot a glance over his shoulder. The dragon pursued, moving its claws in a circular pattern. A fireball grew before it.

Connor pulled up and Phantom whinnied in protest, braking into a hover. The dragon shot past with a shriek of frustration — right into Dar's charge.

Dar swung Rindara Starblade in a mighty arc. The Celestial blade flared white and the Sarkany's head flew off into the battle raging below. The corpse continued its glide, then tumbled over and over before slamming into the ground and digging a furrow in the earth.

Connor saluted Dar, who returned the salute and soared past, heading for an enemy catapult team.

"She'll need healing!" Hannah shouted. Connor spared a look down at Phantom's legs. One looked burned.

No wonder she whinnied…

He swung around, heading for the original enemy division. He easily made out the figure of a brunette in red robes, casting lightning and fire darts into rebel formations. Next to her, a trio of ogres in chainmail slammed down any foe daring to come close.

"Adina!" Connor shouted, pointing.

A pair of Cla'Agik priests chanted. Green light flared on wounded enemy troops. They climbed to their feet and charged into the fray. Rebel soldiers gave way before the renewed assault, retreating as magic spells burst on protective shields. Reserves hustled towards the fight.

"Adina's the key!" Hannah tapped him on the thigh. "We need to take her out or drive her back!"

He looped around for another run, this time heading for the Ja'al sorceress. He sighted an arrow with a blue-glittering head. Hannah held an identical one in her bow alongside his shoulder. As they swung around, they loosed arrows twice more. The shafts missed Adina, hitting an ogre in the chest instead. The shafts exploded in a burst of lightning and hurled the ogre backward to lie in a smoldering heap.

Adina turned to face them, screaming something. One of the white-robed priests threw back his hood. Together the pair cast up a coruscating shield of red fire. Connor and Hannah's arrows burst into flame and fluttered to the ground.

Connor recognized the man at Adina's side. *That's where Berek is!*

Berek and Adina handed dead-black arrows to nearby archers. The shafts writhed like serpents.

Something about the arrows caused Connor's heart to freeze in his chest. *Wait. What the hell are those?*

He pulled up Phantom and dodged left and right. The arrows zipped past, then detonated into clouds of thin black strands, like ebony spider webs. Unable to stop, Connor's pegasus ran straight into the filmy mass.

Phantom beat her wings frantically, but the tendrils entangled her as if she were a giant moth. She struggled, losing altitude. Enemy archers drew a bead on them. Arrows zipped past, narrowly missing one of Phantom's wings.

Connor drew Glittershard. He cut through a few of the strands but with difficulty: they wiggled like earthworms.

This is not good!

Hannah drew Shriek and sliced into nearby tendrils, ducking to avoid another arrow winging past. One cut tendril snapped across Connor's wrist and burned like acid. Phantom's breathing became labored and she faltered, drifting downwards.

"Come on, girl!" Connor called to her, trying to ignore the stinging of the cut filaments. "You can do it."

A lightning bolt burst on their shields and Phantom veered. Brandi's protections fizzled and went out. A fusillade of fire darts exploded on Phantom's barding and Connor's armor. He gasped. Phantom's wingbeats ceased. They plummeted downward.

Great Irial help us! He could do nothing but hold on as the ground rushed towards them.

"I love you, Connor!" Hannah screamed, squeezing him tightly.

Then a great taloned claw of gold and blue swept down before his eyes, gently clasping Phantom around the neck. Phantom whinnied in alarm as another claw grasped her about the withers, behind Hannah. Connor looked up.

A massive True Dragon lifted them all, pegasus and riders, as if hefting a sack of potatoes. He gave them a toothy dragon-grin, then soared upward and towards the rebel lines. Arrows sang past and shells boomed behind them.

"Thank the Great Creator," Connor breathed. He patted the dragon's claw in gratitude.

Enemy artillery opened fire. The dragon suddenly swung left, then right. Two glowing shells spat past them, trailing sparks. Twenty feet above the dragon, they detonated.

Hot fragments of stone peppered them. Connor gasped again. The dragon took the brunt of it. He swept left and right, avoiding a sparkling ballista bolt but another shell detonated on his left, lashing him with hot metal shards. Blood and smoke streamed from the dragon's wings.

He's taking the damage to protect us! Looking down, Connor saw his centaur escort gallop towards them at full speed.

"Land!" Connor yelled up at the dragon. He pointed down. "There! My guard comes to join us! Don't risk yourself!"

The dragon nodded wearily, heading for a clear spot near the edge of the battlefield. He slowed as he neared the ground, then released Phantom and stumbled to a crash landing ten yards away, bowling over two Skullhead knights.

Connor's pegasus staggered upon landing but stayed on her feet. His centaur guards thundered to a halt near him.

"Captain! Shield wall!" Hannah screamed to them. The centaurs formed a barrier, shields and swords up.

"Stay behind us, Highness!" Captain Brightgrove called. The dragon retreated to stand next to them.

Connor slid out of the saddle and fumbled for his belt pouch, his arms and legs aching as adrenaline wore off and the pain of his injuries set in. Hannah tumbled off, landing on all fours. He pressed a healing potion into her hands. She downed it as he fed one to Phantom, then swallowed another for himself, trying to ignore the flavor of beets, lemon peel and cloves. The burning of his injuries eased though everything still ached.

Connor searched for his bow but it was gone. He tapped the brooch on his tunic and his guardian blade flowed out of it, hovering in front of him. Glittershard flared azure. Brushing sweat-matted hair out of his eyes, he strode to the dragon's side.

Wild combat raged all around them. Connor saw a trio of rebel Halflings dance and dodge away from the looping axe swings of a pair of Skullheads, stabbing with spear and sword. A centaur and a Torosci knight hammered away at each other, whirling and slamming each other's shields. Knots of struggling warriors formed a hellish, chaotic background and clouds of smoke billowed up into the air. A fireball exploded in the distance. He heard the guttural shout of an Ogre over the din and the crunch of metal and bone. Dragons swooped and grappled in midair, breathing fire and ice, tearing at each other to spiral down trailing smoke. The air stank of fire, brimstone, blood and death.

"Bows! Clear a path!" Brightgrove shouted. The centaurs switched to their bows and loosed. The dragon waited until their shafts found their marks, then then spat streams of flame at nearby enemy formations. Many fell, skewered or roasted, but a phalanx of heavy infantry with shields and spears trotted towards them, accompanied by ogres and Cla'Agik priests.

Adina and Berek advanced behind them. Her robes swirled around her with a life of their own, snapping to deflect arrows and darts, red sigils glittering along the hem. Her braided brown hair whipped behind her like a lash and her eyes blazed with hate. Electricity raced along her forearms. Berek stalked forwards at her side, a cloud of swirling dots of light surrounding him like guardian fireflies, absorbing flames and firedarts alike.

Connor's blood ran cold and he recalled the Nuncio's words about magic from Hades. *Those must be Daemonic spells!*

"Kill the Halfling royals!" screamed Berek. The infantry and ogres responded with a shout.

"Captain Brightgrove, shield wall to the right!" Hannah shouted.

Connor's centaur guard loosed again, then switched to swords and shields against the charge, wheeling about to block the path of the enemy.

The dragon shot a jet of flame at Berek and Adina. They joined hands and raised their free fists to the sky. A green translucent wall arced in front of them and their troops. The dragon's flame curved around it, then, impossibly, shot back at Connor and his allies.

Connor seized Hannah and ducked. The dragon shielded them with his body against his own breath. Some of the centaurs fell, writhing in pain, their armor afire, but the remainder held their ground.

"How Adina and Berek reflect a dragon's breath?" Hannah gasped, drawing Shriek. "I've never seen that before, even during the War!"

"It's Daemon magic, like Father Thomas said!" Connor shouted over the din of battle. He leapt out from behind the dragon.

A Torosci squad charged from the left flank. *"Gurus Ux,"* Connor snapped, pointing his sword in that direction. A ten-foot tall, twenty-foot-wide wall of thick ice sprang up. Soldiers slammed into it and fell backwards, stunned. Those following behind them tripped, falling in a heap on top of them.

Adina shouted and thrust her hands towards him. The ground exploded upward and a cloud of fist-sized rocks shot at him.

"Steelwing, protect me!" Hannah yelled and enveloped Connor in her cloak. It instantly hardened into a metal wall. The stones thumped heavily into it.

"Enemies desist!" Hannah shouted. A bright light flashed over their heads and Connor heard a collective cry of dismay from the enemy, then Berek cursing.

Nicely done, sweetheart!

"Done, Steelwing!" The metal cloak returned to cloth. Connor emerged and Hannah lifted her shield.

Half of the centaurs lay on the ground, but the enemy stood blinking in confusion.

This is our chance! While they're blinded! "Follow me!" Connor shouted and leapt into the fray, slashing with Glittershard. "For Loemin!" His guardian blade danced and thrust before him. Hannah followed at his side.

An ogre swung a mace. Connor and Hannah danced aside and the ogre's strike pulverized a rock. Connor jumped up, planted a boot on the ogre's thigh and vaulted onto its back. He drove Glittershard into the ogre's skull. The creature didn't even have time to scream as its head turned into a block of ice. It toppled over and Connor hopped off.

Connor's dragon ally breathed a fiery cloud at Adina. She cast up a pearlescent, translucent screen and the flame curled around her, lighting the tall grass and nearby corpses on fire. She retreated, coughing, behind a cloud of smoke and flame.

Hannah leapt to Connor's side. She raised her shield and three glowing sling bullets exploded in flame on it. She darted forward and rolled under the wild swing of a Skullhead sergeant with a battle axe. Coming up, she stabbed him in the thigh with Shriek, dodged a spear thrust from a Halfling warrior, and sidestepped a snarling, snapping Fell Wolf. She slammed the Wolf in the face with her shield.

Connor's dancing sword impaled the Wolf in the eye. Hannah spun around the Skullhead sergeant, grabbed the Halfling's spear, and stabbed a nearby soldier in the heart with it before beheading the Halfling.

The sergeant whirled around, cursing and swinging his axe high. Hannah rolled away. The axe bit into the earth. Connor hamstrung the sergeant with Glittershard and the man's leg iced over. He screamed. As he fell, Hannah lopped his head off with Shriek.

Hannah and Connor returned to their positions, back-to-back.

"Move aside, you fools! I need a clear shot at the Halfling scum!" Adina shrieked.

"I'll handle this!" Berek bellowed in return. He shouted harsh words in a dark language.

Three nearby ogres grunted and warped, transforming into growling Tiger Daemons.

Connor gaped. *The Ogres were actually polymorphed Daemons? What the Hell?*

The Daemons laughed and snarled, rushing at them.

Connor pointed Glittershard at one of them. *"Uxil Dlabit!"*

The Daemon halted in mid-stride, encased in a block of ice, but the other two hurtled on. Connor dodged, slashing one in the midsection. It howled with rage, its scale mail armor icing over. Out of the corner of his eye, he saw Berek cast lightning. Connor ducked. The twin-forked bolt slammed into Connor's dragon ally behind him and the dragon staggered backwards. Connor swept his hand and his guardian sword attacked Berek, stabbing and slashing. The wizard cursed and backed away, dodging the darting blade.

"Your right!" screamed Hannah. Connor stepped to his left, avoiding the rush of a Daemon. The Fallen One yowled in frustration and swung. Connor sidestepped and stabbed it in the leg. An arrow zipped by his head. He ducked and another shaft thumped into his side, flaring with red fire. Agony shot through him and he went to one knee. The Daemon clouted him in the chest and he flew backwards, tumbling into Hannah and landing on a dead centaur. He tried to rise, grimacing from the pain in his side.

"This isn't going so well," Hannah gasped, struggling to her feet. Blood ran down her forehead and burns marked her plate armor.

The two Daemons laughed in triumph. Connor heard a whoosh and Dar swooped by on his pegasus, the Starblade flashing in an ebon arc. A headless Daemon keeled over and exploded. Connor ducked, narrowly missing a bone fragment in the eye.

The remaining Tiger Daemon tumbled out of the way.

Dar wheeled his pegasus around and landed near Connor's force, his blade up and glowing with starlight.

"Damn you!" Berek raged. "Damn all of you!"

His fist glowed black. He punched the air at the Daemon frozen by Connor's ice block. The giant cube of frost disintegrated in a hiss of steam.

Connor gripped Glittershard's handle with a white-knuckled hand. *Well, that didn't last long.*

Connor's dragon ally lumbered forwards, jaws agape and swordlike talons reaching. Adina whirled her fists in front of her and made a pushing motion at the dragon. A blue orb of light struck him in the chest. He jerked backward as if hit by a massive fist and fell on his side, head lolling unsteadily.

The two remaining Daemons gathered themselves and stalked towards Connor, but Dar gave his trademark, devil-may-care grin. "Too afraid to fight me, eh? Or are you just little house-kittens for your masters? Poor kitty cats!" He blew them a kiss.

The Tiger Daemons shrieked in fury and charged. Dar leapt his pegasus into the air. The Daemons took wing, howling and hissing as they pursued.

Berek shook his fists in rage. "No! You idiots! The royals!"

With another whoosh, Brandi landed next to Connor. Her armor shone and her red-gold tresses glowed. For a moment, Connor saw what her Celestial ancestors must have looked like.

"*Sanari!*" she said. A pulse of blue light burst from her, washing over the wounded rebels. The pain of Connor's injuries faded and he recalled his guardian blade to his side.

"The Kingdom of Alenar stands with Loemin," Brandi announced.

The enemy force stared, open-mouthed, as injured rebels regained their feet.

Adina gasped. "This must be some trick! That's Celestial magic! Impossible!"

"Nothing will be impossible for God," Brandi replied, walking her pegasus forward. Adina's troops halted their advance, uncertainty written on their faces. Connor's force gathered around him, reforming their ranks.

Connor jerked the arrow out of his armor and strode forward with Hannah at his side.

"The Kingdom of Loemin thanks Alenar," he said, hefting Glittershard.

"Loemin? Alenar?" Berek's face contorted in rage. "Lies! The People's Republic rules supreme!"

Berek and Adina slapped the ground and a black cloud of mist puffed up, withering the grass nearby. Connor's troops drew back, coughing and choking.

"Fear not!" Brandi said. "*Refuto!*"

A blast of white light shot out from her and the mist disintegrated. As when Hannah used Steelwing's light, Berek and Adina and their soldiers threw hands before their faces, blinking and cursing.

"Now, Connor!" Hannah leapt at Berek and Connor followed. The dragon roared, charging alongside the centaur guards. Rebel warriors slammed into the enemy ranks.

Brandi charged Adina, who shot a blast of dark fire at her, knocking her out of the saddle. Brandi jumped up, her blades shining with silver light. Adina sneered and fired a rainbow-colored beam at Brandi's pegasus. Amicus froze in mid-step, immobilized by multi-colored cords rooting him to the ground. Brandi stalked forward to meet Connor and Hannah.

Berek stepped back, then to the side. Magical shields flared over his form. Connor's guardian blade slashed and red light burst from each hit. Berek merely sneered. Connor followed with Glittershard. Hannah also thrust and cut, but Berek dodged with superhuman grace and speed. His hands glowed and yellow circles of light deflected the attacks.

"You will not win!" he snarled. "The power of Darkness overcomes all!" He blasted a sheet of coruscating black flame at them.

Hannah transformed Steelwing into a metal dome and the fire roared over her harmlessly. Connor held up the Sword of Ice and it flashed blue-white. The black fire fizzled and went out.

"Darkness is only the absence of light," he retorted.

Berek flicked his hands. Two copies of him shimmered into place next to him, mimicking his motions. Beams of light and firedarts reached out at Connor.

He dodged as best he could but some attacks got through, pummeling him to his knees. His vision swam. To his satisfaction, he saw Berek's images bleeding from several cuts. The wizard panted with effort, deflecting the strikes of Connor's dancing sword and sidestepping.

Damn it! Which one is the real Berek?

Realization hit him and Connor froze. The guardian blade only attacked one of the images.

It has no eyes to be fooled!

Connor jumped forward and impaled the real Berek with Glittershard. The other two images winked out. Connor withdrew the blade and staggered backwards.

Berek clutched his midsection, now rimed with frost and ice. His eyes faded as he stared at Connor and Hannah. "No! *You* were supposed to lose!"

Connor shook his head, panting. "Evil… always… lies," he gasped.

Face twisted with savage wrath, Berek leapt forward, his hands and arms transforming into living flame. Connor sidestepped and Hannah rolled past him.

Berek swiped a fiery arm at Connor's head and he ducked. Coming up under the taller man's guard, he drove Glittershard into Berek's heart. Berek lurched and Hannah beheaded him as he fell.

"NO!" wailed Adina.

Fighting dizziness, Connor leaned against Hannah, trying to locate the other Riders. In his misty vision, Brandawyn fought Adina. Brandi dodged repeated blasts of sizzling black fire, deflecting them with one of her swords glowing now with a holy aura.

"It's over, Adina," Brandi said, striding closer.

"For you it is, you misbegotten whore!" Adina snapped. She made a grasping motion with her left hand and pulled upward. The air went bone-dry. The ground erupted underneath Brandi, shifting into a mass of mud, then engulfed her completely.

She'll suffocate in there. Connor's throat tightened. "Come on, Brandi…"

"You're my slave," Adina chortled at the earthy prison. "You were my slave before and my slave you will always be!"

A crack sizzling with bright light opened in the mud cocoon, then another, then with an abrupt motion, it broke open and fell to the ground. Brandi stepped out, filthy but otherwise whole.

Wow! thought Connor. *I didn't know she could do that!*

"I am no one's slave," Brandi responded. "I am Queen of Alenar. Christ has set me free, forever. Cease this folly, Adina. If you will repent, I will forgive you."

Adina's brow furrowed in confusion and irritation. "Wait. What? You forgive me? Repent? What in the Nine Hells are you babbling about? I want none of your insipid Christian mysticism!"

"Don't you want peace?" Brandi asked, letting her swords drop by her sides. "To live without strife and war and pain?"

Connor marveled. *After everything she's been through at Adina's hands, Brandi still offers her redemption. I don't know that I'd be so magnanimous.*

Adina smirked. "Peace? A weak dream. I want the reign of power, of the deserving over the undeserving masses. In that way, we will progress society and purify the races. There is no other way."

"You are wrong," Brandi said. Her eyes became pools of light. "There is only one Way, and He leads to the Father. If you do not repent and surrender, I will stop you from your depredations on the people of Loemin."

"Adina is finished," Hannah whispered.

"I have the might of Hades," Adina sneered. "I am not afraid of the likes of an insignificant half-breed Elf slut."

Brandi smiled. "You aren't fighting me, but the One who I serve. He is the One who will defeat you."

Adina's face contorted in anger. "Your puny god has no authority over me!" she shrieked in fury, raising her hands high. Out of the mid-air, a hellish blast of flame shot down. Brandi raised her arms and eyes to heaven. A shield of white light sprang up over her, deflecting most of the blast. Adina shot a stream of firedarts at her. They cracked and exploded on the shield and Brandi's armor.

Adina summoned a whip of flame and lashed at Brandi, but the Alenar Queen spun to the left with impossible speed. The whip cracked on empty air, bursting in a cloud of fire. Before Adina could react, Brandi darted forward.

Adina transformed the whip to a curved sword of flame and attempted to take her head off with it. Brandi ducked, then impaled Adina with both blades. The sorceress stared at Brandi in shock and amazement.

"I'm sorry it came to this," Brandi said, sounding truly regretful.

"I will rise from Hell to curse you and your line," Adina gasped out, blood trickling from the corners of her mouth.

Brandi withdrew her blades. "No, you won't."

Adina collapsed in a widening pool of blood. All fighting nearby ceased as Connor's army and the forces of Torosc gazed on the bodies of Berek and

Adina lying dead on the field. Connor's troops cheered in triumph. Then he heard the roar of dragons.

The nearby copse of trees and the pond dissolved into the forms of Gorlak, Kindri and Tholi, accompanied by a battalion of Colonel Whitson's militia. They charged pell-mell into the fray on the enemy's left flank, driving them towards the city walls.

Well-timed, Gorlak.

Captain Brightgrove cantered over. "Stay here, Highnesses. We'll watch over you. Let Major Gorlak and Colonel Whitson do their work."

Connor nodded numbly, his arm around Hannah. The couple leaned on each other, watching the tide of battle turn.

The enemy force retreated from Gorlak's charge, bringing them closer to the city walls. The town artillery opened up, blasting enemy troops with magical catapult rounds and ballista bolts. The gates of Highmarket flew open and the city guard galloped out, leading a roiling mob of citizens.

The divisions of the People's Republic struggled against the new onslaught for a couple of minutes. Many fell on both sides. Then horns sounded from the PRT units and they began a fighting retreat, pulling back from the city.

"Think we can rest now for a bit?" Hannah rasped. She was filthy, covered in dirt, grass and blood. Dark char marked her armor and one side of her breastplate looked melted. She sagged into Connor, favoring one leg, blood running down her right arm. He held her up despite his own weariness.

"Yes, we can, beautiful," he said, kissing her.

She pulled back and smiled, her eyes bright with love. "Got any more of those healing potions?"

"I think I can find a couple. Or ten," he whispered.

He watched the enemy retreat before the forces of Loemin — his people now.

Yes. My people. You will be free. This is just the beginning.

Chapter Eighteen – Paths Long Forgotten

"How was that, Your Highness?" Hannah asked with a dreamy smile.

"Spectacular, as always, Your Highness." Connor put his arm around her and she laid her head on his chest. She kissed his neck and he stroked her smooth, strong shoulders and back, down to her tailbone.

He rested in her embrace, staring up at the underside of the massive pavilion, as large as a human-sized house. Embroidered figures of spear-wielding centaurs and flying owls decorated the walls of their inner chamber.

Hannah sighed. "I'm glad we finally have a few moments peace, even if we have to sneak lovemaking into the early morning hours."

"I know, and I'm sorry our life has to be like this."

She swatted his shoulder. "Don't be. We're in this together, for keeps."

Thank you, Great Lord Irial. She is a blessing.

From outside their pavilion, familiar sounds came to him: the clank of metal, calls of soldiers in the distance, whinnies of horses and occasional laughter. The faint aroma of brewed jekka, rice pudding, and bacon drifted on the breeze.

He heard Gorlak's voice outside, then the muffled reply of one of the guards. Connor sighed. "As much as I hate to admit it, sweetheart, we do have to get up and get on with the day."

"No." Hannah murmured, nestling closer. "Send them away and make love to me again."

"I only wish. Come on, Crown Princess. Duty calls."

With an exasperated huff, Hannah rolled off him and the couple dressed in matching green and gold: a long velvet dress and slippers for her and leggings, high boots and tunic for him.

A bell rang at the tent entrance. "Come in," Connor said.

"Ah, young lovers awake now! Good. I bring breakfast." Gorlak ambled into the massive inner chamber, the size of a large living room. A Halfling orderly followed him, pushing a cart laden with covered bowls and trays. Gorlak gestured to a carved wooden table on the opposite side of the tent. The orderly spread a tablecloth and began laying out ceramic dishes and silver utensils.

Hannah gave him a brilliant smile. "That's very sweet of you, Gorlak."

The Goblin waved a hand. "Not at all. Many challenges in early marriage even without war. Need time for each other."

"And how would you know this Gorlak?" Connor asked, pulling matching carved wooden chairs to the table.

Gorlak raised an eyebrow, black eyes amused. "It surprise you to know I married before?"

Connor halted and set down a couple of chairs. "Really?"

Gorlak nodded. Hannah put her hands on her hips. "Why didn't you tell us?"

"Not a happy memory." Gorlak's demeanor turned somber.

Hannah blinked and her cheeks reddened. "Oh. I'm… sorry Gorlak."

He patted her hand. "It okay. Goblin marriages not like yours. More like business arrangements."

"What happened to her?" Connor asked, setting the chairs by the table. The orderly finished arranging eight place settings and bowed, then departed.

Gorlak poured himself a mug of jekka. The bracing aroma filled the tent. "Don't know. Her family not approve of me: not ambitious enough. After first four kids, she demand to have me removed in favor of more wealthy leader. Since she related to chieftain, I go."

Connor gaped at him. Hannah gasped. "You have *children?*"

Gorlak nodded. "Two male, two female."

Sweet Irial. Connor gazed at him with sympathy. "And something tells me you don't know if they're alive or not either."

Gorlak stared at the wall of the pavilion, eyes distant. "No. But you need understand: Goblin children property of tribe, not parents. After short time, they taken to be trained in whatever chieftain and chieftain's wives decide. I not know mine very well at all. Anyway, they grown now."

"But still, they were your children. I think it's pretty heartless for your wife to separate you from them for her own gain," Hannah said, taking a mug for herself.

Gorlak gave a rueful shrug. "Goblin society heartless. In any case, I not allowed to interact with them often — always on missions for chieftain. Then our tribe work for Halkith the Grey near Forester to find pegasi of White-horse Peak. That is when I meet Grey Riders for first time. And you know the rest."

Gorlak had a family? And his wife had him removed out of greed! Connor's mind whirled as he took a plate and loaded it with bacon, sausage, fluffy rolls, tropical fruit salad and honey cakes.

The trio sat at the table and ate in silence. Connor struggled for something to say. Finally, halfway done, he turned to Gorlak. "I know we seem a bit flabbergasted, but I guess I never thought of you with a family and grown children. You seem so young."

Gorlak set down his fork and peered at him. "How old you think I am?"

Hannah exchanged a look with Connor. "Thirty?"

Gorlak tossed his head back and laughed heartily. "Ha! Thirty! Well, thank you a thousand times! Such gallant people. No, I am forty-seven."

Connor blinked. "You don't seem like it."

Hannah nodded in agreement, taking a bite of mango. "I hope I age as well as you."

Gorlak winked. "Again, I thank you. Goblins not show age very much until last years but few get there. Almost all die before that in combat, by execution or in accidents. I actually quite old for a Goblin. Most not live past fifty years or so."

Connor felt a pang of fear and shock. *Fifty? And he's forty-seven? That means he's near the end of a typical lifespan.* He tried to imagine a world without brave Gorlak in it and his throat constricted.

Hannah's eyes glistened and she nodded, sipping her jekka. Their dismay must have been obvious because Gorlak paused, staring at them intently.

"Please, do not worry about me," he said in a gentle, warm tone. "You give me something I could never dream of. If only other Goblins would seek the Light! Last two years have been happiest of my life. I would never serve Darkness again. Jesus is my God and my Lord. I am content."

Hannah took his hand and squeezed it. "Please don't plan on leaving us any time soon," she whispered.

Gorlak slowly lifted her hand to his lips and gave it a light kiss. "I do my best, Princess Hannah," he replied with a sad smile, "but is not in my hands. Do not worry. All will be well."

Connor had difficulty swallowing, so he covered it by taking a sip of jekka.

The bell from the tent entrance rang again.

Connor cleared his throat. "Enter."

The inner tent flap drew aside. Megan, Dar, Eric and Brandi entered with Malcolm Ashford in tow.

"Ah, I see you began without us," Eric said with a grin. "Good idea to get started before Dar got here." Dar shoved him in the shoulder and Eric laughed.

Hannah, Gorlak and Connor rose from the table. "Connor will more than make up for it," Hannah said with a wry look at him.

Connor nodded to Malcolm. "And welcome, Oldfather."

Malcolm's blind eyes glinted and he bowed. "I am greatly honored that Queen Brandawyn invited me to share a meal with you."

The new arrivals arranged themselves at the table, bringing over chairs for the larger folk.

Hannah gave Brandi a sidelong look. "I would think this is a family affair, but Gorlak and Oldfather Malcolm are here. Any special reason?"

Brandi took a bite of honey cake and savored a sip of jekka before answering. "I'll let Malcolm tell you."

"Wait." Megan waved a hand and set down her cup. "We need a few precautions first. Even though this camp is fairly secure, we know that the enemy has Companion Pin automatons and we can't be too careful."

She stood and held her arms out, then turned in a slow circle, incanting phrases in the arcane language of magic. A whirling cloud of silvery motes spread from her fingertips and flew out to the underside of the pavilion ceiling and the walls, adhering there in a shimmering coating.

She put a finger to her lips and gave a satisfied nod. "That should do it."

She reseated herself next to Dar and appropriated a miniature berry muffin from his plate.

Malcolm inclined his head at Brandi. "The capital city of Loemin was my home long before I moved away, closer to Havenridge," he said. "I have special knowledge that I think will be very useful."

Connor spooned up some rice pudding studded with cashews and raisins. "Do tell, Oldfather."

"To be blunt, Highness, you have succeeded beyond our wildest dreams. Most of Bluevale — excuse me, Loemin — is now in rebel hands and the defection rate from regular Torosc military units is very high. However, though we have the capital encircled, we have not captured it."

"And whoever controls Aldath controls Loemin," Connor murmured.

Brandi sat back in her chair, hands wrapped around her mug. "Our latest intelligence indicates many people in the city want to switch sides and help us, but there are three whole divisions of Skullheads manning the walls. To make matters worse, Red Veils are there to intimidate the locals. The regular Halfling soldiers would gladly join the rebellion at this point but with Arlene Culver and the Count Balris in charge, they won't dare try it."

Connor thought this over, imagining different possible ways to take the capital but none of them appealed to him. "A siege would result in a lot of casualties and possibly a plague of some sort."

Hannah nodded in agreement. "And a frontal assault would be just as bad. Knowing Arlene, she would push the Halfling regulars to the front with the Skullheads poised behind to slay any of them who attempt to surrender."

Eric popped a piece of bacon into his mouth and smiled at Oldfather Malcolm. "Which brings us to our scholar."

A sudden idea dawned on Connor and he snapped his fingers. "Yes! You know the city very well. Even, I assume, in ways that Arlene and Balris do not?"

Malcolm smiled. "Neither of those august personages are from Loemin — much less from Aldath — and they are unaware that I was privy to secret information during my time as archivist here."

Hanna's eyes narrowed. "Interesting. Do you know of a way we can get at Arlene and Balris without raising the entire garrison? If we can take them out, we can throw their command structure into disarray and allow sympathizers the opportunity they need — and allow us to get troops inside."

That's my warrior girl. Connor thought with a little smile.

Malcolm sat back in his chair. "Yes. There is a hidden passage near the northern city wall that was used to bring in important visitors for secret conferences back in the time of the Paragons. It has connections to various access tunnels and public works under the city. Legend has it that Saint Alyssa herself once used it. It is called The Quiet Way."

Dar and Eric exchanged a glance. "And no one in Aldath will know of this?" Eric said. "I find that hard to believe."

Malcolm shook his head. "There was so much chaos during the time of the overthrow, and so much destruction, many things were forgotten or lost. I stumbled upon a map of the Quiet Way in my youth. Once I realized what it was, I hid the parchment, but when they renovated some of the government buildings, the bastards from Hellsfont just knocked things down instead of going about it like normal people. The map is good and buried."

But he's blind. What good is a map? "How do you know the details?" Connor asked. "With all due respect, you couldn't have seen them anyway."

Malcolm smiled. "I have not always been blind, you know. I lost my sight about ten years ago. But I assure you my memory is still good. I memorized that particular map because it was so unique."

A germ of hope grew in Connor's mind. Maybe this would be a way to take the final step to victory and minimize losses. "Can you provide enough details for us?"

Malcolm now turned his face to Connor. "I could dictate it for a cartographer. The only unknown is whatever else has happened to the tunnels in the meantime. The Paragon Age was thousands of years ago."

No one spoke for quite some time. Connor tapped the tabletop, lost in thought. *A hidden path, with many uncertainties, but with a possible victory at the end, freedom for our people, and a minimum of bloodshed. It's almost too good to be true.*

"What other options do we have?" he asked.

Dar picked up his mug from the table and shot a sidelong grin at Brandi. "I suggested a night raid by air, similar to what we did in Meridian when we rescued Hannah. But people don't seem to like that one."

Brandi held up a hand. "It is certainly an idea that plays to our strengths, but the enemy is well aware of our aerial capabilities and you've all seen their patrols. I think they're expecting it."

"Let me be devil's advocate for a minute. Going underground into an area no one has seen for a very long time?" Dar asked. "Didn't we just do that in the tunnels near Duarvar? We barely made it out alive, and that was an area no one had visited in five months. The forces of evil have literally occupied Aldath for centuries. Do you think they would have missed this secret passage all this time?"

Connor had to admit he had a point, but his intense desire to free his people won out. "Yes, there is a risk, for sure, but the other alternatives, such as an extended siege or frontal assault, would cost many lives and I am not willing to do that unless there was no other way."

Dar raised an eyebrow. "What about the risk to you, the heir? Would your people agree to that?"

Again, no one spoke.

Connor found his fist clenching and forced himself to relax. *Dar isn't wrong — I should be safeguarding myself as the heir to Loemin.*

He turned his gaze to his companions. "What do you think?"

Brandi exchanged a glance with Eric, Dar and Megan. "I think I speak for everyone when I say we will follow you to whatever end you choose. It is your kingdom and your people, Connor."

For a moment, the enormity of his position weighed on Connor like a mound of boulders. Not only would his own army spend their lives for him and Hannah, but these, his dearest friends — royalty of an allied nation, of all things, and no less in need of succor than Loemin — stood ready to risk everything as well.

I really am responsible for the fate of my nation and people, he thought with a humbling sense of awe. *And even the fate of another kingdom. Do I dare take the riskier road?*

Then he recalled the forlorn looks on the faces of the people in Haven-ridge and the other towns. His eyes rested on the golden badger motif on Hannah's gown. *But there's no Loemin if we don't eliminate the last remnants of the People's Republic of Torosc. Our people deserve better. And if I can give it to them at the risk of my life, so be it.*

Hannah gave his hand a squeeze and he knew her thoughts. He rose from his seat. "Hannah and I will try the ancient road with whoever will join us. I won't think less of you if you don't want to risk the chance of freeing Alenar."

"As if you could stop us," quipped Dar with a grin. He stood alongside the others.

Gorlak nodded vigorously. "I small. Can hide in a backpack."

This got a chuckle out of them, dispelling the intense mood.

"We should probably bring Varani and Alex," Eric suggested.

Megan laughed. "Can you imagine the reaction if we didn't? Even if we all died, we'd never hear the end of it!"

For a poignant moment, the smiles on his friends' faces reminded Connor of them when they first met: eager, unafraid and ready to take on the world. He found it hard to imagine that they were all rulers of kingdoms.

How far we've come. How much we've learned. Yet, despite a World War and all our new responsibilities, deep down, we're still the same.

"Thank you." He took Hannah's hand in his own. "I couldn't have asked for better friends."

"With allies like this," added Malcolm, his blind eyes sweeping over them. "Aldath will belong to Loemin again. I am sure of it."

Chapter Nineteen – A Little Detour

Arlene peered out the window at the metropolis of Aldath, swathed in nighttime. An armored hippogriff bearing a rider flashed through the light from mage-globes on the city parapets. In the East Courtyard below her, ogres in scale mail hunched over cookfires under the watchful eye of Skull-head commanders nearby.

She frowned. Everywhere she went in the city, she sensed anticipation, as if everyone awaited a climactic event.

She raised her eyes to the scene beyond the walls and her lips tightened. Hundreds, if not thousands, of campfires formed a vast semicircle around the capital city.

"Damnable little bastards," Arlene hissed under her breath. *They have us pinned here with Three-Nation Lake at our back. If only we had enough boats, but no… the local traitors set them afloat days ago and they've drifted all over the lake by now.*

A rap at the door made her turn. Arless Octavio bowed as he entered. "Milady. Do you require the regular service tonight?"

She considered, then discarded the idea. "No. My mood is otherwise." She beckoned him over to the window.

He joined her, gazing out impassively over the scene.

"They must have some kind of weakness, something we can exploit," she said with a wave of her hand at Connor Loemin's army.

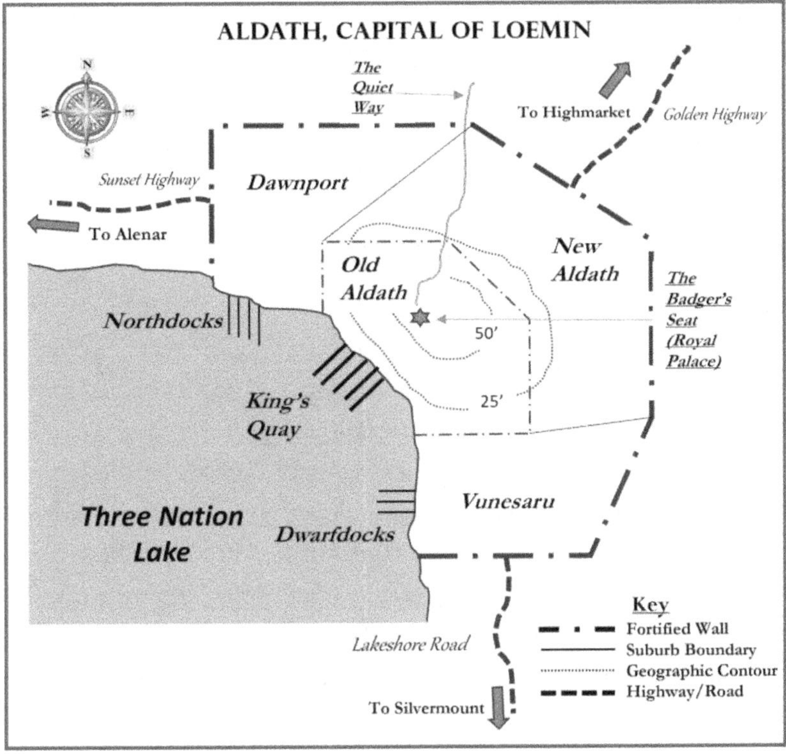

After a while he shrugged. "Perhaps, milady, but we have yet to detect it."

She chewed her lip. "How far away is Lord Golvadu?

"The last reports placed his army about a week away, near the Southern Spur in Silvermount."

"We don't have a week," she hissed.

"Lord Balris seems more optimistic."

She huffed in derision. "Balris? Yes, I know. Between his pet project and Golvadu, he thinks we'll have them between the hammer and the anvil. But I don't hold out a lot of hope that the old goat can actually *get* here without losing a tenth of his army. He's essentially traveling through hostile territory, now that most of the countryside follows that idiot Prince Connor and his bitch."

"Yet hold out we must," Octavio, said, clasping his hands behind his back. "Have no fear. The rebels will find out the hard way that standing up to the might of the People's Republic and our allies has a steep price."

"Our allies from Hades are what worry me." Visions of Balris' latest project flitted through her mind. "What the esteemed Count is trying to do is certainly within his capabilities, and with the records we recovered from the ruin of George Oxbridge's house, we have a better chance, but his ultimate goal is concerning."

She leaned on the windowsill. *Maybe Lord Golvadu's wariness of Daemonic "assistance" is well-founded.*

Octavio said nothing for a few heartbeats. "Well, the rebels are out there and we're in here, in a fortified city. Daemons or no Daemons, when the Archon arrives, we have a chance to break the siege."

"Perhaps, but what's the end game? We can't fight the entire population of Loemin." She recalled recent correspondence with Golvadu. "Now, if we could get the Morlanese or the Pirate Kings of Jered to contribute forces to the cause, that would certainly change the game. They did not suffer losses during the War nearly as great as Torosc."

He leaned against the nearby wall. "The Morlanese and the Jeredans would exact a steep price for helping."

Arlene smirked. "Oh, I'm sure the Archon has already thought of that. And he's already considered how to maintain control if that happens. Count on it." She returned her attention to the scene outside.

Octavio flicked a dead fly off the windowpane. "For the future, that may be a factor. However, what to do about this current situation? Maybe we should consider a decapitation strike. Imagine what it would be like if they lost even one of the so-called royals? Devastating to morale, I gather."

"Easier said than done, Arless. They're all Grey Riders. And they have the ability to strike us first." She glowered at the sight of the opposing army. *Grey Riders. How many times have they done something unexpected and thrown our plans into disarray?*

"Agreed, but we are watching for any air assaults. They would be foolhardy in the extreme to try that now."

What are the chances they can get in here and wreak havoc? "We know very little about this city, don't we?" she asked, spinning away from the window.

"You and I, yes. But the Secret Police have some limited information."

"Are there any ways that the Riders could sneak in and open any of the gates? Maybe from across the lake?"

He shrugged. "A possibility, but not likely. We are watching that approach."

"How about from another direction?"

"I don't see how, milady."

She remained silent, lost in thought. *Thanks to the many defectors, the Riders have ample information about Aldath. They could strike supplies, communications, magical support units, maybe even us here in the Royal Palace. They've have proven before that they can take an unexpected approach. What am I missing?*

"Milady?"

We need extra eyes out there, ones that don't need to sleep. She turned to face him. "I'm going to put you on special assignment."

He met her gaze, his eyebrow raised.

She drew herself up to her full height and lifted her chin. "I want you on constant patrol around the palace. Take whatever resources you need. I have a feeling the Riders are about to spring something unexpected."

He inclined his head. "Of course, milady. I will employ some of our *unique* troops in key locations to make sure all approaches are covered."

She smiled. "Just be wary, Arless. If the Riders do try to infiltrate somehow, that little Loemin bitch has a special sword that can chop undead into moldering chunks in no time — including you."

"Understood, milady. Will there be anything else?"

The more she thought about her preparations, the more she relaxed. *Perhaps there's a way out of this. We have assets that they do not know about and Balris' little project can turn the tide, if we time it right. Let the Riders try their worst. We have a few surprises for them.*

Her demeanor improved and she turned her gaze to his handsome features. With a wolfish smile, she ran a hand up his sleeve to his chest. "Yes. I find my mood is better now. Let us begin."

<<>>

Alex shot a glance at Varani. "So, what do I call you now?"

She adjusted a strap on her breastplate. "Varani."

"No, I mean, you're a member of the Aldenar family. Aren't you a

Duchess or something?"

She yanked the strap tight and looked at him sidelong, eyes twinkling. "I'm still the same person, Alex."

He refitted one of his pauldrons. "I just don't want to make some kind of error in protocol."

She gave a gentle smile. "We're beyond protocol."

The happy light in her eyes warmed his heart and an aura of calm joy surrounded her. *I like this new Varani. Not that the old one was bad.*

"What?" she asked.

He realized he had been staring. "Sorry."

"No. What is it?"

"You're different now, Khyla. Sorry. Varani."

Her smile turned gentle. "Love will do that to you." She reached out and took his hand. "Don't think I don't appreciate all your compassion and encouragement before I talked to Eric. You were the first to believe in me. I cannot thank you enough and I haven't forgotten."

Her blue eyes shone with something deeper and his heart turned over. "I hope that we can be better friends, then," he finished, feeling awkward.

Those eyes lanced into his. "More than friends, Alex."

They stood in silence. His heart skipped a beat at the implication. "But you are of the Royal House. I'm just a simple soldier."

"You're not simple to me."

"You're the sister of a prince, Lady Varani—"

"Alex," she interrupted in a stern tone, "No titles."

Titles. He shook his head. "That's the point, Varani. I don't have one."

"Do you think I care?"

He pressed his lips together. "Maybe you don't, but the people and nobility of Alenar will. Many of the noble houses will cause trouble, particularly if they see an opportunity for themselves with the Royal Family."

She frowned. "So what? You told me you can trace your family name all the way back to the Paragon Age. I doubt that any of the remaining nobility of Alenar can claim so much."

Alex shook his head. "It's a fine lineage, but not from the aristocracy. Do you think they'll want one of their princesses to get involved with a common retainer, no matter how old his name?"

Her eyes flashed. "They will if I command them! Or if my sister-in-law the Queen does!"

He sighed. "Varani, I've heard Brandi and Megan talking. The ancient laws of Alenar predate the Archons of Torosc and they are very strict. Even a Queen can't rule by edict. The government has a say in the workings of the royal family."

"My private life is not a political matter!"

The fire in her eyes made him smile. "I'm with you, but let's be patient. We don't need a controversy already; we haven't even freed Alenar."

She made a visible effort to control her aggravation and took both his hands. "Agreed, but I will not let anything stand in our way," she said firmly.

His heart soared at her gentle touch. Yet he doubted. *What do I have to offer her, the sister-in-law of a queen?*

A young lad's voice interrupted them. "Lady Varani and Captain Fejer?"

Varani abruptly dropped his hands and they turned. A page trotted up to them and bowed. "If you are finished arming, Prince Eric requests your presence."

"We will be there presently," Varani replied and the page left.

"I'm not giving you up because of some stupid title," she hissed to Alex. "You were a friend when I had none, you listened to me and encouraged me through a tough time. You've always been there for me. I want to be with you. I'm not letting this go."

Her intensity made Alex pause. He squeezed her hand. "You're right. We need to address this. Can we talk to Brandi after everything in Loemin is resolved, at least?"

In answer, she kissed the back of his hand, her eyes boring into his.

"Lady Varani?" called the page from the tent entrance. She shot an annoyed glance in that direction but Alex raised an eyebrow and she relaxed.

"Come on. Connor and Hannah have a kingdom to reconquer," he said.

<<>>

Connor paused in the tunnel and held up a fist. Only a faint scrape on stone and a light jingle of mail told him the others halted.

He waited, listening for sounds in the streets overhead. The rhythmic thump and rattle faded into the distance and he relaxed.

Ogres. At least four of them, and two wagons, heavy laden. Interesting.

Still, he waited, scanning the passage ahead. The familiar heat signatures of mold, insects and the occasional rat glowed pale green against the darkness of cold stone, but nothing else. He beckoned to the Riders and continued on, passing a side corridor and then another.

I'm more at home here than in a throne room or battlefield. But I can't serve Loemin very effectively doing dungeon crawls. Maybe I just need to move on to other things in my life. He smirked. *Or maybe I'm getting old.*

The occasional heat signatures of plant life became a vast array directly in front of him, forming a wall that spanned the height and breadth of the tunnel.

Oh, troll turd! He sighed, then held up a fist and clenched it twice. He shifted his sight to the normal spectrum just before a pale white orb flared to life over his head.

Dar and Eric joined him, hands on hips, surveying the fallen rocks, twisted metal and broken beams cluttering the passage ahead. Mold and mushrooms festooned the blockage. A narrow gap stretched into the mass, not much bigger than a dinner plate in diameter.

"Well, a couple of thousand years is a long time," said Eric with a wry smile.

"Do you think someone collapsed it on purpose?" Dar mused.

"Let's ask Gorlak," Megan suggested. "He's better underground than any of us."

Gorlak squirmed his way up to the front of the formation.

"What do you think?" Hannah asked.

The Goblin eyed the collapse for a few heartbeats and ran his hands over the stone and metal. He peered into the narrow gap for a while, then shook his head. "Could be on purpose but I not think so. This look like someone else sink a shaft from surface and not make good construction."

"And we know from the Vault of Safety that underground areas can get damaged by earthquakes," Brandi pointed out.

Connor's eyes roamed the passage. Like most of the Quiet Way, the smooth walls and regular floor showed care in its construction. He even noted a few faded numbers and letters etched into the walls, as if pointing to different destinations.

Not much use to us now, hundreds of years later.

Connor pressed his lips together and reached into the map case at his belt. "On to our contingency plan then."

Dar looked at him in mock surprise. "What? No complaints about how this is slowing us down? About keeping on plan and on schedule?"

"Blow it out your ear, Your Highness," Connor retorted, unfolding a map.

Eric elbowed Dar and the pair grinned.

Connor studiously ignored them. He inspected the map, following the lines with his finger.

Hannah joined him. "We're not getting through that blockage, are we?"

"No." Connor replaced the map. "We'd need the dragons and even then we'd make a lot of noise. Actually, it looks like the turnoff just behind us is our best bet. It comes out near the Eastern Gardens, right by the palace. According to Malcolm's notes, there's a servants' gate that will give us access to the lower halls and storage areas."

They rejoined the others. He explained the situation.

"Nothing for it," said Brandi, hands on her sword hilts. "We made it this far into the Royal District without problems, so thank God for that."

Megan extinguished the magic light and they set off. Connor thought ahead to when they would emerge. Despite the fact that the dark of night covered the city, Connor knew it was precious little advantage. True, shadows would hide them in the visible spectrum, but much of the enemy force could see infrared, which made going aboveground all the riskier.

All it will take is one sentry to look in our direction at just the wrong moment.

They filed down the passage two abreast. Their path turned to the right, then left, then right again and stopped at a dead end. He signaled for light. A rusty ladder rose up from floor to ceiling, ending twenty feet overhead at a round metal door with a wheel. He saw more illegible writing next to the portal.

"Well, they were organized and disciplined in Old Loemin at least," he murmured.

"That's a good sign, Connor." Brandi said with a smile. "They built well and built to last. Your city has good bones, as they say. It can be remade."

If we survive.

Without another word, Connor clambered up the ladder and tried the wheel. As expected, it didn't budge. He looped an arm around a rung and dug into his case for a tiny amber pellet and a little aluminum wand. He jammed the pellet into the interface between the wheel base and the door, then touched it with the wand, whispering an arcane word.

The pellet burst into golden sparkles that suffused the wheel gears and disappeared into the portal. *Lord Melinor, your little toys keep on amazing me.*

Connor tried again, wrenching the wheel to the left. It resisted, then slowly gave way and he eased off, turning it so that it made no sound. Rusty powder sifted onto his gloves. He looked down at the others. "Light off."

The magic globe winked out and he readjusted to infrared.

Dar swarmed up the ladder and Eric followed.

With a deep breath, Connor turned the wheel the last little bit and firmly pushed up. It moved slowly, but eventually gave way with the ripping of dry roots and vines overhead. He opened it just enough to slip through and rolled to the side as Dar caught the door.

Connor scuttled under a nearby bush. He froze, eyes darting left and right. A vast garden spread out before him, several hundred yards long and a hundred wide, surrounded on all sides by iron fencing. Tall, brooding trees crowded out the stars of the night sky near the edges of the area. Pathways of broken flagstone meandered between what had originally been flowerbeds, now a conglomeration of weeds and random plant life. Vines and moss covered the remnants of statuary and fountains.

Thankfully, no Ghost Creepers.

The musty smell of mold and the woodsy aroma of a profusion of plants filled the air. He waited, listening and trying to see through the vegetation to the streets outside the park. The avenues looked empty, but magical lamps illuminated the area by the wide front gates. In the distance, he heard the beat of drums and occasional voices or growls of some Fellbeast.

Not going out that way anyway.

In his mind's eye, he went over Malcolm's map as the others clambered out from the underground passage.

"Here's another place that will need rehabilitation," Hannah breathed as she joined him.

Connor pointed to the right-hand side of the park. "If we follow the fence there, a gate leads out directly opposite the palace."

Hands on their weapons, the Riders crept through the gardens, trying to stay on the walkways as much as possible. Several times they had to detour around fallen trees or paths made impassable by a tangle of thorny plants. The street and lamps on buildings outside the park cast a dim light everywhere. Connor considered using infrared vision again but decided against it: with all the light pollution and plant life, his ability to discern details would be hampered.

We're basically operating on the same vision as humans.

He congratulated himself on making it halfway across when Hannah clutched his arm. She tapped Shriek and put a finger to her lips.

"Undead nearby," Connor whispered to Dar, eyes darting around the trees and bushes. "Pass the word."

Dar whispered to the others. Connor put one hand to the brooch on his tunic and the other hand to Glittershard.

"Where are they?" He whispered to Hannah.

She shook her head. "Shriek doesn't give direction. Only presence."

An unfamiliar, musky scent mingled with the odor of rot drifted to him and he frowned. *What the hell?*

Something massive moved at the base of a nearby tree. He drew Glittershard.

A four-armed, ten-foot-tall Troll detached from the shadows in the foliage, joined by five others. More rose up out of the tangle of bushes and trees behind them. Then Connor saw their rotted limbs, cloven skulls and red-glowing eyes. They lumbered forward and a charnel stench flowed out from them. He fought to keep from retching.

A pale blond man with eyes the color of live coals soared up over the undead trolls and hovered there.

"Well, well, what have we here?" His white fangs gleamed.

Chapter Twenty – Retribution

No! Not him! Connor summoned his guardian sword and the weapon glittered into being before him.

Brandi held up her crucifix. "Begone, Servants of Darkness!" A light flashed from her hand.

The undead trolls cowered, hands raised before their faces. The vampire clutched a skull medallion on a chain around his neck. A light flashed in his fist and the trolls recovered, thumping forward. Megan stepped behind the armored Riders. Varani, Alex and Hannah raised their shields.

The vampire smirked. "Nice try, Brandawyn, my dear, but that won't work here."

"Is that who I think it is, Brandi?" Megan asked.

Before Brandi could answer, the vampire halted the undead trolls with an upraised hand and bowed in midair. "Arless Octavio, at your service. Your lovely sister and I shared a wild night of passion when she turned me to a vampire, for which I must thank her."

Brandi glared at him, standing tall. "It was not my will or choice, Arless Octavio. Adina Hightower forced an evil presence to possess me."

"Really?" he leered. "But you enjoyed it nonetheless at Adina's behest, did you not? And it led to your ultimate death. The gods of the Ja'al prevailed."

A smile curved Brandi's lip. "Prevailed? Hardly. I am here, and Adina Hightower is no more. What does that say about your gods?"

Octavio feigned a yawn. "Religious debates bore me." He waved the undead forward. Brandi transformed to her Celestial aspect, her wings unfurling behind her.

"What is this?" Octavio snarled, floating backward.

Brandi soared up into the air and thrust her hand skyward. A shimmering globe of light sprang up, covering their side of the park. Everything went dead quiet.

Connor tried to shout to the other Riders, but no sound came out. He shot a look at Octavio.

The vampire retreated from Brandi, his mouth open in a silent bellow, but again, Connor heard nothing.

Brandi's silenced the area to prevent him from calling for help! But that means no spells from the rangers or Megan! And we can't use Glittershard or Steelwing or Dar's teleporting armor either. Great! Just great!

Gorlak activated his cloak and fluttered up after Brandi and Octavio, levering a crossbow bolt at the vampire that he dodged. Below him, the trolls charged towards the defensive line.

The trolls met the Riders and all became a maelstrom of flashing blades, whirling bodies and an eerie silence. Shriek flared white every time it hit. Dar's sword and Eric's spear blazed.

Connor slipped behind a ruined statue, gauging the battle. Seeing an opportunity, he made a beeline for a trio of undead harassing Alex and Varani. One of the trolls saw him coming and swung a mighty backhand. Connor ducked under it and slid, slashing the monster's wrist with Glittershard. The troll's mouth opened in a silent roar as its arm frosted over. Connor's guardian blade impaled the creature in the side.

The troll staggered and tried to kick him, but Connor kept moving, ducking around a dry fountain. The undead thumped forward, swinging its good arm. It missed him and broke off part of the statuary instead.

Connor dodged around the remains of the fountain and stabbed the troll in the thigh, covering the limb in a sheen of ice. At the same time, the guardian blade stabbed the troll in the other leg. The undead fell to its knees, still vainly swinging fists covered in frost.

Connor jumped to the fountain's ledge, leaped in the air, and beheaded the monster. An icy troll head thumped silently to the weedy turf.

Connor's peripheral vision alerted him just in time. Another troll loomed out of the trees and he narrowly dodged. The errant blow hit a nearby bough and shards of wood showered him. He rolled away. His guardian blade stabbed the undead in the calf. It tripped and sprawled headlong. Hannah charged into the fray and beheaded it. Shriek flashed soundlessly.

He sprinted to her side. The other Riders stood panting and limping amid a pile of undead trolls. A motion in the sky caught his eye. Octavio swooped down and away from Brandi and Gorlak, holding forth his glowing medallion. To Connor's horror, the dismembered trolls knit back together. Flexing their limbs, they arose.

A memory flashed in his mind. *Dylany, the undead Daemon from the necropolis! She used the same spell!* A chill raced up his spine. *More Daemonic magic!*

The other Riders braced themselves for an onslaught of more than eight undead behemoths. Hannah mouthed to him. "Help Brandi! Kill Octavio!"

Connor backed up, drawing his bow and reaching into his arrow case. He directed his guardian blade towards the attacking trolls. It darted off, slashing and thrusting.

Connor took off away from the main battle, trying to get a bead on Octavio. The vampire fluttered like a butterfly, spinning away from Gorlak's crossbow bolts and dodging Brandi's swords. Occasionally, he took a swipe at Brandi or unleashed a bolt of dark fire at her. Most of the time he tried to escape the dome of silence but she cut him off each time.

Connor laid an enchanted arrow to his bow, aiming at the swooping, diving vampire. He loosed. Octavio looped away and the arrow sizzled past, trailing a glittering tail in its wake.

Damn it!

He spared a glance for the battle against the trolls. His companions fought on, but they looked winded and battered. A troll slammed Varani to the side and Alex chopped off its leg. As it fell, he pulled a groggy Varani to her feet as Hannah arrived at their side, shield up. Another troll leapt at her. She sidestepped and the swing shattered a stone bench near her.

Connor loosed again. Octavio once more flitted out of the way.

It's like trying to shoot down a moth! Sweat broke out on Connor's brow. *I have to end this, and fast.*

Dar chopped off a troll's arm and another undead slammed him to the side. He tumbled into an overgrown flowerbed, striking his helmet on a stone bench. He weakly tried to rise. The trolls pursued, fanged mouths open in silent bellows, but Megan blocked the way, her staff flaring white. A translucent white hemisphere leaped up over her and Dar. The trolls swung repeatedly but the white globe rejected each attack with mild flares of light.

Megan gritted her teeth, despair and panic written on her features. Two more enemies joined in. Eric slid to a stop near Dar and Megan and impaled one with his spear. The troll dropped. Hannah, Varani and Alex took places next to Eric, limping and forming a shield wall near Dar. A crowd of trolls advanced, faces twisted in rage.

How much longer can they last?

Connor tried to track Octavio again but Gorlak distracted him, waving frantically. The Goblin pointed to his bow, then at Connor and at Octavio.

Gorlak, you're a genius.

Connor waited. Gorlak fired. Octavio spun out of the way, right into Connor's line of action. He led the shot perfectly. Octavio's eyes grew wide and he gestured with the medallion — too late. Connor's arrow slammed into his chest and detonated silently in a cloud of blue flame, blowing the vampire back into a tree trunk. His medallion shattered.

Connor whirled back to the main fight. The trolls froze in place, then dropped to the ground, their limbs and heads falling off.

Connor replaced his bow and trotted ahead as Brandi landed near Octavio. The vampire jerked the arrow out of his chest and snapped it in two. A few glittering gashes marked his otherwise perfect pale skin and most of his tunic had been blasted off by Connor's magic arrow.

How is he still moving? Connor wondered.

Brandi waved her hand and the globe of silence vanished. Gorlak landed at her side as the other Riders approached.

"Repent," Brandi said to Octavio. "You shall have mercy if you turn from evil."

Octavio's eyes narrowed and he smirked. "Who? Me? Too late, my little sex kitten. You fight against powers against which there can be no victory. Hell is coming."

"Really?" Eric said with a chuckle. "Well, Hell already made an appearance in the War of the Dark Wave. Not very impressive."

"I don't know, Eric." Dar limped forward with Megan's help. "We could just kick their asses again. Makes no difference to us." He downed a potion and light flared on his injured knee.

Octavio's eyes narrowed. "We have the knowledge of ages past. Do not trifle with us."

Hannah ignored him and addressed Brandi. "How do you typically bind up a vampire? I think he can give us some good intelligence."

"As if I would treat with the likes of you, you sawed-off little slut!" Octavio lunged forward, Hannah drew Shriek but he sidestepped and leapt into the air, turning towards the castle.

Almost too fast to follow, Brandi shot up at him and Hannah tossed Shriek to her. Octavio snarled and took a swipe at her with a glowing claw but Brandi beheaded him. This time Shriek let out its triumphant wail as the vampire's headless body thumped to earth.

In the streets past the city gardens, the rhythmic thumping of drums halted. Then they heard loud voices raised in anger. Horns blared.

Hannah's eyes widened. "Oops."

Brandi landed, growling in frustration. "Stupid, stupid, stupid! I should have thought of that! Quick! Run for the servants' entrance!" She handed Shriek back to Hannah. Connor dismissed his guardian blade.

The Riders gathered themselves and sprinted across the gardens. Connor took Hannah's hand and raced alongside the others. Tree branches and vines lashed them and they stumbled more than once.

"There!" he hissed, pointing. "Servants' gate!"

The sound of galloping hooves and the snarling howl of werewolves approached from one of the nearby boulevards.

Irial protect us!

The Riders dashed through the gate and ran for the wall of the castle looming up ahead. They skidded to a halt next to a barred wooden door with a lock on it.

Connor shot a glance down the avenue. The light of torches and spell globes illuminated the buildings and pavement in an ever-advancing wave. The jangle of armor and the thud of boots echoed in the deserted street.

Megan tapped the lock with her staff and it popped open. Without even taking a chance to look inside first, they rushed past. Connor entered last and eased the door shut, peering through the crack at the scene outside.

A trio of horsemen galloped to the front gate of the gardens. Three Fell Bears with glowing red eyes prowled at their sides. Behind them, a squad of infantry advanced, accompanied by a pair of ogres and two hulking werewolves.

Hannah's voice whispered in his ear. "Megan says to draw back. She's going to put a locking spell on the door."

Connor joined her in the darkness, shifting to the infrared. Megan's warm shape stepped next to him and she murmured softly. A faint luminance raced around the door seams.

"Let's go." Eric's voice floated back to him. "There's a way up. I see a storeroom. We can regroup there."

Connor followed and the Riders pressed into a large chamber crammed with boxes, barrels and crates.

"That was close," Eric said.

Megan spun towards her sister, eyes flashing. "Yes, and unnecessarily so! Why did you silence everyone? We almost got killed, not to mention the alarm being raised at the last second."

Brandi stepped back, confused. "I… We couldn't risk Octavio alerting anyone."

"Why didn't you just silence him then? Why the whole area?"

Brandi frowned. "And no one else would have heard all the clashing of arms and bellowing undead trolls?"

Megan clenched her fists and glowered at her sister.

She's not as angry as she is frightened. Connor thought.

"Megan," Connor said, "I don't think there was a good solution in any case. Octavio had us right where he wanted us. We were fortunate to get away."

Megan blinked rapidly and Dar put his arm around her. "I just felt so… helpless!" she fumed. "If I can't speak, I'm almost useless!"

That's what she fears: helplessness, Connor realized. *She has all this angelic power and yet, for a short time at least, she had little ability to protect the one person she loves most in the world.*

"I know how you feel, Megan," he said simply, "but you're not supposed to do everything. There are times when we have to pick up the slack for each other. We're a team and always have been. Besides, you've saved my life more times than I can count."

Megan stared at him and sniffed, then leaned her head on Dar's shoulder.

Brandi hesitated, then gripped her sister's arm. "I'm sorry Meg. I… I did the best I could. I messed it up there at the end, I know."

Hannah took Connor's hand. "I didn't think too clearly either. I should have realized that Shriek just does what it does, regardless of silence spells or lack thereof."

"Hey," Dar said, kissing Megan's head. "It worked out okay. I'm fine. Besides," he gave a roguish grin, "It will take a lot more than a bunch of measly trolls to finish me off. I'm too annoying."

Megan tried not to smile and pushed his shoulder. "You have that part right!"

Eric chuckled. "You forgot loud and opinionated. But we'll let that pass for now."

The Riders all broke into smiles and the mood lightened.

Megan held out her hand to Brandi with a shy smile. "I'm sorry, Bran, for losing my temper."

"Nothing to be sorry about," Brandi said, kissing her on the cheek. "It was a bad situation all around."

Connor gestured at the storeroom. "Now that we have a little breather, we should probably make sure everyone is healed up before moving on."

Brandi knelt and beckoned to Connor and Hannah. "Let's have a look at the two of you. Uncharacteristically, it looks like you were relatively untouched." Her eyes twinkled.

Hannah made a wry face. "I know. I'm hoping it's a trend."

Brandi examined them for a few seconds, then let her hands drop and looked Connor in the eyes. "And thank you both."

"For what?" he asked.

"For your support. I didn't have a great solution and I was afraid —"

Connor held up a hand. "Brandi, I don't know that we could have done any better. We're fine and we can move on."

She nodded and he noted a look of sadness in her eyes.

"There's something else, I can tell," Hannah said in a soft voice.

Brandi cast a look over her shoulder at the others. "I don't know. I guess I feel responsible for Octavio's condition, and his death. I understand that I was under Adina's control, but still…"

Connor gripped her shoulder. "You didn't really have much of a choice either, did you? I'm sure you fought against it as well as you could, Brandi, but you're not perfect. None of us are. I think your God understands."

"Yes. I — ." Brandi sighed and wiped away a tear from the corner of her eye. "Thank you."

"Brandi?" Varani whispered from the other side of the room. "I think Alex's ankle is sprained. Would you mind?"

Brandi waved to her, then regarded the Halflings for a second. She smiled and kissed both their cheeks before leaving them. "You are the sweetest friends."

Hannah squeezed Connor's hand.

Eric sauntered over and sat on the floor next to them. "Thanks for that."

"For what?"

"The support. She really needs it sometimes."

Connor watched Brandi for a second. "She's battling some terrible memories, isn't she?"

Eric's jaw worked and he nodded. "She always will, though she now has memories of the glory of Heaven to balance them. Still, I'm glad you said what you did. I've told her many times she was not at fault. I think she needed to hear that from someone other than me or her confessor."

Brandi, Dar and Eric finished using their healing magic. The others arose, looking more energetic and not as battered.

"Ready?" Dar asked, drawing Rindara Starblade.

Connor tapped his brooch and the guardian sword flowed out to hover before him. "Just hope that we don't have to take on a castle-full of enemies."

Without another word, the Grey Riders left the storeroom and headed out into the passages of the Royal Palace of Aldath.

Chapter Twenty-One – Reclamation

Brandi let out a steady breath. The faint outlines of footprints leading into the service hallway glowed in her vision. From the bowels of the palace, she heard chanting voices, a short scream or growl of some beast. The stench of stale sweat, blood and offal fouled the air.

So far, so good. How long will our fortune hold?

She extended her Celestial senses. Three silver auras approached. "The men are on their way," she whispered to Megan.

Dar, Connor and Eric crept back to them, their forms glowing with thermal signs of exertion.

"Done," said Eric.

"How many were there?" she asked.

Connor shrugged. "Two Skullhead warriors and a pair of Halfling wizards. Took them by surprise. Let's go."

They continued with only the occasional scrape of a boot or clink of armor to betray their passage.

"I hope Malcolm's map is right," Megan murmured next to her. "Otherwise, we could be circling around in here for days."

"He seemed confident in it. And Connor memorized it," Brandi whispered back. "We'll be fine."

As if in confirmation, Connor held up a fist and they halted. He eyed the left-hand wall, frowning.

"What is it?" whispered Hannah.

"I think the Royal Hall is on the other side." Connor touched the wall.

Megan scooted to the front of their group and leaned her staff against the wall. She placed two fingers over one eye and murmured in Arcana. An iridescent, ethereal sphere in the shape of a tiny, walnut-sized eyeball materialized in front of her. Her eyes took on a sheen that matched the little sphere and she waved her hand at the wall. The eye floated through the stone.

Despite the tension, Brandi smiled. *She works that spell so easily now. Uncle Stephen would be so proud.*

"It's the throne room," Megan whispered. "Balris is there, as well as Arlene Culver and some Daemons: War Fiends and Deathmists."

Brandi chewed her lip, exchanging a look with Connor. He made a rueful face and shrugged. "Well, what did we expect?"

"They've done something to the twin thrones on the dais," Megan continued. "They're covered in some kind of red muck and an interlocking network of bones."

Brandi frowned. "That's disgusting. But why?"

Megan shook her head. "No idea. There are Vampire Roses and some kind of tall, purple reeds in planters. I see…" her voice trailed off. "Bones and skulls, in cages and scattered among the reeds and roses."

Brandi's mind raced, trying to recall something that Petrus and Johanna had told her. "Okay, bones in the planters. That means the two plants work together somehow to feed on victims."

"But Daemons, plus Arlene and Balris?" Eric murmured, taking Fidelis from his belt. "That will be a challenge." He extended his weapon to spear length.

"How's the lighting?" Hannah asked.

"Good point." Megan said. "Red flames in firepits scattered around, so it's not dark. Probably so Arlene can see – she's human."

"Can they see the Ethereal Eye?" Brandi asked.

Megan shook her head. "Not yet. But I better make sure they can't." She beckoned at the wall and the little eye floated through. She closed her eyes, then clenched her fist and the eye popped like a bubble. She held fingers to her temples for a second.

Dar put a hand on her shoulder. "Okay?"

She nodded. "It took a lot for me to maneuver the Eye so that they couldn't see it. Give me a minute."

Brandi turned to Connor. "How do we get in?"

He considered for a few heartbeats, then nodded. "There should be a door that opens behind a set of bookcases just ahead. I'm ninety percent certain."

Dar smirked, drawing Rindara from its scabbard. "Good enough, though I hope we don't end up one hundred percent dead."

The Riders slowly crept along the hallway until Connor stopped them with a raised hand. Megan tapped the wall with her staff and whispered. A seam opened in the stone. Dar, Eric and Alex slowly eased the panel to the side. The back side of a massive wooden bookcase loomed in front of them but a gap of about three feet remained between it and the wall. Brandi held a finger to her lips and peeked in between the shelves.

Arlene stood at the base of the dais, eyes on the twin thrones, hands on her hips. True to Megan's word, a network of bones rather like a spider's web covered the chairs.

Balris lounged on a marble bench nearby, tossing a pair of flaming Halfling skulls from hand to hand. In the background, six War Fiends stood guard, two near the dais and four others next to the double doors at the far end of the throne room. Deathmists hovered in shadowed corners. Lurid red flames danced in iron fire pits.

At the sight of the Daemons, Brandi's heartbeat accelerated and she let out a slow breath. *Easy. Just like training.* She reached into her soul for the confidence and surety of her Elohir birthright.

Arlene frowned at the thrones. "They sure don't look like Gates."

Balris smiled. "Now, now, Lady Arlene. Trust to the power and arcane knowledge of Hades. I assure you they will work as intended."

A stab of fear hit Brandi's stomach. *Gates?*

Arlene shook her head. "How long until they're done?"

Balris shrugged. "Tomorrow morning. They just need to set a little. Don't worry. You'll have enough allies to break the siege soon."

Arlene shook her head. "My lord, this will not be a Skull Gate. We cannot bring in the numbers quickly enough."

Brandi's hands became clammy. *Just like during the War! How in God's name did they manage that? Is this more of the Daemonic magic Father Tom told us about?*

Balris stood up, juggling the skulls. "Two Daemons every half hour will be enough. The rebel force doesn't know we have them and they don't have the numbers for a frontal assault. Slow and easy does it. Besides, Golvadu is on his way. Once we have enough reinforcements, the so-called Heir of Lo-emin will be caught between two armies."

Arlene turned to face him. "Forgive me, Excellency. I do not share your optimism. Lord Golvadu must travel through a lot of hostile territory."

Balris hissed in frustration and tossed the Halfling skulls towards the ceiling. He pointed and a stream of fire darts pulverized them in midair. "You worry too much, Lady Arlene."

Brandi forced herself to unclench her fist. *This is a disaster! The Army won't know what hit it.* She motioned the others back through the door. Eric and Alex pushed it closed.

Megan set her jaw. "If they're making a Gate to Hades somehow, then we can't let them bring in any more Fallen Ones."

"There are Daemons all over the place." Varani whispered. "First at Highmarket and now here, and there's going to be a Gate. Where are the Elohir?"

Brandi shook her head. "I don't know."

"Maybe Father Tom's speculation about Selaan was real," Eric mur-mured. "Maybe the Celestials think they've found him and are closing in. They would spend every effort to get him."

Oh God. Balris here and Selaan potentially roaming around free. Brandi tried to push aside her anxieties and focus. She locked eyes with Connor. "It's your call."

Connor scowled. "We have to strike now. While they're unaware."

Brandi nodded. "Everyone, gather around me." She closed her eyes, raised her hands, and silently prayed for protection and deliverance. In her internal vision, filmy networks of glittering silver, white, blue and gold drifted down on the Riders. Megan whispered under her breath. Additional protec-tive screens of red, green and amber settled on her companions.

Despite Brandi's training with her Celestial mentors, the thought of du-eling with a Daemonic Count made her break out in a cold sweat and she tried to quell the butterflies in her stomach. *Trust in what they taught you,* she counseled herself. *Your Elohir heritage is far stronger.*

Eric gave her shoulder a squeeze. "You okay?"

She nodded without speaking, giving him what she hoped was an encouraging smile.

Eric laid a hand on Gorlak's shoulder. "The dagger you carry is just as deadly to Daemons as Fidelis or Rindara. Hang back and choose the time to strike."

Gorlak patted his belt. "I hide and use Demonspike wisely. Maybe they not care about one humble Goblin."

One humble Goblin. Brandi thought for a second and a sudden inspiration struck her. *Humility! Something that Daemons can't understand.*

"I have an idea," she whispered. She concentrated and touched Gorlak on the center horn in his forehead.

He gave a little jump. "That a weird feeling."

She smiled. "Spell of Insignificance. They'll disregard you unless you attack. If you stop attacking and don't move, it resets."

He smirked at her and winked.

Connor motioned to Varani and Alex. "The firepower they're going to unleash in there is likely to be very intense. Stay in the passage with Gorlak until we engage, then hit them when they're vulnerable. Don't go in too early. If any Daemons look weak enough, finish them off, but make sure to get your shields up. You've seen the results with minor Daemons and these are a lot stronger."

The couple nodded. The Riders exchanged nervous glances. Brandi's heart hammered in her chest. "We have to get as close as we can so we can use Rindara and Fidelis. They're the most potent weapons against them. Move fast, strike hard and don't stop until they're dead."

Hannah took Connor's hand and he nodded. "For Loemin."

The Riders crept into the hall around the bookcases. Connor pointed at Balris and Arlene and the front rank charged. Then a dark symbol flared on the floor stones. A harsh clanging sound echoed off the walls and waves of red fire erupted at the Riders, curling around the protections Brandi had laid on them.

"Lord Balris!" Arlene exclaimed. The War Fiends snarled and surged from their stations. The Deathmists floated closer.

Brandi reached out to Megan. As their hands touched, a silvery white sphere grew over the Riders, glittering and shimmering. Megan's pointed her staff at the entry doors. A golden flare of light raced around the seams, welding the portal shut.

Connor drew Glittershard and activated its frost edge. His guardian blade materialized next to him. "You occupy a palace that does not belong to you," he announced.

Balris merely sniffed and inspected the Riders as if he had just discovered a new species of mold. "So you say. Possession is nine tenths the law."

Dar chuckled. The tiny stars on the sword blade flared. "Spoken like any common thief. Congratulations."

Balris ignored him and spoke to Lady Arlene. "Only six. This will be over soon."

Arlene stepped next to the rank of War Fiends and drew a pair of stiletto daggers. They multiplied into six and hovered overhead.

Dear Jesus! Did she always have those? Brandi gripped her swords.

Balris whispered harsh arcane words and a green sheath of flame sprang up around him. A ball of lightning crackled in his fist. The Fiends raised their arms. The spikes on their armor glowed fiery red.

So it begins.

The War Fiends unleashed their spikes. The missiles slammed into the sphere, dissipating in clouds of steam and ash.

"Ah! Some skills then?" Balris smiled. "This will be more interesting than I thought." He gave a low whistle.

The purple reeds in the planters vibrated, emitting a soft, shrill whine. Brandi gritted her teeth against the sound. Her vision swam and she had trouble focusing. At the same time, the Vampire Roses undulated and a sickly sweet, mesmerizing aroma wafted out at them. She fought to maintain her focus as the Deathmists drifted closer.

Ugh! So that's what the plants do! Damn it!

A motion made her turn. Connor and Hannah, glassy-eyed, staggered towards the Vampire Roses.

The Daemon Count burst out laughing. "Oh, this will be so much fun! Take them apart slowly, one at a time so the others can watch!"

"No!" Brandi shouted. She tried to concentrate on a counterspell but the whining sound muddled her thinking. Dar turned to follow Connor and Hannah but Rindara flared and he stopped, blinking in confusion. Eric gritted his teeth and the head of his spear blazed with fire.

Damn it! We can't fight them like this! Megan… got to … dispel… can't think.

Megan shot a desperate glance at Brandi.

Then, as in the fight against the Stone Lurker swarm, Megan threw her hands to the side and sang her glorious song.

"Irae Angelorum!" The universe vibrated with holy energy and bright light shot out from her body in all directions.

The blast hit the enemy formation with the force of a giant's punch. The Deathmists tumbled backwards in midair and the War Fiends fell to their knees, hands covering their faces. Balris grimaced and stepped back. His lightning ball fizzled out. Arlene gasped and fell against a nearby pillar. The purple reeds went rigidly erect, then flopped over, completely wilted. The Vampire Roses shriveled and curled in on themselves like weeds dried in the sun.

Megan wavered, then caught herself on a nearby bench. Dar supported her with one arm. Eric leapt to their side, the golden, burning point of Fidelis aimed at Balris.

Brandi ran to Megan while the enemy reeled. With no time for anything more complicated, she tapped her sister on the forehead and imparted a potent healing spell.

Megan gasped with pain but revived instantly, clinging to Dar's side for support.

"What is this?" Balris growled, blinking and scowling at Megan. In contrast to his previous arrogant bluster, he sounded uncertain. "Half-elves cannot master Celestial magic!"

"Those with Elohir blood can," Brandi said, and transformed. She unfurled her wings to their full span.

"So! You are related to our misguided brethren." The Daemon Count sneered. "Then this will be all the sweeter!"

He clapped and a blast of green light shot out backwards to his allies. War Fiends rose, snarling and activating their armor spikes to red-hot luminance. The Deathmists surged forward like waves of grey doom.

Without another word, Brandi swooped at Balris. He shot up into the air away from her. She pursued. He pointed behind him, unleashing a set of misty little purple orbs that swirled at her like evil moths. Most detonated on

Brandi's shields but one exploded on her armor in a crackling burst of lightning and fire. Pain tingled where the vile magic touched her. She continued her pursuit, whispering a healing spell under her breath.

The sounds of a titanic battle rang out below them in the Hall. She ignored it all, casting white-hot beams of light at Balris. He stopped in midair, drawing a hooked sword that dripped acid. She struck, dove and dodged, testing his defenses. Neither her blades nor his succeeded in piercing armor. The two broke apart, half-Celestial and Daemon, hovering and breathing hard.

Balris leered, his cat eyes mocking. He floated away from her, touching his blade with his free hand. A corona of red flame now augmented the venomous edge. "How is your darling husband? I'm sure he's a fine toy. He'll be fun to play with before I kill him."

The edges of Brandi's vision tinted red. She gritted her teeth. *Remember the training.* She sneaked a glance at the battle below. Her heart leaped when she saw Eric impale a Deathmist and then tumble away for the inevitable explosion.

She focused on the red haze, drawing on her Celestial power, willing it away. "You mean Eric?" she asked, drifting sideways. "He'd destroy you without breaking a sweat. Maybe I should let him take over." She gestured at the battle.

A War Fiend stood encased in a block of ice near one of the fire pits. Connor and Hanna swirled about in a deadly dance with Arlene and her hovering magic stilettos. Each time they got close to her, she vanished in a swirl of shadowy vapor, reappearing again a few yards away.

Damn! How many tricks does she have?

"Your lackeys aren't doing so well, Count," she said.

He merely grinned. "War of attrition. All this noise will bring the guards, and then you and your little crew will be fighting dozens. They will die and become food. And yes, I'll dine on your little husband, after I've had my fun, of course."

The red tint returned and her rage increased. Brandi prayed under her breath for peace and focus. *Remember what Johanna said: Evil is weak, love is strongest.*

Balris darted at her and she whirled to the side, then rained down blows on him. He barely deflected her strikes and swooped away, heading for Eric as he battled a War Fiend. She cast a ball of light in his path and Balris veered aside, slaloming between pillars and hurling gouts of green fire at her. Stung by the flames and forced to slow her pursuit, she watched him disappear behind a bookcase. She tried to follow but a dense cloud of black smoke erupted from the area, crackling with purple sparks. Her exposed skin stung and her head swam.

Coughing, she retreated and landed near Megan, wincing from the burns. "You okay?"

Megan nodded, spraying a Deathmist with fire-darts. "Just lovely!" she snarled in a husky, malevolent voice. She gestured and a golden shield of light sprang up before her, shunting aside a flaming spike that turned a stone bench into lava.

Alarmed, Brandi looked into Megan's eyes and saw them glowing red. "Meg, your eyes!"

Megan gritted her teeth, deflecting another Deamon spike. The crimson light in her eyes faded. "Just get Balris."

Varani and Alex stormed in behind a wounded pair of War Fiends surrounding Dar and Eric. The captains swept blades at Daemon necks and the Daemons collapsed, decapitated. Varani and Alex hid behind their shields but the blasts hurled them backward into a wall.

Loud shouts rang out from deep within the Palace. The clatter of armor and growls of beasts carried to them. A great blow struck the entry doors from the other side but it merely flexed. A roar of anger echoed from beyond.

Brandi took wing again. *Balris and Arlene are the keys. Behead the snake.*

Balris reappeared, healed of his injuries. He soared up over the bookcase, firing a storm of small bolts of electricity. One hit Brandi in the center of her breastplate and she lurched backwards. Others hit Dar and Eric and they staggered. The War Fiends hurtled at them, slashing and battering. The Riders fell back under the onslaught.

"*Sanari!*" Brandi shouted. A blue-white disk of light shot out from her and washed over her companions. Brandi's wounds stopped stinging and her weariness faded.

"Lady Arlene!" Balris shouted. "Break open the doors!"

"I'm a little busy!" Arlene retorted. She jumped over a slash from Connor and kicked him away, then swept her hand at Hannah. Arlene's stilettos darted out like arrows. Hannah ducked and activated Steelwing. The flying knives bounced off the cloak's metal surface. Connor pointed Glittershard at Arlene but a swirling tornado of black mist leapt up around her and she vanished, leaving behind an empty cube of ice.

Seeing Balris momentarily distracted, Brandi soared at him. He spun out of the way, parrying her blades. He took a slash at her and made a beeline for the double doors. She intercepted him, driving him back with a lightning-fast combination of cuts and thrusts, relaxing and delving into her Elohir powers like Johanna had taught her. He tried to deflect her attacks but Brandi's speed and accuracy took its toll rapidly. He soon bled from arms, legs and shoulder.

I'm winning! Thank God!

"Damn you!" Balris pointed up at the ceiling and then down. A swirling eye of flames opened and a shaft of fire shot down. Brandi barely dodged in time, throwing herself behind a pillar. The flame scorched tiles and crisped Roses and purple ferns. Brandi popped out from behind the column.

"Now you're making me angry!" Balris snapped and held up a fist in front of his face. His hand glowed deep red and a jeweled bracelet on his wrist flashed. A blast of lurid rainbow light shot out in all directions.

The force of the spell hurled Brandi backwards through the air. She slammed into a pillar. She gasped as a rib cracked and her helmet hit the stone with a ringing sound.

Brandi looked about her with bleary eyes. Grey Riders and their adversaries alike lay on the floor in heaps, gasping.

What was that? Have to get up… Balris…

The Daemon Count panted from exertion and drifted down to stand on a ruined statue. "See," he wheezed, holding his shoulder. "I told you it was futile." He pointed a hand at the double doors.

No! The red haze returned, stronger this time. Brandi struggled to rise, fighting both fatigue and Daemon rage. She shot a beam of light at his eyes. He ducked and a swirling red snowflake spun away into the ceiling.

Her weariness threatened to overwhelm her. *Jesus, help me!* She stood shakily. Balris advanced on her, limping.

Then a small figure rather like a Halfling-sized bat floated in behind Balris. "Hey you," said Gorlak.

The Daemon Count whirled and took Demonspike right in the midsection. Gorlak twisted the magic dagger and fluttered backwards. "Surprise," he said with a wry grin.

Balris cursed and swung his acid blade. Gorlak tried to twist out of the way, but the impact slammed him into a wall and he slid to the floor. Balris doubled over, clutching his middle, a white light growing in his hands.

Brandi rose to her feet and marched forward. *Our Father, Who Art in Heaven. Help me save them.* The red haze dissipated. *I will end this, for Connor, for Hannah, for Loemin.*

Balris whipped around, his face twisted in pain and rage. His ribcage glowed white, and purple ichor oozed down his armor. "The unfit will never rule this land!" he thundered, eyes blazing like stars. "The Dark will overtake it and we will make it an outpost of Hades!"

Breathing hard, she readied her blades. "Not while I live."

He thrust with his sword, his other hand hurling dark fire at her. Whirling with blinding speed, Brandi sidestepped and decapitated him with both blades, staggering with fatigue. The Daemon Count's head tumbled off and his corpse detonated. The blast knocked her back into a wall and she groaned.

Somehow, she regained her feet and stumbled into the center of the hall. To her relief, all the Riders stood, covered in dust, Daemon ichor and their own blood — but they stood. Gorlak joined them, wincing and holding his side, his armor rent and his flesh blistering from acid. Brandi quickly applied a healing spell.

Connor and Hannah limped up to join them. "Where's Arlene?" Connor asked, eyes darting all around.

Holy Lord! Suddenly realizing she had lost track of her, Brandi spun. The Riders swiveled their heads around, searching.

A whirling tornado of dark mist coalesced right behind Varani. Arlene appeared and gestured to a stiletto dagger lying on the floor. It leapt to her hand. She wrapped an arm around Varani's shoulders from behind and laid the dagger to her carotid artery. "No one move!"

Everyone froze. Shouts from the entrance doubled in intensity and something large hammered on the portal. Dull booms reverberated in the Hall.

"You've lost, Lady Arlene," Megan panted, leaning on her staff. "There's no way you can get out and they can't neutralize my locking spell in time."

Arlene's lip curled in a sneer. "Wrong. I'll tell you what's going to happen. I'm going to very slowly take my young friend here to the doors, which you will open. Then you will surrender and receive your punishment."

"Don't let her!" Varani shouted and Arlene poked her with the stiletto, drawing blood from just under her collarbone.

"Shut up, bitch." Arlene slowly stalked to the side, angling for the doors. "I know how to make you bleed out very slowly, so don't test my patience."

Connor smiled at her. "One last chance to surrender." He dismissed his guardian blade into the brooch at his shoulder.

What is he doing? Brandi wondered. *He needs that!*

"Surrender?" Arlene sneered. "I hold all the cards, runt."

Connor shrugged, then unpinned his brooch and tossed it past her. "Don't say I didn't warn you."

"Fine," Arlene said, shadowy smoke swirling around her. She raised her dagger.

Connor gestured at his brooch and the dancing sword leapt up in the air, shooting toward him like an arrow. Arlene's eyes widened and she twisted but the guardian blade stabbed her in the lower back.

Arlene lurched, gasping, blood running down her side. In one smooth motion, Varani spun, whipped Arlene's weapon from her hand and impaled her in the neck with her own stiletto.

Arlene choked, falling to the floor. She stared up at them, a widening pool of blood forming under her. "I was... supposed to..." Her voice devolved into a gurgle and her eyes stared at nothing.

Alex embraced Varani, who dropped the dagger as if it were aflame.

Dar gave Connor a tired but wry grin. "Neat trick, there, Crown Prince."

Connor knelt by something shiny on the floor. "Thanks. I've been practicing." He held up Balris' bracelet. "This should be proof of his death."

Gorlak grinned at Brandi. "I like that spell of Insignificance, Majesty. Do that again sometime." She smiled weakly at him, squeezing his shoulder with a gloved hand.

Eric shattered a nearby window with Fidelis, then summoned Stealth. He sent the hawk golem into the night sky. "And that should alert the generals."

Dar gestured to Alex and Varani, then lifted Arlene, handing the body to them. "Not to be macabre or anything, but we have to show the people evidence of their freedom. Connor, do you remember the way to the Royal Balcony?"

"What about them?" Alex asked, jerking his head towards the double doors to the Royal Hall. Shouts, roars and loud thuds echoed in the hall.

Megan nodded wearily. "Unless there's another Daemon lord around, the spell will hold for hours. We have to let the people know that Balris and Arlene are no more."

Connor led them back to the maintenance corridor. Varani and Alex carried Arlene's corpse. Brandi followed, her legs feeling like lead. Eric put his arm around her.

"Hang in there, sweetheart," he said. "Just a little longer."

She brushed a hand over sandy eyes, feeling about a hundred years old. Their path ended at a corridor empty of guards.

Connor pointed at a large, spired set of double doors. "Here."

Megan tiredly pointed her staff while leaning against Dar. With a word from her, the portal swung wide. The cityscape of captive Aldath greeted them under a night sky.

"Light," Dar whispered. A luminous ball popped into being ten feet over his head. Megan tapped Connor with her staff. A shimmering cloud of glowing dust settled on his head. She closed her eyes, utterly spent, and Dar lifted her in his arms.

In the streets below the palace, townsfolk and Halfling soldiers gathered in large crowds, drawn by the commotion. Skullhead Legionnaires, Fellhounds and Goblins pelted down the streets and came to a skidding halt. The crowd gasped at the sight of Arlene's corpse, held up by Alex and Varani. Connor stepped up to the railing and raised Balris' bracelet over his head.

His voice rang out, ten times louder than normal. "People of Aldath! Your deliverance is come! The despot Balris is dead! Behold his bracelet of evil power! See, Arlene the oppressor is no more! Rise up! Free Loemin!"

For a few heartbeats, no one moved. Then, with a thunderous roar, the people of Aldath cried aloud. "Free Loemin! Free Loemin!"

Halfling troopers drew swords and maces, citizens grabbed anything that could be used as a weapon and they turned on the soldiers of the People's Republic. The enemy fought savagely for a few seconds but, then, overwhelmed by sheer numbers, they fell in dark pools of blood. The emboldened citizens and soldiers raced off, raising the cry in the darkened streets as lights blazed to life in lanterns and windows.

Connor laid one arm over Hannah's shoulder. He looked up at Brandi. "I won't forget this."

Brandi smiled back, her heart warmed by the satisfaction and pride mirrored in his eyes. "It was my honor to be here."

Hannah smiled. "We couldn't have done it without you. You were magnificent against Balris, truly."

Balris. Brandi sighed. "The battle wasn't only against him. It was against myself, and my Daemonic heritage."

Eric kissed her head. "And you vanquished both of them. As we all knew you could. You don't have to fear it anymore."

She gazed into his eyes. *He's right. A fight against real Daemons, and I won. Megan and I both did.* The memory of her struggle against Daemon rage remained, but now she felt no dread.

Magical lights flared and a thunderous boom rang out from the area of the city near the East Gate. Two young golden dragons swooped down, breathing fire. Silvery trumpets blared and Brandi heard a roar of many voices heading towards them from the Gate.

Brandi's heart soared.

"It's all over but the celebrating," Connor said with a satisfied sigh.

Chapter Twenty-Two– Novo Ordo

I wonder what Hannah wants. Alex Fejer stopped at the arched doorway to the library and nodded to the Halfling guards. The soldiers saluted with their halberds and one passed through into the room beyond.

The guard soon returned. "The Crown Princess will see you now, Captain."

Alex entered and bowed low.

Hannah Loemin stood next to a tall, spired window. A gold and emerald coronet gleamed on her braided chestnut hair in the fading evening sunlight. She wore a green velvet gown trimmed with gold, with the embroidered emblem of a golden badger at her left shoulder.

Alex read the motto sewn under the insignia: "Fidelis Ad Mortem".

"Faithful unto death" Well, we certainly faced <u>that</u> many times.

With a little smile on her face, Hannah walked to Alex, her green velvet slippers making little sound on the burnished hardwood floor. He knelt and kissed her hands. "Your Highness."

"No honorifics, Alex. We're shield-mates."

He smiled back. "Yes, Your —I mean, Hannah."

He arose and she looked up at him, silent for a little while.

"I thought I should talk to you while Connor is busy with arrangements for the celebration," she finally said. "You will be joining us after the official announcement by King Seamus and Queen Miriam, won't you?"

"Of course, and thank you, Hannah. I'm honored."

She headed towards the window and beckoned to him. "Also, did I hear correctly? Do we see some allies from the north soon?"

He gazed out the window at her side. "Yes. Two regiments of Dwarven Strikers from Merdail, a Heavy Brigade from Gorostol and four Elven Ranger Companies from Terenai arrive today. A mixed regiment from the Alliance will be here by next week. We hear that an allied armada is on the way, but I have no further information. Of necessity, they are keeping the details classified to avoid interception by PRT naval forces."

He saw her eyes twinkle in the window's reflection. "So, they finally managed to cobble something together. Good. I wonder if Father Thomas had something to do with that."

He smiled. "Well, the Messenger Orb certainly came in handy. Torosc will have to think twice if they want to try to reclaim Loemin. We aren't in this alone any longer."

"Very true. We will need all the friends we can get." Hannah fell silent and he took in the scene in the streets outside the palace. Far below, the streets teemed with multitudes of Halflings in the best finery they could find. Their human, Elven and Dwarven neighbors moved among them, clad in similar raiment. Fresh flowers hung in garlands from every balcony and storefront window. Halfling troops in gleaming plate mail sat astride barded Centaurs in an honor guard near the palace gate.

"I'm surprised that the people have nice clothes for the occasion," he observed.

Hannah shrugged. "After the fall of the city, most of the PRT sympathizers and collaborators fled and left everything behind. We had an idea of how much they had stolen but the quantity of fineries and treasures they stored away surprised us."

Alex's eyes wandered to the royal balcony on their right, from where the Royal Family would officially claim the Crown of Loemin.

Hannah tilted her head. "Now that Loemin is free, we begin rebuilding. It will be a long road. We have to establish a completely different form of government, but it will be worth it in the end. You understand why?"

"Yes," he said. "After so many centuries, none of the old Loemin noble houses remain and you want to convert the nation to a royal constitutional meritocracy, like Deran."

"Right. Seamus thought it best. You also understand that I have to stay here while Brandi and Megan continue on with Dar and Eric. There is a lot to be done."

His heart sank at the departure of the Alenar sisters — and Varani. He paused before answering. "Yes. Of course. And I will remain here with you. It is my duty."

Hannah leaned her hands on the windowsill, silent once again. Alex's mind wandered. A starling pecked at something on a ledge next to the window. Another one landed near it and the two birds regarded each other for a moment. They chirped and hopped around. Then as if coming to an agreement, they soared up into the sky.

At least the birds get to be with the one they care about. A sadness verging on bitterness arose in his chest and he struggled to suppress it.

"Duty," Hannah murmured. A piper emerged from a tavern outside the palace and began to play. People nearby broke out in spontaneous dance, laughing and whirling. "Alex, I have a new assignment for you."

Still distracted by morose thoughts of Varani, he murmured, "I am ready to serve you as always."

"Indeed." She turned around and gazed up at him. "You have served us faithfully, Alex, through many dangers. Connor and I appreciate it. But things change and we need to adjust."

He looked at her sharply. "Of course. What sort of adjustment?"

"An assignment away from the Palace."

His mind whirled. "Hannah, please don't send me away. There are many things —"

She held up a hand. "No, it's not what you think. Your loyalty is what makes us confident in this next step. We would like you to transfer to High Princess Megan as her liaison officer and accompany the Alenar royals to reclaim their homeland."

He wasn't sure he heard correctly. His heart skipped a beat. "I'm sorry, what?"

She turned to face him, a little smirk on her face. "Shall I repeat myself?"

"No, High… I mean, Hannah, er…" he stammered. "But my place is here with you."

She straightened to her full height and raised a teasing eyebrow. "Am I, or am I not, Crown Princess of Loemin, one day to become Queen? May I not reassign my staff at my pleasure, to wherever I designate?"

Wild thoughts chased each other around in his mind, buoyed by a sudden hope.

"Well?" she asked, eyes dancing. "Do you accept?"

"Well, of course, Hannah, but…"

She took his hand and gave it a squeeze. "Rewarding faithful friends is one of the advantages of being a princess. Alex, I see now how you look at Varani and how she looks at you. It would be a crime against Heaven for us to separate you. She needs you, you need her, and Brandi and Megan need you both."

A warm, happy feeling spread through him and he gave her a sheepish grin. "Is it that obvious?"

"The eyes don't lie, Alex." She smiled. "Love is obvious to those who can recognize it. Please, go, with our blessing. We have more than enough eager hands here to help us. Take Varani's hands and go on to a future together."

A future? Then he remembered the laws of Alenar and he pressed his lips together. "But Varani is of the Royal House. I'm just a simple soldier."

Hannah's eyes became amused. "Yes, there is that. But what of it?"

"Well, the noble houses of Loemin might be no more, but the nobility of Alenar are still there, in hiding. Once the nation is freed, all the old regulations will apply and those of Royal Blood need the concurrence of the Lords and the Senate to marry. It's in the laws."

"Which Brandi can change," she reminded him.

"After many months of legal wrangling, maybe," he replied. "After reconquering the land and eliminating the remnants of old Torosc and…" he shrugged.

She paused, then drifted over to a nearby desk. "Well, I have something that may help. You are perhaps wondering why we had you take a blood test earlier."

He blinked. "Well, I thought it was to see if I was magically contaminated from the battle against Balris and the Daemons. Megan said that the Daemonic spells were particularly dangerous."

"In part, true. Prolonged exposure can warp and transform someone into something, well, diabolical, but even temporary contact can be damaging.

Thankfully, we are all fine. Did you know that Lord Melinor Indidarc is in Aldath?"

His eyes narrowed. "No… I didn't."

"Yes. He and his whole extended family arrived yesterday – including his natural-born children and their families, as well as Saren and Terenil. I spoke to him about you and Varani. He took a keen interest in your test data."

The tension in the air increased. "My test data? Why?" Alex whispered.

"You remember the old scrolls and books we found in the Vault of Safety? And the Heritage Stones?"

"Yes," he replied slowly, his eyes narrowing.

"Lord Melinor used them and the results were very interesting. Let me show you."

She handed him a scroll. He snatched it and read, then stepped back, holding a chair for support. *Wait!*

"Is this real?" he breathed.

She nodded, beaming at him. "It is. As you're aware, your surname is very old. But there's a little tidbit you aren't aware of. In the north, before there was a Deran, one of the small Paragon Kingdoms was called Terra Dei, or God's Land. Among their nobility was a family with the name of Fejer. We don't know much about them — and maybe the materials from the Vault will tell us more — but you are of their line. As a matter of fact, the Heritage Stones confirmed primogeniture; if there was a Fejer Barony to inherit, it would be yours."

He put a hand to his face, rubbing his jaw, shaking his head. *This is unbelievable!*

"Yes, Alex, you *are* worthy of Varani in spirit and now in lineage," she said softly. "Knowing her, I doubt that she gives two pins about your bloodline anyway, but I sensed that your standards of honor wouldn't allow you to try for her hand if you felt unworthy, no matter what she might insist. This," she waved at the scroll, "removes all possible objection."

We have a future? We can be together? The very air became lighter and he felt weightless. Overcome with gratitude and a swelling of emotion, Alex knelt, pressing Hannah's hand to his forehead.

"I —" his voice broke and he cleared his throat before continuing on. "I can never thank you enough, Hannah."

She gently kissed his cheek. "It's the least I can do for a faithful friend," she said, lifting him up.

He stared at her, still overcome with a swirl of emotions and wild happiness. *Praise you, Jesus!*

"Well?" she said with mischievous grin. "Don't just stand there! She's waiting for you."

<<>>

Evening cast long shadows on the street below as twilight descended like a velvet blanket. Vast crowds of people stood with lanterns, tapers and torches in the wide boulevard and plaza before the Palace. The murmur of thousands of voices floated up to the royal balcony. High in the sky above the city, Tholi and Kindri floated on thermals, their golden scales shimmering like coins.

Connor smoothed his green velvet doublet for the hundredth time and tried not to fidget. Hannah elbowed him.

"You look fine, darling."

His thoughts winged back to a wintry day in Deran, just before the meeting of the Northern Alliance Council, when he and Hannah stood in a guest chamber of the Royal Palace of Oakmoor.

Now it's our palace, our city, our land and our people. And finally, the Alliance and other nations are arriving to help us.

He smiled at her. "These ceremonial things always take too much time to prepare."

"But they are mercifully short."

"Thank Irial."

The door to the balcony opened and his family came to meet them.

"Ready for the show?" Seamus asked, eyes twinkling. The crown of Loemin's king glittered on top of his head. A single large emerald carved into the shape of a badger glowed with internal light above his forehead.

Connor's eyes swept his family: Brendan and Cerys, Deena and Darren. Behind them, all the Grey Riders filed in, smiling and trying to look official. They wore grey hauberks with the silver emblem of a pegasus at the left shoulder. Varani and Alex shared a sweet, secret smile. Dar waggled his eyebrows at Connor and he grinned back.

"Let's do this," Connor said to his father, taking Hannah's hand. "The people have waited long enough."

"Indeed," Seamus said with a wink.

Miriam gave Connor a kiss on the cheek and shared a significant look with Hannah before taking her place at Seamus' side.

Connor shot a glance at his mother and his wife. *Now, what was all that about?*

Seamus nodded to Megan, who then thrust her hands overhead. A cloud of shining motes like dust caught in sunlight floated into the air around the balcony, alighting on Alex, Miriam and Seamus.

Alex bowed to the Royal Family and strode to the edge of the balcony. Varani's eyes shone with pride.

"People of Aldath!" Alex's voice resounded over the scene with the force of a dragon's roar, echoing and rebounding all the way to the city gates. "People of the Free Kingdom of Loemin! Attend! Your King speaks!"

He bowed again and took his place at Varani's side. She squeezed his hand and gazed at him with adoring eyes.

Seamus stepped to the edge of the balcony, hand in hand with Miriam. Dar and Eric gestured and bright globes sprang up above them, illuminating them in the fading daylight.

"People of Loemin!" Seamus' voice boomed out exactly like Alex's. "Rejoice! Your captivity is at an end. The reign of evil is over and our land is free. All those of my house here assembled, as well those of our line yet unborn, pledge our loyalty and service to you forever. Faithful Unto Death!"

"Faithful Unto Death!" The crowd below roared in response, then broke out in cheering. Seamus held up his hands.

Miriam smiled at the people and her voice projected outward to the limits of the city. "Sing praise to Irial, the Creator, the Worldmaker, the Supreme One over all creation! In his great wisdom and mercy, he has seen fit to return our land to us. It is now up to us to care for it, to care for each other, to remain vigilant against evil, and never again to allow the Dark One to gain a foothold in our souls."

The vast assembly cheered again, waving banners and flags of green with the golden badger.

Seamus raised a hand and the people stilled. "We know that we have a daunting task before us. Our nation has suffered for hundreds of years under the Archons and even before that endured centuries of instability from the Paragon Wars. Now that the PRT and its sympathizers have been driven from our midst, the long time of rebuilding begins. But our people are strong and diligent and not afraid of hard work. Together, we will make Loemin better than ever."

He gestured towards Brandi and she joined him at the balustrade. "We wish to thank our well-beloved friends, the Grey Riders," he said, "for their invaluable and loyal assistance and service in reclaiming our land. We could not have done it without them. This morning, one of my first acts as King was to sign a Pledge of Alliance with the Kingdom of Alenar and its heirs in perpetuity. Our Kingdoms henceforth shall be like brothers, sharing in each other's trials, rejoicing in each other's triumphs, aiding each other in all things. One of our first actions as an ally of Alenar will be to assist them in throwing off the yoke of the PRT as we have done here in Loemin."

Brandi bowed to the King and Queen then returned to her place at Eric's side.

Miriam waved her arm to encompass the entire city. "Let it be known the next week shall be a celebration of freedom in our land and this day, the 28th of Marcius, shall be known as Freedom Day, to be observed every year as long as our Kingdom endures. Furthermore, know that from the treasuries of the People's Republic of Torosc within our borders we recovered much of their ill-gotten gains. We will henceforth tabulate the value and distribute to each man, woman and child in our Kingdom a proportional share of that treasure."

The assembly gave a collective gasp, then spontaneous chants of "Loemin! Loemin!" broke out. Miriam and Seamus let the wave pass until the crowd stilled again.

He and Miriam raised their hands. "Raise your voices and sing, O People of Loemin!" they cried out in unison. "Your new day of freedom dawns! Praise Irial!"

"Praise Irial!" The people thundered in response, then broke out in wild applause. Heralds in the courtyard blew trumpets. Fireworks carved glittering trails in the darkening sky above, then boomed and sizzled in a vast array of bright colors. A military band played the long-suppressed anthem of Loemin and people sang along and clapped their hands.

Connor basked in it all, content not to have to worry about fighting or war or evil plots — at least for a little while. He let his eyes roam over his friends gathered on the balcony with him and his thoughts winged away to Andyn and Khyron, Buck and Carine, so far away yet near in spirit. A tear stung his eye as he realized it was the end of a crucial time of his life and the beginning of a new one.

We will always be the Grey Riders. We survived it all, endured it all, and emerged victorious.

He flicked the tear away and squeezed Hannah's hand. "We can build a future now," he said as music played, people danced and fireworks glittered in the evening sky. "We can create a nation based on the rule of law and bring hope to our people and generations yet to come."

She put an arm around him. "Yes. For our children."

He nodded, then something in her tone of voice made him look again. Connor's mother raised her eyebrows and flicked her eyes at Hannah.

Hannah gazed out at the city with a serene countenance.

"Hannah?" Connor asked.

Her smile radiated peace and happiness and she placed Connor's hand on her belly. He stared at her, a bright joy growing in his heart.

"You mean…?"

She kissed him. "Yes. For *our* children, Connor. For our future. For Loemin. Forever."

Chapter Twenty-Three – Hope Unlooked For

Joshua Page set down his hammer on the workbench and lifted the breastplate up to the light. He gave a grim smile.

Well, even though it's going to the Army of the People's Republic, at least it's my handiwork. No one can say I don't give my best effort. That, and I can use the leavings to make armor for the people who really matter.

He inserted the straps and checked them. The door to the armory swung open behind him and slammed into the wall.

"You there!" a rough voice bellowed. "Page! When are we getting our armor, you lazy fat lout?"

Joshua slowly laid the armor down on the table and turned around. "It's done, on time, as promised, Sergeant Sadam."

A burly, bearded human soldier swaggered in, accompanied by two surly-looking troopers. The trio wore dull chainmail under the black and grey surcoat of the 5th Torosc Dragoons and they carried maces and swords at their belts.

"On time?" Sadam demanded, squinting up at Joshua. "We put in a rush order!"

"Which had to take its place in line behind all the other rush orders from the Army. With my apprentice conscripted last month, I can only do so much. I'm only one man."

The sergeant's face darkened. "Well, you'll be half a man if you don't deliver what we ordered, right quick."

Joshua's hand tightened on the edges of his leather apron but he smiled instead. "It's all here, Sergeant, four breastplates." He moved aside, gesturing at the armor on the workbench.

The troops pushed into the workroom and Joshua hid his clenched fist behind his back. Visions of pummeling them danced in his brain, but he took a deep breath.

Easy. Think of Richenda. Think of what Jeremy would say.

The soldiers minutely inspected each breastplate, muttering to each other. Finally, the troopers took two apiece.

Sergeant Sadam spun on his heel. "Acceptable. Barely. I have half a mind to reduce the fee for late delivery and marginal workmanship."

That would be double the mind you already have, Joshua thought. Instead, he said, "I see. So, you think I produce substandard goods. Interesting. I delivered a set of banded mail to Major Rogers last week and he had no objections. Perhaps you're saying that the Major is incapable of assessing armor quality and you are that much more capable. I will mention that to the Major when he comes back tomorrow for a repaired vambrace."

Sadam started and his eyes flicked nervously around the room. "Er, well, no. I didn't imply that at all."

Joshua smiled again and held out his hand. "Then I'm sure the contract price is sufficient."

The sergeant looked torn between an urge to berate him and flee. With a snort of derision, he tossed a small leather bag of coins onto the table. He nodded at his troopers and the gathered up the armor, heading out the door.

"You're not the only armorer in Alford, Joshua Page," he snapped over his shoulder as they walked away. "The problem is that you common folk don't know your place! Well, times are coming when everyone in Coastwatch will know! Mark me! Times are coming!"

Joshua followed them to the door. He watched the Dragoons head off down the main avenue towards the garrison. A trio of Skullhead knights trotted their steeds past Joshua's shop, their nightmare helms gleaming in the sunlight. Townsfolk averted their eyes and gave them a wide berth. A mother shooed her children into an alleyway by a shuttered storefront across the street.

Joshua's eyes fell on the sign on the front wall of the establishment.

"Closed until further notice," he read. A handbill was nailed to the wall next to the sign. Joshua didn't need to read it to know what it said. *Another business taken over by the government for "conspiracy and crimes against the PRT",* he thought bitterly. *When will this end? How much more do we have to endure?*

He forced himself to breathe evenly and unclench his fists. After a few moments contemplating the scene, he returned to his shop and set about arranging his tools for the next day's work.

The door to the house opened and closed behind him. "I'm proud of you," said Richenda.

"I'm not."

Her loving arms encircled his waist and a pair of lips planted a kiss on his back. "Why? Because you didn't pound them? No one hates bullies more than you, love, but for everything there is a season."

He turned around, gazing into his wife's upturned face. "You think you're pretty smart."

Richenda Page lifted a stray blonde hair over a pointed ear and wrinkled her nose at him. "I know I am. And don't you forget it." She ran her fingers through his long dark hair.

He felt the tension leave him at her touch. He kissed her. "Busy morning?"

She unslung her healer's bag from her shoulder and sat on a nearby stool. "The shortage in medicines because of the uprising is making things challenging, but I managed to find enough in town."

He looked deep into her amber-gold eyes. "Speaking of town, how are things?"

Her expression darkened. "Bad to worse. There's another edict about a special tax assessment for funds to fight 'internal enemies of the People's Republic', to the tune of a ten silver per household per month."

He stared at her. "Ten silver a month? Where do they think they're going to get the money? We're stretched thin enough as it is!" His anger returned and he took a deep breath.

"Then I probably shouldn't mention the platoon of regulars encamped near the south gate, or the fact that Ryan Silverman saw Kaftu prowling around near the woods wearing PRT livery."

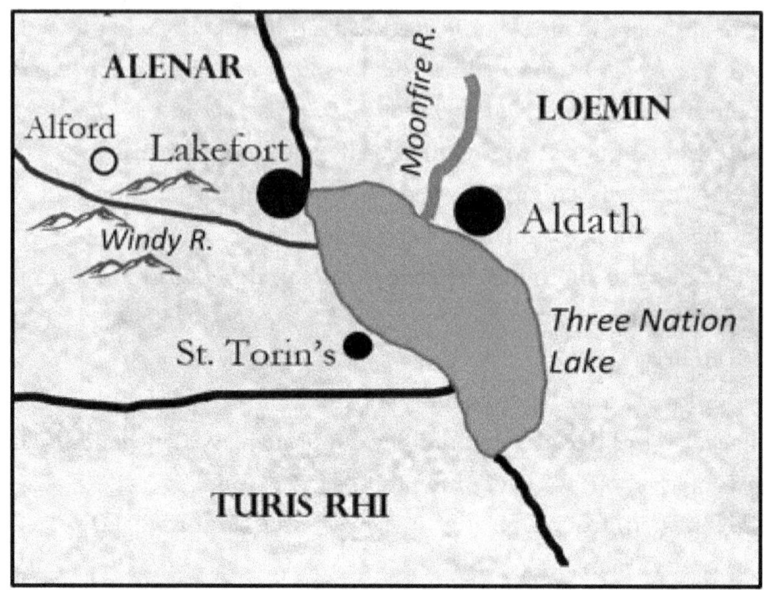

He swore under his breath, gripping the workbench as if he throttled Sergeant Sadam instead. *Hyena-folk in our cities? Dirty mongrel Kaftu! What's next? Dark Elves?*

"Hey."

He looked up.

She fixed him with a stern gaze. "You can't change everything, Joshua. Our time will come."

He almost asked "When" in a petulant voice but knew it would sound, well, petulant, so he nodded instead.

"So, what did you make me for lunch?" she asked with a twinkle in her eye.

He scoffed. "Me? I've been working here the whole time!"

She hopped off the stool and swept up her bag. "Too bad. When your brother shows up, we'll have him make it."

"Jeremiah? Ha. That'll be the day."

The couple headed next door to the house. As they entered, Richenda tapped a blue-gold gemstone embedded on the inside, just behind the door-jamb. A light flashed and shimmered throughout the room.

"Now we can be a little more open," she said. "Have you heard anything lately?"

He eased himself into a chair at the kitchen table, wincing as a flash of pain hit his knee. *Too much standing. Have to take breaks.* "There's supposedly a new King crowned in Aldath, Seamus IV. Also, wild rumors of the death of a Daemon prince when the king invaded the capital. And that's the news I've been able to corroborate via more than one source."

Richenda brought a flask of ale to the table and poured each of them a cup. "Loemin is right on our doorstep. No wonder the Republic is putting more troops in here and levying extra taxes. They think we're next."

He took a swig and brushed his jaw with his hand. "And they'd be right. People are fed up. All this talk of the Grey Riders and exiled royals is making everyone jittery."

She sat with him. "Do you think it's real? Have they found someone to take up the Crown of Alenar?"

He shook his head. "The White Throne has been empty for hundreds of years. We hear rumors from time to time about a new age of freedom, only to find out they were trash. Will the Riders come? Have they found successors to the throne? Or is it just more bait rumors to ferret out dissenters? I don't know."

The couple heard a quadruple tap on the back door, followed by a single knock. Richenda raised an eyebrow and opened it.

"Greetings, sister-in-law," Jeremiah Page said, giving Richenda a peck on the cheek. He breezed into the kitchen as if he owned it. "What's for lunch?"

Joshua scoffed. "Whatever you make. We've been working all morning."

Jeremiah grinned, his dark eyes dancing. "And I haven't?"

"Painting signs isn't work."

"You try it. On second thought, don't. We don't want anyone going blind." Jeremiah set down his painter's bag and opened the pantry, rummaging around.

Richenda scooted around him and swatted Jeremiah in the hip. "Don't take up the whole kitchen, Jeremy. Lord, I would have to get two of the largest men in Alford in my house."

She sidled over to Joshua and sat on the arm of his chair. He put his arm around her.

"We're not the largest and you know it," Jeremy's voice came back to them, muted, from the inside of the pantry. "The Pendrake brothers are bigger. We're just athletic."

He turned around, bearing half a loaf of bread, two paper-wrapped packages and a bowl of peppers, cucumbers and a mango. "See? I knew there was lunch in here somewhere." He drew a knife from a sheath on his forearm and began peeling the mango.

Richenda rolled her eyes and moved to Jeremy's side, opening the paper packets. "I'll take over from here, thank you." She laid sliced ham, cheese, bread and vegetables on the table.

Jeremy dropped into a chair and took a swig from the ale bottle, earning him a swat in the arm from Richenda.

"Don't contaminate my ale," Joshua growled.

Jeremy's ever-present grin returned. "Nothing to worry about. We're related." He continued peeling and slicing the fruit.

"Any news?" Richenda asked, slicing the peppers and cucumbers.

Jeremy's eyes shot to the doorjamb and Joshua waved a hand. "We're fine. No one can hear us outside the house."

Jeremy's expression turned somber. "Scouts sighted pegasus riders in the hills near Alford, over by the ruined tower."

Jeremy and Richenda exchanged a look. "Really?" he said. "How many?"

"Four. Looks like three Elves or half-Elves and a human."

Pegasus riders again, like last time, except those were PRT agents. Joshua absently accepted a plate from Richenda. "What does Colonel Severin say?"

"He's unsure. After the incident at Tinbore last month, he's really cautious."

Richenda set down two more plates and the three ate in silence. Joshua mulled over the situation. If it really was the Grey Riders, they needed to make contact, and soon, before Republic intelligence agents found out. He doubted if the Riders were strong enough to fend off the inevitable swarm of PRT attackers. On the other hand, if they were just more spies, the rebellion could ill-afford another disaster like Tinbore.

He made his decision. "We should investigate. Immediately."

Jeremiah asked. "Shouldn't we wait to see what they do?"

Joshua shook his head, running his hands through his long, dark hair. "No. If they're legitimate, there's not a moment to lose."

Jeremy dusted off his hands and drained his cup. "Say no more." He strode to a window and opened it. Putting his fingers to his mouth, he let out a short, warbling whistle. Seconds later, a tiny, winged monkey a little larger than his hand fluttered in and alighted on his forearm.

"Well, Coraline," Jeremy said, giving the Tree Flitter a slice of mango, "We have a job to do. Ready to spy on someone?"

Coraline bobbed her head and chittered, then bit into the fruit with miniature sharp teeth.

Joshua stood. "Full kit," he said. Jeremy pursed his lip.

"No arguments," Joshua said. "We need to be ready for anything."

"I'll come too," Richenda said.

"No," Joshua said, then held up a hand when she opened her mouth to protest. "If all of us suddenly disappear from town, that will raise suspicions." He smiled. "Don't worry. No unnecessary risks."

"You better not," she warned with a kiss on his cheek.

"Guaranteed." He tried to ignore Richenda's worried expression.

Jeremy ran a hand over his short, black hair. "Well, well, well, Coraline. What do we have here?" he said.

Coraline shifted on his shoulder and bobbed her head, giving a short chirp.

Jeremy peered through the underbrush at the figures in the woods. Four people — two men and two women — set up camp as four black, winged horses cropped grass nearby. Drooping branches of willows and tall, heavy-leafed banban trees crowded the area but the travelers had managed to find an open space large enough to accommodate three times their number.

Far enough from Alford to avoid patrols. Campsite is well-hidden and with plenty of foliage overhead to sift out campfire smoke he mused. *They have a ranger.*

Briefly, he wondered if he needed to go back to his brother but discarded the idea. Best to find out more before reporting in.

He watched the four. They were obviously two couples, the way that the women interacted with the men. As if to confirm his assessment, the younger woman leaned against the dark-haired man and he put his arm around her. The women were also obviously related, based on their similar facial features, physiques and red-gold hair.

Only one human — the dark-haired man. The others are half-Elves. Interesting. He continued observing for a while. He noticed that the older of the two women wore chainmail under her tunic, like the two men, and had her hair in a braid. The younger woman wore a traveling outfit of a long tunic and breeches and a silver circlet held her hair in place off her forehead. The half-elven man put a hand on the pommel of an ornate dagger at his belt and Jeremy's eyes flitted to the bastard sword on the human man's back.

Jeremy rubbed his chin. *They wear armor, so the older of the two women and both men are warriors for sure. The younger woman could be a wizard or a healer. Or both.*

He withdrew a miniature cord necklace with a dull brown gemstone from his belt purse and slipped it over Coraline's head. The necklace blended in with Coraline's fur perfectly. "Let's have a closer look, shall we?" He tapped the jewel and immediately, a translucent overlay of Coraline's perspective leapt up over his own eyesight.

"Go, Coraline."

The tiny flying monkey jumped and flapped her wings, heading for a branch of a banban that held a trio of other Flitters.

Jeremiah watched his quarry. The human's dark eyes flicked to Coraline and Jeremy held his breath, ready to recall her if anything should go awry. To his relief, the man did nothing. The people's words became intelligible as Coraline alighted on the bough.

"What are those animals, Megan?" the human man asked the woman with the circlet, nestled into his side.

She smiled. "They're called Tree Flitters. Inoffensive little things. They eat fruit and insects. Some people keep them as pets. They're fairly intelligent and can be used to guard nurseries from vermin since they're protective of their own young."

"Kinda cute. Maybe we should get some. Hey Eric," the man called over his shoulder. "Want a few Tree Flitters for the castle?"

"I'll put it on my list of future improvements, Dar," the blond Elven man replied. The woman with the braid smiled and shook her head.

Castle? What castle?

Tree branches swayed from a sudden wind. The Flitters next to Coraline became alert, looking up at the sky. Coraline froze. Jeremiah sensed her alarm and wariness.

Something is coming.

The two couples at the campsite rose and moved the pegasi aside.

To Jeremy's astonishment, a pair of gold dragons drifted down out of the sky and landed in the glade. More amazing, a Goblin wearing black leather armor and a silky black cloak sat in a saddle atop the larger dragon.

"Greetings," the Goblin said, hopping down out of the saddle. A silver crucifix glinted against his camouflage tunic, similar to the one that Joshua always wore.

Wait. Christians with a Goblin? Goblins are evil. What is going on here?

"Go closer," he whispered to Coraline through the link.

The Flitter's eyes flashed to the dragons and she balked.

"I don't think they'll hurt you, baby," he whispered. "Go on."

Reluctantly, Coraline flew to a branch of a closer tree.

"What news, Gorlak?" asked the older of the two women.

"Town of Alford is near, Queen Brandawyn," the Goblin replied with a bow. "Enemy soldiers encamp around it and Tholi sees Kaftu patrols in woods. Soldiers checking people coming into town and leaving."

At the goblin's words, Jeremy's heartbeat accelerated. *Queen! Wait! The rumors! Could this be one of the exiled royals?*

"Just like the other towns," Eric continued. "The PRT is taking steps to avoid what happened in Loemin. We can't use the same ploy Hannah and Connor used in Havenridge."

The larger of the two dragons lowered himself to lie on the ground. "Yes," he said in a deep voice. "I saw many archers and two light ballistae among them. They are watching the skies."

"Did they see you?" the queen asked.

The smaller dragon shook her head. "We were careful, Majesty."

"Then we'll have to be clever," the queen continued. "What about the nearby area? Are there farms where we could observe and try to figure out if there are sympathizers?"

Gorlak nodded. "Yes. Farms and groves and a few ranches."

"Well, we have to do something," the younger woman said. "Alex and

Varani will be back from their own reconnaissance in three days and I'd like to be able to start coordinating."

They all began to discuss the region around Alford.

This is strange. Jeremy's mind raced and he only listened with half an ear. *A Goblin means evil, but he wears a crucifix. If the older woman is a queen, that means that her relative is probably a princess.*

The group continued the discussion, using many terms and names he didn't recognize.

And they all talk as if they oppose the PRT. They're either ridiculously good actors, or they're not evil, Jeremy mused. His eyes began to feel sore and he rubbed them. He would have to break the link soon or risk a splitting headache.

"Those little flying monkeys are charming things," noted the smaller dragon with a smile.

"Would you like a Tree Flitter of your own, Kindri?" the half-Elven man asked with a grin. "Dar is planning on gathering a small herd of them."

That got a round of laughter, especially from the dragons.

Well, I've heard enough to convince me.

"Come back, Coraline."

Jeremy broke the link and waited for her to return to his shoulder. Then, without wasting another second, he drifted back through the trees and brush like a ghost.

<<>>

"I'm not convinced." Joshua said, tossing a stick into the campfire.

Jeremy refrained from grinding his teeth. "I think they're for real."

His brother frowned, the flickering firelight casting deep shadows on his face. "We've been fooled before, and badly."

"That was different," Jeremy reasoned. "The false saviors rode into Tinbore in the open, at the head of a company of troops with fake Northern Alliance livery. They handed out gold like candy and made a big show of denouncing the Republic at every turn. I think we're being too wary with this group."

"They weren't wary enough in Tinbore," Joshua replied stubbornly. "Look what it got them. A town burned, men killed, women and children taken as slaves or sacrifices."

Jeremy felt his frustration rising. "Even if this were some kind of deception, there aren't enough Republic troops to do the same in Alford as they did in Tinbore. They'd need two brigades at least."

Joshua rubbed his jaw. "True. I see the differences." He stood, lost in thought for a while. "Now that you mention it, I realized something else: there are PRT soldiers nearby, but these four and their dragons seem to be taking pains to stay away from them, as if they want to avoid detection. That's too much play-acting even for the People's Republic Intelligence Service."

Jeremy said nothing. From long practice he knew to let his older brother figure things out on his own and then make a decision.

Joshua is decisive when he has enough information. Besides, he's an officer. It's not my call.

Finally, Joshua nodded. "All right. You've convinced me. We should go talk to them, right now, tonight."

Jeremy blinked. "Tonight?"

"Yes. We know the terrain and they don't. More importantly, the new troops at Alford don't either, not even the hyena-folk. We'll have the cover of darkness and less chance of some random patrol stumbling over us. You know the way, so you lead."

Without another word, the brothers doused the fire, gathered their packs and set out. Jeremy loosened his daggers in his scabbards and held his bow ready as they sneaked through the woods. They moved slowly, carefully, navigating by the light of the two moons overhead. Several times, he halted when he saw motion. Each time, he reached into his belt purse and put a pale green gemstone to his eye. When the magical jewel revealed the heat outline of normal forest animals, he motioned them onward.

Then he spied the faint flicker of the travelers' campfire. He motioned his brother closer. "If we approach from the area farthest from the pegasi, it will appear least threatening."

Joshua nodded. They crept up to the underbrush nearby. Once again, Jeremy observed the two couples, the Goblin and the dragons. He dearly wished for Coraline but she needed her rest and Tree Flitters didn't do well at night.

Joshua nodded and they edged in closer.

A tiny red flare burst at their feet and a crystal rod near the campfire glowed white. A bright beam of light lanced towards the brothers, illuminating them even through the undergrowth.

Jeremy froze, hands gripping his daggers.

The people at the fire immediately formed a semi-circle facing him, hands on their weapons, with the dragons on either side.

"Show yourselves, with your hands up," the woman named Brandawyn said.

For a second, Jeremy thought of racing off into the woods, but a warning look from his brother stopped him.

Joshua slowly stepped forward, hands up. "We mean no harm. We only want to talk."

"There are only two of them," said the man named Dar. "Want to make sure there aren't any others, Kindri?"

The smaller dragon nodded, gave the Page brothers an unnerving once-over with glowing golden eyes, then slithered into the forest.

"I promise," said Joshua. "It's just us."

Dar grinned. "Fine, then introduce yourselves."

"Joshua and Jeremy Page, of Alford, Coastwatch."

"Alenar," said Brandawyn.

Jeremy stared at her. She smiled. "The kingdom's rightful name is Alenar, not Coastwatch."

"We are —" Eric began.

Jeremy inclined his head. "Queen Brandawyn and Eric, Megan and Dar, Gorlak, Kindri and Tholi."

Now the interlopers stared. Jeremy felt completely satisfied.

"I should probably ask how you know that," said Eric with a chuckle, "but I'm not sure you'd tell me right away."

Jeremy just smiled.

The Goblin bowed. "Then you know, Page brothers of Alford, these are heirs to throne of Alenar: Queen Brandawyn and High Prince Eric, High Princess Megan and First Prince Darius."

"And you are?" Jeremy raised an eyebrow at him.

The Goblin smiled, black eyes glinting, his short fangs gleaming in the firelight. "No one important."

"I doubt that," Jeremy said but decided not to press the issue. Despite Gorlak's small size, he carried himself like a professional soldier.

The dragon Kindri returned. Eric met her eyes. She shook her head and took up a position behind the brothers, watching the forest.

Trusting but not too trusting.

"I'll come right to the point," Joshua said, lowering his hands. "We're here to find out your true intentions. We've heard rumors that you helped lead the reconquest of Bluevale, which is now called Loemin, and we need to find out if you're here to do the same."

"How can we convince you?" asked Dar.

"Maybe you should start with something that proves your identities."

Megan reached into a shoulder bag next to a log and held out a set of scrolls. "Have a look," she said.

Joshua took them and read. Despite his own curiosity, Jeremy kept his eyes and a disarming smile on the group.

"Those would be very hard to forge," Joshua said finally, handing the papers to Jeremy, "But not impossible."

Jeremy scanned the papers, eyes alighting on the wax seals of the Kingdom of Deran, the Papal Nuncio, the Emperor of Terenai and the High Matriarch of Verian. All of them glittered with a faint luminance.

Geez, Joshua, he thought. *They're even magically enhanced. "Not impossible to forge" my ass. These people are for real.*

"So, you have reason to doubt our intentions?" asked Brandi.

Joshua shrugged. "We can't be too careful these days."

"What would you suggest?" asked Eric. "I know a Heritage Stone would help, but it looks like you're fresh out of them."

Jeremy couldn't help but grin at that. Joshua's eyes flicked to him. "If you're legitimate and not agents of the PRT, then you wouldn't mind taking on a particular mission for us."

Jeremy's pulse quickened.

"What kind of mission?" asked Brandi.

Joshua smiled. "A few weeks ago, a village named Tinbore was razed by the PRT as part of an operation to ferret out rebel sympathizers. Some of the people were taken away as slaves, to a camp where some of our brother officers in the cause are also imprisoned. We'd like you to free them. All of them.”

The newcomers exchanged smiles and Dar rubbed his hands together.

“You’re speaking my language, Mister Page,” he said. “Please, give us the particulars…”

Chapter Twenty-Four – Proof of Life

Brandi surveyed the camp. "Well, I like our chances so far," she said. "Not too many guards."

"The ones you can see, that is," replied Joshua.

She shot him a look. The rebel officer kept his eyes on the prison camp, chewing his bottom lip.

"What makes you say that?"

Joshua paused for a moment. "The PRT are full of tricks. Let's see what Jeremy and Dar say."

Brandi frowned but remained silent. *I've been gone from this land for many years. Much may have changed. I have to trust them. After all, the Page brothers are my people.*

"My people," she whispered. Despite the tension of what they were about to do, the words filled her with elation. *My people. The people of Alenar. The ones I came to set free.*

The enormity of the responsibility contrasted with the satisfaction of finally being able to do something for them. *I will free you.*

She returned her gaze to the stockade. It squatted in the hollow ahead, framed on two sides by trees and to the rear by a hill. Two bright spheres of silvery light hovered above a large pavilion close to the hill. Next to the pavilion, a regular arrangement of vine-covered stones betokened some ancient structure.

Smaller tents dotted the sward near four large cages, illuminated by the light of campfires. Six troopers in black and green livery strolled in pairs near the entrance to the camp.

She adjusted her position in the underbrush, moving one of her blades out of the way. "What are those ruins?" she asked, nodding towards the over-grown stones.

"An old temple of Kurental," Joshua said with a frown of his own. "Destroyed ages ago when the Archons turned evil. There are supposed to be tunnels that go back into the hill — ritual chambers and storage from what I heard. I wouldn't be surprised if the Torosci have taken them over for something dark."

Eric pushed through nearby bushes and crouched at their side. "They're back."

Two shadowy figures slipped through the underbrush with only a few swaying leaves to mark their passage.

"Well?" asked Megan.

Jeremy squatted down under a large shrub. "Trying to infiltrate through the woods on either side won't work."

Brandi sat back against a tree trunk. "Why not?"

"We saw a Red Veil officer near the command pavilion." Jeremy exchanged a look with his brother.

"What does that mean?" Eric asked. "I know the Red Veils are a problem but it's only one."

Dar shook his head. "According to Jeremy, officers rarely travel alone. And the Red Veils are known to have potions made with Troll blood that can camouflage them."

Megan nodded slowly. "And I can't use dispelling magic without giving away my position, so that's not an option."

Brandi stared at the camp again, mulling over options in her mind as she listened to the others. *Guide me, Lord,* she prayed.

"We also saw hippogriffs," Dar added, "so an aerial assault will be a problem. Hippogriffs aren't as fast as pegasi, but they can prevent us from landing and there's no way we can descend undetected with all those light sources."

"I wonder if we can draw them by attacking the guards by the entrance, then slipping off into the forest," Eric mused. "Then some of us could sneak in behind them when they chase the first group."

"No good." Joshua adjusted his gauntlets. "Those are Torosc dragoons. We've used that tactic before and they're on to it by now."

Brandi felt her frustration rising and she wracked her brain for a different approach. She forced herself to relax. *I have to let the Lord guide me.*

Megan and the others held a whispered conference and Brandi's eyes wandered to the tattoo of an armored angel on Joshua's bicep. She smiled. *It looks a lot like an Elohir. Speaking of Elohir, what I would give to have one available, or something equally distracting.*

She mulled over various approaches but nothing obvious presented itself. Her eyes wandered to Tholi and Kindri, lying in the brush nearby.

Something distracting! Well, they certainly fit the bill.

"Do they have any artillery?" she whispered.

The others stopped talking and looked at her.

"Artillery," she repeated. "Particularly ballistae."

A slow smile spread over Jeremy's features. "No, Majesty, they do not."

Brandi returned his smile. "Then I think it's time for Kindri and Tholi to pay them a visit."

<<>>

"Ready for the fireworks?" asked Megan in a low voice.

"Yes, but not understand why I not ride Tholi," Gorlak whispered at her side.

"We need you here on the ground if we go into the old tunnels," she reminded him. "I'm still not much good in there."

He muttered something she couldn't hear. She hid a smile. *He's getting entirely too comfortable as a dragon-rider.*

She returned to her observation of the camp, wondering when the dragons would leap into action. As if on cue, a sharp wind blew and the horses snorted, pulling at their reins, eyes wide. The four hippogriffs clawed the turf, curved beaks upturned to the sky, eyes glittering. The warriors by the command pavilion halted their conversation, hands going to weapons. A woman in banded mail peered up into the night. A red-enameled veil of chain mesh hung from her helmet.

Red Veil commander. That means the others are out there somewhere.

With a suddenness that made her start, Tholi and Kindri swooped down out of the darkness, unleashing blasts of fire at the Torosci warriors in the camp. Notably, they left the hippogriffs alone.

Tents burst into flame and wooden containers blazed. Troops scattered, shouting and loosing arrows at the hovering dragons. More soldiers emerged from the tents, strapping on armor and grabbing weapons. The Red Veil commander screamed an order and, just as Megan had hoped, four similarly attired women shimmered into view near the prisoner cages. They raced towards the hippogriffs.

Just as they mounted up, Kindri and Tholi soared off into the night. The enemy air cavalry launched themselves into the air in pursuit.

Bows twanged near the entrance. Four guards dropped and the burly forms of Joshua and Jeremy Page charged into the remaining warriors. A roiling melee swirled.

"Now, Gorlak." Megan broke cover and raced towards the left side of the camp, near one of the prisoner cages. A crossbowman sighted on her but Gorlak dropped him with a sizzling blue bolt of his own.

Megan paused, motioning with her staff at a trio of guards pelting their way. A dark, cloying fog swirled up out of the grass, covering the enemy completely. She and Gorlak swerved around the cloud. She cast a Storm Force spell for good measure from her staff and the guards flew backwards twenty feet.

At the cages, she cast a spell at the locks and they exploded into fragments. The prisoners scrambled towards the doors and Gorlak flipped them open.

Dar raced to her side, his sword red with blood. "Follow me," he ordered the prisoners. "Are any rebel officers with you?"

A young female Elf in white rags shook her head. "They took them into the pavilion a couple of days ago and we haven't seen them since."

"What's in the pavilion?" Megan asked.

A portly human man gestured. "Tunnels that go deep into the cliff. We never hear any sound from there."

"We'll handle them," Megan said.

"No," Dar said, eyes narrowed. "They've been alerted by now with all this ruckus."

The Elf shook her head. "That far underground, they won't be able to hear anything. Besides, all the guards came out and none went in."

Dar frowned and Megan put a hand on his arm. "I'll be okay. You're needed out there."

A conflict warred in his eyes but he finally nodded. He kissed her hand as he led the slaves away to safety.

"Alright, Gorlak," she said, preparing several spells in her mind. "Let's see what's going on in there."

The Goblin gave her a wicked grin and drew his glittering dagger.

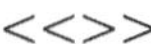

A hard slap brought Major Adam Tolbert to groggy wakefulness.

"Come on, Major," said a cheerful male voice. "No time for dozing."

A cold splash of water left him gasping and alert. He raised gritty eyes to a tall blond man in scale mail with the symbol of the Skullhead Legion emblazoned on the chest. Oil lamps cast capering shadows in the nearly-empty room. "I'd rather keep my eyes closed, Ormond," Tolbert retorted, "if the alternative is looking at you."

A dark-haired woman with smooth, youthful features leaned back onto a nearby table. She wore what could only be described as a chainmail negligee, but that didn't fool Tolbert. The armor glittered with magic. Crimson runes writhed on the head of a war hammer at her hip.

"Well, he can still talk, which is useful." She selected a wicked-looking set of pincers from a nearby table. "We need to make him talk about the right kinds of things."

"If he won't talk, I'm sure there are others who will." Ormond smirked. "You have family in Coastwatch, don't you Major? Maybe some of Roshana's coreligionists should pay them a visit."

A momentary panic rushed through Tolbert's mind at the idea of Gudarta fiends plying their sadistic trade on his wife and children. He struggled to keep any hint of apprehension off his face. *Linda knows the signs. They'll get away. We have allies.*

Ormond straddled a nearby chair. "Let's dispense with the song and dance, shall we? If you're an adherent of the Church of Gariil, I'm an Elohir.

Tell us. Which one of the prohibited churches do you serve? Verian? Irial? Christianity?"

Tolbert didn't answer, keeping his gaze fixed on the door to the adjacent guard room. He tested the bonds on his wrists and ankles holding him to the chair but could barely move his arms.

"We can just pick one," Ormond continued. "It's a death sentence anyway."

"It won't matter," Tolbert answered. "The Ja'al are finished. The Daemons are either dead or have escaped back to Hades. Your time is ending and you know it."

Ormond's eyes flicked to Roshana, who shrugged. "It will matter to you," the Gudarta priestess replied. "And to your family. Do you think that everyone will suddenly rise up now and restore the old kingdoms? Many people are still loyal to the Grand Remaking. The People's Republic of Torosc is strong, despite what you may have heard."

Tolbert chose not to answer.

"It's true we've taken some losses," Roshana continued, laying the pincers down on the table, "but the bulk of our strength remained in Torosc. Additionally, there are still some of our allies from Hades who weren't killed. They're very much alive, as everyone will soon find out."

What? Dear God! Tolbert's mind raced. *If there are still daemons on Damora, no one is safe.*

He thought back to the rumors and stories he had heard. Tales said a mighty Elohir Army had annihilated the Ja'al Dark Wave up north. One source maintained that descendants of the rightful rulers of Torosc's many districts had been found and were coming to reclaim their homelands. Some even said the Grey Riders were on their way. Those thoughts buoyed his spirits.

Daemons or no daemons, he concluded, it won't matter. *The reign of evil in the Southlands will end. It has to.*

"It won't matter when the Grey Riders get here," he retorted.

"Grey Riders!" Roshana laughed out loud.

"That's very funny," Ormond chuckled. "Grey Riders indeed."

Roshana smirked. "Well, you have one thing right, Major. The question of religion is not as important as who is loyal to the Cause. Suppose you start naming those who are no longer supporters of Torosc? It might make a big difference to the health and well-being of your family, not to mention great rewards for you."

Tolbert told her where she could put her rewards.

In one long step, she closed the distance to him and gripped his jaw with her hand. Her eyes blazed. "Don't place so much faith in the Riders. They won't be going anywhere: Shrike assassins will see to that."

She jerked his head to the side, a motion that restarted his headache.

"The pincers or something more brutal?" Ormond asked.

"Neither," she said, standing tall. "I have more elegant methods." She began a harsh, sing-song chant. Ormond took two wax plugs from his belt purse and inserted them in his ears.

Tolbert gasped. The air filled with needles of sound. Tingling, intense pain lanced into his ears, eyes, skin and even his brain. He heard someone scream and realized it was himself.

Abruptly, the hellish song stopped. Ormond removed his ear plugs and smiled genially.

Roshana leered at him. "I can keep this up all day. Give up on any lies about anyone coming down to liberate the old lands. It won't happen."

Tolbert breathed deeply, willing the headache and pain to subside. When he could talk, he raised his eyes to Roshana's. "The Riders will be here. They are bringing the rightful Queen of Alenar and the High Princess."

Ormond snorted in derision. "Now I know you're delusional. Queen? High Princess? I don't see any of them, do you?"

A double-thump sounded from the adjacent guard room. Roshana frowned and nodded at the door. Ormond rose from his chair, but before he took more than two steps, the portal burst open.

A figure in a hooded cloak stepped into the room with a young Halfling man. Behind them, Tolbert spotted the prone figures of two Gudarta warriors in the outer guard chamber. The Halfling removed a medallion from around his neck. The air around him shimmered and he transformed into a wiry Goblin carrying a glowing dagger. A silver crucifix lay against his tabard.

The figure lifted the hood. A gorgeous half-Elven woman regarded the room with amber eyes. Her red-gold hair glowed in the firelight. She wore a grey tunic with the figure of a flying pegasus on the left breast and a circlet of silver around her brow. She carried a staff of shiny white wood. She made a fist with her free hand and golden lightning crackled around it. Her eyes became pools of light.

"My name is Megan Aldenar, High Princess. You were saying?"

Chapter Twenty-Five – Cards on the Table

I'm tired of waiting. Golvadu Fellhammer clasped his hands behind his back and stared at the embroidered wall of his massive pavilion. *We need to get moving.*

"Your Grace?" Ilyan Kalik's said from the entrance.

Shit. What does he want now? Golvadu turned around. "Yes, Priest Kalik? I trust you have good news."

The Vardu cleric bowed, his blue scale mail armor reflecting the light of nearby mage fires. Three Red Veil assassins waited behind him. "The emissaries from Jered and Morlan arrive with their battalions."

Finally! Those dullards sure took their time. "Excellent. I will meet with them now." He smoothed his robes, lifted his staff in his hand and strode to the pavilion entrance. Three Red Veil assassins bowed as he exited, then fell into place behind Kalik.

Hmm, Golvadu mused. *They seem to follow him around a lot lately. Well, no matter. It is only three, and if Kalik decides to betray our arrangement, I can handle him and his crimson bitches without any trouble.*

Golvadu stopped outside and waited patiently, a smug smile on his face. All around his pavilion on the grassy knolls, orderly camps of Torosc soldiery spread like a vast carpet of cloth, leather and steel. In the maintenance yards, catapults, trebuchets and ballistae sat in rows like children's toys. Smoke billowed from a sacrificial altar atop another nearby hill and Golvadu made out the forms of Daemons there: Shock Hind, Tigris Infernalis and Deathhammers.

Yes, despite our recent setbacks, everything is coming together nicely.

Groups of riders approached and Golvadu shifted his attention to them. Two banners fluttered in the breeze as the parties rode up the hill: the rainbow ensign of the Confederacy of Jered and a white comet on a black field, for Morlan. Most importantly, large formations of Jeredan and Morlani troops followed at a slower pace in the distance.

He waited for the ambassadors. Ilyan Kalik bowed to Golvadu and then to the newcomers as they cantered to a halt and dismounted.

Ilyan gestured to two men leading the groups. "Your Grace, may I introduce His Serene Highness, Prince Don Patian of Jered and His Grace Gilbert Bates, Archduke of Morlan." He then swept a hand at Golvadu. "Your Highness, Your Grace, this is Golvadu Fellhammer, First Archon of Torosc."

In a heartbeat, Golvadu assessed the pair. Patian measured him right back with shiny black eyes set in a swarthy face, his dark brown hair under a spired helmet encrusted with jewels. His grey mantle bore the symbols of the Six Pirate Kings.

Bates nodded, pale grey eyes calm. He wore wizard's robes decorated with shimmering runes of power. A gold circlet with the tiny figure of a dragon on the front sat on his blonde hair.

Golvadu bowed and straightened. "My lords. You honor me greatly."

Patian gave him a thin smile in return. "The Confederacy of Jered is always pleased to aid our allies in Torosc."

Bates grinned. "As is Morlan. It is in our interest to see your Republic succeed against the ignorance of the unenlightened."

Golvadu swept a hand at the pavilion. "Please join me inside. You must be tired from your journey."

Once inside, he noticed Kalik lurking in their wake, followed by his three guards. He nodded in his direction. "My lords, you have already made the acquaintance of Priest Ilyan Kalik of Vardu, our emissary from his church."

Kalik bowed low.

Bates gave Kalik a once-over. "Indeed," the Archduke noted. "It appears we are now in common cause against a common enemy."

"It seems you have allies from every corner of the world, Archon Golvadu." Prince Patian said, a dark eyebrow arching over equally dark eyes. "Dark Elven knights as your personal guard, Red Veils, Vardish priests,

Daemons on the hill — and did I not see a high matriarch of Cla'Agik passing by with her retinue as we came in?"

Golvadu curled his fingers at a nearby wine table. It rolled towards him of its own accord. He then beckoned to a decanter on the table and it floated to his hand. "Yes. She has been sent by their Council to assist us. We are united in putting down these rebellions and defeating the Northern Alliance and its lapdogs." With a smile, he poured three goblets of wine and handed one each to Patian and Bates.

Patian waited until Golvadu drank before sipping from his goblet. He nodded, impressed. "A very fine vintage."

"Taken during our campaign in Terenai. The Elves are self-righteous, simpering bastards, but they do make good wine, I have to admit."

Bates also sipped, then strolled towards a tapestry of a black dragon consuming a dismembered knight. "I understand that a Prince of Daemons is also aiding you."

Golvadu kept his expression neutral. "Yes, Excellency. Prince Tarvener is even now in command of the garrison in the capital of Coastwatch."

"Indeed." Bates regarded the tapestry, tracing the dragon's tail with a finger. "I wonder how you manage to control him. Daemons are famous for having hidden agendas."

Golvadu chose his words carefully, well aware that anything he said could find its way to Tarvener's ears. "His Highness Prince Tarvener has proven to be a most reliable and helpful ally."

Patian lounged on a nearby couch, nonchalantly appropriating a tiny honey cake from a platter and popping it into his mouth. "Let us get down to business, Your Grace. I bring twenty regiments of Jeredan regulars and His Excellency Duke Gilbert is in command of two Morlani divisions. This is a significant contribution. We expect a significant reward."

Taking over like he owns the place. Golvadu raised an eyebrow at Patian's presumption and graciously sat in a nearby chair. "Of course, Highness. There are plenty of rewards in the offing. Once we blunt the efforts of the rebels and strike northward, the riches of the nation of Gorostol are only the first of a basket of ripe plums to be picked. However, I understand that the profits may not be acquired immediately, so I am prepared to offer one quarter of our spoils of war to each of you, as assessed in tax from the rebel provinces in the form of coin, materials and slaves."

Bates also sat. "From all the rebel provinces except Bluevale, of course — I'm sorry, it's called Loemin now, isn't it?" He smiled.

Golvadu decided not to rise to the challenge. "Temporarily. That province is landlocked and not large. Make no mistake. We will reconquer it and they will reap the whirlwind. They are only Halflings for the most part."

"Yet you turned aside from Loemin's capital city of Aldath and diverted here to Coastwatch," Patian sipped his wine. "It doesn't give the impression that you were willing to take them on."

Inwardly, Golvadu seethed. He smiled nonchalantly and flicked a finger to a bunch of grapes in a bowl next to Patian. The fruit floated to his hand past Patian's face. The prince didn't even flinch.

"All in due time. We know their game," Golvadu replied, plucking a grape and popping it into his mouth. "We diverted here as a counter to their plans, not because we feared them. If the rebels manage to conquer Coastwatch, then Bluevale will have an ally with a major seaport. If we thwart them, it will be an easy matter to strangle Bluevale later."

Bates nodded slowly. "And Prince Tarvener?"

Golvadu popped another grape into his mouth. "He holds the port, which Brandawyn of Alenar must capture if she is to implement her alliance with Bluevale. Our combined force — with your reinforcements, of course — marches to intercept the rebel army near Tor Aldin."

"A good plan," Patian admitted. "But some of your other plans did not go so well. I understand you are without three of your top allies now, due to the exploits of these so-called Grey Riders."

Golvadu took his time chewing and swallowing. "Everyone rises to the level of their own incompetence, Highness, and they obviously reached their zenith. Or nadir, depending on your interpretation." He finished the grapes and wiped his mouth with a napkin. "Shall we go review the troops?"

Patian and Bates stood, smoothing their attire.

Golvadu nodded at Kalik, standing quiet and impassive in a corner of the pavilion. "Bring Vizkir." Kalik bowed and departed.

Golvadu proceeded outside with his guests. Patian and Bates mounted up. The Prince eyed Golvadu. "You are walking?" Then his eyes flicked skyward and narrowed.

Golvadu smiled. The rush of wings and a quadruple thud beside the pavilion signaled the arrival of Vizkir.

"Your Grace commands?" rumbled a sibilant voice. A massive blue and purple Drake slithered close, shouldering aside guards. His eyes glowed red.

Golvadu inclined his head. "Ah, Vizkir. Good of you to come. If you please?"

The dragon crouched down and Golvadu clambered up into the special saddle on his back. Vizkir straightened to his full height, his head towering twenty feet in the air.

"Shall we?" Golvadu nudged the dragon, who stalked forward down the hill with Bates and Patian riding horses at his side.

Golvadu's eyes roamed over the army and a deep feeling of satisfaction settled in his chest. Each section of the army was laid out with meticulous attention to detail: Kaftu and Ogre camps separated, Goblins quartered away from Dark Elves, engineers encamped near their siege artillery, massive mess tents belching smoke from their roof vents, corrals of horses, pens of Fell Wolves.

If I add the twenty thousand from Jered and Morlan, we number almost fifty thousand. Yes, this will be more than enough to take down "Queen Brandawyn" and her motley crew.

Patian shot him a speculative look. "I heard there were significant defections among the units in Loemin, Your Grace," he offered as they rode. "Have you seen similar events in this province?"

Golvadu again refused to rise to the bait. "Yes, but it doesn't matter. Our forces are more than a match for them. Not only is this host at our disposal, but Tarvener has a division of troops in Tor Aldin."

With their retinue following, the trio passed by the hill with the altar. Bates nodded at it. "How many Daemons?"

"More than forty here so far," Golvadu answered. "Paltry numbers in comparison to the Dark Wave but plenty for our purposes. And Tarvener has others."

Patian smirked up at him. "But there are Elohir lurking about, are there not? And now rumor has it that the Aldenar sisters have Celestial blood. That will make things complicated."

Golvadu decided that he needed to find a way to put Patian in a location where the Grey Riders could finish him off. "Not so, Highness. We have other ways of dealing with them."

"Really?" asked Bates. He sniffed. "So far nothing has proved useful."

Thinks he knows so much, does he? He has no idea what we have planned. But maybe I should let them see it. Golvadu debated with himself, eyeing the hill with the daemons and the altar of sacrifices.

Yes. Maybe it will be helpful to demonstrate our latest gift from Tarvener.

He pointed. "In that case, let me show you something that will spell the end of the Riders."

He guided them to the altar. The Daemons parted, inclining their heads as the party crested the top of the hill. Their eyes raked the Morlani and Jeredan entourage. To Golvadu's satisfaction, both Patian and Bates sat stiffly in the saddle, despite being surrounded by their personal guard.

A lime-green crystal hovered above the altar, pulsing with lurid light and dripping a pale mist. A Deathhammer dragged the bloodied body of a young man off the altar and laid it on a nearby table. Two Tiger Daemons approached, licking their lips.

Golvadu patted the side of his dragon. "Stop here, Vizkir," he said, climbing down. The Drake crouched and coiled his tail around himself, watching the nearby Daemons with a baleful eye.

A dark-haired woman with dusky skin bowed low to him and straightened. She wore blue-enameled chainmail panties and matching halter top that left little to the imagination. A gold emblem of the church of Gudarta winked between her breasts: pincers and a whip surrounded by a circle of flame. Intense grey eyes flicked to Patian and Bates before returning to Golvadu. "Your Grace honors us with a visit."

Golvadu nodded to her. "High Priestess. I would like to show Prince Patian and Archduke Bates our latest, er, gift, from Prince Tarvener."

The woman's eyes gleamed. "This way, my lords." She paused by the altar and lifted a palm towards the green crystal. It floated to her hand and she led them towards a vast open area away from the altar, her shapely little backside flexing as she walked. Golvadu suppressed a smirk at the way Patian's eyes followed her movements.

With that libido, he must have very attentive guards. Kalik's Red Veils could easily exploit that weakness and dispatch him.

The High Priestess swept a hand at the clearing with a sultry smile. "My lords."

Golvadu folded his hands against his chest. Patian and Bates abruptly stopped next to him and their retinue likewise halted. Some of the foreign guards whispered to one another.

"Is that what I think it is?" Patian asked.

"It is." Golvadu nodded at the meticulously arranged True Dragon skeleton laid out on the grass. Small, glittering orbs of dark purple fire glimmered at the base of the skull, the breastbone, and the pelvis. Gudarta priestesses moved slowly and carefully around it, touching glowing metal wands to joints.

Gilbert Bates shook his head. "A True Dragon skeleton? What do you hope to gain by this? Even if you could succeed in animating it, what good would that do? Any experienced free-lance team could defeat it, let alone one as capable as the Grey Riders."

Golvadu nodded. "Of course, Your Grace. But this is a particular Dragon. This one — whose True Name I will not divulge for obvious reasons — was a dedicated adherent of the Dark One, and a potent wizard to boot. He was no ordinary dragon. We have more interesting plans for him."

"Like what?" asked Patian.

The High Priestess raised an eyebrow at Golvadu. He nodded to her.

She lifted the green crystal over her head, then beckoned to the other priestesses. Soon all the women stood at Golvadu's side. They started a sultry chant that sounded like half-song, half-whisper, hips and shoulders swaying hypnotically. The High Priestess raised her hand and the green crystal flashed. The glittering orbs near the skeleton shone in answer.

In one of the empty eye-sockets of the dragon's skull, a red light flickered, then flared to life like a miniature crimson star. The light focused on Golvadu's party. A palpable wave of intense malice and icy resentment flowed over the glade.

"A lich," Bates muttered under his breath.

The High Priestess lowered her hand and the lights faded. "We have almost enough energy from the sacrifices to rejuvenate him," she said. "Prince Tarvener's instructions are working marvelously. It won't be long now."

"Good," said Golvadu. He held out his hand and she gave him the glowing shard. "The Grey Riders will never know what hit them."

<<>>

Brandawyn wasn't next to him when he awoke in the early hours before dawn. The air felt warm on his skin and he smelled jasmine and kalaca flowers from outside their massive royal pavilion. He stared at the fabric walls for a while, then switched to infrared. The thermal outline of her body still faintly glowed on the mattress and he saw similar footprints on the rug.

I hope she got some rest this time.

He switched back to the visible spectrum and turned onto his side. Brandawyn stood next to the huge map table in her Celestial aspect, graceful wings arcing overhead. The light of the two moons shone down on her from an opening in the peak of the roof, illuminating every gorgeous curve of her body. Her red-gold hair glowed with a heavenly aura as she peered down at the map in concentration.

He found himself holding his breath. *I really do have a wife who is semi-angelic, don't I?*

Swinging his legs over the edge of the bed, he padded over to her.

"You should go back to sleep," she said without turning her head.

He couldn't help but grin. "You'd think I'd be unnerved by a wife who can detect me without seeing me, but for some reason I don't mind."

She turned her head and smiled but he saw the worry lines around her eyes. "What's the matter? Another dream?" he asked.

She nodded, turning her attention back to the massive relief map on the table.

He wrapped his arms around her and she laid her hands on his wrists. "It's hard to kiss you like this with your wings out," he teased, brushing his lips against her shoulder and neck.

"You're a rascal and a rogue," she replied with a chuckle, sinking into his embrace. She shifted her wings back into the Other Space and they receded into her upper back. "There. Is that better?"

He rested his head on her shoulder, reveling in their closeness and the feeling of her warmth. "Do you want to talk about it?"

She waited a few heartbeats before answering. "It's very much like the others but this time there's something different."

"Tell me."

She sighed. "Well, I was walking along a hillside through tall grass, heading towards Tor Aldin. Dark clouds roiled above the city, and I saw the castle near the harbor. The tallest pinnacle of the castle was like a tower of light, blazing as a beacon through the murk. Then, Saint Mary called to me and appeared next to me. She wore a blue mantle covered with glittering stars. I felt peace despite the darkness."

She paused, relaxing.

"That seems like some of the other dreams," he offered.

"Yes, but then Mother Mary held out a hand and a shining crown hovered in midair. I reached for it but she stopped me. She said 'Not yet. The ways of God are not your ways.' Megan suddenly stood there next to me. Mary turned and gave the crown to her. Then the dream ended."

Eric mulled over her story. "It's not like the others."

"What does it mean? Does God want Megan to lead Alenar instead of me? Am I supposed to do something different? Or does the crown symbolize something else? Frankly, it worries me."

"Why?"

"There's such a thing as a martyr's crown," Brandi whispered. Her voice hitched. "Does that mean Megan will die?"

He felt her tense in his arms and hugged her tightly. "Not necessarily, dear, and worrying about that will gain us nothing. We're in a war. Death is always a reality. But your sister is very able to take care of herself. And don't forget that smart-mouthed husband of hers. I pity anyone trying to take out Megan and Dar."

His gaze wandered to the tabletop. Small blue and red ceramic plates with numbers and symbols etched onto them lay in ordered groups, showing the positioning of their allies and enemies. A very detailed diagram of Tor Aldin dominated the left side of the huge parchment and red markers dotted its interior. In the castle he saw a prominent round one with a single name: Tarvener.

Farther south, a vast array of red pieces clustered near the highway, near a large red marker with "Golvadu" etched in it. Just by the crossroads leading to the city, a smaller group of blue markers indicated Brandi's army and the mixed force from the northern nations. Just to the east, orderly rows of azure showed Connor's Loemin Expeditionary Force hustling to meet them along the road from Loemin.

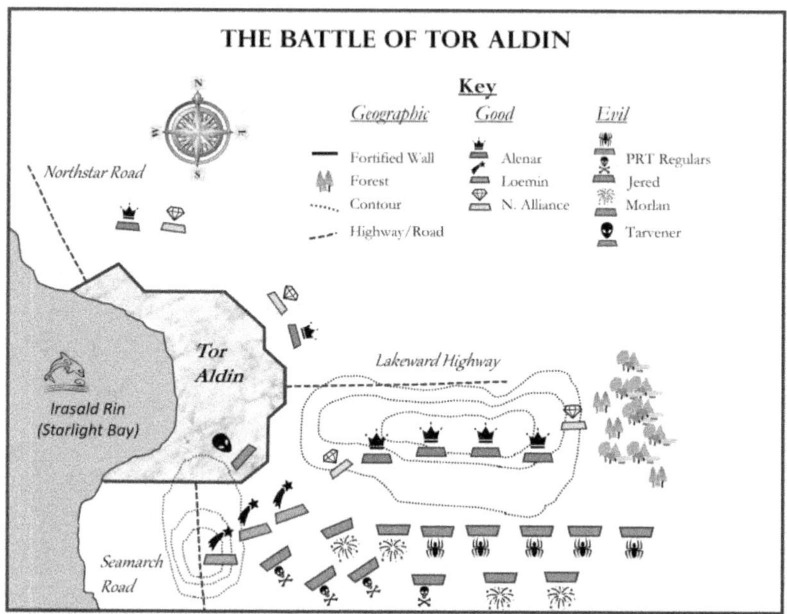

"Inspecting your troops?" he asked to take her mind off the dream and its implications.

She picked up a round blue marker with her name on it. "Yes, though I wish there were more."

"We'll be fine, Bran."

She nodded. "In my heart, I know we will. It's convincing my head that's taking all the energy. Thank God for Varani and Alex. They've been invaluable in coordinating between the various noble houses and army units who turned to our side."

"Thank God indeed." His eyes drifted over the map, along the shoreline, to the islands off the coast, to the borders. *The Alliance fleet is supposed to be on the way. But where are they?*

She tossed the marker in her hand. "Can I be queen? I mean, really?" she murmured.

He kissed her cheek. "Of course you can. Not only is it in your blood, but you have all the right qualities."

"Do I?"

"Brandawyn, honestly. Remember what Father Thomas told you: everything has been leading up to this and you are the exact person Alenar needs. He believes in you. I believe in you, as do so many other people who see you as I do: courageous, kind, caring, honest and dedicated."

She twisted around in his arms to face him and kissed his lips. "Thank you, dearest. But I now understand how Andyn felt when she decided to retire. I wish I could just be plain Brandawyn and live with you somewhere obscure, raise a crowd of boisterous, silly children and live in peace."

He chuckled. "I'm with you on that! But the decision is not ours to make any more. There are so many who depend on us. All we have to decide is how to lead this nation, to give them a brighter future."

"You're right," she replied, dropping her eyes to his chest.

How do I encourage her? "Don't forget our enemies are fighting for money and loot," he added. "We are fighting for home and family and a new nation. That's the best advantage."

"I'm glad you think so," she said.

"I think so, Dar thinks so, Megan thinks so. And Father Tom thinks so. You heard him when we talked to him via the Orb last night."

Her violet eyes met his. "I did, but his latest news shocked me. Have the Elohir found the trail of Selaan? Or is it just a ruse by the forces of Evil, to keep the Celestials away on a wild hootling chase while Golvadu and his cronies try to wipe us out here?"

A faint unease grew in his mind and he shrugged it off. "The deceptions of evil are many. You, of all people know that." He paused. "If the Elohir really can find Selaan, that will help the whole world. If it's a ruse, we'll learn soon enough. The Elohir will come to help when they can. But don't forget that Father Thomas and Sister Karen will be here any day now."

"Not soon enough for my taste."

He took the marker from her hand and held it up to the dim light. "*Brandawyn Regina Alenarensis*," he read. "I'm proud of you, you know."

She raised an eyebrow. "I haven't done anything yet."

He set down the marker. "Really? You didn't help Connor free his kingdom? You didn't sacrifice your life to uncover the Ja'al plot that brought in the Daemons? You didn't rally the people to your side by selflessly rescuing prisoners?" He winked at her. "There must be some other Brandawyn Veronica Therese Aldenar wandering around. I have to meet her."

She pressed her lips together and swatted him in the hip. "You're impossible, you know that?"

"Impossibly in love with you. Impossibly impressed with what we've accomplished so far. Impossibly hopeful about the future. Guilty."

She gazed into his face, eyes burning with desire. She cupped his face in her hands. "I don't deserve you," she whispered.

"Yes, you do. And I'll exasperate you in the future, guaranteed."

"I love you, Eric." She brought his mouth down to meet hers. Every nerve in his body tingled at the kiss and he drew her close, longing to be joined with her once more in exhilarating, blessed union.

"And I love you," he replied when their lips parted.

"Then show me how much…"

Chapter Twenty-Six – Blessed Are the Meek

Brandi lifted her eyes from the map on the table. *We're as ready as we'll ever be. Am I missing something?* Her brow furrowed.

A bell tinkled from outside her pavilion. "Majesty?" asked her maidservant.

"Yes, Joyce?"

"Lord Melinor is here."

Brandi's heart lightened and she walked to the tent flap leading to the antechamber. "Excellent. Please show him in."

The flap opened and Melinor Indidarc shuffled into the tent, giving her a peck on the cheek.

"Hello, Dad," she said, returning his kiss. "How are you?"

"I would settle for a new set of back muscles and a little less gout, if you can manage it."

"You know I would do that immediately if it were in my power. How about some tea?" She led him to the table.

"Actually, that rascally son of mine tells me you have mineral water from Loemin. That will do nicely."

He sank into a chair and she brought him a carved little wooden bowl filled with the sparkling water. He fixed her with dancing eyes. "I must be someone important if a Queen is waiting on me."

She laughed and took a seat next to him, squeezing his hand. "I'm just your daughter-in-law right now."

He sipped slowly from the cup. "Ah, I see why this is so prized," he remarked. "I foresee thriving trade between Loemin and points north."

"As do I. Eric thinks it will be in high demand."

"Speaking of Eric, where is he?"

"Reviewing artillery placements with the generals while Dar is working with the air cavalry and Megan is coordinating with the magical support troops."

"Good. That will keep them occupied." He patted her hand. "Now, how are you doing, my dear? And please, don't tell me you're fine. I can sense your tension from here."

Her smile faded a little. "Honestly, Dad, I know how Connor felt at Highmarket. I'm not an expert in massed warfare. I'm really a battle medic. Yes, I've had lots of classroom training in the time before we came to Torosc, but there's no substitute for experience. Thank God for Lord Kontar and the other generals. I don't know what I'd do without them."

He tipped his head to the side. "And what's so wrong about depending on those with expertise? No one expects you to know everything from the outset."

She tapped her foot absently against the carpet and forced herself to stop. "What if I make a mistake?"

"No general — or monarch, for that matter — has ever gone through a battle without making at least one. But I see no reason for alarm. Thanks to Alex and Varani coordinating with all the lords and commanders, you have a good battle plan, yes?"

She nodded.

"Yes. Then tell me of it. Or, before we speak of that, maybe I should ask if this pavilion is warded against spying."

"It is. Megan took care of that yesterday evening."

"Excellent. Proceed." He sat back in his chair, sipping the mineral water.

"Well," she began, "All of us realize we have an experience gap in commanding large units, so Eric, Dar, Megan and I will let the generals run the tactical aspects, just like at the Battle of Highmarket. Our job is to fly cover and observe the flow of battle, then warn our commanders when we see changes. We're also going to make sure we prevent enemy air units from attacking the army directly. If there is any severe danger to our forces, such as if Golvadu or Tarvener step in, we'll handle it and the army will draw back to the crest of the hill."

He smiled, setting the bowl down on the table. "That sounds prudent and effective."

"So why do I feel so apprehensive?" Her eyes drifted to the walls of the pavilion, as if to see the enemy beyond. "I keep having these doubts and worries, even though I know God is with us."

He covered her hand with both of his. "Well, that is the key, then, isn't it? You have many allies and friends. Trust the Lord. He will not abandon you."

She met his eyes and relaxed. *He always makes me feel so calm, so welcome, so… seen.*

He squeezed her hand and she smiled. "Now, as to preparations. I trust you have put our latest information to good use?"

She sighed. "Yes, and thank you for your help in deciphering the scrolls from the Vault of Safety. The spell of Purifying Light will be an excellent counter to any diseases the clerics of the Cla'Agik can throw at us."

"I was glad to help in my own small way. You are in much better shape than you thought. And I understand the Nuncio and Sister Karen are due here today."

"Yes, thank the Lord! Father Tom said he brought a surprise for us. Do you know what it is?"

Melinor's eyes twinkled. "Oh, I have my suspicions, but I'm sure he brings more than one. Don't worry. He and the Alliance Council had a long discussion before he left last week."

Joyce called to them from the antechamber. "Your Majesty?"

"Yes?" Brandi asked.

"A pair of blue and silver dragons approaches from the north. Each bears a rider."

"There, you see? Let's greet them properly." Melinor said with a grin. He struggled to hoist himself out of the chair and Brandi supported him in walking to the entrance.

He's so frail. A stab of anxiety hit her. *We just found out Gorlak is near the end of his lifespan. Can I cope with a life without Melinor and Gorlak?* Her eyes stung and she blinked rapidly.

Brandi and Melinor emerged from the pavilion into the summer sunshine. Joyce bowed, her wizard's robes swishing against the tall grass. Two large dragons soared in towards them, heading for a clear space to the left of the pavilion.

Chortling with glee, Tholi and Kindri came barreling around the corner. "Yes! They're here!"

Brandi held up a hand with a grin and the young dragons skidded to a halt in a shower of grass and earth.

"Slow down and clear the area, you two," she chided. "They need room to land." With only minor grumbling, the two pair shuffled backwards.

"Well, hello Kindri and Tholi!" Melinor said with a tone of distinct pleasure. "I would comment on how much you've grown, but that would seem to be an obvious understatement."

With shy smiles, the dragons dipped their heads to Melinor. Brandi led her father-in-law away from the pavilion as the two younger dragons fidgeted. Nearby troops hastily relocated horses, camp stools and crates, then stood in admiration, watching the approach.

Despite the overcast day, the dragons' shimmering scales of blue and white shone like jewels and mighty wings spread out wide. They floated down with amazing grace for such huge creatures. Even so, the ground shook when they landed. The pair reminded Brandi of Iron Thunder and she blinked back a tear.

You would be proud of Tholi and Kindri, Grandpa, she prayed. *But of course, I'm sure you can see them from Heaven.*

The newcomers approached and the larger male bowed his head to Brandi. "Greetings, Queen of Alenar! I am Baradellinaru and this is my mate, Feleseniala. We know that Draconic names are a bit difficult for your folk, so please call us Barad and Fela."

Brandi inclined her head. "You have our undying gratitude, Lord Barad and Lady Fela."

"Lord Melinor." Fela inclined her head to him.

"Good to see you again, Barad and Fela. What unusual cargo you bring." The corner of Melinor's lip curved up in a smile.

Father Thomas Williams clambered down from Barad's back, stretching his back as he set foot on the ground. He smiled, perfect white teeth brilliant against dark skin. "I'm sure Lord Barad would have preferred a different package. He is a masterful flier and a great companion, but I think I held on too tightly. And I'm a little stiff."

"Not as stiff as I," remarked Sister Karen with a wry smirk at Father Thomas. She smoothed her black and white habit, then tucked a stray blonde hair over a pointed ear and back under her cap. "I'm not used to all this rushing about the countryside."

Brandi's heart warmed at seeing both of them and she knelt to kiss the Nuncio's ring. He clucked his tongue at her. "Now, now, none of that. Give your Uncle Thomas a hug."

With a sheepish smile on her face, she embraced him and Sister Karen warmly. "Thank you both for coming."

"Our place is here with you," Sister Karen replied, giving the camp a once-over. "Well, you certainly have moved quickly."

Brandi's eyes roamed over her army. Neat rows of tents marched away from her command pavilion. Stockades held horses near clear fields with carts and siege artillery. Humans, Elves and even some Dwarves moved about, many of them casting curious glances in her direction. The clang of hammers echoed from the smithies. She caught sight of Joshua Page near one of the arming tents.

"Of necessity," she murmured. "We had to cut off the approach to the city before the Republic troops could reinforce it. As it is, we have only slightly more than half the numbers of the enemy."

"Then our arrival is timely," Father Tom said.

"Sergeant, please bring the Nuncio's baggage." Brandi motioned to a trio of guards and pointed at the metal-banded wooden boxes strapped to Barad and Fela's sides. "Joyce, will you see that those go onto the conference table? You may need to move a few things around."

"Yes, Majesty," Brandi's maidservant tied her curly brown hair behind her head and pulled back her long sleeves as she beckoned to the guards. The soldiers unstrapped the sturdy containers and hefted them inside the pavilion after her.

"If you don't mind, Majesty," rumbled Barad as he cast a sidelong look at Kindri and Tholi, who fidgeted even more. "May we borrow your draconic aides for a bit? We have news from our clan."

"Please do."

The two elder dragons and their younger charges ambled away from the camp towards a copse of trees on the other side of the hill.

Brandi led Father Tom and Sister Karen into the pavilion, explaining the whereabouts of the other Riders.

Father Thomas stroked his chin. "You had best have them attend us. We have some important things to discuss."

"I can imagine." Brandi noted as she watched Joyce clear the table and direct the troops on placing the boxes. "I'm most interested in what's inside those. You can't have brought that many clothes."

Father Tom chuckled.

"Will there be anything else, Majesty?" asked Joyce.

"Please have the sprites bring Prince Eric, Prince Dar and Princess Megan here," Brandi replied. "And place a locking spell on the entrance. We don't want to be disturbed."

"Yes, Majesty." Joyce curtseyed and left with the guards. Brandi soon sensed the tingle of magic and a faint light raced around the tent flap. *It's good to have a maidservant with magical talents.*

Sister Karen, Father Tom and Melinor exchanged small talk. Soon a light flashed at the tent flap. It opened, admitting Dar, Eric and Megan, then flashed again as the spell reapplied itself.

Father Tom motioned to the table, where one of the cases now lay. "Please, gather around."

"First of all," he announced, "we need to ask your forgiveness, Brandawyn."

Now Brandi chuckled. "Forgiveness? For what? You haven't offended me."

He smiled in return. "Well, it is customary for the nations of the Alliance to bestow gifts on new rulers upon their coronation, but financial circumstances made it difficult just after the war, with all the reconstruction. However, they have seen fit to make amends."

He touched his signet ring to the lock on the container. With a faint hissing sound, a forest green light raced around the seam and he opened the case.

A beautiful suit of gleaming plate armor greeted Brandi's eyes. The metal shone blue-white and Brandi gently touched the breastplate. She ran her fingers over the embossed symbol of the House of Alenar: a crenelated tower with a cross etched in it and a shining sun hovering above. The motto of her house was engraved on the figure of a scroll beneath the symbol: *Ad Deum, Ad Vitam.*

"I've never seen it's equal. And with my House heraldry on it," she breathed. Her throat tightened. *The symbol of my family, after all these years.* Eric put his arm around her and planted a kiss on her head.

"Impressive, isn't it?" Sister Karen said, looking extremely pleased. "It's made of a metal called Heavensteel, a special alloy invented by Celestial artisans in ages past. It is very strong and has a special feature: if any magic attack is aimed at you, the armor will try to deflect it."

"So, it's quite old then," Megan said.

"Most likely," the nun replied.

Brandi lifted the breastplate, wondering at its weight. "It's so light," she said, looking at her amazed reflection. "Who made it?"

"We don't actually know." Karen said with a shrug. "As a matter of fact, free-lance mercenaries hired by your friend Andyn found it on an expedition in north-eastern Terenai. Once I analyzed it magically, we had it engraved especially for you."

Brandi shook her head. "This is beyond belief, Sister Karen, Father Tom. Thank you, both of you."

"You are most welcome." Karen reached into the case and Brandi now noticed two other containers inside: one flat and narrow and the other one more like a cube. She handed the flat one to Brandi.

"From your friend Lord Bydecy, another prize from a free-lance team in the mountains of Astarel. He said 'I think it's better in Brandi's hands than mine'. Direct quote."

Eric laughed. "That sounds like him, the rogue. Being the Lord Regent of the Institute hasn't changed him much."

Dar and Megan chuckled.

Brandi opened the box. A longsword lay on a padded cushion within. Celestial runes ran up and down the scabbard. The guard formed angel wings and a single large pearl gleamed in the pommel. Brandi read the lettering and translated to Humana. "To the Greater Glory of God", she whispered.

"Let's have a look, then," Melinor urged gently.

Brandi's senses tingled and she felt an overwhelming sense of peace and purpose as she grasped the handle and drew it. The mirror bright blade sang like a church bell and she lifted it before her eyes. The surface swirled with opalescent colors.

Those colors on the blade. They're mesmerizing. I've never seen them before. "I've seen a lot of magic weapons," she managed, "but this one?"

"It's rather special," said Sister Karen. "Your Elohir mentor, Lady Johanna, examined it magically and confirmed that it is also of Celestial make. She also said it's a paladin's sword, but could not determine the origin or former owner."

"A paladin's sword?" Brandi asked, her brow furrowed. "Are you sure I can use it effectively? I didn't complete paladin training in the Academy and was never consecrated."

Father Tom smiled. "We asked Lady Johanna the same thing. In her words 'I don't think that will be a problem for Brandawyn. The touch of the One God has consecrated her for all time'. I tend to agree."

A memory flashed in her mind, a memory of a loving, peaceful Presence who held her gently before she was brought back to life. She swallowed with difficulty and cleared her throat. "Well, then. When you say you have a surprise for me, you aren't kidding, are you?" Brandi slid the weapon back into its sheath.

The Nuncio reached into the case and took out the cube-like box. "Well, to be honest, though those gifts are long overdue, there is something else that will be very helpful in the days to come."

Brandi's senses tingled so vibrantly that she thought her hair would stand on end. "What is it?"

Without a word, Father Tom lifted the top of the box and withdrew a glittering platinum crown. Brandi's heart skipped. *It's the one from my dream!*

The crown reminded her of a cathedral with stained glass windows, of rainbows, and of the sparkle of sunlight on a baptismal font. Seven points surmounted it with a cross capping the center point. Two gold chains hung down from the left and right temples, as long as her thumb, ending in rubies. A single diamond in a triangle-shaped setting glittered from the center, where the wearer's forehead would be.

"I don't believe it," Megan breathed. "The Crown of Saint Alyssa. Does this mean that —."

"Yes." Father Tom nodded, lifting the crown from the box. "It has lain dormant since Saren DeMey returned it to me after the Battle of Oakmoor. It has chosen a new bearer."

All eyes swiveled to Brandi and she felt dizzy. *This is it. I'm the heir of Saint Alyssa. The Crown is mine.*

Father Tom shook his head. "It has chosen Megan."

What?

Megan turned pale. "Me?" she squeaked.

Father Tom chuckled. "Don't look so terrified, Megan. You're of the bloodline of Saint Alyssa too."

"But…" Megan stammered. "Brandi's the heir."

The Nuncio shook his head. "God's ways are not our ways. I received a dream that told me to put my hand on the Crown. The name that whispered in my head was yours, not Brandi's."

But this is what we need to counter Golvadu and Tarvener. Why Megan? Awe and wonder gave way to jealousy and confusion. *Why not me? I'm the Queen! I'm supposed to lead our people to victory, to glory!* She clutched Eric's hand.

Megan stared at the Crown, appearing to ignore all else in the room. To Brandi, it suddenly seemed as if her sister took on a more powerful, regal quality. Now Brandi felt betrayed, as if Heaven itself held out the Crown to mock her, then snatched it away at the last second. The edges of her vision tinted crimson.

It's not fair! I'm the true ruler, not Megan. Or is she planning on usurping the throne with the power of the Crown?

Brandi gritted her teeth and closed her eyes, struggling against her envy. *No! I have to resist. I can't give in!*

"Sweetheart?" Eric's concerned voice cut through her mental struggle.

She blinked. The others regarded her with expressions of concern. "I'm… I'll be okay."

Father Tom frowned. "You don't look like it."

"Princess Megan looks a little unnerved as well," Sister Karen observed, her eyes narrowed.

Brandi locked eyes with her sister. Megan's lips formed a thin line and the rims of her eyes glowed like coals, but Brandi saw the sheen of tears as well. *She feels it too. She's being tested, tempted to envy and greed and pride.*

"What's the matter?" Eric asked, putting his arm around her. Dar did likewise, leaning his head against Megan's.

"Overwhelming feelings of betrayal and envy because the Crown has chosen Megan," Brandi managed.

Megan winced. "It's the same for me. I have an intense desire not to trust her, to imprison her so she can't harm me."

An overwhelming feeling of betrayal and bitterness struck Brandi again. *Haven't I gone through fire and death and vampirism and a thousand humiliations?* She raged. *I made the sacrifices! I deserve to rule our people! Why should Megan get the privilege?*

Almost before she could stop herself, she growled. "The Crown is for a Queen and a Queen alone! It is mine!" The red haze intensified.

Megan's eyes blazed and Dar tightened his grip on her. "No, Brandi! The choice has been made. There is no going back. I am the wielder of the Crown! You will submit!"

Brandi took a step forward but Eric's strong hands stopped her. She angrily turned around.

"Brandi," he held her shoulders in a viselike grip but his gaze reflected only love and understanding. "This isn't you."

No, he's right! What was I thinking? Brandi's will strengthened. She bit the inside of her cheek and shivered.

Father Tom laid a comforting hand on her shoulder and on Megan's. "Be at peace. We are here to help you."

"What's going on?" Megan asked in a tight voice. "We've felt these emotions and temptations before, but not like this."

The Nuncio smiled at the sisters. "Your Daemonic bloodlines are reacting to the Crown and attempting to turn you against each other."

"But why now?" Megan asked in a plaintive voice. "Isn't the Crown a holy relic? Can't it protect us? Look what I'm turning into!"

Father Tom put a hand on her arm. "The Crown is a powerful artifact, but it doesn't rule your mind or your soul. You still are a person with free will. Besides, I will point out that you are both resisting the temptation, are you not?"

"But I can't let my Daemonic side control me," Brandi gritted through clenched teeth, fighting against a powerful inclination to turn on Megan again. "I have to conquer this or I'll never be free of it!"

Father Tom smiled. "You don't have to do it alone, Brandawyn," he said in a serene voice. "The prayer of humble servants of God is powerful and effective."

Brandi took in a shuddering breath, willing herself to calmness like Johanna had taught her months ago. *Humility. Yes. Just like Johanna said. Humility defeats pride and envy.*

"Please," she whispered. "Help me."

Eric hugged her close and her heart soared from his love. The others laid hands on the sisters. The Nuncio led them in a quiet prayer and Brandi felt a wave of strength and stability.

"Now," whispered Sister Karen. "Trust in the Lord."

Brandi closed her eyes. Awash in the prayers of her friends and family, she recited along with them in her mind and the red haze diminished. Her thoughts of envy and jealousy faded to an incomprehensible muttering the more she concentrated. Eventually, they faded altogether.

Brandi opened her eyes to see the others regarding her expectantly. "Thank you," she said, feeling embarrassed and miserable. Her earlier jealous words still stung.

Everyone heaved a collective sigh of relief.

Father Tom patted her back and Megan's. "The Lord provides His grace to the righteous."

Brandi fought to speak past the lump in her throat. "Me? Righteous? Did you hear me? I was going to fight Megan over the Crown, a holy relic of our saintly ancestor!"

Megan took her hand. Her eyes brimmed with tears. "It's no different than what I thought, Bran."

"How can I rule our people when I can't control my Daemonic side?" Brandi said, her heart wrenching with guilt. "I thought I had figured it out after overcoming Balris but now I failed, again. I'm not worthy."

Father Thomas' arms encircled her and Megan. "None of us are worthy," he said in a quiet and gentle voice. "Neither I, nor Sister Karen, nor Dar, nor Eric nor Megan. And neither, for that matter, was Saint Alyssa herself, if you think about it. We're all sinners, Brandawyn. God understands. He just wants us to get back up again, ask for forgiveness and move on. He will always take us back. Always. No matter what."

Brandi said nothing. Tears rolled down her cheeks. *I'm so sorry.*

The Nuncio gave her and Megan a hug. "You have prevailed," he soothed. "God doesn't expect us to be perfect. Just faithful. And I am completely confident in both of you."

Eric kissed her head. Brandi cast a look at her sister through . "I'm sorry, Meg. The thoughts in my head —"

Megan threw her arms around her. "No worse than what I was thinking!"

Brandi took a deep breath, then pulled back and touched her forehead to Megan's. "Forgiven?"

"Forgiven."

Dar pulled Megan into his embrace. Brandi leaned back into Eric, warm and grateful for his presence and faith in her.

"You're going to be fine," Sister Karen said with a gentle smile.

Father Tom grinned. "You may think it odd for me to say this, but I think this is actually a good sign."

Dar looked at the Nuncio like he had a third eye in his forehead. "Are you feeling well, Father Tom?"

Brandi wiped her eyes as the others chuckled.

"I am quite well, Darius," replied the Nuncio. "Think about it. Why would their Daemonic sides react so strongly? I believe it's because the power of Good is so potent in this room, with all of you, with the Crown of Saint Alyssa. And that fills me with hope."

"Me too," said Megan. She smiled at Brandi and a wave of warm affection surged towards her.

Her sister's smile took her back in time, to when they had arrived in Deran two years ago and met the Riders. *We faced the world together, depending on each other, relying on our love to pull us through. She's fighting the same battle as I am. She always has been. And I know she would do anything for me. So how can I do any less for her?*

In an instant, she saw that part of being a Queen meant giving up her own ideas of the greater good in favor of God's plan. *I have to trust.*

Brandi reached out to hug her sister and planted a kiss on her cheek.

"The Crown chose you for a reason, Meg. Take it and bear it to victory. We'll be right beside you."

Chapter Twenty-Seven – Fog of War

Brandi leaned her hands on the saddle horn. The skies above roiled with grey clouds and the sun struggled to peek through, occasionally sending down shafts of light. A half mile away downslope, beyond her forces, the might of the Torosci army stared back at her, a vast seething carpet of metal and magic and hatred. *So many.*

She gazed out at the orderly ranks of her army, arrayed in colors of their regiments, cities or noble houses and wearing a grey and burgundy armband of the Royal House of Alenar. "Well, this is it then, Lord Kontar," she said, surprised at how calm she sounded.

Field Marshal Kontar grunted. He settled his helm on his head and climbed up into the saddle on the back of a purple and red Sarkany, his plate mail clanking. "That, Your Majesty, is the understatement of the year," he said as he gathered the reins.

Despite the butterflies in her stomach, she smiled up at him. "But I see banners of the old noble houses of Alenar and their military units: the Trident Company of Khorpoint, the Chinook Legion from Lakefort, the Cougar Battalion from Kentridge, to name a few. There are even Knights of Saint Michael and Black Kestrels."

"Indeed." The Field Marshal's eyes twinkled. "It was your own labors in aid of the rebellion that brought this about – that and the work of your liaisons."

But will it be enough? She forced herself to breathe evenly. She remembered Eric's words: *"God would not bring you back to life for nothing."*

Turning to their left flank, she spied the lean figure of her father-in-law among the troops. She counted four sergeants and two healers by his side. Garbed in white and silver, carrying his black wooden staff, he looked like a sage or saint of legend.

"I wish he had gone somewhere safe," she murmured.

Lord Kontar chuckled. "Lord Melinor? Begging your pardon, Majesty, but the day he does that is the day can no longer move. He has more cunning and spirit than a man half his age. No, Majesty, let him aid us. He is wise enough to conserve his strength and remain where he is, no matter what happens."

He's so sick. How can we ask him to help in the battle? But he insisted, even when I tried to forbid him. One of the few times he's been upset at me. She turned her eyes away. *My faith certainly is being tested.*

Kontar pointed in the direction of the nearby city of Tor Aldin. "I see that Prince Eric returns from his reconnoiter." A pegasus swooped down towards her position and her heart lifted at the sight of her husband in the saddle.

Kontar settled himself atop his mount. "The time has come for me to check final preparations and command the center of the formation. The enemy will move soon, mark my words."

Brandi's heart skipped a beat at the sight of the enemy. "Fare well, my lord," she said to Kontar. "May God bring us victory."

Kontar inclined his head. "May He see us safely through our trials, Majesty." He tapped the dragon on the head. With a deep nod at Brandi, the Sarkany stalked forward and the Alenari troops parted to let them through.

Eric landed and trotted his pegasus to her side, lifting the visor of his helm. "We're all set," he said. "Counterspells laid in, all healers ready, magical ammunition prepared, troops itching for a fight. Varani and Alex are there to coordinate the battalions from Merdail, Gorostol and Terenai should Tarvener attempt to break out of the city and attack, which I doubt he will."

"If only we had arrived a couple of days earlier," she fretted. "We could have stormed the city. Between us and Father Thomas, we could have taken out Tarvener."

Eric held up his hand. "Sweetheart, there's no way we could have arrived sooner, what with all the harassment by Kaftu raiders along the way. Let

Tarvener stay where he is. He has a large city to manage, not to mention the seaport. He can't attack us and still hold Tor Aldin, no matter how powerful he is personally."

A Daemon Prince. But Eric's right. Even when Tarvener conquered cities during the Dark Wave, he didn't do it on his own. He needed armies of thousands.

"I see your point," she mused, tapping her saddlebow. "But I still have a feeling I'm missing something."

Eric took a deep breath. "Well, I'm convinced he's not going anywhere, at least not until Golvadu gets him some help."

Why am I so edgy? Her eyes flicked to the enemy camp more than once, always drifting to the area with the altar. She nodded in that direction. "That worries me."

"Me too. But we can't get close enough to see what's going on. They almost destroyed Stealth when I sent him up last time. But don't worry. That area is far away. We'll see what they're up to long before any trouble can get to us."

She nodded absently, trying to hold down a nagging premonition of doom. "And the Hill Sprites?"

"They await your command." He smiled. "The world's best spies and messengers if you ask me."

"Thank God for them," she murmured, eyes flicking to two small humanlike figures with dragonfly wings, no more than a foot tall each, standing on the cross-beam of one of her battle standards. Lady Tinira and Lord Esdan smiled back at her and waved. She waved back, happy to see familiar, loyal and friendly faces.

Eric took her mail-gauntleted hand in his. Though heavily armored, she still felt his reassuring squeeze. "We'll be all right, Bran. Remember the plan: Let the generals and lords do their job, advise them of what we see, make sure our troops can see you and only intervene when there is a need. God is with us."

She reached out with her Celestial senses and felt his confidence, faith and love as a warm wave of comfort. *Yes. God, is with us.* She straightened in the saddle and picked up her own helm.

Trumpets blared from the enemy lines. The more martial side of her Elohir lineage and her Daemonic bloodlust simultaneously blazed to life. She exerted control over both of them. *Follow the battle plan.*

Eric raised his hands and murmured under his breath. A glittering cloud of dust motes settled on her. "Go be their Queen, my Brandi," he said with a proud smile. He drew Fidelis and activated it. It grew to full spear length and the head glowed golden fire. "I'll be right with you."

Her heart swelled with fierce love. She leaned over in the saddle and kissed him firmly. "With you at my side, I can do anything."

She settled her helm on her head and left her visor open. With a gentle kick to Amicus' side, they lifted off over her army. She stopped in a hover over the center, eyes roaming over the many banners and flags. Her army lifted weapons in salute and cheered. Dar, Eric and Megan flew to hover next to her, accompanied by Tholi and Kindri and their dragon allies.

Now she understood what Connor must have felt, standing on the battlefield at Highmarket. *So many. All willing to give their lives for our country — for me.* A lump rose in her throat and her eyes stung, but she swallowed and sat straighter in the saddle. *I will ensure they do not give their lives in vain.*

When she spoke, her voice reverberated over the field and nearby hills just like Connor's had done in Aldath. "Raise your eyes, oh my people!" she called. "See our enemies! Look upon their banners! See the symbols of oppression, of thievery, of looting, of despoiling, of evil! Now is our time to throw off the yoke of slavery!"

The Knights of Saint Michael raised their lances in salute and the troops cheered. Guidons waved pennons of the Chinook Legion and the Trident Company. Emboldened, she spoke with increasing conviction. "Remember that they fight for Darkness, which always loses against the Light. Just as David slew Goliath with only five smooth stones and the help of God, we will vanquish the foe. Loemin has already defeated the People's Republic and stands at our side. Today, it is our turn. Today we throw off our chains! Today we reclaim Alenar!"

Her troops roared their approval. The Black Kestrels banged their shields with their swords, eyes upraised to her. She waved to Marshal Kontar and held her position.

The enemy host advanced amid the rattle of drums and chanted cadences. To quell the knot in her stomach, she recalled the day of her return to life and the words of Saint Mary: *"Talitha koum."*

"Young girl, arise." Arise indeed! Alenar will also rise again.

Her nerves calmed. She saw the PRT army for what it was despite their greater numbers: a swarm of ants, come to ravage and plunder. She would stop them or die trying.

Both sides unleashed artillery. Magical screens shunted aside many of the blasts. Arrows arced from one army to the other and cavalry galloped towards her army's flanks. Connor and Hannah's expeditionary force, closer to the city and the seashore, swiveled around to bring centaur cavalry into position. She saw immediately that the enemy had a disadvantage ascending the hill to her waiting force.

"Airborne units coming for us!" Eric shouted, pointing.

Several dragons, Dwerrolves and War Fiends arrowed towards their position.

She pulled back. Eric flew between her and the enemy, joined by Dar and Megan. She held her bow in her hand, a glittering blue arrow nocked and at the ready. Her family members engaged the Daemons as Barad and Fela swooped down, attacking the dragons. Dar, Megan and Eric made short work of the War Fiends but a pair of Dwerrolves shot through the aerial dogfight. Brandi promptly skewered them with her arrows. The shafts burst in icy explosions and the Daemons fluttered downward, detonating before they hit the ground.

Below, the PRT divisions and their allies rammed into her army. Magic flared so bright in places she had to look away. Cavalry charged, wheeled and charged again. Arrows and spells darted between the armies. Infantry dueled it out on trampled high grass wet with blood and ichor. Occasionally, a Daemon met its demise in a gory explosion.

Brandi followed the plan though her instincts urged her to dive into the fray. From her vantage point high above the battle, protected from enemy interference by Megan, Dar and Eric, she spied tactical maneuvers as they developed. She swooped down several times to warn Marshal Kontar or other generals about enemy units attempting to outflank them, artillery moving up to new positions or spellcasters bringing magic to bear. Each time, her commanders modified their tactics to blunt the attack.

Despite not being in the thick of the fighting, she felt a thrill of success. *It's working! So far so good.*

Megan, Dar and Eric continued to dispatch enemy airborne attacks. Each time, the Crown of Saint Alyssa proved to be the deciding factor. Megan deflected spells, healed her allies and devastated dragons, pegasus riders and Daemons alike with timely attacks of her own.

On occasion, Cla'Agik priests unleashed clouds of noxious pestilence. Clerics and mages in Brandi's army cast Purifying Light spells to nullify the plagues. Brandi watched as Father Tom and Sister Karen, surrounded by armored knights, send waves of healing spells to revive and fortify her divisions against repeated assaults.

Finally, unable to make headway against the Allied defenses, the PRT force drew back to regroup. Brandi swooped down to land near Marshal Kontar.

"Your Majesty." The Dwarven general inclined his head, wiping off a battle axe covered in blood and Daemon ichor.

"Well done, Marshal. We're holding," she said. "Golvadu hasn't been able to turn our left flank — Lord Melinor, Father Tom and Sister Karen are seeing to that. Connor's Expeditionary force holds the beach and the hill slope against the Jeredans and Morlani legions on the right flank, near the sea."

He nodded. "And your influence is making a difference. See how the troops hold up their heads, how they pull back the wounded and risk their lives for each other? It's because they can see you above us, directing the battle, alerting the commanders, and it gives them hope."

Her heart soared. "And seeing their dedication gives me hope in return. We have to hold out as long as we can. We have the strategic high ground. No matter how many Golvadu throws at us, he can't break through to the city. Speaking of the city, is Gorlak ready?"

Now the Marshal grinned. "Oh, aye. That little schemer is already there, pretending to be an archer, ready to take down the South Gate guards with that pretty dagger of his and open the portal."

She shot a glance at the ocean nearby, dull under grey skies. "Any sign of the Northern Alliance fleet?"

He shook his head. "The sprites are watching for them. We'll know the instant they appear. Have we seen anything from Tarvener?"

She kept her eyes on the enemy ranks. "A couple of probing sorties from the North and East Gates but the mixed regiments have repulsed them each time. Other than that, nothing."

Kontar grunted and readied his axe. "Well, we can't let down our guard. The bastard is probably just waiting for the right time."

"We'll stay alert. If he tries anything, we'll be ready," she said with more conviction than she felt. *If anyone can ever be ready to fight a Hadean Prince of Daemons.*

Kontar stared at the scene before him. "We've done well so far, but they have the advantage in sheer numbers."

Brandi watched healers moving among her troops. *How many will never go home?* She dreaded the answer but asked anyway. "What are our casualties?"

"My guess? Around ten percent so far, but we're giving twice that to the enemy."

One in ten? Her heart sank.

He shot her a sympathetic look. "Don't take it on yourself, Majesty. We knew this would be hard. I see the enemy mustering for another try."

"I'd best get to my station. I need to have eyes on them." She flew up to her position over the army and stared out at the enemy formations. Past the lead units, rank on rank of enemy waited to join the fight, held back only by their fellows before them.

The feeling of looming disaster came again. Brandi took a deep breath, trying to ignore it. *How much longer can we keep it up?*

Chapter Twenty-Eight – Strike and Counterstrike

Golvadu wrung Vizkir's reins in his hands. *How much longer are these miserable incompetents going to keep on fucking up a perfectly good battle plan?*

Drums rolled and trumpets blared. Once again, Golvadu's army advanced up the slope towards the enemy. Artillery shells arced and sizzled overhead and flights of arrows sang through the cloudy spring sky.

Golvadu's eyes narrowed. *We should have rolled over them by now. The Loeminites and the battalions from the Northern Alliance keep blocking our assaults along the beach. Brandawyn's forces are outclassing the Morlani raiders and Jeredan legionnaires. It's as if they have some invisible force inspiring them.*

"Something wrong, Lord Golvadu?" Prince Patian asked.

Golvadu looked down at the Jeredan Prince from his perch atop his Drake. "Not really. We are wearing them down. It's only a matter of time."

He spotted the Papal Nuncio, standing with Sister Karen near the center, then the hated figure of Melinor Indidarc behind the lines on the Allied left flank, guarded by soldiers and healers.

Damn Melinor! Between him, that idiot priest and his woman assistant, they're neutralizing our assaults on their left flank. And it seems like Brandawyn Aldenar is reading our minds. We can't even get light cavalry around them to hit their camp or supply area.

"Why hasn't Lord Tarvener sallied forth?" asked Lord Bates. "He could devastate them from behind."

Golvadu frowned. "It's not as easy as you might think. You've seen his attempts, correct? Be realistic. He can't monitor all three gates, man the walls and watch the ocean while trying to attack the besiegers."

"But he is a Daemon Prince, no? He can take out entire squads by himself," Bates noted.

Golvadu gritted his teeth and forced himself to give a matter of fact answer. "He is, but then he would have to face all of the Riders, plus the accursed Christian priest and his pet priestess at the same time. Even he can't overcome that many, especially now that we know the Aldenar bitches are part-Celestial."

"Pity," Patian intoned. "If we had arrived here weeks ago, we might have joined forces or encamped before the city, but …" He shrugged, blandly refusing to look Golvadu's way.

Golvadu only barely restrained himself from unleashing some of Tarvener's forbidden Daemonic magic at him. Instead, he gave a mocking nod. "I do not have Your Highness' insight. Had I known that Balris would get his head handed to him and that Loemin would fall in two months, I would have bypassed Aldath altogether and come straight here. Perhaps in the future, Your Highness can gift me with your clairvoyant talents to assist in planning."

Patian shot him an acid look.

"Well, we must not bicker amongst ourselves," Bates interjected. "Lord Golvadu is right. We still outnumber the rebels and while we cannot get to Tarvener now, we will grind down the Alenari."

Patian nodded curtly and returned his attention to the battle.

Golvadu's irritation remained. He watched Megan Alenar swoop down to a harried rebel company, uncork a blast of blue-white light and hover, guarded by the two young gold dragons. The rebel force regrouped, its wounds healed, and surged into the fight with renewed vigor. Nearby Cla'Agik priests tried to do the same for Golvadu's force, but Megan gestured with one hand as if scattering seeds in a field. Crackling bursts of light exploded by the Cla'Agik and they cowered or fell, their healing spells fizzling out.

That little slut is making this a lot harder than it has to be. His irritation turned to **rage**. *I think it's time to put her in her place. Maybe a little Daemonic magic from Hades is in order.*

"If my lords will excuse me," Golvadu smirked, spurring Vizkir forward. "I have to go bitch-slap a pretend princess."

<<>>

Brandi saw Golvadu and his mixed company of Daemons and Ogres advancing on Megan. She shot a look down at her forces, torn between a desire to help her sister and knowledge that her position above the battle gave her army a distinct advantage.

They're trying to distract us. Wait for the counterpunch.

She held her ground as Dar and Eric soared in, loosing shining arrows at the enemy. The Daemons swept in at Eric and Dar and the dragons. Barad and Fela led the counterattack and soon the sky became a tapestry of diving and soaring figures. Several Daemons perished and detonated in mid-air but the airborne enemy kept Brandi's allies occupied and away from Megan.

Just as Brandi predicted, two battalions of Jeredan legionaries suddenly wheeled about from the rear of the enemy force and headed towards the Allied troops directly under the aerial battle, joining up with the lumbering Ogre platoon.

Brandi dove down towards the center right of her lines, hovering above the commander.

"General! Counterattack coming! Shore up your right flank where the Ogres are advancing!"

The officer saluted and directed his officers and sergeants. Soon, several companies of reserves trotted towards the battle. Arrows and spells arced out at the enemy.

That should hold them off, Brandi thought, flying upward again.

Golvadu drove straight at Megan. His drake breathed clouds of sizzling acid but Megan shunted them away using the Crown. The Dwarven wizard concentrated his attacks on her, casting arrows of pure darkness, sizzling pin-wheels of clashing colors, flaming meteors, and storms of fire-darts. Each time, Megan deflected, diffused, dispelled and disrupted everything he threw at her.

Brandi shot a glance at her troops. They held against the attack of the Ogres and the Jeredans. Seeing an opportunity to help Megan, Brandi spurred Amicus in her direction.

Golvadu waved his hands in a circular pattern. A glowing black bead shot out from his hand. It burst with a heavy thump that made Brandi's chest hurt. A whirling void of darkness spun and grew where it had detonated, swirling larger by the second. A strong wind pulled nearby soldiers, Ogres and Daemons towards it. Megan's pegasus backed in midair, trying to put distance between them and the vortex.

Golvadu laughed wildly. "Die! You all will die!" A red corona of light surrounded him.

What the hell is that thing!

Without another thought, Brandi yanked on the reins and put Amicus into a dive. Out of the corner of her eye, she saw Father Tom and Sister Karen mount horses and race in Megan's direction.

God, please let us get there in time!

Megan brushed her fingers in the air as if touching emblems only she could see. The swirling rings of Celestial runes around her grew brighter in intensity and pulsed out a hemisphere of light. Where it touched, the vortex faltered, though troops, beasts and mounts from both armies struggled frantically to get away.

Brandi tried to fly past the swirling whirlwind at speed but a viselike grip yanked Amicus closer. The pegasus screamed in terror, beating his wings desperately.

Brandi pointed three fingers at the vortex. "*Perturbare!*" A wave of sizzling light shot out from her hand. The vortex slowed. The force lessened and Amicus pulled away towards the rebel lines.

Sensing her mount laboring, Brandi brought him in for a landing. Father Tom and Sister Karen raised their hands in prayer. A soft white radiance spread outward from them, covering dozens of yards in mere seconds.

Megan's voice rose above the din of war, singing a gorgeous melody in the entrancing, heavenly language of the Elohir. For a split second, it seemed to Brandi that the universe paused, then answered.

"*Fiat!*" Megan shouted. She pointed and a sparkling bead of light shot out from her finger at the vortex. It impacted dead-center. With a thunderous blast, the whirlpool of death exploded. The shields cast by Megan, Father Tom and Sister Karen managed to divert most of the blast, but Ogres, Daemons, Fell Beasts and dragons flew back like rag dolls.

The dwarven wizard and his Drake tumbled through the air. The dragon windmilled his wings violently. Golvadu sawed on the reins and regained control. He steered his mount towards a distant hilltop with a crowd of Gudarta clergy surrounding an altar. Something glittered with green light.

Brandi's apprehension reached a fever pitch. *There's something very wrong over there.*

Megan landed and Brandi flew down to meet her. The People's Republic army and Brandi's force drew apart, warily eyeing each other as they retreated in exhaustion.

"Disengage from battle! Withdraw and stay alert!" Brandi commanded. Her officers sprang into action. "Keep an eye on that hill with the altar. Something's not right."

She trotted Amicus over to Megan. "Hey, are you okay?" Brandi asked. *God, she looks like she just hiked to Oakmoor and back.*

Megan nodded, her face pale. "Just really tired."

Brandi put a hand to her shoulder, imparting a healing spell. Some of Megan's color returned. Eric and Dar joined them.

"Sweetheart?" Dar asked.

Megan gave him a wan smile. "I might need a nap after this."

Dar grinned. "As long as I can join you."

Father Tom and Sister Karen reined in as Marshal Kontar landed his dragon nearby.

"By all that's holy, what the hell was that?" Kontar asked.

"Nullity Globe," Sister Karen replied, brow furrowed in tiredness and worry. "The Globe itself is the size of a peach but its immense pulling power causes the vortex and that sucks in everything near it. The only other time we saw it was at Oakmoor." She exchanged a look with Father Tom. "Hadean royalty conjured one," she finished.

Kontar glowered, muttering.

Brandi swallowed and looked up. The clouds seemed to mock her, hiding blue skies from view. *God help us. If he has access to that kind of magic, how can we survive?*

As she gazed at the murky sky, yearning for sunlight, the words of Saint Mary returned to Brandi as if it had been yesterday: *Talitha koum… little girl, rise up.* An image of peace and love flashed in her memory from the time after her death.

Her tension diminished and her heartbeat slowed. She took a deep breath. *It will do no good for me to lose hope. Everyone is depending on me. I am called to be faithful. If I give my life for them, I know Heaven is waiting for me, my true home.*

As if Heaven and Heaven's Lord responded to her declaration of faith, a section of clouds parted. The sun burst forth with golden rays, illuminating her army in a wave of golden light.

There's my answer. Despite the dire setting, she began to smile. *The light overcomes the darkness.*

"Highnesses!" a high-pitched female voice called. A pair of glittering figures shot in towards their position from the direction of Tor Aldin.

"Esdan and Tinira!" Megan said.

Brandi held out her hands and the two sprites landed in her palms. They fell to their knees, their little bodies heaving with exertion, dragonfly wings fluttering.

"What is it?" Brandi asked.

The sprites tried to speak but panted so heavily their words didn't make sense. Father Thomas poured from a waterskin into his palm. Both sprites dipped their hands into the water and drank, recovering their breath.

"A large battle group sails into the harbor," Esdan gasped. "It flies the flags of many nations: Deran, Terenai, Astarel, others. They fight against Torosc navy units and are aided by Merfolk in the water. The enemy gives way and landing ships are arriving at the beach near Prince Connor."

"The Northern Alliance!" Eric exulted. "They made it past the blockades!"

Kontar nodded curtly. "Then it is time to seize the initiative, Majesty. We can move on Tor Aldin."

Brandi addressed the two sprites almost apologetically. "I know you're tired, but can you send some of your people to Lady Varani and Lord Alex? Tell them to feint attacks on the East and North Gate. Also tell General West to send the combined battalions to relieve Connor. Connor will disengage and send up a signal flare for Gorlak. They'll take it from there."

The sprites joined hands and bowed. "It will be done," replied Tinira. They zipped off without further fanfare.

Finally, some help! Maybe we can turn this around after all.

Her heart rose.

Then a horrid, bellowing shriek rang out from the enemy camp near the hill with the Gudarta altar. Troops from both armies froze and recoiled.

Brandi stared in horror. Behind the enemy lines an immense skeletal dragon hovered, its massive bony wings flapping rhythmically. *It has no wing membranes, so how can it fly?*

Golvadu led the skeletal monstrosity towards the battle lines. He pulled up into a hover as the beast slowed to a halt behind him. "Now you see the might of Torosc in full measure! Behold, from the Paragon Age arises Zulgubrudan, the Immolator of Life, servant of the People's Republic of Torosc."

The skeletal abomination screeched and the air shuddered. Clashing tones vibrated Brandi's core. She froze, wide-eyed, her mind screaming for her to do something. Her body refused to obey. Alenari soldiers cowered and their mounts reared in panic. Even the nearby allied dragons shrank away and averted their eyes.

"What is that thing?" Eric ground out, wincing.

Brandi glimpsed fireball eyes in the dragon's eye sockets and tracers of green electricity coursing over bones and joints. A pale green globe pulsed behind the thing's massive breastbone, like a heart made of sickly light.

A palpable wave of power washed over her and, with it, a fear to freeze her bones. "Dragon lich," Brandi managed.

Chapter Twenty-Nine – Death from the Past

That thing can destroy entire companies! We have to get it away from the army.
"Marshal!" Brandi took the reins of Amicus, her heart in her throat. "Pull back your forces!"

"You can't face this alone!" Kontar objected.

She shook her head. "Withdraw in good order to the high ground and set up defensive positions," she ordered. "If we draw it away from the army, we can take it down. Do not engage Golvadu or the dragon lich. Let us handle this away from the troops."

Kontar bit his lip, then nodded and barked a command over his shoulder. Brandi's army drew back. The skeletal dragon drifted closer. Torosci soldiers, Fell Creatures, Ogres and even Daemons gave way, clearing out a space.

"Oh, great!" Dar snarled, trying to control Virasi as the pegasus pawed the ground, wings flapping frantically. "A cross between Margoth and an evil Iron Thunder. This just keeps getting better and better."

"Steady!" Megan called, and a burst of white light shot out from the Crown of Saint Alyssa, touching Brandi and those near her. The terror vanished like a snuffed candle. The pegasi calmed immediately.

"Remember we are with you, Brandawyn," Father Thomas said in a soothing voice.

Golvadu and the dragon lich halted about fifty yards from the rebel lines. The Dwarven wizard looked down his nose at them. "So. The Christian high priest and his pet woman are on hand to help out the overmatched Grey Riders? Vardu indeed smiles upon us this day. We will be rid of all of you in one fell swoop." He sniffed.

Instead of answering, Father Thomas and Sister Karen closed their eyes and whispered prayers.

Golvadu laughed. "Typical!"

The Nuncio raised his hands alongside Sister Karen. A rapid succession of protective spells floated down over them and the Grey Riders. Brandi relaxed, feeling comforting energy envelop her and then disperse throughout her body.

Golvadu frowned. "Humph. As if that will help." He swept a hand at the undead dragon. "Zulgubrudan will be your doom. He serves me and me alone."

The skeletal head pivoted around to stare at the Dwarven wizard. Miniature purple suns blazed in massive eye sockets. "I am my own master!" Zulgubrudan thundered.

"Submit, slave!" Golvadu snapped, gripping a misty green crystal on a pendant around his neck. He lifted his staff and pointed at the Riders. "Destroy them."

Zulgubrudan doesn't want to be commanded, Brandi realized. *We can use that against him. But how?*

The undead dragon's fireball eyes flicked to Megan, wearing the luminous Crown. He shook his head and ground his teeth. "That… thing… it burns."

"Don't be a weakling!" Golvadu glared at him and his staff glittered. "I command you!" he repeated. The crystal flared and the green throbbing orb behind the dragon's sternum flashed in response.

The defiant tint in Zulgubrudan's eyes faded. "And I obey," he grated in a voice that sounded like the door of an immense tomb. He approached, exuding waves of malice and terror.

Brandi clenched her jaw. Johanna's counsel echoed in her mind: *"Evil relies on fear. It is weaker than Good, so that is all that it has to fall back upon."*

Golvadu spoke over his shoulder to a Skullhead officer in black plate mail near the front line. "Field Marshal, I have business with these bothersome fools. Do not interfere. I will enjoy crushing them myself."

Sister Karen tapped her crucifix and an immense opaque globe of mist leapt up around her to a distance of a hundred feet. "That will keep our duel between us," she told Brandi. Her eyes narrowed. "Go. We will take care of Golvadu."

Brandi loosed an arrow at one of Zulgubrudan's eyes. The lich ducked and the shaft pinged off a massive cheekbone with a flash of electricity. He whipped his head around to glare at her and a deep, menacing growl shook the air.

Got his attention at least. "Your servitude will be your doom, thrall of Evil!" she shouted. She leapt her mount to the side and into the air, zooming past Sister Karen's shield. Megan, Dar and Eric followed.

Zulgubrudan pursued, wings flaring red fire with each beat. He gestured with his forepaws and a semi-transparent globe of sizzling electricity surrounded him.

Megan soared up high. The rotating concentric rings of symbols from the Crown whirled around her. "Do I bother, you, Mighty Zulgubrudan? Well, then. Come and get me!"

"Megan!" Brandi hissed under her breath. *Good Lord! She's been around Dar so much she's becoming just as foolhardy as he is!*

With a hissed curse in Draconic, the dragon lich followed Megan. Brandi pursued with Dar and Eric at her side. She and Dar loosed fire arrows and Eric threw Fidelis. The missiles pinged harmlessly off the lich's screen. Fidelis spun off into the air and Eric recalled it to his hand with a word.

Brandi accelerated, heading for the lich's lower extremities. He pivoted his head around to track her. The skeletal maw opened and a bolt of coruscating mauve light shot out. Brandi pulled on the reins, swerving just in time. The air stank of brimstone and sulfur.

She swooped under his belly. Unable to bring his breath weapon to bear, he swiped at her with his rear claws. Dodging a sweeping blow, she planted two arrows in a thighbone. They detonated in fiery blooms. Zulgubrudan barely slowed.

Dar, Eric and Megan followed with a storm of firedarts. They cracked and exploded on the lich's shield, which flickered in response.

The dragon lich thundered a curse and surged at Brandi and the men. The Riders scattered, using their superior velocity to put distance between them and Zulgubrudan.

Brandi spared a look downwards. Golvadu darted about with unearthly speed, casting a rapid sequence of magic attacks at Father Thomas and Sister Karen. The priest and nun moved as a team, deflecting lightning, casting up shields against thunderous fireballs and dispelling shadowy eldritch horrors that materialized from swirling rainbow voids. The Dwarven wizard laughed raucously. He hurled arrows of deepest indigo at the pair, driving them backwards.

Where is Golvadu getting that magic? I've only ever seen Daemons move that fast!

The dragon lich swerved towards her and Brandi banked Amicus in the other direction. She circled around. Dar and Eric unleashed lightning bolts but the lich's magic shield shunted them aside.

One thing is for sure. We're not going to bring down Zulgubrudan from distance. She stowed her bow and arrows, then drew her swords.

The undead dragon hovered in midair. A red light blazed in his massive ribcage, then a blue and a white one. In rapid succession, he breathed a blast of fire, a triple-forked bolt of lightning and a cloud of hailstones. The fire curled around Brandi's shields. One lightning bolt got through but her armor reflected it back into the cloudy sky. Ice balls the size of apples rained down at her. Brandi felt her magical protections give way and called on her new sword. A silver shield of light sprang up in front of her. Many hailstones burst into clouds of ice but a few penetrated and bounced off Amicus' wings. He whinnied and faltered, then regained speed.

Damn it. Zulgubrudan's magic is too strong! She banked away and upwards, dodging more plummeting hailstones, then turned in a wide circle. Dar and Eric also struggled to control injured mounts.

Zulgubrudan surged to gain altitude and go after Megan. She flew away from him, turning in the saddle. With a wave of her hand, bright clouds of light burst out behind her like a trail of water lilies on a pond. The dragon lich slalomed through them but got too close to one and it detonated in bright flame. He roared in anger and hissed out a grey cloud of mist. Where the mist met Megan's airborne mines, a flash of light and clap of thunder destroyed them.

Megan continued leading Zulgubrudan away from the main battlefield and Brandi's forces. She swung around and headed towards the Riders with the dragon lich in hot pursuit. Brandi, Dar and Eric flew to meet him. Megan unloaded a healing pulse and another protective screen on her family as she shot past.

The dragon lich and the Riders bore down on each other. The Riders split apart just as Zulgubrudan breathed a cloud of crackling green acid. Brandi dove and banked. Most of the acid dissipated on her shields. Some spattered on her. Amicus whinnied in pain.

Brandi pulled up towards the undead dragon, slashing him in the hip and leg, eliciting a howl of pain as she swept past him.

Zulgubrudan swerved and uncorked dozens of firedarts at the Riders. Brandi and Amicus reeled, hit by four each. She yanked on the reins and gritted her teeth, guiding her mount away.

How do we bring him down?

The dragon lich growled a curse. His skull transformed into pure darkness and concentric spheres of lurid red blasted out in all directions. Heart in her throat, Brandi dove her pegasus to get away from the blast. Her armor glittered, reflecting the first wave of hellish energy. The second sphere hit her and the last of her magical protections vanished in a pop.

Brandi had never felt the effects of cold, heat and acid simultaneously — until then. She heard screams and realized it was probably her and Amicus.

Pain blinded her and nausea roiled her stomach. She lost all sense of direction. Amicus struggled to remain airborne under her.

God, which way is up?

Brandi blinked to clear her vision. She sheathed one sword and laid a hand on her pegasus, whispering a healing spell. In her mind's eye, warm golden light washed over a multitude of injuries and her mount recovered his powerful rhythmic wing beats. She swiveled her head around. Looking down, she saw the armies warily squared off, watching Golvadu's battle with Father Tom and Sister Karen.

With the other Riders temporarily disabled, the lich turned his attention to Megan. She led him away from the armies and he cut her off. Megan pulled into a swirling dive towards the city, then veered back towards the highway, firing off a sequence of sun-bright rays behind her. Zulgubrudan took two to his breastbone. He slowed and bellowed in pain, then lashed his tail like a whip. Six bony spines shot out at Megan, glittering with a green radiance. One got through her shields, lodging in Virasi's barding. The spine melted into a gout of acid and the pegasus whinnied in pain, diving down towards the gates of Tor Aldin.

With a cry of triumph that reverberated through the air, Zulgubrudan pursued, casting spears of ice and breathing a jet of plasma. Megan dodged both.

Brandi accelerated Amicus into a dive, aiming for the lich's back. She slashed one of his wing bones with both blades as she passed. Bright sparks of blue leapt up from the impact. Zulgubrudan faltered but kept after Megan.

Blast! I can't hit him hard enough. I need to distract him so that Eric and Dar can get close.

She cast a ball of light in front of the lich's bony snout. He growled in exasperation and slowed to a hover. He waved a claw before his face and the sphere of light vanished.

"Miserable weaklings!" he shouted. "You are no match for me! I am supreme!"

Supreme? He's Golvadu's slave, just like so many — wait! His pride!

She swept around in a tight turn, keeping his eyes on her. "Are we weak? Then why are we still alive? Or are you just incompetent? That must be it! Just what I expected from Golvadu's latest lackey!"

A lurid light flared in Zulgubrudan's eye sockets and he swung around, starpoint eyes burning.

Yes! Now to draw him after me.

Zulgubrudan shot a beam of plasma at Brandi and she barrel-rolled out of the way. She accelerated, looking over her shoulder. Unseen by the lich, Dar and Eric swooped in from behind. She held out her hand and fired a beam of light, hitting the dragon lich in the chest. He snarled and kept on her tail.

That's it! Just a little longer. Another beam of plasma rippled past, leaving the air stinking of ozone.

Dar dove and hacked off an entire wing bone with Rindara. Eric followed close behind, hurling Fidelis. This time the enchanted spear punched through the lich's shields and shattered a bone in his back.

With a hoarse scream, Zulgubrudan lurched and tumbled towards the ground, flailing wildly with his remaining wing. He gestured with a claw. A burst of blue light flashed under him and his descent slowed, though he still fell earthwards.

Brandi landed Amicus on the road, panting and wiping sweat and blood out of her eyes. Her eyes flicked towards the city walls and she glimpsed the wicked points of ballista bolts on one tower.

At least we're far enough away to avoid Tarvener's artillery.

The dragon lich landed not fifty feet away with a heavy thud, staggering to fall prone. He struggled to rise.

Brandi's wounds ached and Amicus limped. Megan, Dar and Eric landed nearby, their armor scorched and dented, their mounts barely able to stand. Her heart wrenched at the disheveled state of the winged horses.

"*Sanari!*" Brandi said. A disk of blue light shot out from her. Magic healing power coursed through her, leaving her lightheaded. Her wounds and those of her family faded though the pegasi still limped. Brandi shook her head to clear the dizziness.

"You think you will prevail?" The dragon lich glared at them with flaming eyes, his head towering thirty feet overhead. "I will outlast you, puny mortals." He lifted a claw and flexed his talons skyward. Black tentacles erupted from the ground, wrapping around the pegasi and pinning them in place.

"Dismount!" Brandi shouted, leaping off. "He wants us, not the pegasi."

If a skeletal dragon could sneer, Zulgubrudan somehow managed it. "Not right now, anyway, little Queen. Later, after I've finished you." He shuffled closer, coming within thirty feet. "I am deathless."

Brandi noticed his limping pace and his useless left wing. Though still mighty, he moved with far less alacrity than before. *He's losing*, she realized. *He's thrown everything at us and we're still standing.*

"No, Zulgubrudan," she said, readying both swords. "Your life ended long ago. Now you are just another one of Golvadu's servants, like one of his Hobgoblins or a Skullhead warrior." She reached into the Other Space and extended her wings through slots in the backplate of her armor.

Zulgubrudan's eyes flared at the sight of her Celestial aspect. "Ah? So, it is true. You have Celestial blood! Well, that will not avail you," he hissed, eyes narrowing. "You have dared to defy the will of the Great Ones and will pay for it."

"You're obviously not Great if you have to dance to Golvadu's music," Dar said, lifting Rindara. His eyes flicked to Brandi and his other hand touched the throat-plate of his armor.

His armor! Dar can teleport!

The dragon lich's eyes swiveled to Dar, blazing. "You have a lot of hubris for one so small."

"And how is it that one so small can still hammer your sorry ass?" Dar retorted with a smirk. "Maybe Golvadu should have chosen a stronger slave."

Brandi caught Eric's eye and gave a slight nod to the side. He sidestepped to the lich's other flank.

"Insolent bastard!" the dragon sneered at Dar. The white, red and blue lights flashed in his ribcage again.

Three things happened in quick succession. Megan made a circular motion with her hands towards Dar and a sparkling net of light flashed on him.

Dar tapped the plate at his throat and said, "Habbakuk!"

The dragon lich breathed lightning, hail and fire at him just as Dar vanished in a cloud of sparkles — and materialized on Zulgubrudan's back. The lich's breath weapons tore into the ground where Dar had just been. Dar swung Rindara high in the air as Zulgubrudan twisted his neck around towards him, jaws agape and sword-like teeth flashing.

This is our chance!

Brandi darted forward, Eric at her side. She drove both blades into the dragon lich's breastbone. Eric heaved Fidelis up through the back of Zulgubrudan's head, bursting through the top of the cranium. Dar smashed into his neck just above his ruined wing bones. Brandi pulled back her holy sword and drove it through the lich's shattered sternum into the vile green sphere. The sickly verdant light flickered and went out.

With a rasping hiss, the undead dragon froze in mid-motion. "Not possible… You are weak…"

Dar leaped off Zulgubrudan's back and tucked into a roll as the dragon lich collapsed. With a loud rattling sound, he simply fell apart, scattering its bones on the ground.

For what seemed like minutes, Brandi simply stared, gasping for breath. She managed to keep hold of her blades with shaking hands and she felt like she had run for two whole days without stopping. A motion at her side made her turn.

Megan staggered towards her, some of her hair burned away, ice coating one leg and her armor blackened. In alarm, Brandi caught her as she collapsed.

"I'm okay, Bran," Megan said through cracked lips. "I'm just tired, so tired."

Dar slid to a stop next to his wife and laid her in his lap. "Meg?" he asked, tears running down his cheeks. He applied a healing spell to her and winced as he did it.

"Thank you, honey," She smiled at him. "I'll be all right. Just need to catch my breath."

"Let's get back to Father Tom and Sister Karen," Dar said. "They'll take care of you."

A gloating laugh from the city drew their eyes. To Brandi's horror, Tarvener soared down from the top of a gate tower and flew towards them.

Brandi's throat clenched. *He's been waiting for this the whole time. Now that we're weakened, he's come to finish us.*

"So, you managed to destroy Golvadu's latest minion? Congratulations!" he thundered, drawing two black scimitars. "A victory, I'll grant you, though a short-lived one. Now you die!"

Chapter Thirty – Light from On High

The clouds in the sky grew darker and Brandi's weariness threatened to overwhelm her. *How can we summon the strength to fight him now?*

Dar wiped blood and sweat from his eyes and raised Rindara. "What? You want some of this?"

Tarvener roared with laughter, flying closer. "As if you could stop me, you second-rate brush tramp. Your crown comes from your woman, not from anything you did. Don't insult my intelligence."

Trumpets sounded from the plains near the city and Brandi shot a glance that way. Alex and Varani pelted towards them at the head of a phalanx of cavalry, the Alenar pennon flying behind them.

Tarvener clashed his blades together. Flame erupted in a wide circle around the Riders, catching on the tall grass. Soon, a ring of fire a hundred yards in diameter surrounded them, cutting off all view of Alex and Varani and their troops riding to help.

He raised his hands in a circle overhead and a shimmering globe rose up from the ring of fire, forming a dome overhead. "That should keep us from being interrupted," Tarvener said with a nod of satisfaction.

Megan removed the Crown of Saint Alyssa and held it out to Brandi. "Here."

"No! Father Tom said —"

Megan pressed it into her hands. "Brandi! I can't go on. You're of the bloodline and you're the Queen. Saint Alyssa would not deny you."

The words stuck in Brandi's throat.

"I'm so tired," Megan whispered, slumping down on the dirt road.

Tarvener landed. He prowled closer, whirling his scimitars and sneered at Eric and Dar. "You're nothing but boy gigolos for two little girls pretending to be royalty."

"Well," Eric retorted. "At least we have a kingdom to fight for."

"That's right," Dar agreed. "How's life on Hades these days, Prince? Ah! I'm forgetting. You can't get back there. Too bad, isn't it?"

"Oh, don't you worry. I'll bring Hades here so you can experience it firsthand." Tarvener smirked, eyes roaming over the Riders. "A little the worse for wear, don't you think? Well, let's make this easy." His horns flared red.

Brandi placed the crown on her head. Instantly, a vibrant tingle filled her body and a myriad of glittering symbols leapt up in her sight.

The black appendages holding the pegasi spread throughout the entire area and entangled the Grey Riders — except for Brandi. She stared in horror as her family fell prone, pinned to the earth by shimmering tentacles. Dar and Eric struggled, slashing at their bonds, but new ones stretched out to replace the old. Megan tried to lift her hand for a spell but the black cords of night held her down.

Why am I spared? The Crown!

Tarvener's eyebrows rose. "Hmm… You have some skills then, but it is futile to resist."

A chill of fear raced down Brandi's spine. *It's just him and me.*

"Surrender and I promise I won't turn you over to the Gudarta clergy." Tarvener smirked. "The Cla'Agik, on the other hand will want to experiment on you. Maybe I'll give you to them. They have healing powers so it won't be too painful. I think."

His eyes flared and a wave of images of fiendish tortures danced in Brandi's mind. She blinked rapidly and shook her head.

No! You'll never take us! Rage built up within her and her vision swam red. She fought against an overpowering, Daemonic anger and fear for her family and her people. *I won't let him win!*

As if sensing her struggle, Tarvener leered.

God help me! She tried to focus on the now-familiar sense of peace and confidence of her Elohir forebears. A vision of the time after her death coalesced in her mind's eye. She remembered being enveloped in God's peace.

I prevailed before, with God's help, and I will again. She recalled her victory over Balris and her racing pulse slowed.

Brandi took a deep breath and touched the Crown of Saint Alyssa. *Our Father, Who art in Heaven…*

The rage faded and with it, Brandi's exhaustion. One of the golden symbols beckoned to her and she touched it.

The entire scene before her froze. Tarvener stopped in mid-step, one cloven hoof a few inches from the ground. A wind-blown leaf halted in mid-air next to Eric.

Brandi's eyes widened. *I think I just stopped time!*

Another feminine voice continued the Lord's Prayer. "…Hallowed be Thy Name. Thy Kingdom come, Thy Will be done…" A tall human woman with red-gold hair shimmered into being before her. She wore a pure white robe with a silver belt. "Hello, daughter."

Brandi gaped. "Queen Alyssa?"

Alyssa smiled. "The same."

Brandi dropped to one knee but Alyssa clucked her tongue. "Now, now. You are Queen of Alenar. Kneel only before God."

Brandi straightened. "Yes, Majesty."

"So formal!" Alyssa's smile became playful. "How about just Grandmother Alyssa?"

Brandi resisted the urge to pinch herself. *I'm talking to a saint?*

She looked at the frozen scene before her. Her heart sank at the sight of the others pinned to the ground and Tarvener, fresh and ready for the fight. "I'm so tired, Grandmother. I have no spells left and I can barely walk. How can I vanquish that abomination?"

"You are of my line, are you not?" Alyssa touched her hand. "You have many special gifts: first, your armor, once made for a Celestial Prince, second, your blade, Sanctus Lux, wielded by the last King of Terra Dei, and third, my crown, which will tie all together."

Alyssa pointed at four symbols hovering in the air before Brandi. "These symbols will link the items. Together, they will strengthen you and help you see past Tarvener's lies and deception. Then, your agility and faith will be more than a match for him."

But can I? Tarvener is a Daemon Prince. Brandi flicked her eyes from the symbols to Tarvener to Alyssa, then to her captive city in the distance. The hated flags of the Skullhead Legion and of the People's Republic of Torosc flew motionless in the ocean breeze above the walls.

Those are my people, my city, my nation. If I take him out, they will see their oppressor is dead. They will be free.

She set her jaw and nodded. "Yes, Grandmother. I won't let him win."

Alyssa cupped Brandi's face in her hands. "That's my girl."

A wave of peace and love reminiscent of Brandi's after-death experience flowed from Alyssa into her. Brandi smiled back through sudden tears. "I will try to make you proud."

"I already am." Alyssa kissed her gently and stepped back. A surge of warmth coursed through Brandi. Alyssa started to fade.

Brandi touched the first symbol. The Crown sent out a pulse of energy that touched her sword and armor. "Pray for me, Grandmother."

"I do, dearest child. Constantly."

Alyssa vanished.

Brandi touched the other three symbols. A spark of golden light leaped from the crown to the sword, to the armor and back to the Crown. A thin, sparkling gold cord linked all three items. Brandi brushed a finger on the time-stop symbol and it winked out.

Time flowed again. Tarvener's cloven hoof landed on the road in a puff of dust and he frowned.

"What just happened?" he snapped.

Brandi gave him a little half-smile. "Wouldn't you like to know? I'm going to give you a chance to repent, surrender and disband your army."

He laughed. "Repent? You forget yourself, little queen. I am a Fallen One. We never repent."

Sudden inspiration struck her and her smile became gentle. "Even your granddaughter, Saren DeMey, wife of Terenil? She is half-Daemon and my husband's adopted sister. She serves the Christ, as do I. How is that possible if there is no repentance, no conversion, no dedication to Good?"

His eyelid twitched. "Spare me. I'll deal with my wayward granddaughter in due time."

"Oh really? Based on your latest attempt during the War, I wouldn't bet on your chances."

He snorted. "I'm not the one who's half-dead."

Brandi brushed her fingers on a symbol and it flared. Exhilarating power surged through her and she felt refreshed, like she had just had a good long nap. Saren's face hovered in her mind's eye. *You will be free of him, sister. I promise.*

Brandi touched another glyph and the tentacles holding her family became limp. Megan, Dar and Eric struggled to their feet. Tarvener sneered and tapped the ground with a sword point. The tendrils re-animated and pulled the Riders back down again.

"I can keep this up all day," he said. "But I have other things in mind." He waved one of his blades up and to the side. A massive clump of earth and rocks erupted out of the ground and soared at Megan, Dar and Eric. Brandi flew up, pointing at the flying earth with her sword and touching a symbol with the other hand. A mighty pulse of air flung the stones and dirt away from her family into the tall grass.

I have to get him away from them. "Nice try, but weak," she said, pulling away from Eric, Dar and Megan.

Tarvener's eyes narrowed. He flicked his scimitar point in her direction and a black gem in the guard flashed. A cloud of black threads exploded out at her. She twisted out of the way but some entangled her right wing. She plummeted towards the ground.

She quickly tapped a symbol. Her armor flashed and the sizzling ebony tendrils flew back at Tarvener. He cursed and slashed them in half. They drifted to the ground and vanished in a puff of smoke. She drifted even farther from her family.

"You're starting to annoy me," he snarled, eyes flashing as he followed. He chanted harsh words and his horns flared red. Brandi sensed, rather than saw, a motion above her and instinctively darted to the side. A flaming meteor the size of an ale barrel plummeted past, exploding on the empty road below with a heavy boom and cloud of fire.

Brandi moved away from the road and touched another sigil. A beam of intense light shot at Tarvener from the diamond on the brow of the Crown, slamming into his breastplate. A clap of thunder echoed in the fields and he flew backwards, bellowing in pain and cartwheeling through the air. Behind her, Brandi heard her army cheering wildly.

Is that because of me or did something happen with Golvadu? No time to look.

She darted after Tarvener, but he righted himself and danced aside. She whirled in midair, slashing, thrusting and spinning with lightning speed. None of her attacks connected and she barely missed taking a cut in the thigh from a red-glowing scimitar. He rained blows and spells at her. Her armor deflected his magic into the grey sky.

He bull-rushed her. She whirled out of the way, casting a pattern of glittering, flashing lights on his face. He swore and dove towards the grassy plain, blinking. She barely missed taking off his right arm with a slash.

She chased him but he pulled up, corkscrewing and accelerating. He cast a cloud of acid in his wake and she banked out of the way, her leg armor deflecting the sizzling fog.

Damn it! I'm faster but he has too many tricks. She took a deep breath and flew higher to get a better view. Below, Eric and Dar doggedly sliced away at the tentacles but for each one they severed, another took its place. Megan fought to raise her hands and cast a spell. The tendrils wrapped around her hands and slapped her in the stomach, cutting off her incantations.

Tarvener flapped his wings and rose to her altitude, panting. "You're going to die slowly, bitch."

She shook her head. "Not if you die first."

He clashed his blades together and a globe of darkness sprang up around her. Knowing what was coming, she folded up her wings and dropped straight down. Emerging from the sphere of blackness, she watched him hurtle through it, swinging his blades on empty air.

She landed on the ground and gazed up at him. "Did you lose something in the Darkness Globe, Prince Tarvener?"

"Oh great! Now she sounds like me," Dar said from his prone position on the ground.

Tarvener flicked a hand at him and an opaque sphere of violet light sprang up around the Riders. "No interruptions, weakling. You'll get your turn later."

Dar tried to reply but no sound came out of his mouth.

"Oh, I don't think you want any part of Dar, Tarvener," Brandi countered. The Daemon Prince shot down at her, his face a mask of anger. She flew up and to the side. He attacked with speed and power and she spent several harrowing seconds dodging and parrying.

He feinted and she spun out of the way. Too late, she realized his intention and a searing pain lanced through her right wing. With a cry of triumph, he darted forward as she faltered. Again, she folded her wings and dropped. His scimitars swished through empty air. She tapped a symbol and her wound healed. She shot upwards, stabbing. Her Paladin's sword bit deep into his leg and a flash of holy fire burst around him.

With a cry of pain and frustration, he flipped in midair, avoiding her backhand slash, then landed on the road, panting. He touched a scimitar to his injury and it knit together. "This is pointless. I will defeat you."

"But you aren't just fighting me, Tarvener," Brandi said, landing as well.

"The Lord of Hosts fights at my side. You cannot prevail against Him."

"There is no such being!" he snapped. His horns glowed again. Twin balls of crackling lightning zipped out at her. She whirled aside and they detonated on her shields. Some of the energy got through and her left arm took a jolt so intense she almost dropped her sword. She retreated, shaking her arm to get the feeling back.

He lunged, his blades shooting firedarts at her. She tapped a glyph again. Her armor and the Crown flared and the magic missiles rebounded back at him. He skidded to a halt, swatting the darts away with his magic scimitars.

"Damn you!" he raged. Uncertainty showed in his eyes for the first time.

Please, God, be with me. Brandi lunged. He sidestepped and swung, but she ducked into a slide underneath the razor edges of his blades. With her left-hand sword, she cut his goat's legs as she skimmed past. He howled in pain. She popped up behind him and slashed his left wing. He whipped around, his swords carving arcs of flame in the air, but she skipped out of the way and bounced up into the air.

Now he's grounded, she thought, noting his injured wing. "Had enough, Prince of Hades?"

His eyes flashed like fireballs and he clanged his swords together. His horns flared red again. The air around Brandi suddenly became hot as a furnace and a swirling globe of fire surrounded her, shrinking in size.

Brandi shrank away from the fiery barrier as it came closer but it singed her wings and arms and legs anyway. Searing pain lanced through her and she bit back a scream of agony.

Holy Lord! In desperation, she tapped three symbols. A minor burst of healing lessened the sting and a sudden blast of magic from the Crown and Paladin's Sword exploded outward. The blazing sphere evaporated with a crack. She flew backwards and skidded in the tall grass near the road. She clambered to her feet.

With a malicious, savage leer on his face, Tarvener raised his blades and lurched towards Eric where he lay pinned to the ground. "Perhaps I'll just take your husband first."

"Not while I live!" Brandi screamed, unleashing another blast of heavenly light. Tarvener took it in the flank and tumbled across the road to the other side.

Brandi flexed her wings and the pain threatened to make her black out. *Oh God, that hurts. Well, neither of us can fly now.* She dismissed her pinions to the Other Space.

Tarvener dragged himself out of the tall grass on the other side of the road, panting. "You can't be doing this!" he croaked. "I have fought wars for hundreds of years and you are a mere child. How is this possible?"

She brushed sweaty hair off her face and readied her swords. "Faith in God makes all things possible."

With an oath, Tarvener charged. She dove out of the way, tucking into a roll. He shot past, scrambling to a halt. She popped up and he attacked instantly. She stabbed at his head. When he blocked it with one hand, she knelt into a back-leg sweep. The jarring impact of slamming her heel behind his knee made her leg tingle, but he toppled to the side with a cry. As he rose, she stabbed him in the arm and stepped back.

Desperation showed in his eyes now. He advanced with a complicated combination of cuts and thrusts. She dodged and parried as best she could but one of his attacks got through, slamming into her armor with such force that the wind left her lungs. He swept both blades high and stabbed downward. She fell to the side and rolled. His attack embedded his swords in the earth. She thrust the Paladin's sword into his armor just above his hip. He gasped and lurched.

She struggled to her feet. Her limbs felt leaden and she struggled to focus through bleary vision. Tarvener bled purple ichor from several deep wounds. He leaned on one sword and placed his hand on his injuries. Red light glowed. Though the bleeding stopped, the wounds remained.

We're both running out of energy. Brandi applied a healing spell to herself. It didn't make her feel all that much better and she knew that even the impressive reserves of the Crown would deplete, and soon. *I will do this. I can do this. I must do this.*

"Give it up, Tarvener. You're finished," she said.

"I will never surrender to the likes of you," he gasped. Taking up his blade again, he muttered a quick phrase. The ground in front of him swirled and warped, forming a wall of earth and stone and blocking her view of him.

He could be anywhere. I have to protect Eric, Megan and Dar. Brandi retreated towards her family, wary of any tricks. With a speed that alarmed her,

Tarvener leapt over the earthen wall, slashing. She dodged and cut him through the neck and chest. Instead of dying in a Daemonic explosion of fire, blood and meat, he simply vanished.

Illusion!

One of the Crown's symbols flared. Going more by instinct, she leaped towards the high grass just as a gout of lava scorched the ground where she had stood.

Panting, she touched a symbol and a block of ice landed on the lava, causing a vast eruption of steam. She touched another symbol and the silence globe over her family vanished.

"Where is he?" she asked her relatives.

"No idea," Megan managed in a tired voice. "The wall went up and then his illusion appeared."

"Dar? Eric?"

"Keep your eyes peeled, sweetheart," Eric said. "He's hiding somewhere, the craven tyrant."

"But where? How can he hide in plain sight?"

See through his deceptions. Saint Alyssa's words came back to her and she felt a chill. *Invisibility!*

Brandi touched her sword to the Crown and put a hand on her chest. Energies surged. She released it in a vibrant blast of magic that made her dizzy with fatigue.

Tarvener glittered into view next to her and she ducked just as his blade swished through the air where her head had been. Kneeling, she drove her lefthand blade into his midsection. The enchanted sword penetrated Tarvener's Daemonic armor with a meaty, ringing impact. He choked and dropped one of his swords but managed to swing around and backhand her. She staggered and he stabbed her in the side with his other blade. Fire burst between her ribs. She stumbled backward, then fell to her hands and knees. Tarvener tried to advance but also dropped to all fours.

Panting, she lifted her head and stood shakily, holding a hand to her bloody side. She laid a healing spell on herself but it only stopped the worst of the bleeding. *I will not give in. I will give my life for my people, so help me God. He will not have them.*

As if nature itself tried to aid her, the clouds above the sea parted and golden rays of light shone down on her city. The tallest tower of the castle reflected the sunlight, like it had in her dream. An image of Mary holding the Crown of Saint Alyssa flickered in her mind's eye.

She stood taller. "God is with me," she whispered. "He always has been."

Motion on the ramparts of Tor Aldin's East Gate caught her attention. Magic explosions burst and a pennant of the Skullhead Legion toppled over the wall. A triumphant surge of joy burst out in her heart despite her pain and exhaustion.

Connor's troops are inside! The South Gate is open! My people see Tarvener losing! They're rebelling!

"Look there, Prince of Hades," she said, nodding towards Tor Aldin. "My people rise up against you. It is over."

Tarvener shot a glance at the city. "They will see you die here in the dust!" he screamed and staggered towards her. He feinted a thrust and she sidestepped. He slashed at her neck. She ducked.

Alyssa's voice echoed in her head. *Now, daughter.*

"Alenar!" Brandi screamed and swung an uppercut with the Paladin's blade. The holy sword rang like a church bell and flared golden, beheading the Daemon Prince. Brandi slapped a hand on one last glyph. A shimmering sphere rather like a giant soap bubble leapt up around Tarvener's corpse. With a thunderous boom, he exploded, smearing the inside of the globe with gore and bones.

She fell to her knees and dispelled the protective sphere. Bits of armor and bloody meat thumped onto the road.

The magic tentacles pinning the pegasi and her family dissipated in puffs of black smoke. Eric, Dar and Megan limped to Brandi's side and hauled her to her feet. Eric embraced her, kissing her face.

The dome of magic dissipated like morning fog and the fires in the grass died out. Varani and Alex rallied their force and raced towards them. Alex thundered to a halt at their side.

"Your Majesty!"

Brandi waved a tired hand. "We'll be fine, Alex."

Varani frowned. "You don't look fine. Take a moment to gather yourselves, sister. We'll escort you back to the command pavilion."

"We can make it," Brandi said, then stopped. In the distance on the hills, magical attack and defense spells flashed as Golvadu battled the Nuncio and Sister Karen while their armies held their positions.

Eric smiled. "Thank you, Alex and Varani. Let us have a couple of minutes and you can escort us."

Drums and a skirling pipe drew their eyes to the south side of the city, where Connor's force held the seashore and the hills. Thousands of Alliance troops advanced from beach landings, the flags of many nations snapping in the ocean breeze. A piper in maroon and white livery led the vanguard battalion, playing a stirring marching tune. Hippogriff riders soared overhead. A trumpet blared three times. The serried regiments wheeled as one towards Golvadu's army, then lowered spears behind couched shields and charged, flanked by trotting cavalry.

Even from this distance, she heard many voices shouting. "Tarvener is slain! Long Live Queen Brandawyn!"

"I'm so proud of you," Eric whispered. His arms around her felt like a healing spell.

Around them, Brandi's army took up the cry and surged forward, swiftly joined by the newly-arrived Alliance formations. Golvadu's army held, but hammer blow after hammer blow of massed infantry, cavalry and magical attacks drove them back. Finally, they began a full-scale retreat.

Elation warred with exhaustion and her limbs trembled with fatigue and overwrought nerves. Tears streamed down Brandawyn's face as she watched the battle turn. She turned her eyes heavenward. "Thank you."

Chapter Thirty-One – The Wages of Sin

"No! You idiots! Hold your positions!" Golvadu yanked on the reins. Vizkir backed up, hissing a cloud of small lightning bolts at a phalanx of infantry charging them. Six of the soldiers jerked spasmodically and dropped, but the rest came on, roaring a challenge. All around Golvadu, units of the People's Republic of Torosc gave way before the Alenar rebels and their new allies from the Northern Alliance. The Papal Nuncio and the Elven nun stood next to a trio of black-and-gold-armored Kestrel Knights. The pair looked winded and bloodied, but they remained on their feet.

This can't be happening! Those two refuse to die, then Zulgubrudan gets his ass kicked and now Tarvener is a pile of bloody meat?

"No! You cowards!" Golvadu thundered. Despair, rage and frustration warred within him as he saw his army retreating around him. Hot anger gave him new energy and he sought a target for his ire.

"Damn you!" Golvadu shrieked, uncorking one last blast of Hellfire at Father Thomas. The Nuncio cast up a shield of light. The Daemonic flame burst on it and the Nuncio fell to one knee, but the nun lifted him up. She thrust a hand at Golvadu and a heavy, invisible force knocked Vizkir backwards.

The Kestrel Knights formed a shield wall and the Nuncio and the nun drew back behind it. A platoon of heavily armored Dwarven infantry trotted forward down the hill with gleaming battle axes, accompanied by Imperial Elven cavalry archers on barded horses.

A sudden panic seized Golvadu. "To the air, Vizkir! Back to the command center!" The Drake crouched to spring but four arrows hummed in, trailing sizzling sparks. Two ripped into the Drake's left wing, one hit him in the chest, sizzling with electricity, and the fourth took him in the right eye. The dragon keeled over and Golvadu tumbled off.

The Dwarven wizard staggered to his feet, his temples throbbing from excessive magic use. His troops took up the cry and fell back past him in a wave. "The Alliance is here! Retreat!"

How did they make it past the blockades? We have to regroup! Fury filled Golvadu but his mind couldn't focus.

A strong hand clasped his shoulder. "Come, Lord Golvadu," Ilyan Kalik said, pulling him to a waiting armored pony. "Back to the command post."

Two arrows zipped by Golvadu's head. A trio of firedarts exploded on his shields and he barely felt the impact. He numbly climbed into the saddle, casting about for the figures of Prince Patian and Lord Bates. "What of Morlan and Jered?"

Kalik made no answer but galloped ahead to the pavilion. Golvadu followed, dodging the occasional artillery shell or errant lightning bolt shot his way. Chaos reigned as commanders attempted to rally their troops or to form up for a fighting retreat.

He dismounted at the entrance to his pavilion, dimly aware that Kalik's Red Veil assassins came to join them, though his personal guard were nowhere in sight. He lurched inside, making immediately for a side table. The place was a mess: cushions torn up, tables overturned, strongboxes looted, glasses and dishes shattered. Most of his most prized liquors were gone, but he downed several gulps of Gnomish whiskey.

The heady blast of alcohol made him gasp and his mind cleared. He stared at Kalik's bodyguards in their red armor. *At least someone is still loyal.*

"Where are Prince Patian and Lord Bates?" he wheezed.

"They just arrived," announced Kalik, bowing to admit both men.

"Your Highness, Your Grace," Golvadu began, "We can implement the first contingency plan. After we shore up our center and pull back from the coastline, we can wheel left, then drive them into the sea and —"

"Shut up, you arrogant ass!" Patian snapped, eyes blazing. "All your plotting and schemes and yet you didn't pay enough attention to the seaways to the north!"

Golvadu shook his head, anger growing. "The coast was your responsibility!"

Bates held up a hand. "Perhaps, but the ocean was yours. With the help of the Merfolk and the Navy of Gorostol, the Alliance fleet was able to swing out into deeper waters to the west and move around the bulk of your squadrons."

"Merfolk?" Golvadu asked, feeling the situation rapidly getting away from him.

"Yes!" Patian threw his hands up. "Merfolk from the north mustered in large numbers. Many of your blockade ships are at the bottom of the ocean, thanks to them."

Golvadu sat heavily on the couch. Now the alcohol in the drink felt like a fog. "Why would the Merfolk help land dwellers?"

Bates laughed bitterly. "Have you so quickly forgotten? They died by the thousands in the oceans of the north during the War of the Dark Wave and then you enslaved their southern kin in Vodyanoi camps off the coast. They were only too glad to join the relief force."

"But the Vodyanoi were supposed to have the ocean ways under control," Golvadu finished. His own voice sounded weak and lame in his ears.

Patian scoffed. "Those lazy fish-folk? Torosc let them get fat off tribute and slaves for centuries. The Merfolk rolled over them like Halfling harvesters in fields of wheat."

Golvadu tried to come up with alternatives to the situation but nothing materialized. His thoughts whirled this way and that. Only one stood out.

We lost.

Bates gave a sardonic smile. "I can see that the First Archon needs to ponder surrender terms with the Queen of Alenar. In the meantime, since our arrangement was with the People's Republic of Torosc in this region and the Republic is no longer in authority, our agreement is at an end."

Patian fixed Golvadu with an icy stare. "All your schemes, brought to nothing by a gang of former freelance sellswords. First the Skull Gates, then the Dark Wave, now this."

He gestured to Bates. "Your Grace, we need to move fast. Brandawyn of Alenar and the Alliance won't wait long after securing the field to come after us."

Bates nodded. "Yes. The stink of failure is ripe in this pavilion, Highness. Pray, lead the way."

The Jeredan Pirate Prince and the Morlani wizard swept out of the tent without a backward glance.

Golvadu didn't even blink. He slowly stood and walked to a gnarled staff leaning against a shattered glass case, stepping over the charred body of the Skullhead who had unwisely tried to purloin it. The staff tingled with latent Daemonic magic.

"Priest Kalik," he finally said. "We need to move out with a small force to the east and try to link up with reinforcements east of Loemin. Then —"

Kalik held up a hand and the three Red Veils stepped up behind him. "Actually, Lord Golvadu, there is a slight alteration."

Golvadu stared at him. "Alteration?"

"Yes. Similar to the arrangement with Jered and Morlan, now that you hold no authority in these lands, our own arrangement is void."

Golvadu's eyes narrowed. "What are you blathering about? My agreement with the Vardu High Council —"

"Was for me to coordinate as liaison and support your efforts to destroy the Southern Royals attempting to recover their ancestral lands. We were promised much in the way of treasure and privileges once the restive provinces were pacified and the Grey Riders either dead or imprisoned. Since you accomplished neither, the contract is null."

Golvadu's anger returned. "You egotistical idiot! I live and we still have forces, though they are in retreat."

Kalik shrugged. "I see no coherent force here. Even if you were to make it to Highpoint, it would take months to summon enough power to try to take on Alenar and Loemin, now that they have the Alliance and Gorostol to back them up. It's over, Your Grace. You will come with us now, to make account to the Council."

"Preposterous!" Golvadu fumed. "I am not accountable to your Council! This is mutiny! Red Veils, take Priest Kalik into custody!"

The women remained in place.

"Did you not hear me, you lousy bitches?"

Kalik's smile became icy. "They work for me, Golvadu. They have always worked for me."

Sweat ran down Golvadu's back. He gaped at them, then slowly turned towards the wall of the pavilion.

Think! There has to be a way out of this. His eyes fell on the staff in his hands. *Tarvener gave me this for emergencies. I could blast them! No, I'm in no condition to wield that level of magic, not now. Wait. There is one spell.*

Pretending to be weak and defeated, he turned back around to the traitorous Vardu priest. "Is that your final word on the subject?"

Kalik inclined his head. "As commanded by my High Council."

"Well then," Golvadu pressed a thumb against a knot in the wood of the staff, feeling the miniscule magic runes carved there.

"Sergeant," Kalik said over his shoulder without taking his dead blue eyes off Golvadu. "Take the First Archon in charge and retreat south to our mustering point. There, you will await further instructions."

Golvadu allowed himself a wolfish smile, then recited a short phrase. The runes sizzled under his thumb. The interior of the pavilion warped and misted over. He could just make out Kalik's amazed expression.

"Fuck you," he retorted as he teleported away.

<<>>

Ilyan Kalik stared at the cloud of sparkles where Golvadu had once stood. He said nothing, listening to the sounds of the Torosc, Jered and Morlan armies try to prevent the retreat from turning into a rout.

"Priest Kalik?" The sergeant said.

Kalik sighed. "There's nothing for it. Let's go."

"Aren't you worried about Lord Golvadu's wrath?"

Kalik smirked. "I'm not worried about us. We can make it to the mustering point and escape this confusion. It's Lord Golvadu who has to be worried. This land belongs to Queen Brandawyn now. She's part Elohir and I'm sure her relatives will be arriving soon. Then Golvadu's life will get very exciting."

Chapter Thirty-Two – Finally

"I'm proud of you," Megan whispered with a coy look at her husband.

Dar flicked his eyes at her. "For what? Being heroic? Being a devastatingly handsome husband and superb lover? For vanquishing Daemonic hordes?"

She pinched his side. "For getting into your finery without complaining."

He rolled his eyes. "The Daemonic hordes were easier."

She tried to give him a disapproving look and failed. "Since it's you we're talking about, I can believe it. Now, let's have a look. They'll call us any minute."

Morning sunlight streamed in from the tall windows in the antechamber and she heard voices and footfalls in the hall outside. She inspected him top to bottom, which she had to admit was one of her favorite pastimes. He wore a long grey tunic with a high collar, grey breeches and black boots. A wide burgundy stripe curved from the left shoulder of the tunic to the right hip. An emblem of the Royal House of Alenar and the Grey Rider insignia were embroidered at his left chest. The golden pin of a Colonel — a star within a circle — winked at her from one side of his collar and a black pin of a snarling cat's face surrounded by a circle of thorns marked the other side. A belt encircled his waist and a scabbard held a dagger at his hip.

She nodded, satisfied. "Colonel Lord Dar Cabot Aldenar, First Prince and Commander of the Catbriar Cloaks Special Ranger Regiment. You look very presentable."

He measured her with his eyes as if trying to determine if she teased him, then broke into a grin and kissed her quickly. "I'll take that as a compliment." He took her hands and spun her in a circle. "You, of course, look breathtaking."

Now she did giggle as her white gown belled out around her. Diamond encrusted gold glittered at wrist and ankle and her platinum pegasus earrings twinkled. She paused and gave him a mock curtsey. "Your Highness is too kind." She straightened.

"No. I'm truthful." His gentle, warm eyes transfixed her.

Megan simply gazed at him, smiling, holding his hands and not wanting to go anywhere or do anything. "And you're sweet."

"Now *that* is a compliment."

The sound of boots echoed in the hall outside the door. "Highnesses? All is ready."

She winked and brushed her fingers over his tunic. "Duty calls."

"At least there are no explosions this time," he said, offering her his hand.

"True." She waved her hand to the side and the door unlocked and swung open. "And, at least, if you're with me, I can keep an eye on you."

"And every other body part, too, I hope," he whispered back.

"That's for later, dear," she murmured. The couple left the antechamber, escorted by four Elven guards in shining plate mail. Varani awaited them in the hall. She wore a short black tunic over grey leggings and black boots, a sword belted at her side and silvery chainmail glittering under her clothes. A large gold medallion of the Royal Arms shone against her chest. In her hands, she carried a silver rod of office with a single sapphire at the top.

"Your Highnesses," Varani said with a bow.

"My lady," Megan replied. "Well met."

"Pray follow me." With a tiny smile, Varani led them to the Grand Hall.

Megan marveled at how quickly the people of Tor Aldin managed to repair and clean up the castle. With the state of disrepair and filthiness the Riders discovered upon their initial entry after Tarvener's defeat, she considered it a miracle.

It's amazing what a small army of motivated people can accomplish in three weeks. Many hands make light work!

They stopped at tall, spired double doors embossed with figures of armored angels holding lanterns. Two human guards came to attention, halberds held in salute.

Varani winked as she pushed the doors open. "Time for the show."

Dar grinned at her. "I'm more interested in the party afterwards."

The portal swung wide and, despite knowing what she would see, Megan blinked. Nobles and aristocracy lined the sides of the hall in a panoply of finery, attended by guards. Marble pillars gleamed and sunlight lanced in through high windows. Garlands of flowers added splashes of color and the banners of the noble houses of Alenar draped the walls between the windows. At the far end of the hall, a large round dais held a single, tall-backed throne with three smaller thrones next to it. A massive stained-glass window held the image of a dove crowned by a tongue of flame, descending on a crenelated tower like the one in the Royal coat of arms. The flags of the House of Aldenar and the Papal Nuncio hung on either side of the window.

So beautiful! It's like an epic tale told by a bard. Except this is real. The wonder and majesty of the scene pierced Megan's soul and her throat tightened. Dar squeezed her hand. Her eyes stung and she let out a measured breath.

Everyone turned towards Megan and Dar. Varani raised her chin and addressed the court.

"My lords and ladies, honored citizens, High Princess Megan Diana Marie Aldenar and her husband, First Prince Darius Richard Cabot Aldenar."

The assembly bowed and curtseyed as Varani led them towards the dais. Megan inclined her head to each noble they passed, trying desperately to remember their names. After a while, she gave up.

That's what the Royal Chamberlain is for. At least until I get my bearings.

They stopped at the base of the dais. Megan gave a warm smile to Father Thomas, Melinor and Sister Karen, standing at the base of the platform on the right. Melinor winked at her and Sister Karen smiled back. Resplendent in their own Loemin finery, Hannah and Connor waited by the Papal Nuncio's side.

A side door opened and Alex entered. Attired in a grey uniform similar to Varani's, he carried a staff of cherry wood capped with gold. He rapped the marble floor. "Her Royal Majesty, Queen Brandawyn Veronica Therese the First, and His Royal Highness, Eric Daniel Indidarc, High Prince."

Megan joined with the court in bowing to her sister and Eric as they took their places on the dais in front of the thrones.

"Thank you, Lord Fejer," Brandi announced, eyes sweeping the crowd.

Varani moved to Alex's side and the pair knelt.

"What would you have of us, Lord Fejer and Lady Hylar?" Brandi said in a solemn tone.

Varani held up her rod of office as Alex held up his staff. "Your Majesty, as your Liaison Officers to Alenar, we beg leave to surrender our office now that Alenar is free."

Brandi nodded. "We accept your petition, Lord Fejer and Lady Hylar, upon one condition. We command that you remain as part of our Royal Household, to serve us as designated. Do you accept?"

Alex nodded. "Command us as you will. We are your servants."

Eric gestured to the assembly. "Please join the rest of the Royal Court, Lord Fejer, Lady Hylar."

Varani and Alex slipped back to stand with the other dignitaries. Megan hid a smile, watching them. *Wait until you see what's coming.*

Brandi beckoned to the court. A gorgeous blonde Elven woman approached and knelt, wearing silvery chainmail under a blue tunic embroidered with a golden trumpet.

"Henceforth," Brandi continued. "The duties formerly assigned to our liaisons will be carried out by the Royal Herald, Lady Carawyn of the House of Altair. Lady Carawyn?"

The Elven lady bowed to Alex and Varani and received the symbols of office from them. She slipped the rod into her belt and took up a position at the left of the dais.

Brandi nodded to Megan and Dar. "My well-beloved sister and brother-in-law, please approach."

Anticipation, pride and a small amount of nervousness flowed through Megan. She bowed. "Yes, Majesty."

"Take the formal oath of fealty."

How can I be excited and afraid all at once? Megan's hand found Dar's as they knelt on the floor and raised their eyes.

She and Dar declared in unison, "We do promise and affirm that we will be loyal servants of the Crown and Nation of Alenar, following the dictates and commands of the White Throne and its Monarch, accepting such duties as requested, to support the Royal House in the person of Brandawyn Veronica Therese until life leaves us, to celebrate, improve and bring to fullness of potential the Nation of Alenar. This we promise before God Almighty and those here assembled."

This is it, what I'm born to do. An absolute certainty filled her mind and soul. *I'm pledging my life to my people. They are free, truly free, and I will be their servant for the rest of my life. God, help me rise to the challenge!*

Father Thomas approached, accompanied by Gorlak and Sister Karen, each bearing a satin pillow with a twelve-pointed crown. Gorlak, clad in a black uniform with a silver Catbriar emblem embroidered on the left shoulder, winked at Megan. She studiously refrained from returning the wink, though she dearly wanted to at least smile at him. *Stop that Gorlak! I have to appear regal and formal.*

Father Thomas blessed the crowns. "May the blessing of God the Father Almighty come upon those who wear these crowns as symbols of authority, responsibility and integrity. May the Holy Spirit pour His gifts on Princess Megan and Prince Dar and on their heirs in perpetuity. We pray this in the name of Jesus Christ, our Lord and Savior."

Brandi took up the slimmer crown. "Then I, Brandawyn Veronica Therese Aldenar, do affirm and establish Megan Diana Marie Aldenar, as High Princess of Alenar, in station, truth and authority. Arise, beloved sister."

Megan stood with the crown on her head, heart swelling with both gratitude and joy. *Please, God, help me make lives better. Give me strength.*

Brandi placed the other crown on Dar's head. "I, Brandawyn Veronica Therese Aldenar, likewise do affirm and establish Darius Richard Cabot Aldenar as First Prince of the House of Aldenar in station, truth and authority. Arise, beloved brother."

Dar arose, similarly crowned, and gave her a little smirk.

Now you'll actually have to behave like a prince! Oh, don't worry, dearest. You'll get used to all this pomp and protocol — and you'll do better than you think.

Brandi swept her hand to the two thrones beside her own. Megan and Dar took their places. Megan let out a deep breath as the entire assembly bowed and curtseyed to them. A wave of elation at finally achieving their goals surged over her, tempered by a sudden, overwhelming realization of her responsibilities.

God, I know I'm asking for a lot of things, but I need you to guide me in dealing with my people. Please help me be just, kind and firm.

"Now," Brandi said with a pointed look at Alex. "Is there any boon that anyone would ask of the Crown?"

Alex shot a little smile at Varani and nodded. "I have a very special request of the High Prince of Alenar."

Megan tried to retain a regal countenance. *You better have a very special request, Alex!*

Eric nodded. "Yes, Lord Fejer."

Alex took Varani's hand. "Highness, since you are her only living relative, I humbly ask for the hand of your half-sister, Varani Khyla Hylar, in marriage."

Eric grinned. "Gladly do I give it, if my sister is willing."

Varani grinned back. "I am, beloved brother."

Brandi gestured to Carawyn. "Lady Carawyn, as your first task of Royal Herald, I bid you announce the engagement of Lord Alex and Lady Varani."

Carawyn tapped her staff on the floor. "To all here assembled, attend me. By the approval of Her Royal Majesty, Brandawyn the First of Alenar, and His Royal Highness Prince Eric, the Lord Alex Fejer and the Lady Varani Hylar are to be wed. Any who may object are commanded to speak now or be forever silent."

Utter silence reigned.

Brandi turned to Marshal Kontar in the assembly. "Lord Kontar, as the President Pro-Tempore of the Royal Senate, pray tell the Court the result of last night's vote concerning Lord Alex and Lady Varani."

The Dwarven lord bowed. "Twenty-seven votes in favor and none in opposition, Majesty."

"Thank you, Lord Kontar."

Carawyn bowed to Brandi. "Your Majesty."

Brandi motioned for Varani and Alex to rise. "In anticipation of their nuptials and their ascendancy to the House of Aldenar, I, Brandawyn Veronica Therese, do establish and declare that Lord Alex and Lady Varani be invested as Titular Duke and Duchess of Khorpoint. In this way they will serve both the Royal House and the nation."

Alex and Varani exchanged a stunned look. "I...We... We thank you,

Majesty." Varani stammered.

Now Megan did grin. *Surprise, surprise, my loves!*

Connor and Hannah approached, likewise bearing pillows with nine-pointed gold coronets.

With words similar to those she used for Megan and Dar, Brandi crowned Varani and Alex. "Pray join the Royal Family," Eric said with a smile, gesturing to the first step of the dais. Still looking somewhat stunned, the couple took their places.

Brandi addressed Eric. "My lord, is there any further business for the Court to consider?"

Eric nodded. "The Crown of Alenar has a request of the Nuncio."

Megan and Dar exchanged a conspiratorial look. *I wonder how Father Thomas will take this?*

Father Thomas bowed to Brandi. "Indeed? And what would your Majesties require?"

"We would ask for the services of your most loyal retainer, Gorlak," Eric said. "Will you release him?"

Father Tom considered this, then shot a sidelong look at Gorlak. "I believe that is for Gorlak himself to decide."

Eric smiled. "Please come forth, my friend."

Gorlak, looking a little confused, bowed. "Majesties."

Brandi now favored the Goblin with a brilliant smile. "Gorlak, you have been our faithful companion through many trials. Though it seems little enough to reward you, in addition to your current status as Major of the Catbriar Cloaks, we would entitle you as Baron of Ryefield and Knight Royal Guard Commander."

Gorlak blinked. He opened and closed his mouth and looked at Megan. She smiled at him and nodded in encouragement.

"If I truthful, Queen Brandawyn," he replied, looking down and shuffling his feet. He paused for several heartbeats, then raised his eyes to Brandi. "I not qualified to rule any of the people of Alenar. That for those who understand rulership and management of cities. However, I honored to serve you as Royal Guard."

Brandi inclined her head. "Well said, my friend. If that is your wish, then you shall be Knighted as Sir Gorlak of the House of Aldenar. Prince Dar, as commander of the Catbriars, do you have an assignment for Sir Gorlak?"

Dar nodded. "Indeed. Sir Gorlak of Alenar, it is my command that you guard, assist and protect Lord Melinor Indidarc, who will reside henceforth in the palace in Tor Aldin."

Melinor winked at Gorlak, who grinned back.

"If Father Tom permits," the Goblin said, "I gladly do this."

Father Thomas shrugged, but his eyes twinkled. "Who am I to stand in the way of what is obviously the Lord's will? Go, then, my friend, with my blessing."

Gorlak bowed to Eric and Brandi and took his place next to Melinor, who, in Megan's opinion, looked entirely too pleased with himself.

"Is there any other business to come before the Crown prior to the oaths of fealty, my lord?" Brandi asked Eric.

"Yes, milady," he said. "There is the matter of Tholerios and Kindriana of the Sunfire Clan. Now that they are Knights of the Silver Tower, they have petitioned the Crown to remain here with us in Alenar. As their liege, Lord Barad has given his consent, but there are no accommodations here in the palace large enough for them – they are young dragons, after all, and will grow — and the sea-caves near the city are unsuitable for mountain dragons."

"Could something be found for them in the countryside nearby?" asked Brandi. "I would like to honor their request, but I agree: the castle is not the place for them."

Marshal Kontar raised his hand.

"Yes, my lord Baron of Greymount?" Megan said.

"My community and its dependencies would be proud to host the grand-children of Iron Thunder."

Brandi frowned. "Your fief suffered grievously under the heel of the People's Republic. You have much reconstruction in your future. Do you have the means? We do not wish to impose."

Kontar waved a hand. "It is no imposition. Some of our old mines are no longer used and they are in proximity to the city of Greymount. We had thought to use them for storage, but as homes for dragons, I believe they would be entirely suitable. Besides, in ages past, dragons regularly lived in the mountains nearby and were allies to our folk. We would be honored to offer a home to the young Knights of the Tower."

"Superb," Brandi said. "I would be most reluctant to disappoint Kindri and Tholi since they have been so enthusiastic about remaining here in Alenar. It is settled, then. Many thanks to you, Lord Kontar, and the people of Greymount."

Kontar smiled and bowed, looking satisfied.

Megan nodded to him. *The standing of the Dwarves will rise considerably in the Court when they become hosts for two Royal Knights. And they have dragons living among them again.*

"Is there any other matter for the Court to consider?"

"Ah, actually, there is," said Melinor. He shuffled towards the thrones and inclined his head. "We have received word that the hunt for Selaan was, as suspected, a hoax to keep the Alliance occupied during the wars in Torosc. With that resolved, the Alliance is recommending that Alenar host a number of Elohir as a counterbalance to the inevitable influx of Daemons that will come from the darker portions of Torosc, as well as Morlan and Jered."

Brandi nodded. "Certainly prudent. We received four Elohir yesterday. Am I to assume they would part of the local contingent?"

"Yes, Majesty," Melinor answered. "Lady Johanna and Lord Petrus are on their way to join us here in Tor Aldin."

How wonderful! Megan thought. *We owe them so much.* The idea of seeing her two Elohir mentors filled her with happiness.

Brandi gave a bright smile. "Of course, we will be proud to host them here for as long as they care to stay. Thank you, Lord Melinor, for facilitating this."

"Of course."

Eric took Brandi's hand. "As the last order of business before the oaths of fealty, my Queen, the Royal Bard has composed a song on this most happy occasion of the return of the Royal House to the throne of Alenar. Lady Alicia of the House of Vintre begs leave to perform it."

Brandi's eyebrows rose. "Really? That is excellent. Lady Alicia, if you please."

A brown-haired half-Elven lady in a flowered, sky-blue gown stepped forward, carrying a small harp in her hands. She bowed low to the Royal Family, strummed the harp and sang in a clear, bell-like soprano. Megan closed her eyes, letting herself drift as the Elven words floated on the air over the melody. She translated in her mind.

"From the deepest darkness
From loss and despair
To northern hope winging
Two stars journeyed

Leaving sorrow behind them
Sisterly hands joined
With kind ones to guide them
To refuge and peace

Finding guidance anew
In a land cold and far
New friends beside them
New purpose found

Evil plots thwarting
Ancient treasure unearthing
True loves found
Amid danger and strife

Victory gaining
Against dark power's schemes
New task appointed
Flying to captive lands

Mighty wings gifted
Two stars tearful depart
Promising to lovers
To be united again

In shadows searching
Evil's schemes contending
Yet in victory, loss

TOWER OF LIGHT

Captive to darkness

Faith never failing
Death yet suspended
Sleeping by heaven's gates
Safe in God's arms

Dark Wave arriving
Fire and blood
Bright Riders returning
With Army of Gold

Evil vanquished
Now victory and Glory
Two stars awaken
To see lovers again

Wedded, now blissful
Ancient heritage claiming
Joy to purpose turning
To free captive lands

Royal lineage bringing
An end to oppression
To prisoners, liberty
Hope burning bright

New friends bringing
Crowns ancient restoring
Freedom for the hopeless
And future days renewed

Through fire and war
Through strife and doubt
Two stars return

Triumphant at last

Sing praise to the Almighty
Sing praise to the Highest Lord
World-King Immovable
Sing praise to the Maker
Victorious forever"

Megan brushed tears from her eyes and joined the assembly in applauding. Dar took her hand and squeezed it. His smile and bright eyes filled her soul with joy, a delight so intense it reminded her of her time before she was returned to life, waiting in the presence of God.

Why am I so blessed?

Brandi's ceremonial composure faltered for a few seconds as she wiped her eyes and took Eric's hand. "Thank you, Lady Alicia. That was remarkable. Please see to it that the song is sent to every corner of the Kingdom in celebration, to be sung every year on this day in commemoration."

"As you wish, my Queen." Lady Alicia beamed and stepped back into the crowd.

Eric nodded to Lady Carawyn. The Royal Herald again tapped her staff on the floor. "Now attend! The nobles, aristocracy, knights and gentry of the land will now approach to offer their oaths of loyalty to the White Throne!"

Megan looked over the crowd and prayed for endurance. "I hope you have some rejuvenating spells ready, Dar," she whispered.

"Oh, I think your sister has that covered," Dar replied with a wink.

With that, the first of the gentry processed to the dais and knelt before Brandi and Eric.

Megan sighed, both with happiness and to steel herself against the upcoming, long morning.

Part of the duties of royalty now, she thought. *And I will gladly endure the fatigue.*

Chapter Thirty-Three – Ad Clara Futura

Golvadu slipped behind the gnarled oak tree by the jumble of boulders. He gripped his Daemonic staff, feeling the tingling of heady, Infernal power just under his fingertips.

"Careful," whispered a sly voice in his mind. "Danger ahead. Wait."

Golvadu summoned a spell of far-seeing and his vision narrowed in on the road, almost a mile away. Halfling troops wearing the livery of the Royal Guard of Loemin patrolled in the bright sunlight, searching.

Golvadu shifted the shabby cloak on his shoulders. "Hunting for me in the bushes, the little bastards," he snarled, feeling the weight of his backpack, "as if I were some common bandit!"

A quick glance down at his once-sumptuous robes, now stained with dried blood and dirt, reminded him how accurate that assessment could be.

At least the boots are relatively new. And the farmhand lying in the ditch by the fields a few miles back won't need them anymore — not with a smoking hole in his chest.

With a sour expression on his face, he wrung the Daemonic staff in his hands, waiting for the troops to depart. He took stock of his potion stash while he waited. *I'll have to procure some at the next town,* he mused, tapping the staff absently.

"Good plan," the crafty voice prompted him. "Strengthen yourself for the battle ahead. Always resist the forces of the Light."

The patrol finally regrouped and continued down the road. He waited many heartbeats before breaking cover, heading away from the direction the troops had taken. His mind raced as he tramped through the brush.

Let's see. He mulled over his plans. *Golad. That's where we can regroup. And Veldan Rhi still has garrisons capable of taking out the Loeminites, for a start. Then, I'll have to get into the Main Library and see if I can get the plans for the Skull Gates. I know where we have them locked up.*

He ran through calculations, occasionally pausing to make sure he wasn't followed. He felt confident that his misdirection and obscuring spells would put any search parties off his trail, but it never hurt to be cautious.

Ha! Finished, am I? I am still First Archon of the People's Republic of Torosc! He twisted the Daemonic staff in his grip.

"Be resolute yes, but also wary," whispered the insistent voice in his head. "Make them pay. Insolent, simpering, triumphalist commoners masquerading as the elite."

Thoughts of revenge consumed him for a while and Golvadu's thoughts strayed. The memories of days of hiding, scrambling and scraping for the necessities of life came back to him. More than once, his Daemonic staff came in handy, disguising him or striking down the unwary.

Damn the Grey Riders! I'm reduced to this state by a bunch of low-life free-lancers! I, who should be ruling over the lesser peoples from a position of authority befitting my station and knowledge!

Thoughts of the Riders reminded him of the Battle of Tor Aldin and he hissed in anger. *What a debacle that was! And then there's Morlan and Jered — and the Vardish!* He spat. *Some allies! Cowardly dogs and two-faced liars, the lot of them.*

He paused by a brook and filled his canteen, careful to keep the staff close at hand.

"There must be a reckoning," said the voice. "They must pay."

Yes, Golvadu thought. *A reckoning. But I am patient. First things first. I have allies and the Riders have made many enemies. Now that that Ban is no more, I can bring in Daemons to help.*

He remembered the last time he had seen the Riders and he clenched a fist. *They will not know the time or place, but I will have my vengeance on them and their families. In time, I will be there, when they least expect it, when they are complacent. Then I will dismember their children before their eyes, then I will flay and burn them alive!*

A sound in the brush alerted him and he froze. When nothing appeared, he cast a spell of detection, looking for a hidden automaton such as a Companion pin bird or rat. He waited, using the staff to scan his surroundings, but nothing magical showed up in his augmented vision.

Satisfied that no danger lurked in the shafts of sunlight shooting through leafy green boughs, he continued on. Eventually, he came to what he had sought all day: the crossroads.

There! The road back towards Highpoint. Soon, I will be back in business.

He calculated how long it would take to get to the nearest outpost. There, he could commandeer an escort to Highpoint, then on to Hellsfont. He ran over the military and magical strength in each of the loyal provinces.

Yes, there are still plenty of resources in the right hands. Of course, with the promise of forbidden magic and Daemonic allies to assist them, I will find many willing to take part in the reconquest of Torosc.

Then he stopped. Next to the crossroads, by the four-way signpost, an old human woman leaned on her walking stick. As he approached, she shuffled towards him.

He cast a spell of detection but nothing showed up and he marched forward, impatient to get to the next town. "Out of the way, you wizened bitch," he snarled.

"A moment of your time, Great One," the woman wheezed, fixing him with rheumy brown eyes.

Damned old crone. "I have no time for vagrants," he said, lifting his chin.

"But do you have time to consider your future?" the woman said striking the iron signpost with her stick three times. It rang like a bell.

"What are you? A fortune-teller? Get out of my way before I blast you to ashes!"

She bowed, a sardonic smile curving her lips. "Of course, Great One. But everyone must be concerned about their future, especially one such as yourself."

The Daemonic staff thrummed in Golvadu's hands. "Careful!" the sly voice cautioned. "She will tell you lies."

He scowled at her as he passed. "What are you blathering about?"

She began limping away. "All lives come to an end, my lord, and then there is a reckoning for past misdeeds."

"Reckoning?" The voice hissed in anger. "Misdeeds? You are the First Archon of the People's Republic! Who does she think she is?"

"Shove it up your ass," Golvadu growled at the old woman. "I am not answerable to anyone."

"Yes," whispered the cunning voice. "You are wise and powerful indeed."

The woman shook her head and shuffled down the path, away from him. He watched her go, considering whether blasting her with firedarts was a waste of energy. With a shrug, he decided he wasn't interested and moved on. Then a rushing of wind sounded in the crossroads. Leaves and branches swayed. He whirled.

A golden-haired Elohir woman with tanned skin and eyes the color of agate floated down out of the sky, clad in silvery chainmail and carrying a spear. He stared, frozen in shock.

Where the hell did she come from?

The Elohir inclined her head at the old woman. "Thank you, Mistress Dobbs, for your help in watching the road."

Golvadu's eyes flashed to the iron signpost. *Shit! That was a signal!*

"Always glad to help the Celestials," the woman cackled. "Especially when retribution is at hand." She pointed her stick at Golvadu. "This one conscripted my grandsons into the Army and they died in Deran. See that justice is done upon him."

The Elohir smiled. "Justice tempered by mercy. Again, I thank you. Now go home, please."

With a baleful scowl at Golvadu, the woman hobbled away.

The Elohir turned towards Golvadu. "Despite your many sins, Golvadu Fellhammer, should you repent and pay your debt to those you have wronged, I offer you mercy. Do you accept?" Her spearhead gleamed.

'No!" shrieked the devious voice in Golvadu's head. "This is your true enemy! Take hold of the new power you have, the power you used in Coastwatch! Your Daemonic gifts are more than a match for her!"

A sudden, white-hot rage coursed through Golvadu. *Mercy? Sins? Wrongdoing? Me?*

"Repent for what?" he sputtered, "For running society as it should be, with the fit ruling the unfit? Why should I request mercy for ruling over lesser beings too feebleminded or stuck in their own religious superstition to understand true power? They defied the will of their betters and paid the consequences!"

He energized the staff as Tarvener had taught him. Once again, the surge of raw power lifted him to near-euphoria. *The Dark One will give me victory!*

"Yes!" hissed the voice. "Destroy her and all like her!"

The Elohir shook her head, her eyes sad. "I am sorry to hear that. Perhaps you may yet see the truth and seek forgiveness at the last. But you will not reach your goal, Golvadu Fellhammer. I will see to it!"

"And I'll have your head on a pike outside my castle!" he snapped.

Her spear flared with golden fire. He leaped forward, casting several spells at once, laughing with the energy coursing through him. *Yes! All the power of a Daemon prince at my command!*

She moved with blinding speed and the spear of holy fire struck like a serpent. Searing pain lanced through him. He screamed in helpless rage.

"No!" he pointed the staff and shot spears of pure darkness at her. The impact threw her backwards in midair, her shields flickering. She slammed into the trunk of a nearby tree and fluttered there for a moment. He unleashed a blast of triple Hellfire and brimstone. She dodged aside and the tree disappeared in a cloud of sparking flame.

The Elohir shook her head and set her jaw in a firm line. She touched a hand to her injuries. Her armor glowed and a screen of glowing sigils leapt up in front of her.

Seeing her wounds, Golvadu's lip curled in a sneer. "So, you can be hurt by the magic of Hades!"

"You are winning!" The voice exulted. "Destroy her!"

He shot ice, electricity and dark energy at her. She held up her hand. The screen of symbols flared. The force of the attack pushed her back several feet, but her shields held.

He gritted his teeth and pointed his staff at her. The air in the crossroads crackled with antiproton annihilations as he summoned antimatter. "I will never yield! I have all the power I need!"

"Power without wisdom is useless." She touched three symbols. A fiery corona of power surrounded her lithe form.

Frothing incoherently, he shot the antimatter beam at her. Her screen of symbols swirled and consumed the beam, exploding in a flash of energy. Golvadu fell back and she spun out of the way.

How can she resist me? Tarvener promised me unlimited power! He struggled to his feet, then shot a stream of dagger-like icicles at her.

She moved as quick as thought, sidestepping and fluttering out of the way. Her darting spear struck again and again.

Intense pain wracked every part of his body. Blood ran down his side, his legs and his chest. "I have... the power... of Hades," he gasped. "They promised... victory..."

His vision greyed and he fell to his knees. He saw his own hands, clawed like a Daemon, gripping his staff. His strength left him and he wheezed with effort.

The Elohir, regarded him with a gentle expression. She ceased her attack and stood on guard, with her glowing spear held before her. "You can still be saved from oblivion, Golvadu Fellhammer," she said. "If you will repent."

"No!" he rasped, struggling to rise. His legs refused to obey him and he sagged further down. "I will rule. It ... is all... mine." His vision faded.

"No," cackled the voice in his mind. "You belong to us now. Come, slave. Become food for us..."

He felt himself falling, then the jarring jolt of hitting the hard earth of the road. Everything went dark — the deepest, coldest dark.

Johanna the Elohir sighed as Golvadu collapsed on the highway in a widening pool of blood. A deep chill swept the area.

She took a breath, centering her thoughts on the Creator. *Aid me, Great Lord of All.*

She held up her hand. "Begone, foul servant of the Dark One," she whispered. With her Other Senses, she heard a sly voice hiss, then it gave a shriek of terror. An ominous shadow flickered near the corpse, then vanished. The icy cold fled with it.

I thank and praise you for helping me again, Holy One, she prayed. A warm, peaceful aura filled the crossroads.

Johanna regarded the scene for a few heartbeats. She turned her palm upward and Golvadu's corpse levitated up and drifted across the road, towards a patch of dry earth. She twisted her wrist and dirt fountained up in the air. With another turn of her hand, his body floated down into the hole in the ground. She flipped her fingers and the dirt piled on top of him, hiding his grave completely.

Well, at least Brandi and her family can rest easily when I tell them Golvadu can't menace them anymore.

She imagined their reaction and her smile widened. "Well, maybe not yet," she murmured. "Let them not think of Golvadu or Hades or Daemons for a while. They have earned a little time to celebrate."

Dar strode into his bedchamber and sat on the edge of the massive bed. "That was an incredible party and the food was amazing," Dar said, removing his boots. He could still taste the remnant of witchberry tart on his tongue. *I'm going to make sure to get some recipes out of our many guests.*

"Though it was all a little tiring," he added, stretching out onto his back.

Megan bounced onto the bed next to him, kicking off her slippers and wiggling her toes. "Ugh. I thought my legs would fall off."

"I thought you liked dancing."

"Yes, but every male in the court wanted the honor of a dance with the High Princess. I lost count at forty."

The sound of music, laughter and clinking silverware echoed to them from the royal courtyard below.

Dar flipped onto his side and propped up his head on his elbow. "Brandi had it worse. Not only did they all want a dance, several of them tried to lobby her for their pet projects while doing so."

Megan shook her head. "My poor sister. I'm sure she can't wait to start delegating to us." She scooted over next to him and pulled him close.

"Don't remind me," he replied, laying his head on her shoulder. They rested quietly for a couple of minutes, listening to the sounds of merriment below. "I'm just glad she told the court to continue on in our absence. They'll probably go all night."

A knock sounded on the door to their bedchamber and they sat up.

"Who is it?" Megan asked.

"Maid service," said a voice that sounded suspiciously like Eric's.

Megan howled with laughter. "You had better be wearing a maid's uniform, then, Eric Aldenar!"

Brandi and Eric strode into the room, laughing.

"The style looks horrid on him," said Brandi, flopping into a nearby chair. Following Megan's lead, she also removed her shoes with a sigh.

Dar raised an eyebrow. "Make yourself at home, sister."

Before she could answer, Eric took a seat next to her and took off his boots. "Don't mind if we do. By the way, the fireworks are going to start soon. Why aren't you on the balcony?"

Megan stretched. "Waiting for Connor and Hannah."

"Wait no longer," sang out Hannah's voice from the door. Grinning from ear to ear, she swept in, hand-in-hand with Connor.

"Someone mentioned fireworks?" Connor noted. "And you're just sitting here?"

Dar yawned. "Taking a little rest."

Eric frowned. "You can rest later. Tomorrow's a royal holiday anyway." He and Brandi hauled Megan and Dar to their feet.

Brandi bestowed warm kisses on them both. "Come on. You're too young to act this old." Connor and Hannah laughed.

"Hey," Dar protested. He bumped Brandi with his hip. "I'm the only full human. I'm going to get old first."

"Yes," Eric replied, giving him a playful slug in the shoulder, "but not for another fifty years at least."

"Watch it," Dar retorted. "Or you'll find a levitated eggplant landing on your head one of these days. I can do that spell now, you know."

Eric looked at him in surprise as the couples assembled on the balcony. "When did you learn that?"

Dar shot a smile at Megan. "I don't remember."

Hannah raised an eyebrow at Dar. "Selective memory," she opined. "A sure sign of a married man." Connor scoffed, pulling a pair of chairs near the balustrade.

Dar blew her a kiss. Hannah took Connor's hand and rested her head on his shoulder. The two Halflings stood on the chairs to watch the show.

Eric put his arms around Brandi. Dar did likewise for Megan as the first of the fireworks fluttered aloft and exploded in a burst of color and light. Tholi and Kindri soared up among them, darting and dodging the explosions, much to the delight and cheers of the people in the city below. Starlight Bay glittered below them, awash with moonlight and reflections of bursting sky rockets. From the balcony, Dar saw almost the entire city spread out before him, from Osprey Hill to the north, all the way to Mariner's Quay and Seapark in the south. Everywhere, lamps and lights glowed and people danced, waving sparklers.

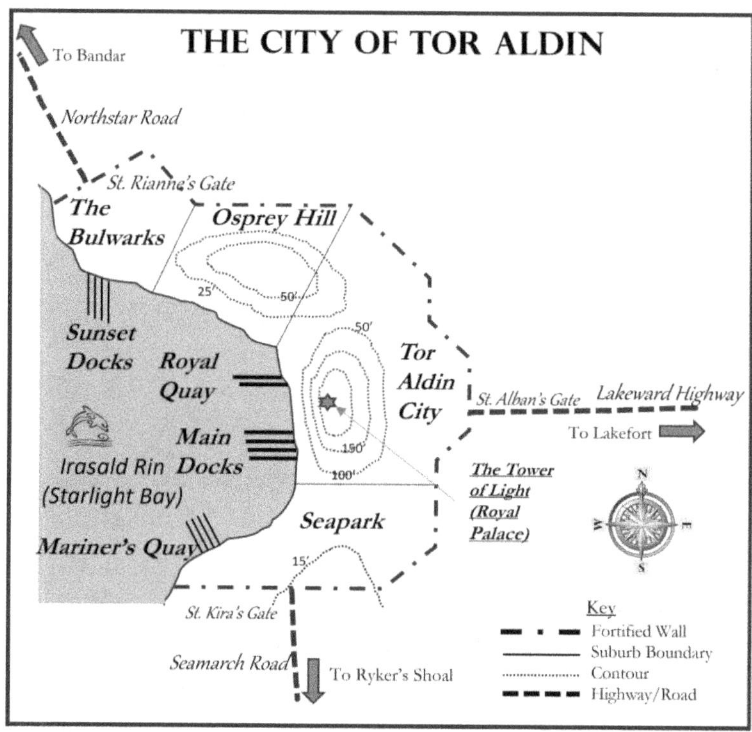

Dar stood quietly with Megan in his arms, smelling the scent of vanilla and roses in her hair, her head resting against his chest.

How many times will we get any relaxation and peace in the future? he wondered. *We've freed Alenar and Loemin and soon, Turis Rhi, but the rest of the People's Republic is still intact and probably itching for revenge. Morlan and Jered can't be happy that we bested them, and I'm sure the Vardish and Cla'Agik will be watching our every move.*

He sighed. *Best to take advantage of the peace and celebration while we can.* His thoughts wandered as the fireworks boomed and sparkled and people applauded.

How far we've come.

As if reading his thoughts, Brandi asked, "Remember when we first met?"

"How could I forget?" Eric chuckled, hugging her. "You didn't trust us at all."

She smacked his hip. "That's not what I meant. I mean, do you remember how naïve and innocent we were? More importantly, how idealistic and optimistic?"

"And we're jaded and cynical now?" Dar asked with a grin.

"Speak for yourself, dear," Megan said, tweaking his chin.

Brandi sighed. "That's not what I mean, you rogue. Yes, we've been through a lot, but I hope we can regain some of that idealism and optimism. We need it. We're trying to rebuild a kingdom."

"I remember not knowing quite what to do all the time," Megan offered. "I wasn't sure my spells would work and there was so much I couldn't control. And the forces of evil terrified me, at least at the beginning. I felt like I was making it all up half the time."

"I'm still that way," Eric said. "But we prevailed by sticking together and working together."

"And praying," added Brandi, "and relying on God."

Dar's thoughts wandered, recalling their adventures: unearthing the secret of Whitehorse Peak and the pegasi, finding the Eye of Truth and clearing Buck's name, searching for the Helm of Shadows — and the battle with Zhinia Margoth. *Every single one of us has died and been brought back to life through miraculous means. Even Megan and Brandi.*

"I remember when we first found the pegasi, out there on the wilderness of Deran," Connor mused. "Iron Thunder was so intimidating at first. I had heard of True Dragons before, but his size completely stunned me. I'm sure glad he was on our side."

"I wish I could have met him," Hannah said wistfully.

Connor kissed her. "You have, in a way. Tholi and Kindri are a lot like their grandfather."

Dar's thoughts shifted to their campaign against the Crossed Swords assassins and bringing Eric's birth parents to justice — then the War of the Dark Wave. He suppressed a shudder, recalling those frantic days of near panic, trying to find the Gate of Stars in time to bring the Elohir.

"You okay, sweetheart?" Megan asked.

He smiled down at her. She gazed at him with bright amber eyes full of love and concern.

God, she's gorgeous. "I'm perfect," he said, giving her a kiss. "And you're perfect. I love you."

"Mmmm," she purred. "Keep talking like that."

The couples lapsed into silence under a starry sky lit by the sliver of Kaliri and the smaller half-circle of Diometrius. Citizens and nobility alike sang and cheered in the castle below them.

Dar soaked it all in and the world narrowed down to just him and Megan, holding each other beneath the light of the moons as fireworks boomed and sparkled and music drifted in the warm summer night. Tears stung his eyes and he swallowed past a lump in his throat. *God, why am I so blessed?*

Megan sighed. "This is like a dream. Who would have thought that we'd end up like this?"

Struck by her words, Dar paused. "End? No, sweetheart," he whispered. Intense love and gratitude spread throughout his whole being and he kissed her head. "This isn't an end. It's a new beginning. It's our future and we're going on to face it, with confidence and faith."

"Yes," she chuckled, nestling closer. "New beginnings and bright futures. What would I ever do without you?"

He hugged her. "Maybe you'd do better?"

Megan laughed, squeezing him tightly. "Absolutely not! You are all I need, whether Princess or pauper or free-lance. All I want is to be your wife and mother to our family. It's a dream, a wonderful dream."

She's right. After all our struggles, it is a dream come true. For the first time in a long time, Dar Cabot felt peace and calm. "And I will always be by your side, my love," he murmured. "Til death do us part."

The End

Appendix - Glossary

<u>Aldath –</u> The capital of Loemin/Bluevale (pop ~125,000). It is a major city positioned on the southeastern shore of Three Nation Lake (q.v.), on the top of a bluff overlooking both the lake and the countryside beyond.

<u>Aldenar, Brandawyn (Brandi)</u> - A half-elven woman trained as a combat medic, she is one of the original Grey Riders and the current Queen-in-Exile of Alenar, an ancient kingdom in the south now in the grip of the People's Republic of Torosc, or PRT (q.v.). The older sister of Megan, she and her family were persecuted for their Christian faith and eventually fled their homeland. During her time with the Riders, she fell in love with Eric Indidarc (q.v.). Later, she was captured by the Ja'al (q.v.) and changed into a vampire thrall by evil magic. When she finally met the Riders again, she insisted that Eric put a stake through her heart to prevent her from seducing and destroying them one by one. After the War of the Dark Wave, she was restored to life by a thorn from the Crown of Thorns of Christ and married Eric Indidarc.

Reserved, kind and devoutly religious, Brandi is quite pretty, with red-gold hair and violet eyes. She is also ambidextrous. Her pegasus is named Amicus (Lat. *"friend"*). Her surname was the more common "Alenar" prior to confirmation of her lineage, after which she changed it to the royal "Aldenar". Through various ancestors in her lineage, Brandawyn has human, Elven, Elohir (q.v.) and Daemonic (q.v.) blood.

<u>Aldenar, Megan</u> - Another of the original Grey Riders and younger sister of Brandawyn Alenar (q.v.), she fled persecution in Torosc (q.v.). After attending college in Terenai (q.v.), she graduated as a wizard and scholar. She and Brandi met the Grey Riders in Deran (q.v.) and helped them solve the mystery of *Whitehorse Peak*. When her aunt and uncle died fighting the Ja'al (q.v.), she was sold into slavery to a Ja'al High Wizard to work in his laboratory. The Grey Riders rescued her but she was poisoned by an encoded, infernal venom. The Riders used a Preservation Net (q.v.) on her as she died. She was restored to life by the power of a thorn from the Crown of Thorns of Christ and later married Dar Cabot (q.v.).

A strawberry blonde like her sibling, Megan is friendly and outgoing, somewhat vain and impetuous, yet fiercely loyal and brave. She is also very attractive, with strawberry blonde hair and amber eyes, and is fond of baubles and fancy clothes. She rides a pegasus named Larinor (Elv. *"ranger"* or *"faithful guide"*). Like her sister, she adopted the royal version of her last name (Aldenar) after she was crowned as High Princess.

Alenar, Daphne, - The only sister of Megan and Brandi's human mother, she spirited her nieces northward away from Torosc to safety. Sometimes thought of as overly serious (like her niece, Brandawyn), she served as a devoted mother-figure to the sisters after the death of their parents. She perished in battle with Ja'al forces along with her brother, Stephen (q.v.). If she had lived, she would have inherited the Kingdom of Alenar as Queen Daphne I.

Alenar, Stephen - Uncle of Brandawyn and Megan Alenar, he was the younger brother of Daphne Alenar. In addition to being a scholar, Stephen was also a skilled warrior and wielded potent magic in battle. Known for his teasing sense of humor, he died fighting alongside his sister against the Ja'al. He would have become the High Prince of Alenar, had he survived.

Alenar – A petty kingdom to the south in ancient times in what is now part of the People's Republic of Torosc (q.v.), it was ruled by the Aldenar family prior to its fall hundreds of years prior to the events of the Grey Riders series. It has several natural harbors, fertile inland regions and some mountainous areas. Brandi and Megan (Grey Riders) are the heirs to the kingdom.

Alford – A large town in southern Alenar/Coastwatch (q.v.), pop ~15,000.

Alphaeus, Robert, Sir – The ambassador of Rokon (q.v.) to the Kingdom of Deran (q.v.).

Alrihan (Elv. *"seven lights"*)– A seaside metropolis (pop. ~200,000) in the nation of Deran. It is ruled by a Duke and Duchess.

Alyssa of Tor Haldin, Saint – Queen of a petty kingdom during the late Paragon Age, Alyssa ruled over Alenar and is an ancient ancestor of both Brandawyn and Megan Aldenar (q.q.v). Her battles against Zhinia Margoth (q.v.) were legendary and all the more remarkable since Margoth was Alyssa's first cousin. After Margoth was finally defeated at the Battle of Three-Nation Lake (q.v.) and disappeared, Alyssa returned to her kingdom. She and her husband and family died ten years later when a combination of wild tribes and opportunistic foreign powers overran her war-depleted nation. She was known for her piety, generosity and forgiving nature.

Her Crown is a relic of jaw-dropping power, bestowing impressive magical abilities, healing capabilities and protections to someone of sufficiently pure heart, though it all comes with a price. It is rumored that the Crown was crafted by the Elohir (q.v.) in her honor.

<u>Arachnia</u> – One of the goddesses of the Ja'al (q.v.) pantheon, the Mistress of Venom and Treachery and High Majesty of Hades appeared as a tall, raven-haired woman of great beauty, yet with fangs and short horns to indicate her Daemonic nature. She arrived on Damora with Torvu (q.v.) and Selaan (q.v.), two other gods of the High Royalty of Hades, to take over of the War of the Dark Wave. She is partial to creatures with poison, such as scorpions, snakes and spiders. At the end of the War of the Dark Wave, she died fighting against an overwhelming number of powerful Elohir (q.v.).

<u>Archon</u> – One of the rulers of the People's Republic of Torosc (PRT). Originally, the Archons were nine in number (one for each of the kingdoms that banded together in the Republic of Torosc) but three were eventually removed and the remaining six became corrupted by their own evil and selfishness, resulting in the PRT. Almost all of them perished during the War of the Dark Wave (q.v.) and the 2nd Archon, Golvadu Fellhammer (q.v.) became the de-facto ruler of the Republic, promoting himself to 1st Archon.

<u>Ashford, Fiona, Lt.</u> – A Halfling officer under Colonel Whitson's command. She is a warrior and mage.

<u>Ashford, Malcolm</u> - An elderly Halfling sage who lives near Havenridge (q.v.). Despite being blind, he has an uncanny perception of people and things near him. His memory is photographic and his granddaughter, Fiona, is a member of the rebel resistance in Loemin/Bluevale. He is a friend and contemporary of Melinor Indidarc (q.v.). He is given the respectful title of Oldfather due to his wisdom.

<u>Astarel</u> – A kingdom to the north of Deran (q.v.), along the coast, it is the homeland of Buck Bydecy, (q.v.) (one of the original Grey Riders, retired at the time of *Tower of Light*). It is a seafaring nation with a robust navy and a racially mixed society comprised equally of Elves, humans, Dwarves and Halflings. It is a member of the Northern Alliance (q.v.).

<u>Balris</u> – A Daemonic ambassador from Hades to the evil nation of

Morlan (q.v.) on Damora. He is sly, calculating and sadistic but prudent, only exercising his skills when necessary. About six feet, three inches tall, he has golden blond hair, black horns and wings, and amber cat-eyes. After the War of the Dark Wave, his whereabouts are unknown.

<u>Baradellinaru</u> – A good True Dragon (q.v.) of the Sunfire Clan. His mate is Feleseniala (q.v). His short-form name is Barad.

<u>Bates, Gilbert, Archduke</u> – A member of the aristocracy of the Magocratic Kingdom of Morlan (q.v.), he is calm, calculating and a good team player. Despite being a wizard, scholar and academic, he is a capable military commander. He is only interested in power and cares little for other people.

<u>Black Kestrels</u> – An elite division of the Knights of the Falcon (Knights of Saint Juliana Falconieri), they are often used as special guards or shock troops. They are distinguishable by their black armor with white and gold accents.

<u>Blood Star Confederation</u> – A massive confederacy of Goblin tribes from Wild Lands near the south eastern borders of Torosc (q.v). Their numbers are rumored to be in the hundreds of thousands. They avoided conflict during the War of the Dark Wave and are thus very strong.

<u>Bluevale</u> – The name of the ancient Paragon kingdom of Loemin given to the region after the fall of the Archons (q.v.) of Torosc.

<u>Brightgrove, Captain</u> – A female centaur commander, she is part of Connor Loemin's Royal Guard.

<u>Bydecy, Buckminster (Buck)</u> - Another of the original Grey Riders, Buck is a tall, rangy, sandy-haired human male warrior. He is a native of Tyler, Astarel, and was elevated to the rank of Baron after the War of the Dark Wave. He is married to Carine Del Rio, a druidess. At the time of *Tower of Light*, he and Carine are Regents of the Grey Rider Institute, a multinational academy dedicated to training freelance specialists such as wizards, healers and warriors. He is the owner of the Eye of Truth (q.v.), a powerful magical gemstone, which he found in a tower built by an ancestor from antiquity, Moridan Bydecy.

<u>Cabot, Darius (Dar)</u> - An original Grey Rider and native of the border town of Forester, Deran, Dar ran into Ja'al (q.v.) Goblin troops in the wilds and headed back to town for help, setting the events of *Whitehorse Peak* in motion. A dark-haired human male, he is a ranger/scout and adept in the

woods. He has a wry sense of humor, a quick tongue and a penchant for bravery bordering on foolhardiness. His sword has a black blade that is covered with tiny stars that flare to incandescent brightness in the presence of evil. The weapon (Rindara Starblade) is deadly to evil things, particularly Daemons (q.v.). He rides a pegasus named Virasi (Elv. *"white star"*). After the end of the War of the Dark Wave (q.v.), he married Megan Aldenar (q.v.), the High Princess of Alenar.

<u>Catbriar Cloaks</u> – An elite regiment of ranger-scouts of the Kingdom of Alenar. It is commanded by a member of the Royal Family, typically the First Prince.

<u>Cerberus Hound</u> – Evil, multi-headed dogs, they were once normal animals (similar to Fell Beasts, q.v.) but were warped by vile magic and now serve Darkness. They have particularly keen senses of smell and can detect hidden enemies. They are exceptionally good trackers.

<u>Chilverton</u> – A large city in the province of Northwatch in the People's Republic of Torosc (q.v.). It is a substantial distance from Loemin/Bluevale, which is why Connor Loemin cites it as his hometown when posing as a locksmith in Havenridge (q.v.).

<u>Cla'Agik (Dw. *"that which rots"*)</u> – The religion of the evil god of Decay and Corruption, his cult is distinguished by scientific curiosity and the attitude that if something can be made or devised, it should be, no matter the consequences. While devotees of the religion are feared for their ability to spread disease, the decentralized nature of the church inhibits them from making any concerted effort at conquest. Understandably for people who experiment on diseases, they are extremely good healers.

<u>Coastwatch</u> – The official name given to the former Kingdom of Alenar after the rise and corruption of the Archons (q.v.) of Torosc. The name was also given to the former royal capital of Tor Aldin, the seaside metropolis (pop. 150,000) where the Aldenar sisters were born and raised.

<u>Companion Pin</u> – Enchanted pieces of jewelry, Companion Pins are keyed to a miniature golem resembling a small animal like a rat, hawk, ferret or cat. The constructs are summoned from the Other Space (q.v.) to serve the bearer of the Pin using a secret code word. They share their special abilities (night vision, enhanced hearing, camouflage, etc.) with their masters. Stealth (a hawk Pin), owned by Eric Indidarc, is an example of a Companion

Pin.

<u>Crossed Swords</u> - Guild of assassins based in Deran and Terenai. Founded and ruled by the Hylar family, the Crossed Swords were used by evil forces to eliminate opposition. Eric Indidarc's real family name is Hylar and he is a son of the guild master; he escaped his former life and was adopted by Melinor Indidarc. In *Assassin Prince*, the Grey Riders joined him in destroying the Guild and bringing his parents to justice.

<u>Crypt Rot</u> – A vile disease imparted on victims by certain types of undead, including mummies and vampires.

<u>Culver, Arlene, Countess</u> – Lady and former ruler of Harlinsville, a city in Deran. She is middle-aged, with brown hair and green eyes. Unknown to her husband, she was a secret agent of the Ja'al (q.v.). When the Dark Wave commenced, she assassinated him and fled to join the invasion force to become a regimental commander.

<u>Curbolg</u> – A hideous combination of cattle and squid, Curbolg Daemons are a cross between a beast of burden, a combat mount and a tank. One of their tentacles can inject a pod into a victim which will spawn into a Curbolg newt once the victim dies. Smaller Daemons can sometimes ride them.

<u>Daemon</u> - Evil to the core, the otherworldly race of daemons spends most of their time trying to overthrow the Elohir (q.v.) or conquer various regions of Damora. They are known as the Fallen Ones because legend has it that they were originally Elohir who turned to the side of evil and worship of themselves (and the Dark One). While many Daemons look like nightmarish beasts, some are very attractive and almost human-like or Elven in appearance. Daemons regard Damora (q.v.) as a free zone, ripe for the picking. Their home world, Hades, is the 4th planet orbiting the star Beta Hydri (G11 spectral class, 24.38 LY from Earth) and is a combination of stunning beauty and stomach-churning grotesqueness.

<u>Damora</u> - Imaginary world setting for the Grey Riders novels. The fourth planet orbiting the star 82 Eridani, it is roughly 1.15 times the size of Earth and possesses similar climate, regions and flora/fauna. The parent star is a G5V spectral class, main-sequence yellow star approximately 20 light years from Earth. It has two moons, Kaliri and Diometrius, which provide both tidal forces and substantial moonlight for the planet's surface. The technology level of Damora approximates the High Middle Ages of the real world,

with significant differences due to the use of magic and scientific advancement.

<u>Dark Faiths</u> - The evil religions on the world of Damora (q.v.). Also known as Dark Powers.

<u>Darlon</u> - Major metropolis in northern Deran, pop ~ 170,000. Home to people of many races, creeds and professions, it is a trading center and university town. Ruled by a duke, it controls trade and access between Deran and the northernmost nations of Astarel, Elder and Rokon.

<u>Deathhammer</u> – A type of Daemon from Hades, a Deathhammer is a hulking brutish beast with pig-like features, fangs and white horns. They can use their great wings to fly but are not particularly maneuverable. As their name suggests, they are shock troops. They have a limited magical repertoire.

<u>Dearborn, Khyla, Captain</u> – A young female human officer who distinguished herself during the War of the Dark Wave and was recruited to travel to Torosc with Megan Aldenar (q.v.). She is skilled in airborne riding, loyal and virtuous but has a very troubled past. She is blonde and blue-eyed. Her pegasus is named Nightflame.

<u>Deathmist</u> – Daemons (q.v.) from Hades (q.v.), Deathmists resemble a cloud of grey fog with red eyes that floats low to the ground and extends silvery tendrils to attack. They radiate extreme cold, can cast lightning and can drain the life-force out of someone by grappling them with their tentacles. They do not speak.

<u>DeMey, Saren, Lady</u> - The half-sister of Eric Indidarc by adoption, Saren DeMey was found by Melinor Indidarc (q.v.) as an infant and raised by him and his wife, Ann. A devout Christian, Saren appears to be a complete contradiction in terms as she is half-Daemon but fights for the forces of good. Dark-haired and dark-eyed, she transforms to a bat-winged, horned half-Daemon at will. Saren continually guards against her daemonic background, as it is a temptation to lust and savagery; however, to the common folk of Deran, she is warm, generous, wise and gentle. After the War of the Dark Wave (q.v.), she was elevated to the rank of Duchess of Alrihan (q.v.)

<u>DeMey, Terenil, Lord</u> - The half-elven husband of Saren DeMey(q.v.), he was an Earl prior to the War of the Dark Wave (q.v.). A skilled wizard and soldier in his own right, he is easygoing, thoughtful and kind. After the War, he was elevated to Duke of Alrihan (q.v.), a coastal metropolis.

Deorfast - A major city (pop ~75000) in the mountains of central Deran (q.v.).

Deran - Constitutional monarchy in the northern lands of the Western continent of Damora. A nation built from the remnants of the Esten Empire, Deran is also a meritocracy, where nobles are elected by their peers and the legislature is based on merit and ability more than family connections. Deran has an advanced network of roads, potent military, and several universities. During the War of the Dark Wave (q.v.), Deran especially targeted by the forces of evil; it was badly damaged and lost many people, both civilians and military alike. The seat of the Christian Church, Saint Martin's Town (St. Martin's) is in Deran.

Diometrius – The larger of Damora's (q.v.) two moons.

Dragon – Exactly as the name implies, the bat-winged, lizard-like Draconic race is comprised of four sub-groups: Balar, Sarkany, Drakes and True Dragons. The Balar are the smallest (20-30 feet long) and True Dragons the largest (up to 100+ feet long). All can use magic and have a social structure of clans. Evil dragons are marked by a glowing red sheen to their eyes, much like other Dark races (Dark Elves, Dwarves, etc). Kidriana (q.v.) and Tholerios (q.v.) are True Dragons, though still quite young.

Duarvar (Elv. "*Stone Castle*") - A fortified city (pop ~ 50,000) in the south of Gorostol (q.v.), it was conquered by the Dark Wave but reclaimed by the Golden Army (q.v.). It guards an important mountain pass into Torosc and has extensive underground holdings.

Dwarf - One of the major races of Damora. The term "Dwarf" comes from the ancient Elven words, *duarfaen* (Elv. *duar* = 'stone' + *fae*/ *fey*/ *fej* - = 'magic', literally "those of stone-magic"). A typical Dwarf male is about four feet six inches tall. Dwarves tend to be burly, sturdy or muscular for their size and can live for almost two hundred years. Males are often bearded (though not all are). They are generally honorable and appreciate strength and resolve in others. Their main talent, as indicated by the name bestowed on them by the Elves, is in stonework and metallurgy.

Dwerrolf – A cross between a wolf and a Dwarf, these Daemons can use minor magic such as fire breath. Much like Skreets (q.v.), they are used as light infantry and fly to their destinations, though they usually land to attack. Their voices are often parodies of children's voices.

<u>Dylany</u> – A female Daemon, she served Zhinia Margoth (q.v.) during the Paragon Age (q.v.) and was changed into a vampire, then tasked with tending a necropolis within Thul Mardil (q.v.).

<u>Eleandir Demaris, Andyn, Lady</u> - One of the original Grey Riders, Andyn is a priestess of the Elven god Verian (q.v.) and a wizard. She has honey-blonde hair and amber eyes, a trim figure and a marvelous singing voice. At the Battle of Hillton, she used a holy relic (the Crown of Saint Alyssa) to destroy Zhinia Margoth. After the War of the Dark Wave, she was raised to the title of Viscountess of Marolpeth, Terenai, and rules that city with her husband, Khyron.

<u>Eldir</u> – A nation of the Northern Alliance, Eldir is a patriarchate and the seat of the faith of Verian (q.v.). Possessing a climate similar to Germany in the real world, it used to be at odds with Rokon, a breakaway duchy, until the need for collaboration against the forces of evil caused them to bury the hatchet. It is ruled by the High Matriarch or Patriarch of Verian.

<u>Elf</u> - One of the major races of Damora. The term "Elf" comes from the ancient word for their race, *Ellfaen* (Elv. *ell* = 'life' + *fae/ fey/ fej* -= 'magic', literally "those of life-magic"). Elves are more slender than humans and possess intriguing eye colors, such as aqua, amber or violet; they also have a slight point to the top of the ear, though this is not usually pronounced or even noted if the ears are concealed under hair, hat or helm. Elves tend to be a bit more reserved than the other races and have an affinity for magic of all kinds. They possess skills for getting along well with animals and a talent for healing trees and plants. Elves who have turned to evil are named "Dark Elves" and are distinguished by a reddish tint to their eyes.

<u>Elohir</u> - Denizen of the planet of Celestia (the 5th planet of the 61 Virginis star, a single G6 spectral class, main-sequence yellow star approximately 28 light years from Earth). Sometimes called "Celestials", they appear to be winged humans. Skin color covers the range of typical shades seen in humans (porcelain, tanned, brown, yellow, dark brown) and their eyes are the color of jewels. Their beauty is often described as 'unearthly'. All possess potent magical and martial skills but are usually reluctant to meddle in the affairs of Damorans. They are uniformly kind, wise, honest and just. Elohir live extremely long lives (~ 1000 years) if not killed in warfare with their evil kindred, the Fallen Ones (or Daemons, q.v.).

Erica Highwater – Hannah Loemin's (q.v.) alias when in Loemin (q.v.) trying to make contact with rebel forces.

Esdan, Lord – A hill sprite (q.v.) nobleman rescued by the Alenar sisters, he is married to Tinira (q.v.). Together with a cadre of other sprites, they assist the Allied nations as reconnaissance troops.

Esten Empire - An empire formed of various kingdoms controlling much of the known world during the second age of Damora (known as the Esten Imperial Age and denoted in calendars by the letters IY (for Imperial Year)). It fell after hundreds of years of mostly stable rule due to infighting, a breakdown in the social order and the influence of evil.

Ethereal Eye - A magical utility spell, it forms a walnut-sized translucent eyeball that can pass through solid objects. The wizard who casts the spell can maneuver the Eye within a short range and see whatever the Eye sees (rather like a very tiny airborne drone with a camera). It does not last long.

Evendale - Small Halfling nation southeast of Deran (q.v.) and northeast of Terenai (q.v.). A republic, Evendale consists of seven districts or counties. It is a land with mild climate and productive farmland. It borders on the Wilderness, which means the Halflings are always on vigilant watch, having been invaded by evil tribes multiple times.

Eye of Truth - A magical diamond, the Eye of Truth is actually a sort of lens that allows the owner to see the true nature of things and people. It can detect evil or good auras, see through illusion and discern truth from lies. It was crafted by an ancestor of Buck Bydecy (q.v.) and is owned by him.

Faldor – A high priest of the religion of Cla'Agik (q.v.), one of the Dark Faiths (q.v.). He is arrogant, powerful and eager to elevate the status of his church.

Fallen One – A Daemon (q.v.).

Fejer, Alex – A human soldier who fought in the War of the Dark Wave (q.v.), he was recruited to accompany the Grey Riders as the liaison officer to Hannah Loemin (q.v.). He is tall, dark-haired and sturdy and has the rare skill of airborne riding. He is an orphan and has endured losses in his life (including his girlfriend, Eleanor, during the War) but is still optimistic and positive. His pegasus is named Onyx.

Feleseniala – A good True Dragon (q.v.) of the Sunfire Clan, she travels south with her mate, Baradellinaru to assist the Grey Riders. Also known as

Fela.

<u>Fell Beast</u> - A normal animal warped by vile magic and forbidden scientific knowledge into a servant of evil. Almost any creature can be made Fell; examples are Fell Bears, Fell Hounds and Fell Rats.

<u>Fellhammer, Golvadu, Lord</u> – A dwarven wizard of impressive ability, he was one of the Archons of the People's Republic of Torosc. After the War of the Dark Wave, when most of the other Archons were killed, he took over as the de-facto ruler of the Republic. Short-tempered, profane and conniving, he is also a creative thinker and a dangerous opponent. He has particular hatred for Melinor Indidarc (q.v.) and the Grey Riders.

<u>Fidelis (Lat. *"Faithful"*)</u> – A magic spear that can contract to the size of a dagger or telescope to the length of a medium infantry spear, it was awarded to Eric Indidarc by an Elohir (q.v.). It strikes with great power against evil things and, if thrown, returns unerringly to its wielder's hand via teleport when called. It has a sharp head that glows like the sun in the presence of evil.

<u>Firedart</u> - A magical attack spell used by wizards and sorcerers. It is essentially a small projectile of flame with a detonable core that looks rather like a tiny comet and has a limited range (about 100 feet or so). It produces the effect equivalent to a 9 mm pistol bullet and rarely misses.

<u>Forester</u> - Large town along the northern border highway of Deran. Forester is ruled by a baron and controls trade along the borderlands. It is the hometown of Dar Cabot.

<u>Gariil</u> – (Dw. *"random"*) The god of chance and luck sometimes also associated with fertility, Gariil can take on male or female aspects. One of the original faiths of Damora, it is still popular in urban areas. The religion is very loosely organized and clergy are often made simply by claiming the title and demonstrating priestly magic. Their temples are often nothing more than casinos or amusement centers. Due to their uncanny ability to turn a profit, they are tolerated in the evil realms of Torosc, Morlan and Jered.

<u>Gate of Stars</u> – A Gate to Celestia (homeworld of the Elohir, q.v.) its location was lost in the mists of time until the Grey Riders followed a series of clues and discovered it. They traveled to Celestia and brought back thousands of Elohir, spelling the end of the War of the Dark Wave (q.v).

<u>Ghost Creeper</u> – An evil, semi-intelligent plant that can detect the

approach of non-evil creatures and set up a wailing sound. Their vines wrap around victims and insert a narcotic that makes them sleepy and clumsy. They are often used by servants of Darkness as sentries.

Glen – The hometown of Connor Loemin's family. It is a farming community in the land of Evendale.

Glittershard – The hereditary sword of the Kings of Loemin, it is a blade of ice. Upon command, it can cast up a thick wall of ice or freeze an opponent in a giant ice cube. The blade's frosty edge can freeze whatever it strikes and is very dangerous to creatures of fire.

Gnome - Half-breeds resulting from the marriage of Halfling and Dwarf, gnomes possess features from each parent: natural affinity for stone and the underground from the Dwarves and a cheerful disposition and natural talent with all things organic from the Halflings. They usually have dark hair, tan-to-dark complexions, and brown, amber or grey eyes. A typical gnome lives about 180 years or so. Handor Lervion (q.v.), brother of Hannah (Lervion) Loemin (q.v.) was a gnome.

Goblin - Short, half-simian creatures who often serve as foot-soldiers for the forces of evil, looking somewhat like horned chimpanzees. Extremely agile and able to use any available weapon that is sized for them, they are also good at hiding in shadows. They dislike sunlight. Their social structure is usually in a hierarchical monarchy, with the chieftain or king of a particular tribe wielding absolute authority. Goblins particularly hate Dwarves since the two races compete for underground areas and resources. They are capable miners and are about the size of a gnome or tall Halfling (a few inches short of four feet tall).

Golad – A very large, populous province in the People's Republic of Torosc (q.v.). Much of the wealth of the PRT comes from this area. It was renamed Eastwatch when the Archons came to power.

Golden Army – The massive military force brought from Celestia (q.v.) to Damora (q.v.) by the Grey Riders to put an end to the War of the Dark Wave. It reputedly numbered in the tens of thousands of Elohir (q.v.).

Gorlak - A Goblin formerly in the employ of the Ja'al, he switched sides after the Battle of Hillton when his life was spared by the Riders. After his capture, he was asked to join the household of the Papal Nuncio (Edward Simpson, who died soon after from pancreatic cancer). Under the Nuncio's tutelage and care, he flourished and now serves as a spy, with devastating success since few would ever entertain the idea of a Christian Goblin. He was made an honorary Grey Rider and awarded the rank of Major in the Army of Deran (q.v.) in recognition of his efforts during the War of the Dark Wave.

Gorostol (Dw. *"friend alliance"*) – A large and somewhat eclectic nation south of Terenai (q.v.) and north of the People's Republic of Torosc, or PRT (q.v.). Originally founded by Dwarves, over the ages it attracted folk of all races. It is now a buffer state between the oppressive PRT to the south and the Elven Empire to the north.

Grand Remaking – The ultimate plan of the Ja'al (q.v.) that motivated the War of the Dark Wave (q.v.), the Remaking sought to refashion the world of Damora to fit the ideals of the Dark Faiths.

Greenvale – A small village in Loemin/Bluevale near Havenridge (q.v.). It is the home of Lieutenant Fiona Ashford (q.v.).

Greymount – A large city (pop ~50,000) in central Alenar near the foot-hills of a mountain range. Part of the community was built by Dwarves so there are extensive underground holdings.

Grey Riders – The formerly free-lance mercenary group famous for defeating a lich, destroying an assassin's guild and bringing the Elohir (q.v.) to help defeat the Ja'al cult (q.v.) and their Daemonic allies in the War of the Dark Wave (q.v.). The original members were Buck Bydecy, Dar Cabot, Eric Indidarc, Connor Lomin (Loemin), Andyn Eleandir and the Alenar (later Aldenar) sisters, Brandawyn and Megan. After the departure of the Alenars, they added Hlerv (Handor Lervion) to their team, but he perished while trying to rescue his sister from the Ja'al. Khyron Demaris, an old beau of Andyn's, later joined the group.

Guardian Rod – A magic item, it is used for securing campsites in the wild. It is half metal and half crystal. When planted in the ground and activated, it sends out detection motes (think motion detectors) in a 70-foot radius. If anyone other than the Guardian's owners pass the motes, an alarm bell rings and a bright light illuminates the sector where the intrusion occurred.

Gudarta - The evil goddess of torture and suffering, the seductive and sadistic Gudarta is a member of the Ja'al (q.v.) pantheon. Her priests and priestesses usually wear revealing and scanty (but highly enchanted) outfits designed to distract and seduce others. After the War of the Dark Wave and the destruction of the Ja'al, she has formed a separate religion on Damora dedicated to her alone.

<u>Habakkuk</u> — A suit of magical chainmail with the ability to teleport its owner and up to one other person for short distances. It is owned by Dar Cabot. Using it is extremely draining for the bearer.

<u>Half-Elf</u> - The offspring of a union between an Elf and human, half-elves are a mix of their parents' heritage: magically talented, strong, adaptable and capable of learning new skills quickly. If it were not for the fact that they are noticeably larger than elves by a few inches in height, they would be indistinguishable from elves due to their predilection to inherit their Elven parent's eye color, hair color and ear shape. Half-elves live to between 100 and 150 years.

<u>Halfling</u> - The smallest of the races, Halflings (from the Elven for "those of hearth magic" - *haliv-fae*) prefer pastoral villages and countrysides to large cities, though they are at home in any setting. As adaptable as humans, Halflings have a talent for craftsmanship (with things other than stone) and farming. They are known for their skill in the kitchen and the durability of their finished goods. Their hair color (blonde, brown or black), skin color (porcelain to dark brown) and eye color (blue, green, black or grey) remind the other races of miniature humans. They live about 100 years or so.

<u>Halkith (the Grey)</u> — A Ja'al commander charged with finding a herd of battle-trained pegasi, he conducted a campaign of terror on the borderlands of Deran (q.v.) near Forester, the hometown of Dar Cabot (q.v.). He died in battle with the Grey Riders.

<u>Harlinsville</u> — A mid-sized suburb of the Deranese capital of Oakmoor, Harlinsville has about 35,000 inhabitants. It was ruled by Lord Dunston Culver and Lady Arlene Culver — before his murder and her escape to join the Ja'al (q.v.) in the War of the Dark Wave (q.v.).

<u>Havenridge</u> — A medium sized town in Loemin/ Bluevale (q.v.) It is a farming community near a stretch of forest. Like many towns in the PRT, it is riddled with spies and agents of evil.

<u>Heavensteel</u> — A special lightweight alloy crafted by the Elohir (q.v.), its formula and method of manufacture are closely held secrets and, rumor has it, extremely difficult to implement for any but the Elohir. It can be used for

both armor and weapons.

<u>Hellsfont</u> – A fortified metropolis (pop ~ 400,000) in the province of Eastwatch, Torosc. It is aptly named since many evil religions have seats of power in the city.

<u>Heritage Stone</u> - A magical item, a Heritage Stone is used to prove paternity and lineage. It uses magical analysis of DNA from a blood sample to ascertain the relationship of the subject to a predetermined DNA pattern associated with a target family or person.

<u>Highpoint</u> – The capital of the Republic of Torosc, Highpoint is one of the largest cities in the world with a population of over half a million. It sprawls along the ridges and foothills of a mountain range in the central province of Silvermount (formerly the kingdom of Gandar). It overlooks a large river and an inland sea (the Great Star Sea).

<u>Highwater, Devyn and Erica</u> – The aliases that Connor and Hannah Loemin adopt while infiltrating Havenridge (q.v.), Loemin/Bluevale.

<u>Hootling</u> – A fictional creature of great stealth and slyness, similar to the legendary "snipe" of the real world.

<u>Human</u> - Humans are much like people in real life, with the exception that they can use magic in the same manner as elves, Dwarves, Halflings and other denizens of Damora. Humans are energetic, adaptable, learn quickly and are endlessly curious about Damora and its people, flora and fauna. The origin of the word "human" has no Damoran equivalent as it does not translate from any Elven or Dwarven syntax.

<u>Humana</u> - Language of the human race on Damora. It is the equivalent of English in the real world.

<u>Hylar, Harkin</u> – Eric Indidarc's biological father, he was the head of the Crossed Swords assassins' guild. In *Assassin Prince*, Eric and the Riders captured him after infiltrating the main compound of the guild. Harkin was executed for his crimes a few weeks before the War of the Dark Wave (q.v.) broke out. His wife, Taramis, died in battle against her biological son, Eric.

<u>Hylar, Varani</u> – Eric Indidarc's half-sister. They share a common father, Harkin Hylar (q.v.).

<u>Indidarc, Eric</u>- One of the original Grey Riders, Eric is the adopted son of Melinor Indidarc (q.v.). Able to use magic and martial weapons with equal proficiency, Eric is cheerful, optimistic and friendly. He treats everyone he

meets with the same courtesy and kindness, whether a beggar or noble. His birth parents, the Hylars, were the leaders of an assassins' guild from which Eric escaped at an early age. Eric has violet eyes and blond hair and is a half-Elf. His pegasus is named Niveral (Elv. *"snow bright"*). He is the High Prince of Alenar by virtue of his marriage to Brandawyn Alenar (q.v.).

<u>Indidarc, Melinor, Lord</u> - High Wizard of the nation of Deran, Melinor is a nobleman and confidante of royalty in the Kingdoms of the Northern Alliance. He adopted both Eric Hylar/Indidarc (q.v.) and Saren DeMey (q.v.) after his own children were grown. A formidable mage with knowledge of magic, science, medicine, literature and history, Melinor is fluent in several languages. He is kind and somewhat absent-minded, but singularly focused on thwarting evil plots in the known lands. He is a widower; his deceased wife's name was Ann.

<u>Irae Angelorum (Lat. *"wrath of angels"*)</u> – The phrase that Megan Aldenar (q.v.) uses to initiate her most potent Celestial magical talent (*Aura of Heaven*), an area-effect burst of holy fire that burns nearby evil creatures to ash and blinds enemies. The spell is very costly and drains the user's strength.

<u>Irial</u> - The Halfling god of harvests, craftsmen and home, Irial is a benevolent deity who sometimes counts elves and humans among his adherents. The precepts of Irial are hospitality, kindness, courtesy, respect for people, animals and nature, and steadfastness in the face of hardship, whether caused by nature or evil designs. Another of Irial's names is Worldmaker.

<u>Ja'al</u> - Also known as the Manipulator Church (for their penchant for twisting words, lying and otherwise using others callously for their own ends) the Ja'al were one of the Dark Faiths and worshipped a number of harsh and cruel deities. They valued world domination, rule of the strong over the weak, eugenics, personal gain at the cost of others, and treachery. The Ja'al brought in the Daemons using Skull Gates (q.v.) and ushered in the War of the Dark Wave. After the arrival of the Elohir (q.v.) at the end of the War, the tide quickly turned against them and the Golden Army (q.v.) systematically annihilated the Ja'al. There are few, if any, Ja'al at the time of *Tower of Light*.

<u>Jekka</u> – A drink from Gorostol (q.v.) made from a dark brown bean that grows on vines, it is a cross between coffee and chicory and is highly prized for its invigorating qualities and smooth flavor.

<u>Jered</u> – A large nation south of Torosc (q.v.), it is a confederacy of

kingdoms originally established by pirates. Possessing miles of coastline, a multitude of islands, and a tropical climate, Jered is wealthy, powerful, and an ally of Torosc (q.v.) and Morlan (q.v.) in opposing the Northern Alliance (q.v.).

Johanna – An Elohir (q.v.) from Celestia (q.v.), she was assigned to tutor Brandawyn and Megan Aldenar after the War of the Dark Wave (q.v.), since the sisters were identified as having royal Elohir blood through an ancient ancestor. Johanna is about six feet four inches tall, of athletic build, with blonde hair and gem-like eyes the color of agate. She has a wry sense of humor and her husband's name is Petrus.

Kaftu – A race of hyena-folk similar to the creatures of African legend, Kaftu are often found either terrorizing the countryside or in the employ of the forces of evil. Their society is matriarchal, with males only used for mating, brute labor and some specialized tasks. They have no regard for life other than their own and even see Kaftu from other tribes as competitors.

Kalar, Ahlana II, PhD – The Queen of Deran, she is thirty years old, with a dusky complexion, brown hair and black eyes. A scholar and wizard by trade, she met King Phillip at a religious retreat in her teens and never forgot him — nor he, her. She is sunny, optimistic, and resourceful and has an impressive arsenal of magic devices.

Kalar, Phillip IV – The King of Deran, Phillip is in his mid-thirties and has extensive experience in both the freelance sell-sword profession and military matters. Ahlana is his wife. A cautious and thoughtful man, he has learned the value of thinking before acting as well as the need to act swiftly if needed. He has black hair and blue eyes and tends to worry over possible outcomes. He is a paladin (a holy warrior dedicated to a religion — in this case, Christianity).

Kalik, Ilyan – An opportunistic priest of Vardu (q.v.), he is always on the lookout for an advantageous situation for his religion to exploit. Despite his apparent low rank, he appears to have the ear of the Vardish High Council. He has had dealings with the Grey Riders in the past.

Kaliri – The smaller of Damora's (q.v.) two moons.

Khorpoint (Elv. "*sharp*" + Humana "*point*") – A major city (pop ~ 75000) in the north of Alenar. It is so named because it takes up most of a pointed stretch of land that juts out into the Great Sea. It has a large seaport.

<u>Kindriana (Kindri)</u> - A young female gold Dragon (q.v.) in the equivalent of the teen-age phase of life, she is a friend of the Grey Riders through her grandfather, who was a mentor to the Riders until his death at the Battle of Oakmoor. Kindri is intelligent, cautious and protective of her younger brother Tholerios (q.v.).

<u>Kontar of Greymount, Lord</u> – A warrior from an ancient noble family of Dwarves in Alenar, he is a rebel against the People's Republic of Torosc and an expert battlefield commander. He is Brandawyn Aldenar's Field Marshal.

<u>Kurental</u> (Dw. *"Creator god"*) - Benevolent Dwarven deity and god of stone, mountains, and creation. The main god honored by the Dwarves of Damora, his church is allied with Verian (q.v.), Irial (q.v.) and Christianity in resistance to the evil religions.

<u>Lervion, Handor (Hlerv)</u> - A Gnome wizard and spy, he joined the Grey Riders in *Eye of Truth* and helped them clear Buck Bydecy's name and avenge the murder of Andyn Eleandir's husband. He was secretive and somewhat aloof in order to protect his secret identity as the heir of a shipping magnate's fortune. After stealing the *Helm of Shadows*, he escaped to his hometown of Meridian, Gorostol and freed his sister from her Ja'al captors, only to lose his life in the process. Before the end, he regretted not appealing to the other Riders for help in his quest and is now celebrated as a hero.

<u>Lich</u> - An undead wizard. Liches are created when a wizard or sorcerer makes a pact with Dark Powers in order to forestall his/her own death, gaining immense magical power and undead status in the bargain. They exude an aura of terror but are greatly harmed by holy spells and items.

<u>Loemin</u> – A petty kingdom south of Gorostol (q.v.) in ancient times, it fell under the sway of the Archons of Torosc (q.v.) and was subjugated hundreds of years prior to the events of the Grey Riders series. Centrally located in the north of Torosc, it is landlocked but controls one shore of the massive Three-Nation Lake (q.v.). Geography is mostly rolling hills and plains with some mountainous areas. It was ruled by the House of Loemin, a Halfling Royal Family, during the time of the Paragons (q.v.).

<u>Loemin (nee Lervion), Hannah</u> – The sister of Handor (q.v.), Hannah was studying at a military academy at the time of the death of both her parents. Temporarily reunited with her brother in *Assassin Prince*, she tragically

lost him while trying to escape from the clutches of the Ja'al (q.v.) and her conniving uncle. A brown-eyed brunette, she is fit and very attractive but acts like the girl next door. During the War of the Dark Wave, she commanded troops in the southern nation of Gorostol (her homeland) and has a keen tactical mind. She is married to Connor Loemin (q.v.), the Crown Prince of the lost ancient southern kingdom of Loemin.

Loemin, Connor - Another of the original Grey Riders, Connor is a Halfling spy who hails from Evendale. Serious, but with a somewhat ribald sense of humor, Connor appears stoic and sober most of the time. He is knowledgeable about traps, curious about ancient ruins and secrets, and wields a broadsword, a rather heavy weapon for a Halfling. Dark-eyed and dark-haired, he has a muscular build but has an almost uncanny skill for moving unseen. He has a magical brooch (a reward for his prior exploits) that summons an animated sword from the Other Space (q.v.). After the War of the Dark Wave (q.v.), he and his family were confirmed as the hereditary rulers of the captive southern kingdom of Loemin (q.v.). As the eldest child of his parents, he is the Crown Prince. His pegasus is named Phantom.

Loemin, Brendan – The younger brother of Connor Loemin (q.v.), he almost died in a plague called the Whispering Death, a disease that left his voice is at half strength. Due to his royal heritage, he is an Archduke of Loemin. He is the father of Deena and Darren (q.v.).

Loemin, Cerys – The sister-in-law of Connor Lomin (q.v.) and the wife of Brendan (q.v.), she is an Archduchess of Loemin. Her children are Deena and Darren (q.v.), aged 11 and nine, respectively.

Loemin (Lomin), Janey - Deceased wife of Connor Lomin. Along with her daughter, Rose, she perished in a plague known as the Whispering Death.

Loemin, Liam II – The last King of Loemin, who, with his Queen, Siany, spirited away the magical heirlooms of the House of Loemin prior to the takeover of his Kingdom when the Archons (q.v.) of Torosc came to power. Not trusting the Archons, they hid the sword Glittershard (q.v.) and the magic cloak Steelwing (q.v.) in a Safehouse (q.v.) along with important records and other magical devices.

Loemin, Miriam – A High Priestess of the church of Irial (q.v.), Connor Loemin's (q.v.) mother is practical, confident and even-handed. As a high priestess, she has significant martial and magical skills and commanded a company of ecclesiastical troops of her own in the city of Glen, Evendale. After the War of the Dark Wave (q.v.) she became Queen-in-Exile of the Loemin as Queen Miriam the First.

<u>Loemin, Seamus</u> – The husband of Miriam (q.v.), he is a former army officer who handles security and logistics for his wife's temple district. He is calm, insightful and maintains an even keel under pressure. After the War of the Dark Wave, he became King Seamus the Fourth of Loemin (q.v.).

<u>Lordwain, Berek</u> – A blond Ja'al wizard in the service of the PRT (q.v.), he was highly placed in the Ja'al cult (q.v.) and helped them in closing Celestial Gates at the start of the War of the Dark Wave (q.v.). He is equally at home commanding large military units or working in a small group. While he is an ambitious and smooth operator, he is more practical and less fiery than his mistress, Adina Tenspire (q.v.). He detests the Alenar family but acquiesced to Adina's initial scheme to turn Brandawyn Aldenar (q.v.) into a vampire.

<u>Margoth, Zhinia</u> - A former Paragon Queen who used fell and evil magics to transform herself into an undead sorceress (a lich) near the end of the Paragon Age. Vicious, conniving, and cruel, she appeared as a skeleton with pinpoint eyes of purple light, clothed in rotting royal robes and wielding a skull-headed staff. Her battle standard was a fanged skull with a crown of flame. Andyn Eleandir (q.v.) destroyed her at the Battle of Hillton, Deran, in the year 1085 PIY using a powerful holy relic. Her despotic and repressive Paragon realm was called Thul Mardil, The Black Cage.

<u>Mercato, Karen, MD</u> – The personal physician to the Papal Nuncio to Damora and a member of the Order of the Three Magi, she is also an Elven Dominican nun. Her talents run more to healing, science and medical knowledge, though she is more than capable of defending herself.

<u>Merdail</u> (Dw. "Holy Land") – A large, mountainous kingdom southeast of Terenai (q.v.), it is the Dwarven homeland. Over the centuries, it has become more eclectic as humans and halflings have come to help till the land while the Dwarves concentrate on underground endeavors. It is ruled by a king and queen.

<u>Merfolk</u> – Mermaids, Mermen and Sirines of legend and myth. Despite a somewhat rocky history with land-bound peoples (particularly humans), merfolk communities often form alliances with land nations for mutual protection and assistance. Mermaids and Mermen look exactly as detailed in fairy

tales (human torso and fish body) while Sirines have human bodies with webbed hands and feet.

Meridian – The capital city of Gorostol (q.v.), it is a large metropolis in the foothills overlooking a beautiful lake known as the Kaljirre (Dw. "*sky mirror*"). It has over 200,000 inhabitants.

Messenger Bag – A leather sack with a teleportation field inside it that can send small objects to a companion Bag at another location by use of a special token.

Minrikard (Elv. "*Guardian Steel*")– An underground kingdom ruled by Dark Elves (q.v.) within the eastern districts of the People's Republic of Torosc. They sat out the War of the Dark Wave and are relatively unscathed.

Moonfire – A river in central Loemin. It runs south from the mountains in the north of the country and empties into Three Nation Lake (q.v.).

Morlan – A nation to the south of Torosc allied with the Dark Powers, Morlan is ruled by a Wizard King. There are many schools and academies devoted to magic. The terrain is hilly or flat plains, punctuated by numerous lakes and rivers. The climate is warm and humid much of the year and it contains vast tracts of verdant jungle. It is allies with Torosc (q.v.) and Jered (q.v.).

Navarre, Colleen (Lady) – Former cavalry officer and commander of Beta Company, Third Regiment (the Fire Eagles), Third Division, Royal Army of Deran, she was elevated to the rank of Baronetess after the War of the Dark Wave (q.v.) and now serves the King of Deran, Phillip IV.

Neralia - Evil goddess of child sacrifice, murder and domination, Neralia is one of the members of the Ja'al pantheon. She, like her peer Gudarta (q.v.), set up a separate religion dedicated to her worship and precepts on Damora after the demise of the Ja'al (q.v.) after the War of the Dark Wave (q.v.).

New Faith – Another name for Christianity on Damora.

Northern Alliance - A multinational pact similar to NATO in the real world, the Alliance is composed of Deran, Astarel, Rokon, Eldir, Evendale and Terenai (all q.v.).

Oakmoor - The capital city of Deran (q.v.), home to over a quarter of a million people. Oakmoor is based on three large hills at the confluence of the East River and Lonmar Rivers. It has several suburbs in addition to the main city proper.

Octavio, Arless– An extremely wealthy and arrogant young merchant in the Deranese city of Fenbluff, he was turned into a vampire by Brandawyn Alenar (q.v.) while she was still a thrall to Adina Tenspire (q.v.). After the War of the Dark Wave, he took service (in more ways than one) with Arlene Culver (q.v.) and continues to serve the Dark Faiths.

Ogre - Large, human-like creatures with fangs and odd-colored hair, ogres are brutish, violent, and not particularly bright. Their leaders are usually the more intelligent members of a particular tribe. Some of their number are smart enough to use magic. They are usually over seven feet tall and three hundred and fifty pounds. Used as shock troops by the forces of evil, Ogres are also greedy and selfish.

Ormond – An officer of the Intelligence Service of the People's Republic of Torosc. He was part of the Tinbore (q.v.) operation.

Ostor (Dw. "Spur") – A large town in north-central Loemin (Bluevale).It is near the spur of the Rampart Mountains that form the northern border with Gorostol (q.v.).

Other Space – A pocket dimension that some creatures, such as those with mixed Elohir (q.v.) or mixed Daemon (q.v.) lineage, can use to "store" physical features such as wings or horns to enable them to mingle more easily with the races of Damora. The Other Space can also be used to summon creatures or objects but is not well understood by any except Elohir or Daemons, who rarely speak of it.

Oxbridge, George – A Wizard of the First Circle of the Ja'al (q.v.) High Council, George Oxbridge was charged with research and development of the Skull Gates (q.v). He purchased Megan Alenar from the Ja'al hierarchy after her capture. The Grey Riders killed him in a spectacular battle in Book 5, *The Skull Gates*.

Page, Jeremy (Jeremiah) –_A human resident of Alford (q.v.), Alenar, he is a limner/painter and, secretly, a rebel sergeant opposing the PRT in his homeland. A strong and burly man, he nevertheless is very stealthy in the woods and knows the territory near his hometown very well. His brother is Joshua Page (q.v.).

Page, Joshua – A rebel lieutenant living in Alford (q.v.), Alenar, he uses his profession as an armorer as a cover to spy on PRT forces in the vicinity of his homeland. Like his brother, Jeremy (q.v.), he is strong and burly and a competent combatant. He hates bullies and thinks carefully before acting. His wife, Richenda, is one of the town healers.

Page, Richenda – An Elven healer in the town of Alford (q.v.), Alenar, she is married to Joshua (q.v.). While her husband and brother-in-law use their martial skills to oppose the PRT, she applies her healing and interpersonal skills to find out information that can be used against the People's Republic.

Papal Nuncio – Official human envoy of Christianity to Damora, appointed by the Pope. The Nuncio at the time of Tower of Light is Thomas Williams (q.v.).

Paragon Age – One of the major epochs of the history of Damora, it was ushered in by the event known as the Skyfire, when humans first appeared and brought Christianity with them. Records prior to this time are sketchy and incomplete. The age is so named because of the rise of rulers of petty kingdoms who were all superior practitioners of a particular branch of a freelance career (i.e. warrior, healer, mage, etc.). It ended when some of the Paragon rulers succumbed to evil influences and tried to expand their nations at the expense of their neighbors. Alyssa of Tor Aldin and Zhinia Margoth were two Paragon rulers.

Patian, Donald, Prince – A Prince of one of the reigning houses of the Confederacy of Jered (q.v.), he is a powerful magnate in his own right and can command divisions of troops. Arrogant and lustful, he has temper but is pragmatic.

Pegasus (pl. Pegasi) – A winged horse. In the Grey Riders novels, they are omnivores due to their part-raptor heritage and can be domesticated. They are wildly expensive to acquire and maintain and are the fastest flying mounts alive.

Pentak – A large town in central Loemin (q.v.)

Petrus – An Elohir (q.v.) from Celestia (q.v.), he is six foot eight, strongly built and has dark hair and eyes the color of tourmaline. He is married to Johanna (q.v.) and is, like her, a mentor to Megan and Brandawyn Aldenar (q.v.).

Preservation Net / Bead – A small bead of amber imbued with a mighty spell affecting spacetime. If broken over an object, it releases a Preservation Net, a magical effect that reduces the flow of time to one ten-millionth of normal for anything it covers. Preservation Beads are extremely expensive and lose their potency after a time period measured in weeks.

Purifying Light – An area-effect spell that disrupts and dispels magically induced plagues and diseases over a wide area.

Puup - Buck Bydecy's (q.v.) pet pigeon who somehow manages to avoid getting killed despite being in or near several battles. By the time of *Tower of Light*, he has retired to the gardens of the Papal Nuncio's residence in Saint Martin's, Deran.

Quiet Way – A hidden passage into Loemin's capital city of Aldath (q.v.), its existence has been forgotten for hundreds of years.

Red Veils – A cadre of assassins operating in the People's Republic of Torosc, or PRT (q.v.), they are distinguishable by their red armor and chain-mail veils that cover the lower halves of their faces. They are always female. Their hidden identities, superior training and reputation for viciousness make them much feared in the PRT.

Rindara Starblade – A magic bastard sword owned by Dar Cabot (q.v.). It has a night-black blade that glitters with the light of a thousand stars and is especially potent against daemons and the undead.

Rokon – One of the smaller members of the Northern Alliance (q.v.), Rokon was originally a duchy of the Patriarchate of Eldir (q.v.) but broke away prior to the forming of the Alliance. Eldir and Rokon have since re-solved their differences, attributable to the need for teamwork as required by the Alliance charter. Rokon has a climate much like Norway in the real world.

Roshana – A priestess of Gudarta (q.v.) attached to the Intelligence Ser-vice of the People's Republic of Torosc (q.v.).

Sadam, Sergeant – A PRT dragoon soldier stationed in Alford, Alenar (q.v.). He is basically a bully.

Safehouse – Safehouses were carefully hidden storerooms set up by na-tional organizations, royal houses or other groups to secure valuable items and knowledge. They were typically used in the time of the Paragon Kings (q.v.) and after, up through the Esten Imperial Age (q.v.). They were heavily protected by magic and other obstacles to prevent the unauthorized from plundering their secrets.

Saint Martin's (Town) - Major port city in Deran (pop ~ 80,000). It is the seat of the Christian church and the base of the Curia, the ruling council of

Christianity on Damora. The Papal Nuncio (q.v.) makes his residence there.

Saint Michael, Order of - Christian military order of knights and warriors dedicated to protecting the innocent against evil, often used as heavy assault infantry or cavalry.

Screen of Air – An obscuring spell used to hide people or objects, it puts up an atmospheric distortion that is difficult to see beyond. It can hide light sources completely if done properly.

Selaan – One of the ruling High Kings of Hades and a former member of the Ja'al (q.v.) pantheon, Selaan is known as the Changeable One. He is the god of Trickery, Deception and Chaos. Quixotic and capricious, he seldom remains on one thought for long but his impressive memory makes up for this shortfall. It is thought that his natural form is a golden-skinned, dark-haired man with white wings (in mockery of the Elohir) but since he never retains one form for very long, this is disputed. He took part in the War of the Dark Wave (q.v.) and supposedly escaped back to Hades when his forces faced defeat.

Sending Mirror – The Damoran equivalent of a cell phone, it can be used to communicate over distances by showing an image of another person who has a similarly designed mirror. Useful range varies. The signals can be tracked, however, and the more powerful the mirror, the easier it is to track.

Sentinel – A large fortified town in southern Gorostol (q.v.) near the border with Torosc (q.v.), Sentinel is one of several outposts designed to keep a watch on the southern lands. It has a population of over 10,000 people.

Severin, Colonel – A militia commander in southern Alenar (q.v.) who is also secretly a rebel.

Shamlin, Gregory – A Halfling farmer who lives near the town of Havenridge, Loemin/Bluevale. He has a wife, Marilla, and several grown children.

Shock Hind – Deer-like bipedal Daemons, they have serpent tails and can use weapons in their human-like hands. They have several effective attacks, including electrical shock from their tails, goring with their antlers, weapon strikes and magical spells. They are heavy infantry.

Shriek - A magical infantry sword found by the Grey Riders near Twinspire Mountain. It makes its wielder stealthier and does great harm to undead. It was owned by Handor Lervion (q.v.); his sister, Crown Princess Hannah Loemin (nee Lervion), now carries it in his name since his death.

<u>Silvermount</u> – A large district in the People's Republic of Torosc (q.v.), formerly the Kingdom of Gandar.

<u>Skyfire</u> - A mysterious event from antiquity that changed the history of Damora. Legends say that visitors from another place arrived on disks or globes of fire and brought with them the Christian faith. The location of the actual arrival and the details of the event are lost in the mists of time. It is thought to have taken place more than 5000 years before the events of *White-horse Peak* (the first of the Grey Riders novels).

<u>Skreet</u> – Small Daemons from Hades, Skreets look like a cross between an eagle and a boar. Used primarily as skirmishers, light infantry or air patrol, they tend to swarm opponents. Able to use a variety of weapons, they also have limited magical abilities.

<u>Skullhead Legion</u> - Paramilitary guard force formerly in the service of the Ja'al cult leadership. Known for their brutality, greed and utter disregard for life, they are often used as shock troops. They are fanatical and fight to the death. After the War of the Dark Wave, their numbers were severely depleted but the remnants took service with other evil churches or governments.

<u>Skull Gate</u> – Horrid structures made of iron bars and the bones of sacrificial victims, the Gates were the brainchild of the Ja'al cult (q.v.). Fully thirty feet tall and twenty wide, they were spacetime portals to the world of Hades (q.v.), the homeland of the Daemons (q.v.). Though some Gates were destroyed by free-lance mercenary teams prior to the War of the Dark Wave, many remained and became veritable thoroughfares for daemons to enter the world of Damora when the War began. After the arrival of the Golden Army of Celestia, all the known Skull Gates were destroyed by the Elohir over a period of half a year. It is hoped that there are no more on Damora (q.v.).

<u>Sprite</u> – Small (~ 12 inches tall), faerie-like beings, the race of sprites frequent woodlands and wild areas uninhabited by the larger folk of Damora. They keep to their own company and society though they form alliances with Elves (q.v.) or Halflings (q.v.) on occasion and have been known to form friendships with other races. There are four known sub-races, including the more outgoing and martial hill-sprites.

<u>Starsilver/Starsteel</u> – Special alloys made with a combination of titanium, iron, and other trace minerals, they are highly prized for their light weight, superior strength and malleability. The original technique for forging the

metals was devised by the Dwarves during the Paragon Era and one of the few artifacts to survive that time period. The alloys are expensive but durable. They are commonly used for high-end weapons and armor and can be enchanted with special effects.

Stealth - Eric Indidarc's enchanted familiar. Summoned from the Other Space (q.v.) via a magic item called a Companion Pin (q.v.), it transforms to a realistic hawk upon command.

Steelwing – The magical cloak of the Queens of Loemin, Steelwing forms a metal "bell" around its wearer, on command, that can reject most projectiles. At another command word it blasts a flare of light in all directions, blinding enemies.

Stone Lurker – Carnivorous subterranean monsters with five appendages, Stone Lurkers hide in caverns and caves by constructing stone cocoons that they attach to ceilings and galleries. There, they wait for the unwary to pass below, whereupon they rappel down on black silken cords. They can project tentacles from their mouths to ensnare and trap. They are repulsed by light and holy magic. Each is about the size of a large dog and none are particularly intelligent. They tend to jealously guard territory.

Storm Force – A magic spell that explodes outward from the caster with a high-pressure wave of air. It can lift human-sized creatures off their feet.

Tarvener – One of the regional rulers of the world of Hades (q.v.), he is a Daemon Prince in his own right and can command legions of troops. Nonetheless, he is subservient to the High Kings and Queens (such as Selaan (q.v.)) and, despite serving as the Captain General of the invading Dark Wave, is required to follow their directives. After the end of the war, his whereabouts were unknown. Attractive and highly intelligent, he is a good planner and personally formidable in battle. His grand-daughter is Saren DeMey (q.v.), whom he intends to bring back to Hades with him. His knowledge of Hadean magic is encyclopedic.

Telepost – A system for sending letters and small packages by teleportation throughout the major cities of the known world. A leftover technology from the Paragon Age (q.v.) it is difficult to maintain and very expensive, so its use is noteworthy.

Tenspire, Adina – A female human priestess of the goddess Gudarta (q.v.), she is beautiful, shapely and blonde (though she changes her hair color on a whim). While involved with the Skull Gates project, she hunted down and eventually captured Brandi and Megan Alenar, keeping Brandi for herself and transforming her through vile magic into a vampire slave. Adina is the mistress of Berek Lordwain (q.v.), though she is not above taking her pleasures wherever they present themselves.

Terenai (Elv. "*Realm of the Elves*") - The hereditary homeland of the Elven people, Terenai lies due south of Deran and also shares borders with Evendale, Gorostol and Merdail. A verdant and fruitful land, it is heavily forested in places. It is ruled by an Emperor (or Empress) and is the oldest of the nations on Deran. Its capital city is Mil-Tereth (Elv. "*King's Palace*").

The Ban – An agreement between the rulers of Hades and Celestia to not meddle directly in the affairs of the people of the world of Damora (q.v.). It stipulated that they could have a small number of advisors and observers and interplanetary gates in hidden locations for travel but nothing more. The Ja'al (q.v.) eventually concocted a plan to violate the Ban and bring Daemons into the world for the War of the Dark Wave (q.v.) which ended in disaster for the forces of evil.

Three Nation Lake – A very large lake in the People's Republic of Torosc (q.v.) bordered by Loemin/Bluevale, Alenar/Coastwatch and Turis Rhi/Watercliff.

Tholerios (Tholi) – A young male gold Dragon (q.v.), he is one of the grandchildren of a friend and mentor to the Grey Riders who died at the Battle of Oakmoor during the Dark Wave (q.v.). He is bold, impetuous but very loyal and clever. He sometimes chafes under the authority of his older sister, Kindri, who has charge of him until he comes of age.

Tigris Infernalis (Lat. "*infernal tiger*") – A Daemon of particularly savage nature it is sometimes referred to as a "tiger Daemon". Looking like bipedal tigers with a ruff of horns and bat wings, they are bloodthirsty, cunning and arrogant. They are difficult to control but fearsome combatants.

Tinbore – A mid-sized town in Alenar that was decimated when agents of the PRT discovered that many were rebel sympathizers.

Tinira, Lady – The wife of Esdan (q.v.), she is a hill-sprite noblewoman who was rescued from an evil fate by the Alenar sisters. She now serves them as a representative of her people.

Tolbert, Adam, Major – A militia battalion commander in

Alenar/Coastwatch (q.v.), he was captured at Tinbore (q.v.) along with some of his officers.

Torosc – (Dw. *"kingdoms"*) An oppressive land south of Gorostol (q.v.) ruled by a council of six Archons, also known as the People's Republic of Torosc (or PRT), it is an amalgamation of several petty kingdoms welded together during a time of upheaval. It is the center of activity for evil forces with designs on world domination. One of its provinces, Coastwatch (the former Paragon Kingdom of Alenar), was the home of the Alenar sisters prior to the death of their parents. The plot for the War of the Dark Wave originated in Torosc, which, at the time, was the seat of the Ja'al (q.v.) cult.

Torvu – One of the High Kings of Hades and another member of the Ja'al (q.v.) pantheon, the god of Death is a tall, powerfully built man with pale skin, dark horns in his forehead, dead black eyes, and dark hair with a bone-white stripe down the middle. He was killed by the Celestial Royal Family during the War of the Dark Wave in a running battle that took several days.

Tree Flitter – A tiny winged monkey found only in the Southlands, Flitters are intelligent and can be trained as pets. They feed on fruit and insects and are protective of their masters, becoming excellent spies. Jeremy Page (q.v.) has a Tree Flitter named Coraline.

Troll - Large, brutish bipedal creatures similar to ogres but taller and heavier. Trolls are hairless and can have four arms rather than two. They prefer mountains and forests and will kill and eat anything edible. Cruel, greedy and selfish, they can nonetheless be outwitted by smarter creatures. Some more intelligent of their species can learn to use rudimentary magic. Trolls have the unnerving talent of being able to blend in with trees and rocks by merely holding still.

Turis Rhi (Elv. *"Sea March"*) – Similar to Loemin (q.v.) and Alenar (q.v.), it was an independent kingdom in ancient times but fell during the late Paragon Era. It is just south of Alenar. The rulers of the Kingdom (the Rhivan family) are in exile in Deran, just like the Aldenar sisters and the Loemins.

Underdark – Colloquial term for the underground world beneath the surface of Damora. It is a wondrous and dangerous place, with Dwarven communities providing islands of safety amid the darkness.

Vampire Rose – A semi-intelligent plant similar to a Ghost Creeper (q.v.), a vampire rose emits a mesmerizing perfume that attracts the unwary.

Once within range, the plant entangles its victim in its branches, stabbing with its thorns and draining blood. In combination with Ghost Creepers, Vampire Roses are a formidable security system.

<u>Vardu</u> – One of most feared of the evil religions on Damora, the faith holds that the power of death over life is the key to domination so it naturally is connected with war, assassination and the undead. They are rule-followers and will honor contracts to the letter but will turn on allies in a second if it suits them. Prior to the Dark Wave, they competed with the Ja'al for adherents but now reign supreme in many regions where the Ja'al are no more.

<u>Vault of Safety</u> – A Safehouse (q.v.) built by the Royal Family of Loemin to hide certain valuable items, including magical family heirlooms.

<u>Venris, Lord</u> – The Dwarven ruler of the city of Duarvar (q.v.) in Gorostol (q.v.). He lost an eye in the War of the Dark Wave.

<u>Verian (Elv. "Lord-Highest")</u> - Elven god of forests and nature. Followers of Verian worship in open structures usually in groves or copses of trees. Verian teaches that liberty, love, kindness, right living, charity and respect for creation are paramount.

<u>Vizkir</u> – A large Drake (Dragon, q.v.), he is the personal mount of Golvadu Fellhammer (q.v.).

<u>Vodyanoi</u> – Half-fish, half-human creatures of the ocean, the Vodyanoi are a parody of merfolk, with the heads of fish, feet that end in fins and human-like torsos and arms. They are almost exclusively devoted to evil but difficult to control due to their capricious and independent nature. They are sworn enemies of Merfolk (q.v.).

<u>War Fiend</u> – Slender, human-sized Daemons (q.v.) from Hades with double bat wings and a dragon tail, War Fiends are savage, intelligent and versatile. They are used as anything from combat wizards to medium infantry. They have access to a deadly array of battle magic and are swift, agile fliers.

<u>War of the Dark Wave</u> – A world-wide conflict on the planet of Damora (q.v.), it was started when the Ja'al (q.v.) cult gathered armies, subverted the civilized nations, and summoned Daemons (q.v.) in a quest for world domination. The Daemons were brought in via Skull Gates (q.v.). The Ja'al also used dark magic that closed the existing interstellar gates to Celestia, preventing the Elohir (q.v.) from coming to the aid of Damora. It ended when the Grey Riders found a legendary gate that the Ja'al had missed (the Gate of

Stars) and travelled to Celestia, returning with a massive army of Elohir. The war ended with the complete destruction of the Ja'al, massive loss of life on all sides and the death of two Daemon gods. At the time of *Tower of Light*, the people of the planet are attempting to rebuild.

Whitehorse Peak - A large mountain north of Forester, Deran, so named because its geology and snow-fall pattern reminded the people nearby of a white-maned horse. It is the site of the recovery of the pegasi (as described in *Whitehorse Peak*) that the Grey Riders eventually own. Its dwarven name is Kelematris (Dw. *"Mountain -Horse"*).

Whitson, Colonel – A Halfling colonel of militia stationed near the town of Havenridge, Leomin/Bluevale. He is secretly a rebel commander opposed to the People's Republic of Torosc (q.v.).

Wild Lands – Any territories (above or below ground) not controlled by civilized nations.

Williams, Thomas, Cardinal, CSC – The Papal Nuncio to Damora, "Father Thomas" (as he prefers to be known to his close associates and friends) is a Christian Cardinal sent to Damora upon the death of the previous Nuncio, Edward. He has dark skin, curly hair and piercing green eyes. He is an avid reader and has a healthy respect for the people and creatures of Damora.

Zulgubrudan – An evil True Dragon (q.v.) wizard, he lived and died during the late Paragon Age (q.v.). Due to his devastating magical attacks, he was known as the Immolator of Life.

ABOUT THE AUTHOR

A route to fantasy fiction through the aerospace industry may seem an odd one to take, but PG Badzey has been writing stories since grammar school and has never stopped, even though his path took an unconventional turn for someone interested in writing. A trained systems engineer, he kept up with creative writing and coursework throughout a career working on the C-17 airlifter, the International Space Station, the Delta IV Rocket and the James Webb Space Telescope. He has enjoyed and been influenced by JRR Tolkien, C.S. Lewis, Katherine Kurtz, Christopher Stasheff, Terry Brooks and C. Dale Brittain, to name a few. He is the author of the first six novels in the *Grey Riders* series, *Whitehorse Peak, Eye of Truth, Helm of Shadows, Assassin Prince, The Skull Gates* and *Gate of Stars*, all of which received 5-star ratings from Readers' Favorite. Other publications include short stories published in *Dragonlaugh*, an online fantasy humor magazine, and *Brevity in Paradise* (the Orange County Writers Guild (OCWG) anthology). PG Badzey has studied martial arts for many years and is active in his parish community. He lives in California, is a member of the OCWG and the Realm Makers online Christian speculative fiction community and has taught seminars on fantasy writing in Orange County Libraries.

ABOUT THE ARTIST

A product of Fullerton College's Entertainment Arts Program, Matthew Bostic brings a background in illustration and the comic book industry to his artwork. With a resume that includes apprenticing as an Inker on Ultimate Spiderman and Ultimate X-men for Hack Shack Studios, his vibrant and evocative images bring the world of the Grey Riders to life. *Tower of Light* is his second novel illustration project (after Book 6 of the Grey Riders saga, *Gate of Stars*). He is a dedicated father and a resident of Arkansas. His fantasy work can be seen on Instagram @thedragonsmaw and at bosticart.com.

Find out more about the World of the Grey Riders at
www.pgbadzey.wordpress.com